THE TUESDAY MAN

THE
TUESDAY
MAN

DAVID DANIEL

 A DUTTON BOOK

A special thanks to Richard Marek

DUTTON
Published by the Penguin Group
Penguin Books USA, Inc., 375 Hudson Street,
New York, New York 10014, U.S.A.
Penguin Books Ltd, 27 Wrights Lane,
London W8 5TZ, England
Penguin Books Australia Ltd, Ringwood,
Victoria, Australia
Penguin Books Canada Ltd, 2801 John Street,
Markham, Ontario, Canada L3R 1B4
Penguin Books (N.Z.) Ltd, 182–190 Wairau Road,
Auckland 10, New Zealand

Penguin Books Ltd, Registered Offices:
Harmondsworth, Middlesex, England

First published by Dutton, an imprint of New American Library, a division of
Penguin Books USA Inc.
Distributed in Canada by McClelland & Stewart Inc.

First Printing, July, 1991
10 9 8 7 6 5 4 3 2 1

 REGISTERED TRADEMARK—MARCA REGISTRADA

LIBRARY OF CONGRESS CATALOGING IN PUBLICATION DATA:

Daniel, David, 1945–
  The Tuesday Man / David Daniel.
    p.   cm.
  ISBN 0-525-93318-2
  I. Title.
PS3554.A5383N6   1991
813'.54—dc20   90-25795
                                                                        CIP

Printed in the United States of America
Set in Garth Graphic
Designed by Leonard Telesca

PUBLISHER'S NOTE
This is a work of fiction. Names, characters, places, and incidents either are the
products of the author's imagination or are used fictitiously, and any resemblance
to actual persons, living or dead, events, or locales is entirely coincidental.

For my shining Star

The road up and the road down is one and the same.

—Heraclitus

Haven

PART ONE

The small house on Martha's Vineyard was spartan and un-cluttered, one of the two ways a house can go when its sole occupant is a man who has ceased to live with self-deception. In the kitchen Eric Thorne eyed the little black-and-white TV on the counter as he oiled his Fin-Nor deep-sea reel. The reel had been a gift on his eighth birthday, which made it thirty years old. Like most things Thorne owned, the reel was kept in good working order.

Upon hearing the geriatric idle of Rufus McCoy's Stude-baker truck, Thorne went to the screen door and hollered for his friend to come on in for a minute. They were going to take McCoy's 18-foot Whaler out toward Cuttyhunk, where the blues were running.

"You want coffee?" Thorne asked.

"I want to get movin'. The wind's southwesterly. It'll take us a good hour to get out there." With deep blue eyes set in a sunburnt face and his hair a salty gray, McCoy looked like the ocean he had fished commercially for over fifty years.

"Now go easy. Just because you've got the 'gone fishing' sign out permanently doesn't mean everyone else does," Thorne said. "A few days more and my angling is over for a spell."

"All the more reason. Once the cop business gets going full steam again, you're gonna regret every vacation minute you wasted. C'mon."

When he'd retired five years ago, Rufus had gone right on

fishing. Summers he ran clambakes for tourists, who jacked up the population of Martha's Vineyard by a factor of ten. Thorne's father, who had been Rufus's friend and partner all those years, had simply retired. He hadn't lived out a year.

Rufus paused by the door, his eyes finally, reluctantly drawn to the television screen. A man was walking through a crowd of well-wishers toward a podium hung with patriotic bunting.

"That the guy says he's gonna set the world in balance come November?"

Thorne was impressed that Rufus had even a hint as to Timothy Murphy's presidential agenda. Rufus was an Islander, with all the isolationist habits that implied. "His platform calls for starting here," said Thorne. "He's going to make rose-tinted glasses mandatory for persnickety old curmudgeons. You know any?"

Rufus scowled. "Optimism's an off-island luxury, like politics. Those birds come and go, but life out here stays the same."

"Simple and hard for all us hard and simple folk." Thorne snapped off the television set and gathered his gear.

"They're a bunch of talkers," Rufus insisted. "They don't make the fish bite any better. Reminds me—you got a filleting knife handy?"

"Top drawer, on the left."

Rufus found the knife. "You're as shipshape as your old man was. Place for everything, everything in its place. Me, I wouldn't find my brain some days if it wasn't prepacked."

"Have you double-checked lately?" Thorne said, trailing him out.

Ray Russo—short, barrel-chested, with a watermelon belly and wire hair—eyed with twitchy alertness a half dozen television monitors. On screen the red, white, and blue cards held by members of the crowd in Shea Stadium formed a shifting geometry of images. It was the curious nature of that form of display, invented in arenas like this for sports events, that no individual participant could see the effect of his efforts. Vision required distance. In that, thought Russo, it was like the political process itself.

Around him, technicians for the cable network were taking instructions by headphone from their director. The cards flickered again and went to a final formation, and Russo ventured his first, tentative smile. How many candidates ever had their own personal symbol? he wondered. An image that would call the name to mind instantly? This candidate does.

A falcon flashed on huge screens in the stadium. Placards danced, styrofoam boaters waved, a covey of balloons broke free and climbed into the almost blue New York sky. And the tens of thousands of Murphy supporters broke into cheering, which went on for a long time.

Maura Ames cheered with the rest of the crowd in the May sunshine. For nearly a year she had been working on the campaign, and just like when she had been chosen as a convention delegate from Massachusetts, this rally was a high point for her. The cheering increased as Senator Murphy came on stage. He acknowledged the crowd with upraised arms, then, shaking hands with the others gathered there, made his way to the rostrum. The noise went on.

A handsome woman in her mid-forties leaned into the aisle and squeezed Maura's arm, and Maura was delighted to see a familiar face. Anna was her name; Maura had met her only briefly the night before last at a party the woman had hosted at her home on Long Island. Maura was surprised to be remembered.

"Wild, isn't it?" Maura said above the noise.

"Truly. Listen, darling. I'm having a little pool party after all this. I'd like you to come and get wet."

"Wouldn't I love to, but I should head back to Boston."

"There are too many 'shoulds' up there. This isn't Boston."

It certainly wasn't. Sunshine and noise and excitement. "There are other flights. . . ."

Anna glanced toward the stage. "Have you noticed that field director? The hunk in Brooks Brothers and Burberry cologne? He definitely noticed you the other night."

Maura was embarrassed and flattered. She had seen Vaughan Belnap at the rallies during the past two days—and he was handsome, though a little too Ivy League smooth for her taste.

"He's been asking about you," Anna confided, and her tone suggested the topic had not been politics.

"Did you tell him I've got two grown children and an almost grown husband?"

Anna smiled conspiratorily. "I don't give away secrets."

"My goodness," Maura laughed, "is that a secret?"

"You have to decide your own secrets, darling. But do come by for a cocktail and a dip later. The party that swims together wins together. I'll have someone run you to the airport for a late flight." Anna touched her shoulder and drifted off.

The governor of New York, a Murphy partisan, was tapping the microphone, quelling the noise at last. Maura's excitement grew. Her months of hosting fund raisers, stuffing envelopes, making phone calls seemed to come to a point. The speaker mentioned the familiars: the youth of the candidate, the wisdom acquired through life experience and a Yale education, the war record—details Maura knew by heart from the countless mailers she'd sent.

"Ladies and gentlemen," the governor declaimed, his words coming back with a faint reverberation, "tireless workers, supporters, *friends* . . . I give you . . . the next president of the United States."

"You hearing that? Guy must have balls this big," said John Bricklin, the White House senior party advisor. He was known for his erudition and oratory, but this was a sport shirt and slacks meeting: a handful of close advisors and the president sequestered in the wooded hills eighty miles northwest of Washington at Camp David. The president had called a time out and switched on the television on the mantle above the rustic stone fireplace, proudly pointing out that the set was an American brand. Bricklin didn't have the heart to tell him that only the name was American—everything else was Korean.

The president's Filipino steward had opened a bottle of MacAllan twenty-five-year-old single malt. No one said a word about the origin of that product. President Peter Hawes unfortunately had to settle for spring water, which sat better with the mild nausea he'd been experiencing lately.

Ron Zelnick, the party's platform strategist, sat with a fistful of salted peanuts, popping them into his mouth one at a time, chewing with intense concentration as he watched the TV. At twenty-eight he had achieved a spot among these men who were twice his age. The tanned, prematurely bald dome of his head, ringed by hair the same dark color as his eyes, gave him a shrewd, monkish look. He had come to Washington only three years before, with his Harvard MBA newly framed, but he had climbed fast, in part because he possessed the habit of weighing what a word, even a gesture, was going to cost the men for whom he worked—and, by extension, himself. He cleared his throat. "You have to admit, Mr. President, spending everything on one shot shows major chutzpah. It's going to win Murphy votes, especially among the undecided. People are going to see him as bold." Zelnick projected a quick string of numbers: costs, poll results, percentage points. Today's stadium event came out a good deal all around.

President Hawes listened. He had grown to value the young advisor, though he also sensed an overeagerness in him that needed the tempering of time, experience, and humor.

"Well, I'm not going to vote for him," Hawes declared at last, bringing general laughter to the group. More Scotch was splashed over ice.

Glibness came easily to a lame duck whose vice president was in the Deep South at that moment oiling the juggernaut that appeared certain to roll the party into office for another term. There were pressing campaign issues before this group right now, but still the president kept his eyes on the screen, listening to the speaker's opening words, not believing them all, but wishing, just a little, that eight years ago he had had the nerve to say some of the things Timothy Murphy was now saying.

Ray Russo's eyes had the furtive flicker of an auctioneer's scanning a crowd for bids. He studied his candidate's video image for flaws. In his years of political management he had worked for many candidates, some winners, some losers, but of all of them, Tim Murphy was his first thoroughbred. True, there had been a lot of grooming needed, habits to break—like one Tim had had of nodding when he talked, as if wanting to affirm the veracity of what he was telling you. But intuitively, he knew how to excite a crowd, to play on their visceral instincts. With the national convention six weeks away, he was showing the good signs.

They'd come a long way since that day in Indiana a year ago when Russo had held his breath and stood with the thirty-odd reporters that had formed a ring around the tall, virtually unknown senator.

Murphy had bent forward and with his teeth and right hand undid the thong that secured the hood over the head of the bird perched on his gloved left wrist. The watchers seemed to exhale as one when the hood came off. The falcon's black eye blinked. Head-feathers shone with a small rainbow. Talons shifted on the gauntlet.

"Couldn't it claw your eyes out, senator?" one of the reporters asked, a wire of nervousness threading her voice.

"There's risk anytime we get close to a powerful counterpart," Murphy replied. "But there's also the chance to go from mutual fear to mutual trust."

No one needed to pursue the obvious symbolism. New relations with old enemies was a theme Murphy had been urging for months. But rhetoric was forgotten for the moment. With an upthrust motion of his arm, Murphy launched the falcon into the air. Instinctively everyone ducked as the powerful wings beat the air and the bird rose. In a moment it was high above the cornfields, climbing toward the blue blanket of Hoosier sky. Jesus, it had worked! They'd loved it.

Russo had wanted a press conference in the local grange hall to announce Murphy's candidacy. Murphy had argued for doing it here, on his family's farm. They'd fought—Tim hadn't kept up with his falconry; what if the bird had grown wild? That reporter's question posed a moment previously had been Russo's secret nightmare for the past week. In the end Murphy won.

The bird was a speck now, moving over the acres of lush farmland, and Murphy was chatting with the crowd. A reporter was trying on the gauntlet, others were examining the hood. After a big feed on barbeque and corn, and lots of pictures (Murphy on a tractor, Murphy with a new calf— the press had tried everything but having Tim and his wife Linda pose like Grant Wood figures), they had moved out here to the field.

Nevertheless, not all talons had been withdrawn. The reporters quizzed the senator, who had turned forty-two in March, as to why he would take on older, more experienced candidates in his party, which itself was going to have a struggle against seven years of popular incumbent rule. They grilled him on controversial issues. And that young man from the *LA Times,* Hugo Boss suitpants tucked into gum boots—like you couldn't be too careful what you stepped into in a farmyard—asked: "In her book on you, senator, Lorraine Patton wonders if beneath your calm exterior, you're not a man living with deep—one is tempted to add, even 'schizoid'—contradictions. Comment?"

While Russo winced, Murphy had smiled, and with an off-hand bit of business that Robert DeNiro might have admired, he plucked a haystraw and slipped it between his teeth. "Mel, flying over this part of the world, what do you see?"

"Corn," came the reply, and laughter.

"Seamless green miles of it," agreed Murphy. "But go in among the rows—" he pointed with his straw, "where the stalks close in above your head, and there's as much life and death and drama going on in a square yard as in a city block. I like to think I'm more complicated than I look too, Mel. Don't we all?"

Soon someone pointed and said the bird was coming back. Murphy tugged on the gauntlet and, directing everyone to stay put, walked forward alone a few dozen paces. And, with the others that morning last June, Russo had squinted and watched the falcon moving in on its narrowing gyre.

All fall and winter the polls had shown Tim running third. Then, a month before the Iowa caucuses the frontrunner, Florida Congressman Royal Hanson, had pulled up lame. A tale about a Christmas party on Hanson's yacht had leaked, and the white stuff hadn't been snow. Murphy had picked up some support but so had others in the race. It looked as if conventional politics, and not the men, were going to decide the outcome. Again questions about Murphy's contradictions, raised in Lorraine Patton's book, *Heartlander,* had come up; but overall the book had stirred interest in the senator by bringing him to the public's notice.

Russo and his strategists urged Murphy to ease off on some of his more outspoken views—Central America, gun control—but Murphy resisted. He even publicly bemoaned Hanson's fate, denouncing the media for digging too deep to find skeletons. And this intuitive move by Murphy was proved right. Americans *were* worried about becoming embroiled in another Vietnam. They *were* scared about the absurd ease with which dangerous firearms are available. They *were* nervous about how much information on every citizen was filed in the computers, and how quick the media were to use it. In Iowa, and then New Hampshire, Murphy had come in second. In Michigan, Wisconsin, and New York he had taken a slim lead.

Then, five weeks ago Murphy had told Russo he wanted to change strategy, wanted to stake the rest of his campaign fund on one big rally televised nationwide. It would be followed by a West-to-East barnstorming trip, and then he'd put campaigning to bed and get back to his Senate seat, where he was being paid by voters in his home state to be. Russo said no. Again Murphy won.

Indiana and Ohio had been Murphy's outright; the momentum had swung. California, New Mexico, and New Jersey were now a week away, and Murphy had a lead of three to six points in most polls. Stadium rental and the cable TV time had cost every cent and then some. As of right now, Russo thought, the Murphy campaign is bust.

One monitor carried a scan of the crowd in the stadium. Russo felt a tingle in his stomach as he checked the faces, listening to words that he himself had helped choose.

"As I sat for three years in a North Vietnamese prison camp," Murphy recalled, "I was filled with an acid hatred of the human systems that had condemned me to that fate and condemned many of my fellow soldiers to death."

The candidate's face appeared semitransparently over the crowd. "I sickened with a loathing of violence that can infect a people when their aims and purposes have gone astray."

The crowd-shot dissolved till the screen showed only Murphy, watching them with the intent, easy gaze of a batter studying an outfield shift. He spoke slowly. "I itched with disgust at leaders who had abdicated their sacred trust to the very people they claimed to serve.

"But in time . . ." Pause, hand stretched out as if to grasp a phrase. "I don't know, maybe it was that diet of rice. I'm a corn and beef-fed boy myself."

The stadium crackled with laughter. Russo shook his head in admiration. Those were no one's words but Murphy's spur-of-the-moment own, tossed out in that offhand, Midwestern way that could undercut any intensity. But he did not lose his tack. "In time, I came to see that such things as war and waste and want could be made obsolete. I came to see, as I sat in that jungle prison, that America could carry the banner for a revival in the soul of our planet.

"That was twenty years ago. I still believe this. But to *do* it, America needs to give her people purpose. For only then can people give America purpose . . . and, in turn, can this nation help give the world purpose. Purpose to break out of our prison camps of poverty. Of hunger. Racism. Despair. Self-satisfied prosperity. . . ."

Cheers erupted with a roar. It was as if the Mets had won another World Series. Even the TV crew—cool professionals—murmured assent. And case-hardened cynic Ray Russo drew a cigar from a humidor in his jacket pocket and for the first time thought: Sweet Mother of Jesus, he's going to go all the way.

Hank Frizzel lay on the big bed in his Riverside Drive townhouse watching his forty-two-inch TV set while the six-foot silver blonde knelt beside him, rubbing cherry-scented love oil into his shoulders. Her name was Corinna—Corky to her friends—and at the moment, except for a black garter belt and stockings, she was naked.

She whined and shifted position to relieve a cramp in one of her long legs. "Hank, when's something interesting gonna happen?"

"When I tell you it is. What is this, the boob tube?" He nudged a breast out of his line of sight. "I'm *watching* this guy."

Corky shuffled her knees again, making the king-size water bed undulate as ripely as her flesh. Frizzel went on studying Timothy Murphy, whose bigger-than-life-size image was talking in stereo about America.

". . . a land where good men should not have to labor without purpose, nor good women labor without equality. We need to awaken this slumbering giant of a land from eight years of somnambulism. . . ."

"Awaken us from this *speech,* you mean," railed Frizzel.

He was a small, quarrelsome man with a taste for large things. The nosey face between receding wavy hair and a retreating chin gave him a look of moving ahead at speed. Which is how he saw himself. In six years he had gone from driving a diaper service van to hosting his own New York radio talk show and penning a weekly column for the *National Insider,* both copyrighted under the title "The Crank's Corner." The name was a station executive's idea, but the rap was pure Queens-born Frizzel, who sounded like a character out of a Jimmy Breslin column—except Frizzel's words were sautéed in acid. He hunted the sacred cows and publicly slaughtered and filleted them each week, collecting a nice bounty for so doing. He had paid for the townhouse as well as the Jaguar in the garage downstairs. Corky, the tall blonde, came more or less free.

Her fingers pinched at the sinews of his shoulders, making him yelp. *"Hey.* Pay attention."

"Sorry. I got watching the speech."

"Let me worry about the speech, okay?"

"That guy's gonna be our next president. I just know it."

"Oh?" Frizzel turned to her with a stare of amazed innocence. "On what do you base this brilliant political analysis?"

"I *feel* it. He's good looking. And he's real honest."

"You believe that, you're a bigger bimbo than six feet. Murphy's got spots on his white hat like all of them. He's just got the hat stashed someplace. But I'll find it."

"You gonna talk about him on your *program?"* The girl-voice rose a half pitch above its usual whine to register surprise.

"No, I'm watching this for my sexual health."

Corky's red-nailed fingers roved over his stomach to his belt. "I got better ways."

Frizzel poked the remote tuner to sag the volume. "Talk on, Mister Candidate. Give us something to remember you by. I'm going to x-ray you, and when I do, I'm writing you out of the story and writing my own ticket to the big time. Phil, baby . . . Geraldo—you guys can punch out and go collect residuals. Hank Frizzel is coming."

Corky giggled.

★ ★ ★

The phone connection wasn't good. Maura Ames's voice faded in and out like a distant radio station, making her husband, who was in Boston, press the receiver tighter against his ear.

"Martha's Vineyard? I thought you were in New York. What about your flight?"

"It's just a small breakup-junket, Martin. We've all been campaigning so hard. Did you see me on TV?"

"I looked for you," he admitted. "What a crowd."

"Incredible. I'll tell you all about it tomorrow. I'll get the bus from Wood's Hole."

Dr. Ames's plans for a quiet dinner at home with his wife drifted away. "All right. Enjoy yourself." Did his disappointment come through in his voice? "See you tomorrow."

"Goodbye, hon."

"Bye." After a moment's indecision, he added, "I love you." But she had already hung up.

Maura Ames replaced the phone, feeling a twinge at the small lie she'd just told. Not actually a lie—an omission. She hadn't informed her husband that the breakup party had only two guests. But the rest had been true; she had been working hard, and she did need a break. And she definitely would be home tomorrow. She patted her crisp brown hair, in which just a tinge of gray was starting to show, and crossed the cafe terrace.

She was aware that the rum drinks made her walk with care, aware too that she was being watched appreciatively. Vaughan Belnap rose to pull out her chair.

At the pool party on Long Island the hostess had practically shoved the two of them together. After that the link had been easy. Vaughan was a Philadelphia attorney who had caught the spirit of Timothy Murphy's campaign early and signed on as an organizer. At the party he had huddled with Maura, talking politics, art and fashion, and she'd been drawn by his charm, which overlay his obvious determination. His interest flattered her. He was due back in Washington tomorrow, but today, he insisted, should be set aside for all Murphy supporters to relish their triumph. The suggestion to carry the conversation over to the Vineyard had come as a natural extension of the day, and she'd surprised herself by accepting.

"All is well at home, I trust," Vaughan said, with a lift of his brows, and Maura thrilled a little at the ambiguity. She was certain this wouldn't end up as an affair—in twenty years of marriage, she'd been faithful to Martin—but just being here, enjoying the late afternoon with an attractive man, was exciting.

Part of her wanted to talk about Martin, and to ask Vaughan about his wife and his family . . . but she didn't. "All is well," she affirmed simply.

Only scattered tables were occupied—guests enjoying the lull before the Memorial Day invasion. At the end of the terrace a fringe of beach-plum trees waved in the sea breeze, and across the island, over Vineyard Sound, clouds soared. "Sunset's going to be spectacular," Maura said. "Can we drive someplace and watch?"

"Done." Vaughan nodded at her camera. "Can you capture it with that?"

"I'll try. Something to remember the weekend by." She grinned. "You'll forgive me if I don't take your picture too."

As they left, Maura noticed a couple sitting in a far corner of the terrace. She realized that the man was familiar to her. She stopped and gripped Vaughan's arm. "Isn't that—?"

She didn't have to complete the question; Vaughan turned, and neither had any doubt that the man in sunglasses and sport clothes sitting beneath the fluttering awning of the cabana bar was Timothy Murphy. Her surprise was mostly at the unexpectedness of seeing him here. The woman with him was not Linda Murphy.

"He's probably doing what we are," Vaughan murmured.

"Catching a breath of ocean air between flights. Great minds think alike."

In truth Murphy seemed anything but relaxed, Maura thought. He was leaning toward the woman, gesturing sharply with his hand. Was he angry? Whatever. Maura was simply excited at seeing the candidate. "I'm going to take his picture," she whispered, raising her Nikon.

Sixty feet away, Murphy went on talking, unaware that any attention was being paid him. The woman, who was small and pretty, with yellow hair, was equally oblivious, intent only on Murphy's words. Then Murphy did turn, sweeping his gaze in their direction as Maura triggered the shutter.

Maura sat astride Vaughan Belnap, who lay on his back beneath her. A single lamp was lit, over which she had draped her apricot silk panties, painting the room with soft light and shadows.

The evening had moved with a seductive inevitability from a barefoot walk on Town Beach at sunset to checking into the guest house. Maura had insisted on getting a room of her own, so they had taken two adjacent, linked by a shared door, closed now. There had been a good dinner and better wine. And now this best part of all.

Straddled atop Vaughan's hips, filmed with a dew of perspiration, Maura swayed in the mellow light, feeling at once graceful and lewd. Reaching, he cupped her breasts, pushing them up and together, then lifted himself and drew his face to her. He bore the mingled scents of wine, cologne, and the musky male warmth the Vineyard sun had kindled.

Maura was rousing toward climax, her nipples electric under the man's knowing touch. She hadn't meant for this to happen. God knew none of this had been planned when she left Boston two days ago . . . and yet, somehow, tonight had been coming during the past year.

With the children gone, marriage had settled into a pattern of separate lives . . . Martin's with his medical practice, hers with the campaign. There was little juncture anymore. Lovemaking came randomly and was quickly forgotten in the weeks that intervened. Still, tonight was one time only. She knew that. Her nuptial love would remain, because it was deep. In fact, now maybe guilt would draw her and Martin nearer . . . this small, intense . . . (she was getting close) thing, with this attractive man (ohh, God) working her expertly now toward their mutual pleasure.

Her head was tipped back, eyes half closed. A moan escaped her throat. Vaughan quickened his tempo, and for just a moment their bodies jarred, then the rhythm was there again and it was all moving toward . . .

She stopped.

Her head came up.

"What?" Vaughan murmured, the pleasured glaze dimming from his eyes.

"Shh." Maura had turned and was looking at the closed door between the adjoining rooms. She'd heard something.

He grabbed her rump, which had prickled suddenly with goosebumps. He pulled her to him, but she resisted and climbed off. Crouching in the semidarkness she whispered, "Someone's in my room."

Perhaps he heard the faint sounds now too, or the certainty in her voice. His arousal was dwindling, his body girding instinctively for a threat. He got up. He put a finger to his lips, signaling her to stay quiet; then, penis abobble, he padded over to the door. He pressed his ear to the panel. Straightening, he turned the lock and opened the door.

From where she sat on the bed, clutching a sheet to her throat, Maura could see the other room only by a muted spill of lamplight from the courtyard outside. Vaughan stepped across the threshold and was standing with his back to her just inside the other room.

"Well?" she asked.

He drew a sudden, audible breath.

"Vaughan? What is it?"

Now he seemed to be humming, making a low buzzing

sound deep in his throat. He stepped backward clumsily, and half turned.

Maura gaped in shock. From the base of his throat down, his chest was wetly dark. All at once loud voices were talking in the other room. It took her a second to realize a television had been switched on.

His eyes wide, Belnap stepped toward her; then his knees buckled and he fell heavily on the carpet. Maura was out of the bed in an instant.

He lay there, his limbs twitching, blood pumping out of a ripped throat. Instinctively she pressed her hand on the wound, aware in her numb terror that it was like trying to stanch a ruptured garden hose. Blood pushed between her fingers. She glanced around frantically. Could she reach the telephone?

A dark figure was standing in the interconnecting doorway. In one hand, swinging from its strap, her camera, in the other, a knife. Unwilling to abandon Vaughan, Maura said, "Who *are* you!"—her voice near hysteria now. "What do you *want?*"

The figure stepped forward. Details registered fast: a tall, beefy man, hair fuller on the sides than on top. Still couldn't make out a face. Naked, she felt doubly vulnerable, but she stayed with Belnap. "Take the camera," she pleaded. "I've got money . . . take it."

The man moved closer.

Under her palm Maura felt the bloodforce fading, the spasms weakening, even as adrenaline sped her own systems. She had to do something if she was going to save Vaughan, save herself.

She drew her hand away and rose. Fighting panic, she grabbed a pillow from the bed and clutched it to her.

She had covered but a short distance when the man came in, leading with the knife. She swung the pillow. Suddenly the air was a blizzard of feathers. She hurled the empty sack aside and lunged for the door.

The man moved quickly, cutting off escape. From the

bedside table, Maura seized the lamp, still draped with her panties, and flung it. The cord yanked loose; the room fell into full darkness. The lamp thumped on the carpeted floor.

She took a step, stumbled. Her back touched a wall; pebbled vinyl pressed cold on her bare flesh as laughs erupted from the adjoining room. A canned sitcom track.

Laughter.

In room twenty-one Maura Ames screamed.

2

Hiram Kirk checked the dial of his watch, just visible in the amber glow of the safelight. It was 7:05 A.M. Time.

Using the thumb and forefinger of his left hand, he drew an 8 × 10 print out of the fixing bath, washed it, and clipped it on a line. He did the same with two others. For a moment, as they dripped, he leaned close and studied them. For another moment, he doubted he was seeing things right. At last he frowned. Only three frames of the roll had been exposed. Shots of a sunset.

When they had dried, he slipped the prints into an envelope which he took, along with a camera, and left the darkroom. There was nobody else in the long, ninth-floor corridor of the J. Edgar Hoover Building. Five minutes later, in a deserted secretarial bullpen on the second floor, he picked up a telephone and punched in a number. It was early, but his call was expected.

"Whatever you thought was on that film," he said to the person who answered, "wasn't." He braced for what came.

"Dammit! That photo gets out, it'll screw up everything! I *want* it."

"There might be a way," Kirk said. He was looking at the Nikon on his lap. A social security number was engraved on the body.

When he hung up, FBI Special Agent Kirk sat on the corner of a desk a moment looking at the lights blinking silently on telephones around the empty office. No matter what time of day it was, somebody was always calling the cops.

A police ambulance was leaving as Eric Thorne parked his six-year-old Wagoneer and picked his way through a growing crowd of the curious. The ringing of church steeple bells drifting faintly from several directions told him it was 11 A.M..

Clad in a baggy, blue hospital shirt, gray pants with big pockets on the thighs, and boat shoes, Thorne had an overnight growth of whiskers that sprouted in the ravines of his face like sagebrush. His wife had once called the face "homely, with Yankee character," though neither face nor character had been enough apparently; his wife was five years gone.

The young summer officer standing at the front entrance of the Captain James Inn, looking both nervous and grim, nodded to Thorne and let him pass.

The Captain James was not one of the big old homes that had been turned into quarters for visitors craving the charm of creaky floors and draughts. This place had been built new and had two floors, modern conveniences, Lagoon Pond views—and rates that would double next weekend. Alden Post, the Vineyard Haven police chief and Thorne's boss, was standing on a rose-colored carpet in the foyer, a clipboard gripped protectively across his midsection, devouring a cigarette. He looked like a man awaiting a hail of bullets.

"Where the hell you been?" he asked Thorne.

"Fishing."

"We got a situation here. *Not yet!*" Post hollered past him at a reporter from the Cape Cod *Times* who was trying to ride his press card by the cop at the front entrance. "Come on."

They moved across the lobby. "I heard bits on the scanner," Thorne said.

Post gazed around a moment, then stubbed his cigarette among the marble chips in the pot of a ficus tree. Wiry, gray, with permanent despair etched in his face, Post was a man simultaneously proud of his family's long past as sea captains and resentful that its heirs had fallen to public servitude. He took it as a personal badge of honor that he hadn't set foot off the island in years. "Nothing like blood to draw flies and reporters," he said gruffly.

For an instant the foyer seemed to teeter, giving Thorne the impression that the carpet had lurched under his feet. Then it steadied. "The scanner said someone's dead."

"*Two.* This way."

Thorne trailed Post through a doorway, up a staircase and along a hallway to an alcove occupied by a Pepsi machine and an ice maker, where Post turned. "The way it looks, we've got an interrupted burglary, sometime between 8 and 10 last night. Victims were stabbed. No valuables left behind." As Post told it, his cigarette breath came at Thorne in hot waves. The state police forensic team had crawled over this place. The victims were on their way to Hyannis for autopsy.

"Do you know who they are?" Thorne asked.

"Off-islanders." Post frowned at his clipboard. "Vaughan Belnap, of Philadelphia. Mrs. Maura Ames, from Boston. They had rooms twenty-one and twenty-three at the end there."

Just then Jimmy Dow and Warren Stubbs came out of one of the rooms. Along with Thorne and Post and two others, they were the year-round police force in Vineyard Haven.

Stubbs's big, inexpressive face was as pale as a daytime moon. In Thorne's four years on the force, he had yet to see Warren smile. It wasn't going to happen today.

"Hello, Ric," Dow said quietly. Short and panther-lean, with Indian hair and eyes, he'd been Thorne's friend since they played football in junior high school. "A bad one," he said.

It was bad. Terrible. There hadn't been a murder on the Vineyard in years. Now two. Thorne still couldn't believe it. Yet, even as he struggled with acceptance, a part of his mind was clearing off a mental desk, readying.

"Prints?" he asked Dow.

"The staties tried hard, but we don't know yet. Looks like the killer wore gloves."

"What about a weapon?"

"A knife, which hasn't turned up yet."

Post said, "I talked to the inn staff. No one saw or heard anything. There were 'Do Not Disturb' cards on both doors this morning. Finally the chambermaid just knocked. Business was so-so last night, but tonight they're booked."

Thorne shook his head. "Not any more."

Twenty-one was quiet. Thorne stood inside with the door closed and drew a slow breath, trying to quiet his mind too, but adrenaline was making the surface choppy. It had been a long time.

Years ago, in another place, he'd had a partner named Mike Pulaski, whose belief it was that every crime scene tried to tell you what had happened. With a sacerdotal turn of phrase Pulaski had called criminal investigation "seeking after the word."

His own visits to murder scenes always brought Thorne to an awareness of his own mortality. During the years before coming back to the Vineyard, he had been at several dozen such scenes: outdoors, in homes, automobiles—each different, yet all alike. Killer and victim had shared a brief, ultimate moment, leaving only mute objects to bear witness. Like a deaf communicant in a church of whispers, Thorne listened now in vain for the word.

Hotel rooms were the toughest. Impersonal, carrying the invisible imprints of a thousand transient strangers, they defied you to find hints. Thorne tried to fit faceless people into this room with the whaling murals on its vinyl walls and Gideon bible on the blond veneer dresser, but he could not. He knew too little yet. Only enough to feel anguish, and a strong wish to be someplace else.

For half an hour he explored the rooms, careful to disturb none of the chaos that the perpetrator and the state police crime team had each made in turn. He checked the windows. He squatted amid wafting feathers to peer at shapes outlined in tape on the stained carpet. The bed linen in both rooms was gone. White smudges assured him that the state team had been thorough in looking for prints. The traps had been removed from the sink and tub in both bathrooms. The team would have taken lab samples and photographs. Autopsy results would be available tonight or tomorrow morning. In a notebook Thorne made notes and sketches of his own.

Post was still standing outside smoking. "Well?"

It was the tone you used when you expected someone to look stupid. "Put out the cigarette, Alden."

Thorne walked him through the scenario point by point: where the killer had entered from next door; where Belnap had fallen; where the woman may have backed away, perhaps trying to fend off attack with a pillow. There was an umber splash on the wall, two feet above the baseboard, six feet from the door, with a few feathers glued to it. Post didn't look any happier with the analysis than he did with anything else.

There was one thing Thorne was having trouble fitting in. "Her room was there, but both ended up in here—what was their relationship?"

At last Post's mouth dipped at the edges in a shark's grin. "You're doing just fine without me, but I'll give you a hint. The pair of them were naked as snakes." He slapped the clipboard at Thorne's flat stomach. "You're the one used to play detective. You get to handle this."

Objections sprang to Thorne's mind—he was on vacation, and he had given up homicide work when he'd left Boston—but before he could voice them, Post jerked a thumb over his shoulder. "Which means you can talk to the wolfpack of reporters who'll be on the next ferry. But shave first, so we don't look like yokels. And put on your uniform. This ain't the big fuckin' city."

Lorraine Patton sat before her computer screen at the D. C. Writers Guild, thinking about dolphins, trying to keep her anger positive. She had, that morning, come from viewing a film which documented that the intelligent marine mammals were still being slaughtered by holdout members of the tuna-canning industry. Now she was composing her column for a community weekly newspaper, the focus this time on the almost sure extinction of certain species of dolphin.

The office was a fourth-floor commercial loft in a Washington neighborhood tourists didn't visit. These days the Writers Guild consisted of an IBM PC, a printer, answering machine, and Lorraine.

Formerly there had been Ethan Ross, with whom Rain had co-founded the guild and established the weekly, each all the while holding a paying job—Ethan as a political science professor, Lorraine a waitress, a skill she'd learned in the West Virginia coal-mining town where she'd grown up, and which might well have remained her life work.

A year and a half ago, five months after Ethan's death, she had sold a piece to the *Post* Sunday Magazine entitled "The Unsentimental Education of Timothy Murphy." Her thesis was that Murphy's hardworking Midwestern boyhood, Ivy League education, and Vietnam experience had been the crucibles for a nontraditional legislator who just might be a person America was in need of. A week after the article appeared, an agent from New York called.

It wasn't an instant match. Rain's publishing credits were few, and Murphy was only beginning to attract interest outside of his home state of Indiana; but the agent was aggressive, and a small publisher liked Rain's proposal. Last fall, *Heartlander: The Making of a Leader* appeared, with a dedication to Ethan Ross. The book was a brief, unvarnished portrait of Murphy, whom Rain saw as a refreshing lawmaker, a curious if contradictory blend of John Kennedy and Ronald Reagan in his broad personal appeal to the American imagination. It had gotten good reviews, including a note from Murphy himself. More practically, the book ended her immediate worries about money. She bought a newer car and some furniture for her apartment. Rent on the office loft was low enough that she intended to keep the place until the lease ran out. Now, the publishers having rushed to capitalize on Murphy's momentum (and compete with the inevitable spate of campaign bios), *Heartlander* was due out in paperback in a few days.

The telephone rang. Rain looked up from her keypad and waited for the answering machine get it.

"Cute message, doll," said a male voice after the beep. "Listen, this is Hank Frizzel calling from the Apple. I read your book. Even liked some of it. But there's stories you didn't tell. Call me." He left a number.

Well, what do you know, Lorraine thought. Hank the Crank—just as overripe in person, as he was in his alleged journalism. She rewound the tape and played it again. "Stories you didn't tell." Now what did Frizzel mean by that?

She considered his request for a moment, then decided she liked the company of dolphins a whole lot better.

Midday heat shimmered from the valley floor as the motorcade whistle-stopped through a series of desert towns, homing westward toward the distant, vaporous skies of Los Angeles. In the backseat of one of the limos, Senator Murphy sat with Ray Russo, rehearsing the text of an address Murphy would deliver at a dinner in Irvine that evening. Russo only half listened. He was preoccupied with the protocols of the black-tie crowd that had paid three hundred dollars a plate to be there tonight. Keep them happy, and the war chest would runneth over. Displease them, punch the wrong buttons, and Murphy's share of the Orange County vote in the upcoming state primary wouldn't fill a doggie bag.

The limo slowed, prompting Russo to glance ahead through the smoked-glass divider. Some kind of commotion appeared to be going on. Traffic had reached an impatient standstill, and he could see the blink of police car lights. He pressed the intercom button.

"What is it, driver?"

"Looks like a demonstration, sir. There're people with signs."

The activity was centered at the next intersection. Police had set up barricades, bottlenecking the main road to a single sluggish lane. As the limo crept nearer, Russo could see a crowd gathered in front of a drab, dilapidated building, which had logs sticking sideways out of the top of its stucco walls like an Indian trading post. A peeling sign said: VETERAN'S DROP-IN CENTER. CLOSED was whitewashed messily across the windows. Picketers milled beyond the barricades.

Russo groaned. "Driver, radio ahead and let the cops know who we are. We get stuck in this mess, we'll have long beards before we get to L.A."

"Hold it," Murphy said, speaking for the first time. He leaned forward, eyeing the activity outside. "What town is this, Ray?"

"East Buffalo Chip, from the looks of it. Driver?"

"It's Las Alas, senator."

"What does that translate as?"

"Uh . . . 'The Wings.' "

"Pull over."

"Jesus, Tim," Russo protested, "this isn't part of our—"

But Murphy had opened his door and stepped out.

Wasting no time, Russo scrambled out too. He flagged the trailing car. Three government security men emerged from it. "Let's stay with him," Russo instructed needlessly.

All four of them set off after the candidate.

Through heat and dust, Murphy took in details: nervous-looking sheriff's deputies trying to hold back a growing crowd. But from what? What was going on? The detail he didn't have to question was his own quickening excitement.

Years ago, at college, he'd been in a New Haven bar one night, prior to The Game. A drunken argument over whether Yale would make it a perfect season by trouncing Harvard became overheated, and someone crashed a bottle against the bar to add jagged emphasis to his words. Murphy had been sitting a few booths away with friends, unconcerned with football; but at the shattering of glass, followed by instant silence in the room, he slid out of his seat and, with his hands spread calmingly, moved straight toward the kid gripping the bottleneck. One of Murphy's pals managed to pull him back, and the bartender quickly got the situation under control; but afterwards, Murphy, a quiet, hardworking honor student, made a discovery about himself. At the moment of crisis his impulse had been to step forward.

In his dozen years of public life, starting as a state rep, followed by the past two terms in the Senate, Murphy had occasionally felt again that instinct, irrational and potentially dangerous, to plunge into the action. And as a U.S. senator, he found many people ready to caution him but few willing to pull him back.

Beyond the barricades stood an inner ring of police clad in flak vests and cradling shotguns. On the other side of them Murphy noticed for the first time a group of eight or ten men. Garbed in old and unmatched military uniforms, they were sitting in the road, where they had padlocked themselves to a long, heavy-link chain. Other picketers tried to join them but were kept back by the cops. The crowd seemed polarized and growing irritable in the heat. Then Murphy saw something that blew a chill across his heart. The seated men were holding grenades.

Just outside a barricade stood a man with a gold star affixed to the front of his straw ranch hat and a walkie-talkie in his hand. Judging him to be the person with authority, Murphy approached.

Russo was hurrying through the crowd after Murphy, his photo-gray glasses darkening in the glare, like a presentiment crossing his mind. This was no damn place for a politician. Safety aside, it was a heads-you-win-tails-I-lose situation. Hell, did you stand with law and order or with vets?

What made it worse, Russo saw now, was that the rear cars of the L.A.-bound motorcade had parked. The members of the media trailing the campaign like camp dogs came trundling out with camcorders and notebooks, their nostrils whiffing the ripe smell of a story.

Russo spotted Murphy conferring with a tin-star cowboy. The sheriff waved some of his deputies over. Then, flanked by the security men and the deputies, Murphy was led past the barricades into the enclosure beyond.

At the sight of the wedge of police and the gray-suited man moving toward them, the rag-tag army of picketers began to close ranks around their chain-linked comrades. Reading their jumpiness, Murphy stopped. He instructed his escort to go back. There was hesitation, especially by the federal guards.

"Back," he snapped, and reluctantly they responded.

His raised voice quieted that part of the crowd nearest to him, and wavelike, the silence began to spread. He was going to get one try at this, he thought, and it was either going to work, or there'd be hell to pay. The sheriff had given him the gist of the situation. Over the outcry of veterans groups, the state had shut the drop-in center a week ago. Here in Las Alas, where the unemployment rate was high, the vets depended heavily on the center. Now it was gone. A few days ago there'd been a break-in at a National Guard armory in Fresno, a case of grenades stolen. This morning a group of men had showed up, slung a long chain around the vet's center door, and handcuffed themselves to it. If the center wasn't reopened by noon, they threatened there was going to be real trouble.

Maybe it was a bluff, as the sheriff had tentatively suggested. But if it wasn't . . .

Murphy felt a droplet of sweat roll over his breastbone, behind which his heart had begun to pound.

In the faces of the demonstrators, he read long-suppressed frustration that easily could burst forth in violence. These were the men who had not readjusted well; who had fought the other wars of substance abuse, bad marriages, scrapes with the law, losing them all, until finally they'd retrenched in their roles as "vets," men unwilling to let go of the past, because they had no real present or future. To them this rundown building was Hamburger Hill. It represented the only turf they had held from a powerful enemy, and they couldn't afford to lose any more.

He glanced at his watch. Ten minutes till noon.

Resisting an urge to wipe his brow, he surveyed the protesters the way he had scanned the cordon of police, looking for one person . . . one face.

The man sat in the middle of the line, with a rusty scraggle of beard and a ranger hat, staff sergeant's chevrons striping his army shirt. He wore wraparound sunglasses, but through the smoked lenses Murphy felt a gaze locked on his own. Warily, the man cradled a grenade like it was an egg he was ambivalent about hatching.

Forcing himself, Murphy moved nearer. Five feet from the sergeant he stopped. Hesitating only one breath, he brought his right hand to his brow in a salute.

Russo pressed his belly against a barricade. There was no script for this. Tim was on his own.

"Sergeant." Murphy's voice rang firmly yet respectfully. "My name is Tim Murphy. I'm not a policeman. I'm not from Las Alas or even California." He gestured toward the highway. "I was passing through."

One corner of the the veteran's beard cracked open. "Then haul ass outta here. This ain't your war."

Among the crowd there was a tensing. Deputies' shotguns shifted.

"Actually, sergeant," Murphy said, "it is my war. And yours, each one of you. And everyone's in the whole country. We're all Americans."

The sergeant exchanged glances with his comrades, then he turned back. "Americans, huh? What the hell you know about being American?"

Didn't the idiot know who he was *talking* to? Russo thought. In the sudden silence he heard the motor drive of cameras, the snapping on of cassette recorders, and, distantly, the wailing of sirens. His gut was cramping.

And then, God help us, Murphy dipped his head and

smiled! The burn-out in the soldier suit was cursing him, and Murphy was smiling!

"As a matter of fact, sergeant, that's something I've been asking myself for years now. I don't have an answer . . . but I have some thoughts."

"Yeah?" piped up another protester, a man with a wild bird's nest of hair. "Stick 'em where the sun don't shine."

"Listen up, you clowns!" roared the sheriff. "You got any idea who you're sassin'? This here's U.S. Senator Murphy. Running for *president!*"

The name registered. The face. Murphy had been in the papers, on TV. Whoever in the crowd had not known did now as murmurs swelled through the factions. The tenseness didn't go away, but it changed. Murphy was the point man now.

Sweat was running down Russo's cheeks like the monologue running in his mind. Okay, Tim, wrap it up. Let's get out of here. Let the pros take over. The shakers and spenders are going to be waiting in L.A. That's where we've got to swing the big stick. Forget this sad little drama. These losers don't even vote . . .

Murphy gestured toward the crowd, the knot of reporters, and beyond them the encircling line of lawmen. "You've got an audience, sergeant. Why don't you have your say."

"What is this shit?" the soldier hissed.

"It's what you wanted, isn't it?"

The man's fingers twitched on the grenade, as though reading there some Braille of warning. Suddenly, he pulled the ring pin. Everyone else gasped, expecting to die.

Nothing happened. The soldier held the spring lever clamped.

Except to draw a slow breath, Murphy didn't move. "Tell it," he coaxed softly.

Russo felt midway between cardiac arrest and wetting himself. He wanted to flee, but his legs wouldn't have moved.

"This is your chance to do something," Murphy went on.

"Or would you rather use that grenade and let it all end with just a noise?"

Beneath the fringe of his beard, the soldier's throat worked. "People would hear it," he croaked. "Seems all people *react* to anymore is noise and blood."

"Oh, they'd react all right," Murphy agreed. "Peter Jennings would say your name on network news tonight, and you'd be in tomorrow's paper. And folks would shake their heads and cluck their tongues. Poor mixed-up vets. Then what? Where are you? Is this center going to open up again? Are other vets going to get a fair shake? Or will people just look at them with fear and hatred, wondering when the next one is going to snap?"

With a cricket-squeak the spring lever rose a fraction of its arc.

Like an electric current sparking along the line, tension widened the eyes of the other men as they glanced at the sergeant; but if he felt their fear, he kept it hidden behind his sunglasses.

"Doesn't matter," he said. "This government . . . this whole country's finished."

With his free hand he took off the sunglasses and dragged a sleeve across his tortured brow. Startled, Russo saw that one of his eyes was gone. What remained was just the scorched and shriveled hole it had been ripped from.

Tim didn't flinch. "So tell it, at least," he challenged. "Give it an epitaph."

Silence stretched to the tenuous length of a breath. At last the soldier replaced his sunglasses. Slowly at first, but soon hemorrhaging out of him as if from a wound, words came. His theme was how America had lost its chance to reclaim its soul. Not a whisper issued from the crowd. Russo stood rooted.

"We didn't want it to go down this way. But what other way is there? You sent us off to kill and be killed, and what good did it do anyone? The haters won out. Some of us came home, and what'd we get? Hassle, man. Shame. We didn't even get a sorry-ass parade.

"You closed down this place and others like it, and you're gonna have to reap the harvest. The only way out I see is . . ." He gazed at a distant point, as if seeing some fiery apocalyptic end to his pain. "Is . . ."

"Sergeant," Murphy broke in quietly, almost plaintively, "isn't there another way?"

"You tell me, man. What way?"

"You said it yourself. What was ever gained by violence?"

"Who are you? Some dude in a suit."

"It's just a uniform, different from yours, but I've been there too."

"Sure, in the movies. You and Rambo."

"What's important is that, win or lose, we're all here now," said Murphy. "In Las Alas—'The Wings.' "

Moving carefully, he drew off his suitcoat, dropped it on the street. He unsnapped the link on his left shirt cuff and began turning back the sleeve. When his forearm was exposed to the elbow, he held it out.

Russo jumped as someone touched his shoulder. "Sir," one of the campaign aides whispered urgently. "We're going to be late."

"Are you crazy?" Russo hissed under his breath. "For what? A few hundred *rich* fucks who're going to back the senator anyway? Wake up. We *won!*"

All around people were craning their necks for a view, but Russo already knew what was happening. He knew the symbol that had been inked in the skin of Murphy's forearm years ago in a Viet Cong prison camp. The veteran gazed at it wonderingly, then slowly lifted his eyes to Murphy, who held his hand out, waiting.

Gay Head rose from Vineyard Sound in a huge upthrust fist of pale clay that took the stain of sunset on its knuckles. Thorne cut the outboard, and the boat's momentum died with the noise.

"Much better," said Jimmy Dow from the rear seat. "Good idea borrowing Rufus's boat. Those phones and reporters were getting to me."

Thorne lowered the anchor partway to create drag and bring the bow around into the long, glassy swells. The muscles in his lean arms clenched as he tied the line off. Straightening, he peered at Gay Head, etched by weather and time to a lunar starkness. The Indians who had occupied the Vineyard as far back as 4500 years ago had long since been wiped out or assimilated. Their descendants peddled souvenirs and junk food from stands atop the cliffs. "Ever wish you lived in your ancestors' days?" he asked.

"Negative. They've found fossil teeth in that clay from sharks a hundred feet long." Jimmy spread his arms dramatically. "What kind of world needed predators that big?"

"An obsolete one. About five-foot-ten does just fine now. Here."

Thorne tossed him one of the two envelopes that had come over on the six o'clock ferry from Woods Hole. Thorne opened the second. Inside were results of autopsies performed on the stabbing victims found at the Captain James Inn. A lot of the data were technical analyses: stomach contents, blood and urine, conditions of various organs. He skimmed, pausing when something caught his attention, like the detail that Maura Ames's body had contained only traces of seminal fluid; Belnap had not ejaculated. This gave credence to the idea that the victims had been interrupted by their killer, but it answered none of Thorne's questions.

Dow said, "The lab found latent fingerprints of both decendents and three other people in the rooms. No ID on the three yet. They'll be checking the prints against those we took from the inn staff."

"Autopsy showed that a single stab wound killed Belnap," Thorne reported. "Severed his carotid artery. Maura Ames was stabbed twice. The wounds were made by a long, double-edged knife, delivered with downward thrusts. Her collar bone was broken by the force."

They went on examining the reports, remarking aloud on details that struck them. Questions kept mounting. At last Thorne flopped the pages down. "So where are we?" he asked.

"Bobbing out here in a big ocean?" Dow shrugged. "Maybe we'll get lucky and something on the inventory will turn up in hock. Or the fingerprints'll give us our man."

"Maybe."

"But you don't think so."

"The ends don't butt right."

"Keep going."

The Whaler's stern had swung around to the southwest. Far off in Rhode Island Sound a tanker was plying northeastward on a brilliantly sunlit sea. Thorne watched it a moment under the flat of his hand, then drew his gaze back. "Figure someone hits a guest room for valuables and gets interrupted. But in a tourist resort, who's going to know you? And is a couple in bed likely to chase you? So you do a fast fade. There's a long, lucrative season ahead. You definitely don't kill people, then wait around for us to come looking."

"It's a puzzler," Dow granted. "Every suspect we've talked to has a skintight story. Which points to the killer being an off-islander. You think the victims recognized him and he panicked and killed them?''

"There's another way to read it. This report says a long two-edged knife. Not your basic burglar tool. The ransacked drawers and luggage could've been a cover for a different motive.''

Dow looked surprised. "Think we're dealing with a freak?''

Thorne shook his head. "Three stabs for two victims doesn't read that way. No, suppose the idea was murder, but planned.''

"You serious?''

He was, sort of; it explained some things. But as they went on talking, they raised many more questions than they answered. Around them dusk began to gather. Finally, while Dow pulled anchor, Thorne started the motor. He switched on the running lights, and they made their way back to moorage in the brooding dark.

Ray Russo laid a fresh cigar on the linen place mat in the Cafe Chablis patio at Irvine's Registry Hotel and signaled for the waiter to bring him another Grand Marnier Centennaire. He leaned back, slipped his fingers beneath his cummerbund. He felt great.

Even his chagrin at his abject fear that afternoon had faded. The Las Alas incident—as network news reports were already calling it—had been a coup. News teams had cranked footage of Murphy convincing the vets to give up their grenades. Members of the print media had come to tonight's affair just long enough to get some flavor for their stories (including the surprising turnout in this bastion of conservatism) before they disappeared to polish their versions of the Las Alas incident for the next editions. Less than an hour ago California's governor announced that he had found funds to reopen the Las Alas vets' center and a dozen like it around the state.

Russo saw that the waiter bringing his liqueur was also

guiding a guest. Smiling with pleasure, he rose. "Prudence. God, you're ageless. And beautiful."

"And you, sir, are a practiced liar." Prudence Winters held out jeweled hands and smiled. Her small, even teeth had the patina of antique ivory. "Hello, Raymond."

She settled into the chair he held out for her and told the waiter to bring a glass of chablis. "One of the concessions to advanced decrepitude," she complained to Russo. "I cannot drink honest liquor anymore."

"Nor does the president, I hear," Russo said, watching her.

Prudence raised her brows. "Is this a spy mission?"

He laughed and said no, and they drew their chairs closer to the table, nearer the dance of the candle flame. He asked and was given permission to light his cigar.

Prudence Winters, widow of Senator Clarence Winters, had aged well. At sixty-six she was every bit as lovely as she had been a decade ago when Russo worked for Senator Winters, and her voice had never lost the charming rhythms of her Baton Rouge childhood.

"I was surprised to see your name on the guest list tonight, Prudence," he said. "Surprised and pleased. I knew you'd begun wintering out here after the senator died, but somehow I don't expect you to be among Murphy supporters in the Land of Sunshine."

"Duke Wayne Airport may be across the street, but open minds aren't extinct here. Anyway, I'm just looking. I have a vested interest in the other party." She crinkled her eyes, and he smiled acknowledgement of their shared secret: that Prudence was the widowed president's woman.

"I thought maybe you believed that if you can't beat 'em, join 'em. I learned to do that long ago, after the senator lost." While to others Russo sometimes used ruder names for the woman's late husband, to her, Clarence Winters was always "the senator." "In fact, it was he who eventually encouraged me to join up with Tim. Did you know that?"

Pru nodded, remembering. "Clarence wasn't bitter about

his loss. He always had the grace to take responsibility for his actions.''

A rare quality in American public life, Russo thought. Even caught red-handed, most people sniveled and pointed fingers.

"Besides," Pru said, "Clarence felt that young Mr. Murphy probably was right for the state. And now perhaps he's going to be right for the country. Tonight's speech was inspiring. Is he as good as he seems to be, Raymond?''

With no hesitation, Russo said, "Yes. He is.''

"I'm glad, because triumphant days like today come too seldom in anyone's life. The bad days are far more common. Remember that.''

"I shall.''

They ordered coffee and talked. And maybe because of their acquaintance over the years, Prudence turned to the topic of her husband's political fall. Russo would never have brought it up himself, but the subject intrigued him, and he attended fascinatedly, like a pigeon near a park bench, waiting for dropped crumbs. Details of the late senator's trouble had reached very few ears.

At the time, Russo had been a factotum for Winters, who had held term continuously since just after the Second World War. When his close associates discovered that the senator was keeping regular if secret company with a former Redskins quarterback, they approached him, knowing full well that a public revelation of the story would grab instant and damning attention in an otherwise lean season for politics and Washington sports. Even so, with his clout, Winters might have held his legislative seat; but there was his family to consider. He chose not to seek reelection, and the matter quietly faded. State Senator Murphy won his first federal term.

"The irony was, Clarence was an honest and deeply moral man," Prudence insisted. "Unfortunately, he was a lustful man too, as I discovered soon after I married him. But in all other ways he was moderate, and he always kept that one small failing quiet. In fact, I came to understand it because it mirrored a part of me. An undeveloped part, you understand.''

Russo frowned. Was she telling him that—?

She smiled as if reading his thoughts. ''I'm saying that I too liked men.'' They both laughed and watched smoke drift away on the dry night air.

When the maître d' appeared and told Russo there was a long-distance phone call, he took it at the inside bar.

''Ray, glad I found you,'' said the campaign press agent back in Washington. ''This may or may not be important. The Boston *Herald* contacted me a half hour ago. They're looking to confirm that one of our people was a *murder* victim.''

''*What?''* Russo experienced an odd little spin of vertigo. ''Who?''

''Remember Vaughan Belnap?''

Russo sank onto a bar stool. Belnap had helped coordinate the rally the day before yesterday. He was *dead?* ''Details,'' Russo demanded.

Details were scarce. There had been a second victim too, a woman who did volunteer work for the campaign in Massachusetts. Both had been stabbed. The police had delayed in order to notify family first. Two facts stuck in Russo's head: the time and the place of the killings.

Back at the table he tried to resurrect the former mood, but Prudence Winters finally said: ''Raymond, don't suspect me—I'm too old to do anything save think it—but you look as if someone had reached under the table and tweaked your future.''

Vineyard Haven police chief Alden Post paced in his stark little office like a badgered animal yipping at the outside world that had invaded his domain. "Boston, Philadelphia . . . Godsake, why don't you put in for *Hawaii* while you're at it?"

With thinning patience Thorne reminded him that he hadn't asked for the case, that he was supposed to be on vacation this week.

"If this were some wacko holed up here on the island," Post went on, "that'd be one thing. But you're talking about maybe chasing around half the country. I've got no budget for that. Contact those people by phone."

Thorne had considered it, and if there were a way to pursue the investigation without leaving, he would've jumped at it. But there wasn't. "It's not the same," he said. "You can't *see* what they're saying." He didn't mention the courtesy of speaking in person to the victims' families because Post wouldn't accept that. What Post did accept, though grudgingly, was that an effort had to be made. The state police had helped with lab analyses, but the crime had happened here. It was Post's jurisdiction—and Thorne's job.

Dropping into his chair, Post examined a thumbnail, chewed a corner of it, made a spitting noise. "You take your own car, I'll authorize limited costs for a few days. *Limited.*"

"All right. And I'd like Jimmy Dow's help with some details here while I'm gone."

Post was resigned. "With the understanding that he's back in the rotation come Saturday. When the tourist invasion starts, I want to be at full strength."

"If we don't handle this right, you won't need any help at all."

"What the hell's that mean?"

Thorne covered the two steps to the door before he turned. "You know it, and I know it, Alden. If folks are scared, the summer trade will dry up and blow over to Nantucket and the Cape. Then we can all sit around and twiddle our nightsticks."

By the time Thorne reached Boston, the rain that had threatened during the drive up from the Cape was falling, smudging the skyline that he hardly recognized anymore anyway. It had been four years since he'd left here, and he hadn't been back. The sight of the city roused memories, but he pulled back from them and focused on directions.

Dr. Martin Ames had his practice in a three-story whitestone near the Fine Arts Museum. Judging from the signs in the lobby, there were more doctors in the one building than on all of the Vineyard. Some of the specialties seemed like linguistic jokes.

The waiting room was desolate, the empty armchairs and well-thumbed magazines giving it an air of futile expectancy. A red-haired receptionist with a tuneful brogue told Thorne that the doctor had canceled appointments for the week but was expecting *him*. She showed him in.

Martin Ames was older than his wife had been, a knotty, athletic man with a horseshoe of gray hair around a sunfreckled scalp. He exuded energy as he came across his examining room to shake hands. He told his receptionist she could go for the day, and he shut the door behind her.

"I appreciate you're calling . . . and coming to see me." Ames pronounced the words carefully, as if he were sifting among many possibilities to find the right ones. "I don't think I'm ready for a trip to the Vineyard. This has been a very . . . difficult week."

The sudden aroma Thorne caught wasn't routine medical office smell; more like 80-proof double-bonded. "Yes, sir. I'm sorry to say we don't have more leads than what I told you about on the phone. We're pretty clear on the sequence of events last Saturday night. And the lab results have filled some gaps. Two sets of fingerprints in the rooms belonged to inn employees. A partial third set may belong to the person we want. So far though, there's no match in any police file."

"So as for suspect, or motive . . ." Ames's words trailed off.

"Nothing yet," Thorne said, watching his eyes, though all they showed was bleakness.

"That's why you're here?"

"Partly."

"Should I be on the examining table over there?"

"I'm just hoping to fill in some background, sir."

"I'm not being much of a host. Have a chair. Uh . . . drink?"

Thorne's acceptance surprised him. The corners of his mouth twitched upward in an uncertain, maybe even grateful smile. "I'm taking solace from friends. I've got Jack and Johnny and . . ."

"Whatever you're drinking."

From a cabinet he got a bottle of Black Jack and poured some over ice cubes, which he took from a tray in the stainless steel sink.

"You a handicap golfer?" Thorne asked conversationally.

Ames showed surprise, glancing around to try to see what might have tipped it off. "How'd you know that?"

"Your left hand's less tanned than your right—from wearing a glove would be my guess."

Ames's chuckle tried for lightness but just missed. "Low eighties," he said, clinking his glass against Thorne's.

He drank his own quickly. It seemed to steady him. But the bottle was half full—or half empty—so Thorne decided to be direct. "Doctor, how was your marriage?"

In the fluorescent light, the man's eyes glittered, his smile gone, and Thorne awaited an angry retort. It didn't come, though. Ames refilled his glass and settled into a desk chair whose ridged vinyl back exhaled softly. He wheeled forward on a lucite carpet protector. "Evidently not as good as I thought," he said quietly, and for a time that was all he said. Thorne didn't hurry him. Growing up among laconic people, he had learned to read men as much by their silences as by what they said. And on the topic of marriage he had some thoughts too.

"Maura was a freshman at B.U.," Ames resumed after a sip of bourbon. "I was doing a residency when we met. We got married the next year."

Their lives grew through a process of accrual: a son, a daughter, a practice. He called it ideal: a nice level of luxury and enough activity to keep any of them from having to examine the parts too closely. "Then, before we knew it, the kids were grown and flown. We sold the Weston house and moved in town. I sometimes wonder which comes first—the conditions, or the terms *Time* magazine invents to name them. Empty nest syndrome, midlife crisis . . ."

He talked looking at his hands, turning them over, considering them from varied angles, as if they had failed him in some way, or something had slipped irretrievably through them. "Marty finished Belmont Hill School this month, and Julia studies with Martha Graham in New York. We were supposed to go down for a recital next weekend."

"Tell me about your wife," Thorne coaxed.

Ames drank again. "Twenty years ago Maura was excited about politics. Majored in it. She got clean with Gene, she marched. Even got busted once." He gave a forlorn laugh at the remembrance. "But then, with raising kids, and being a doctor's wife . . . well, she got busy. This past year though, it was like old times for her. She really caught the campaign bug. I was proud of her. Although I don't think I let her know that."

"We all do the best we can," Thorne said. "Doctor, did you know Vaughan Belnap?"

As he had doubtlessly often done in the past few days,

Ames played with the name. He studied the ice cubes in his glass as if he were searching them for subliminal images of people performing sex acts. At last he shook his head. "Never heard of him before all this. In fact, I honestly don't think Maura had either before last weekend. My guess is they met at the rally and . . . things happened."

"The Murphy rally in New York?"

"She flew down Friday, excited as a kid going to Disneyland." Ames picked up a yellow Kodak packet and handed it across the desk. "These came today."

Thorne opened the packet and took out snapshots: people in imitation straw hats holding campaign signs, a band in striped shirts, swimmers splashing in a pool.

"Always the efficient one, Maura," said Ames with a laugh. "She couldn't even wait to bring film home; she popped it in a mailer and sent it out from the Vineyard."

Thorne went through the prints. Maura Ames smiling prettily in an airport waiting area, a shot of the Murphy falcon, a man and a woman sitting at a patio table. He brought this last print closer. The man was familiar but, in the setting, a surprise. The picture had been taken on the Vineyard—Edgartown, he thought, though it could have been Oak Bluffs, which were the only villages on the island where alcohol was sold.

He held up the snapshot. "Senator Murphy?"

"That's him."

"Who's the woman?"

"No idea. She's not his wife. I've seen too many campaign brochures not to know that."

Thorne studied the picture a moment. "You mind if I hold onto this awhile?"

"Be my guest. Is that evidence of something?"

He didn't know yet. There were more questions, a few more answers, and outside the rain fell, slowly drowning the city the way Ames went on drowning his pain. When he poured the last amber splash of liquor, Thorne said to him, "You ought to go easy."

"Physician heal thyself, huh? Not to worry. Alcohol's a

pickling agent, and that's what I'm hoping for. Just temporarily. I've got children and this practice. Yesterday I had the best Goddam graveside manner y'ever saw. So today . . . cheers." Magnified through the bottom of the tumbler, his teeth were horsey. As he rinsed the glasses in the sink he looked out a window. "It's coming down out there. I'd better call a cab."

"Can I give you a lift?"

The doctor turned back, and for the first time his energy seemed to fail him. He balanced on the counter and let his breath out in a sigh. "A ride maybe. A lift? A boost of spirit? I don't know. That's going to take some doing."

While the windshield wipers and idling engine kept rhythm, Thorne printed his name and the Vineyard Haven police phone number on a page of his notebook and tore it out. "We don't get much call for business cards. If you think of anything, or if you just want to talk . . ."

"Thanks." With care Ames folded the notebook page and put it into his shirt pocket. They shook hands, then Thorne watched him get out and dodge unsteadily between parked cars and up the short, puddled walkway to his building. A sodden *Murphy for President* sign was pegged in the tiny lawn. Ames's bare head shone wetly a moment in the outside lamplight as he unlocked the door and ducked in.

At an intersection a car ran a stop sign, forcing Thorne to brake. The yellow Kodak packet shot out from beside the passenger seat where it must have fallen from Ames's pocket. Thorne retrieved it. He pulled to the curb, put on the map light, and went through the snapshots again. Beyond the one he already had borrowed, none interested him. He thought about just mailing the prints back, but he knew they were one of Ames's last links with his wife. He locked the Jeep and hiked down the block.

As he started across the street, he heard a muffled yell. Looking up, he saw a shape plummeting from the rainy, black air. There was a thunderous *bam*. He ran, full of sudden misgiving.

A body lay twisted on the buckled trunk of a Cadillac. Inside the car a stuffed cartoon cat was climbing the cracked rear window on suction-cup paws. Passersby seemed to arrive from nowhere, their umbrellas bumbling together on the sidewalk. Thorne shouldered through to the victim. He probed a limp wrist for a pulse beat, aware as he did so that his own pulse was hammering in his head.

"God, it just happened, he just fell," gasped one of the onlookers.

"Or jumped," said another. "Somebody should call a doctor."

Thorne didn't reply that the victim *was* a doctor. Or that he was dead.

The producer of WENC Radio's evening programming gave a thirty-second signal, cueing Hank Frizzel to begin his wrap-up.

"So, to all the small-brained small-business yoyos who think that doing their own TV ads is high camp, listen up! The public has had it up to *here* with tender chickens and insane stereo prices! Therefore, I'm urging the governor this week to make it a capital crime for any merchandiser to do his own commercials. Bunch of amateurs! The only thing pro about you clowns is your *egos!* From the 'Crank's Corner,' this is Hank Frizzel." He paused, then gave his signature sign-off: "Hang in there, Baby."

As Frizzel left the studio, the producer sitting beyond the glass wall aimed a finger-and-thumb pistol at him and bent to a microphone. "Bull's-eye, Hank."

Frizzel could see the switchboard already lighting up with telephone calls. "Too easy. Like shooting turds in a toilet. I need some *moving* targets for a change."

"Don't argue with success. You're top gun in the average Joe's everyday struggle. Just keep firing. You know an easier way to hold up the bank?"

Frizzel twirled a raised forefinger in small loops. "Let's hear it for the tax man."

He went down the hall and locked himself in his office.

On his desk lay a briefing sheet for his next show—an exposé of the business practices of a well-known evangelist. He pushed it aside. Among the memo slips was a note from Corky, who'd stopped by on her way back from shopping and would have dinner ready at home. The o in her signature bore a tiny smiling face. Terminally cute. He could picture her: Stouffer's meals in the micro while she sat watching *"America's Funniest Home Videos"* or some such dreck, waiting for him to get there to try out a new love toy she'd bought in Times Square that day. She was starting to bore him a little. Beneath the garter belt and lace chiffon teddy she was just a fuzz-brained broad looking for home and hearth. He skimmed the other memos, then canned them all.

What really irked him was that none of his so-called contacts had called back with a word on Timothy Murphy. But as he pondered this, his peeve started to turn to interest. Wasn't it his long-held belief that politicians were slugs? That they all left slime trails? So Murphy was just more careful than most about covering his. Finding it posed a challenge. Ah, but when I do, thought Frizzel—now there was a moving target.

"Alcohol in his blood. Sink full of dirty dishes. His neighbors said he hadn't been himself. Shit, you're reaching, guy."

Thorne took a faint hope from Mike Pulaski's words.

At 2 A.M. Pulaski's desk lamp was the only light on in the maze of dark cubicles that was the detectives bureau of Boston's Area C police station. Pulaski was tipped back in his chair, the rim of lamplight revealing just his meaty chin and the mashed end of his nose. Thorne didn't have to see the skeptical eyes. They were a fixture with Pulaski, like the generic form of address and the bad cigarette habit. The two men had come close to being friends once, but then Thorne had left the department. Pulaski was a lieutenant now. Outside, the rain made little squirrel-claw sounds on the soot-blackened window panes.

"Ames was okay when I left him," Thorne heard himself saying. "Half drunk, true. A little somber. But not suicidal."

"I call a cannonball onto the trunk of a Cadillac somber *and* suicidal. A Hyundai, maybe, but no fucking way a Cad."

Thorne gave no argument. The smoke eddying in the room, tinged green from the lamp globe and shimmering with the slide of rain on the windows, made him feel like he was underwater. His eyes were silky with exhaustion. Pulaski sighed. "What do you want, guy? The responding officers went through the house. There was no sign of struggle. No word. The doc was alone when he went out. Christ, some other dude was rocking his old lady's boots when she died. Now if that don't spoil your day, what will?"

Still Thorne said nothing, so Pulaski pushed his advantage. "I'm talking to you because we go back. Damn, why make a tough case tougher?"

"You see absolutely no cause to investigate?"

"Soon as that phone rings, we'll know."

Thorne rubbed his face. "I don't know, maybe I am reaching."

"You want work? You could always try for reinstatement. Okay, they let you wear real clothes today, but down there on the island it must be blue pants and tan shortsleeves with the bright shoulder patch this time of year, huh?"

"Have you ever been there?"

"Shit, that's no vacation, bunch of butthole surfers and New Yorkers. But I can guess. A nice mesh-top cap with a shiny visor, or is it the baseball look?"

"You're wrong," Thorne said, though without conviction.

Pulaski stubbed his cigarette, unamused even by his own levity. "That dink-brain lawyer. The last hard work he ever did was squeezing out of his mother's twat. Why don't you file to reopen? Couldn't you talk to . . ." He huffed bitter smoke. "Ah, that's probably the last thing you want to dig up."

But the image wedged itself into Thorne's mind: Lisa sitting at the deposition, delicate-featured and lovely, letting the man lie about what Thorne had done.

The phone rang, startling him. Pulaski's bulldog face came into the light as he lifted the receiver. He listened a moment, grunted, and hung up. Making Thorne wait, he tamped a fresh cigarette on the desk, fitted it to his lips, lit it, fanned out the match, giving each action a solemn precision. "Not only booze in the blood, tranks too. The doc was prescribing for himself. I buy suicide, guy. Why don't you go get some sleep."

5

The offices of Craven, Belnap & Lowe, Attorneys at Law, were in a rehabbed Georgian in old town Philadelphia. Thorne had called ahead and was met now by a plain, brisk young woman in a black linen skirt and white blouse. She led him into a large private office and offered him a seat. Her name was Carol Marks and she had been Vaughan Belnap's paralegal assistant. In spite of an air conditioner purring away, there was a dew of perspiration on her upper lip. From the cartons and general disarray Thorne judged that someone was either coming or going.

"I don't have a lot of time to spare," the woman said. "This stuff just arrived from D.C. I have to get it sorted. Needless to say, Mr. Belnap's office down there has been closed. Do you mind if I keep working while we talk?"

"Please. If you need a hand with anything heavy, shout."

"It's just paper." She dug her arms into a carton to the elbows. "To answer the question you asked on the phone, any lawyer who's any good has enemies. Mr. Belnap probably had his share, but nobody so vengeful or sick as to kill him."

"Does anyone come to mind?" asked Thorne, opening his notebook.

"No one."

"Did he ever receive any threats?"

"Only of litigation. They come with the territory."

"How about bad business deals?"

She shook her head. "Lately all his energy went into the campaign. Or *most* of it," she corrected, turning away.

They went through the questions as she worked. For the most part her answers were perfunctory, given in the cool manner with which she might have read a court transcript; and yet Thorne sensed she was holding onto some inner tension. She avoided his eyes. Patiently he went on.

"How well did your boss know Maura Ames?"

"I don't think he knew her at all."

"So they met at the rally and decided to go to Martha's Vineyard together?"

"I couldn't say. I was in Washington all last week."

"Does his meeting her fit with your perception of him?"

He thought her control wavered for an instant before taking hold again. She pushed back a sprig of hair. "Politics has more groupies than rock 'n' roll. Maybe the Ames woman came on to him. Mr. Belnap was an attractive man."

"Uh huh. You must've been pretty close to Mr. Belnap. To Vaughan," he added.

It seemed to spring some lock.

Carol Marks flung an armload of folders on the desk and spun around so fast he thought she would come at him. *"Bastard!* What in God's name are you *doing* here?" she cried. "I resent you implying . . ."

Her words trailed off. She gazed about with a look of pained wonderment. "God, am I that obvious?"

"No. Just a little guarded. It's understandable." Feeling cheap about his manipulation, he said more gently, "You seem protective of Belnap and yet angry, as if you want both to accuse and defend him. I had to make sense of your ambivalence."

Carol sank into a charcoal velour couch and groaned. "Guarded and ambivalent? I thought the cops were supposed to chase bad guys, not hold encounter sessions."

Thorne smiled. "We even deliver babies on occasion."

Relaxing a little, Carol confessed to having carried on an affair with Belnap during the ten months he had maintained an office in Washington. She seemed almost grateful for a chance to talk. "Usually it was sex after hours, on a sofa like this one. I kept dreaming that candlelight dinners would come next, and one day the announcement that he was filing for divorce. But . . . after a while I quit kidding myself and just hung in there for as long as he wanted me."

Checking Thorne's reaction and deciding perhaps that it was unjudging, she went on. "What's sad and funny about the whole thing is that I worked with him back here for two years before Washington, and he never once made a pass. It's that town, it affects people, makes them different. Does that sound crazy?"

He asked several more questions. At last, without comment, he handed her one of the prints he'd had made from the snapshot Maura Ames had taken on the day she died. Carol Marks looked at it. "That's Senator Murphy all right, though out of uniform. Is this Maura Ames?"

Strikeout. He told her no and put the picture away. "If I wanted to get some background on Murphy, other than the current party line—where would I go?"

Carol rose and hunted a moment in one of the cartons, then handed him a sheet of paper. It was a flyer announcing the paperback publication of a book called *Heartlander*. "It's pretty fair," she told him. "But truthfully—if you want a lead on the murders, I think you're wasting energy here."

"Oh?"

She shrugged dispiritedly. "Most likely it was just dumb luck. Wrong time, wrong place. My dharma runs that way."

Jimmy Dow was lunching on taco chips and Dr. Pepper when the telephone in the police station in Vineyard Haven rang.

"You sitting around doing nothing as usual?" Thorne greeted him.

"Hey, someone's got to." Actually they had prearranged the call for noon so as to talk before Dow began his shift. He didn't waste time with small talk now. "Here's what I've got so far. One, a definite no on that partial third fingerprint. It's not in any police file. Two, the owners of the cafe in

Edgartown have been up to their eyeballs getting ready for summer, but one of them recalls the victims being there late that afternoon. When I showed him the Murphy photo, he was less certain about the people in it. He was floored when I told him who it was. Probably sorry he didn't get to schmooze with the senator."

"What about the woman?" Thorne asked.

"No ID. No one at the ferry office remembers either of them. And no room registration for Murphy on the island."

"Which could mean he stayed in a private home, or more likely he came over for just the day. He was in California Sunday."

"I suggested asking the *Gazette* to run the photo, but the chief nixed it. He says Murphy isn't a suspect, and we haven't connected him in any way to the case. The truth is Post doesn't want his tit caught in a political wringer."

"He's probably right. Anything else?"

"I talked with the harbormaster about last Saturday. He says the east wind was keeping small boat traffic down, so I'm betting Murphy didn't arrive that way. Ed Pease out at the airport tells me there were a dozen private planes in. Day hops from the mainland. One didn't come in till around four and left at nine. The pilot filed a flight plan that showed a destination the same as the point of origin. It doesn't work for the senator because he would've been at that rally in New York—but the plane flew up from Washington, D.C."

"Yeah? Passengers?"

"Two men, Ed thinks. One might've been black, though he could've been someone from another plane."

"That nails it right down."

"Ed did remember the plane was a white twin-engine Beechcraft with a corporate owner."

"Check on it, okay?"

"Will do, but Post keeps saying Saturday, then I'm back on the beat."

"You've done well," Thorne said.

Dow laughed. "If you can't get out of it, get into it. Old Injun wisdom. Or was it on a Salada tea bag?"

★ ★ ★

Thorne opened the door for some air but stayed in the phone booth. He could see a parking ticket on his windshield. At least the Jeep hadn't been spray-painted with graffiti. The street he was on looked like a DMZ between ethnic and racial war zones. Even with steel grilles over the store fronts, there were a lot of plywood windows. The big sellers seemed to be guns and ammo, liquor and lottery tickets. The citation was probably a courtesy warning to get his vehicle out of here before it vanished. He wondered how William Penn would like the City of Brotherly Love these days.

Tomorrow was Thursday, two days before the long weekend, the unofficial start of summer. On the Vineyard the murders would become a topic of speculation over shrimp cocktail and mesquite-grilled bluefish. Unless he could solve them.

He wiped sweat away with the heel of his hand.

Before he'd lost his job in Boston, he had always found energy in an investigation: people to spin ideas with, the backup of labs, experts, computers. Those things were on a wish list now. Aside from Dow's help, there was no support. And no leads, no new evidence, no answers to the big questions of *who?* and *why?* Even answers to the small questions were scarce. There had been something else in those former days too, he remembered now. Call it the enticement of mystery itself—what his then-partner, Pulaski, had dubbed the "siren song." He listened for it now, but he heard only spooky laughter from a recessed doorway down the street where a group of young men passed a pipe.

Carol Marks had said she doubted any answer was to be found with Timothy Murphy, and Thorne was inclined to agree. Still, it appeared that prior to last weekend the victims hadn't known each other, which made their only apparent link the fact that both had worked for the senator. A photograph taken the day of the murders showed Murphy on an island where no one (least of all Thorne's boss) was ready to place him, with a woman nobody seemed to know. Coincidence or meaningful detail?

Thorne knew from his experience as a fisherman that there were times when you climbed down out of the wheelhouse and took the rudder in your hands. Maybe this was one of them. Murphy was a candidate for the highest office in the land. That meant if you asked questions, you asked them quietly.

Timothy Murphy stopped by the courtesy room at the Stouffer Albuquerque Hotel to pick up messages that had come in for him. Most, he knew, would be matters that could be handled by aides, and he shuffled quickly through the slips. One note, however, made him pause.

"CALL LONG DISTANCE OP # 7, RE VINEYARD."

His heart gave a wild little flutter. Lightheadedness swept over him, and for a moment he only stared at the last word.

"How's it going, Senator?"

He slipped the note into his pocket and turned to see several reporters passing, en route to the hotel bar.

"Gonna give them hell tonight, Senator?"

In his suite he dialed long-distance information. "Operator number seven," he said.

At every place where he stayed overnight while campaigning, Murphy had a private, direct-access telephone line. Only the area code changed, and only his family and a select few others knew the sequence.

A brisk operator, whom he couldn't identify for sure as either male or female, gave him a Nassau, Bahamas, number and connected it for him.

At the next voice which answered, his reaction surprised him, mixed as it was between anger and a tinge of longing. Guardedly he said, "I thought our conversation was over."

"Yes, I thought so too," said the woman on the line, perhaps a little sadly. "And I meant for it to be. But I had to call. Remember my warning the other day?"

That there were some men who might know about him? How could he forget? "That was supposition," he pointed out.

"Yes, but if I'm right, it's serious. Those people who were killed on Martha's Vineyard . . . it may be connected."

He swallowed, desperate to cut off the sensation of icy hands clutching his mind, trying to peel away his sanity. "That *can't* be," he said sharply. "Coincidence. Robbery or something, the papers said."

"Oh, do you think so?" There was a hopeful note in the voice, a tone that said she wanted to believe, and for a moment Murphy wanted that too, wanted to reach across the distance of miles and years and make contact with her, longed for them to share the trivia of each other, the statistics of their respective lives: what their marriages were like, their dreams, what memories they harbored. . . . He felt torn by longing, and an aloneness.

Then the reality of now intervened. The blinking message light on his phone told him he had another call. "Yes, I do," he answered emphatically. "I think all of that's dead."

Ray was on the other line, running him through a checklist of details before the limo arrived to take them to tonight's speech. Afterwards, as Tim put on his jacket and straightened his tie, the conversation with the woman tried to insist itself in his mind, and with it the feelings returned. He squeezed his eyes shut, making the darkness swarm with misshapen, vaguely menacing images. All that's dead, he told himself.

You're dead.

6

Washington sweltered under an El Greco sky. Like a har-
binger of the rain that threatened, a drop of sweat plopped
onto the flyer in Thorne's hands, blurring the name and
address he'd scrawled earlier. The building sat across the
street, a former warehouse by the looks of it, transformed
into business lofts: old brick, stripped oak doors, iron fit-
tings—work space, cheap. He locked the Wagoneer.

Stairs took him past an insurance office, a bail bonds-
man's, a hypnotist's with a hand-lettered sign: QUIT NOW! OR
YOUR $$ BACK! He had to wonder if it had worked; this latter
space was deserted. The D.C. Writers Guild was on the
fourth floor. A woman with short dark hair glanced up from
a computer monitor as he went in. She wore black jeans
and a T-shirt with Jack Kerouac's face silk-screened on it.
She was pretty, perhaps thirty. He gave his name and cre-
dentials. "I'm looking for Lorraine Patton."

The woman studied the ID and handed it back. "What
can I do for you?"

"That's you?"

"Good police work so far."

Like her words, her deep blue eyes were direct, challeng-
ing under their accent line of dark brows. She gave no in-
vitation to sit, so he got right to it. "You wrote a book on
Senator Murphy. I'd like to ask you a few questions about
him."

Her forehead crinkled skeptically. "Have you read the book?"

"No."

"Or tried his office? Senators do maintain offices."

So that was going to be the tone. "I thought about it," Thorne said, "but I'm more after information than propaganda."

"That's pretty cynical."

He ventured a smile. "Standard police issue. Actually the extent of my involvement with government is paying taxes. And I do have a certificate somewhere thanking me for loyal service to my country, signed by Richard M. Nixon."

"Whom I suppose you voted for."

He kept smiling, though he wasn't getting much encouragement. "It's funny, with all the people who swear they didn't, he made the White House twice."

That almost got her, but not quite. "I'm still not sure what it is you're after," she said. "You obviously aren't trying to decide whether to vote for Senator Murphy."

His smile had disappeared. "I'm deciding whether to question him in connection with a double murder."

He had cop's eyes all right, Lorraine thought. As he talked, they would hold hers boldly a moment, then slide away to scan the room. He was tall, close to forty, she judged, with all of it showing on the weathered face. It was a face that would have worked on someone who flew helicopters in cigarette ads. He wore a beige corduroy jacket that was overkill in this heat, gray slacks and maroon knit tie on a pale gray shirt. His hair, brown, with a hair-tonic shine, was combed straight back. The names he gave her belonged to two people she'd never heard of before.

"So the fact that both of them worked for the campaign is their only connection with Murphy?" she asked.

"That, and this. It was taken on Martha's Vineyard by Maura Ames the day she died."

Lorraine looked at the photograph. She recognized the senator talking with a suntanned blond woman over drinks.

The woman sat in three-quarter profile, one hand on the table, holding something—a postcard maybe—her other hand spread in what might have been supplication. Lorraine tried but couldn't place her. "Who is she?"

"I don't know."

"Well . . . Senator Murphy talking to a woman. Not exactly an event for *Ripley's.*"

"Still, his having been there should be news where I'm from. It's a small island. So why hasn't there been a story?"

"Are you sure there hasn't?"

"No publicity, and no one remembers seeing Murphy."

Lorraine nibbled her lip, looking again at the picture. "Are you thinking this was a tryst?"

"It crossed my mind."

"Uh uh. Not unless Murphy's got a political death wish, which I darn sure don't think he has. Besides, by all reports, he's a good husband."

"So who's the woman?"

"Why couldn't she be an advisor?"

"Vaughan Belnap's assistant, who's close to the campaign, said she'd never seen her before."

"An admirer then. Or an old friend."

"Granting the point, that still leaves the senator on the island the day of the killings."

"What about just getting away for a breather? He's been known to do that—take off, no fanfare." With the schedule the man had these days, Rain thought, an afternoon free could be heaven. She felt annoyance at the cop's probing, found herself wanting to defend Timothy Murphy. Not that he needed defense—his integrity was established. Certainly this was a tragic coincidence; nevertheless, it was as if the candidate's fate were linked to her own. And in a sense it was. Even beyond the self-serving fact that his success would help sell the book, she felt that in some way she had discovered Murphy.

"Look, I've been impressed with the senator," she declared. "He says what he thinks. Most politicians sound like

ventriloquists' dummies, with someone else doing the thinking.''

''What was that about cynical?''

She was on a cherished subject and didn't let herself get
sidetracked. ''Murphy was an overachieving farm kid from
the Midwest. He helped run the family feed and grain business, lettered in three sports, even graduated at the top of
his high school class. Yet despite all his activity, he used to
make time to go off into the corn fields to be alone. Did you
know that he raised doves *and* was into falconry?''

''You must've felt like a screenwriter recording all that.''

She suddenly realized she'd said more than she meant to,
and this made her angry. *''You* must feel sly for getting me
to spill all that. The point is, it's genuine. And that's all I've
got to say.''

The cop thanked her and wrote his name and the name
of his motel on the back of the photograph, which he gave
her. ''I'll be there overnight if you think of anything else.''

Rain waited until he reached the door. ''One last point.
I'm not someone who climbs on bandwagons. I do, however, honestly believe that Timothy Murphy is a man for
the time. I think he'd be a good president.''

Thorne winked. ''I say bring back Dick Nixon.''

Ray Russo was marching bow-legged figure eights in a
dressing room backstage at the civic auditorium in Kansas
City, waiting for the candidate to finish with the Q and A.
He peeled open a roll of Tums. His stomach couldn't take
this campaigning like it used to. Midwestern barbeque one
day, Texas chili the next, and those hand grenades for
breakfast yesterday. But hell, after forty-five whose health
was perfect? That was just a line for a resumé. The good
news was, if the campaign succeeded, Russo wasn't going
to need a resumé for a long time. For success, however,
there could be no repeats of today.

Murphy barged through the door. ''Bastards were out for
blood,'' he railed, tugging off his suit jacket, tossing it on a
chair. ''Well, I gave it to them. Boy, did I give it to them.''

Russo tried to swallow away the chalky antacid taste in his mouth. Since Shea Stadium, Tim was the contender. But they were still the away team. They just couldn't give the press fat pitches like today. He knew Murphy's line on decriminalization of illicit drugs. The arguments were strong. But this was the farm belt; you didn't go hinting that the next cash crop might be something for dopers to smoke.

At his campaign manager's silence, Murphy slumped into a chair and pressed his eyes shut with a thumb and fingertip. "I didn't intend to get into the drug issue this morning. But after droughts and falling prices, those people were listening for some upbeat note."

"We'll weather this. We've got momentum," Russo said, hopeful that whatever had rattled his candidate had passed. He retrieved Murphy's suit jacket and hung it neatly, then resumed a gentler pacing, letting his own thoughts settle.

"Let's stick something into tonight's Louisville speech about today's comment," he proposed. "Temper the legalization idea so it comes off as something that's only been talked about, not an action item. Remember—the key issue is ending the drug menace. The only ones who aren't for that are too stoned to vote."

Murphy nodded, and Russo felt their confidence returning. He even took out one of the Ramon Allones that Tim had given him. When he got it lit, he decided to pass the word he'd gotten from headquarters that Hank Frizzel was digging for a story. Why not? Tim thrived on adversity.

When Russo finished, Murphy's green eyes deepened. "Frizzel, huh? Did I just give him his target?"

Russo fanned away smoke. "That was my first thought, but I don't think so now. When today's remark turns up in every newspaper and TV broadcast, Frizzel won't touch it. He'll want something exclusive, juicier. Rots of ruck. We're cleaner than a UPS truck. Right?"

Murphy was still. Like a fullback returning to the huddle slowly, he had learned to conserve energy whenever he could. He'd been speaking four and five times a day for weeks, staring into the lights, facing an openly skeptical electorate. The cities between Des Moines and here were a blur of short flights and hotel suites. Thankfully there was only one speech remaining.

"Right?" Russo said again. "Is there anything we should sweat? I mean, you're not pulling a Gary Hart, are you? Or you're not buddies with Fidel and that's how you get these great cigars?"

"And you're not getting shaky on me, *are you, Ray?*"

Russo had meant it funny, but he was stung by the lash of Tim's voice. He mumbled apologies. "I'll just be glad when we get back to D.C."

"We'll both be glad," Murphy sighed, his voice even again, as if he'd never snapped. He rose. "I'm going to take a swim, then work on tonight's text. If you think today's speech went well . . ." He threw out his arms and gave a mock scream.

"Enjoy the cigar," he said. "I'll see you on the plane."

Someone at Boston's Area C police station was taking his sweet time finding Pulaski. A canned voice came on the line at intervals, reminding Thorne that his call was being recorded. He looked doubtfully at his dwindling pile of coins.

The phone booth was adjacent to a car wash, from which issued a wet hiss and the drub of big octopus mops. Nearby a young father and his brood struggled with a coil of vacuum cleaner hose, a modern Laocoön, as they spruced up their Voyager. Thorne could imagine them going from here to fetch the wife/mother, who'd be ready with a picnic basket, then setting off on a holiday adventure. Watching them, he sensed the closeness that knit them together. Of course, it was possible that family was a self-deception he'd refused to indulge in, but the truth was he probably never would know. He'd been an only child, raised by his father when his mother had died young. Since his own divorce Thorne had settled again into a pattern of being alone, and although the wish was occasionally there to find someone and start over, he knew too that with each passing year the weave of life grew tighter, the strands of will, habit, and choice less ready to be fashioned into a new design.

"Hey, guy. How's fantasy island?" Pulaski came on the line.

His mind refocused. "I'm in Washington."

"Yeah? Well, same diff. You break that double murder yet?"

"Trying. Tell me something. When Dr. Ames died, did anyone find a slip of paper with my name on it? In his shirt pocket maybe?"

"What's that flopping noise?"

"Giant squid attacking a Buick. Come on, Mike, I'm short of silver."

"Slip of paper? Yeah, it was there. Punch a hole in your theory?" A pause. "Guy, you're wasting time trying to tie the doc's dive to those killings. I'd like to help you—hell, I'm only ten bodies behind in the workload—but what's to hang a case on? Look, let me tell you something. After our talk the other night? I spoke to O'Keefe, the chief of detectives. You're right. Reinstatement's a long uphill spit into the wind, but—"

"I said I wasn't interested."

"—that don't mean impossible," Pulaski said. "If we could make that lawyer look shaky . . . and if you could show something—like closing that double ice job. The point is, don't get lost on a suicide while the main trail runs cold. Crack that and we'll get you back here, because, guy, why don't you admit it? You're a detective, not a hick-towner with his feet on the desk."

"I *like* my job, dammit."

Pulaski's laugh was wheezy. "Shit."

It was a tossup who clapped his receiver down first.

Clement Jones sneezed.

Disturbed after who knew how long, the heavy velvet drapes covering the balcony doors released a cloud of dust. Like a lot of the once-rich furnishings in the villa, the drapes had been neglected, so the outside-facing surface had faded to a ghost-version of its former royal blue. Jones paused, sneezed again, then pushed open the glass doors and stepped into the blaze of tropical sunshine.

From the balcony he was able to look beyond the tiled courtyard with its pool and enclosing fringe of palmetto to where a margin of jungle appeared to merge with the Caribbean. It was an illusion that didn't reveal the limestone cliff on the southeastern end of Bootleg Cay that dropped to the sea far below, which made the remote Bahamian island ideal for his purposes. With an excitement of anticipation he watched a float plane settling on the sea. Shipment number three had arrived.

He wondered if the old dude was upstairs in his tower room watching the plane too. Jones hadn't communicated with Bootleg Cay's owner since their first exchange of messages, which had set the operation in motion. Luckily, direct contact wasn't essential, the old man having instructed his servants to cooperate in any way Jones required. So let him stay up there in his turret and watch TV, or whatever it was he did all day. Jones would get the old man's majordomo, Childers, to off-load the shipment and stow it in the cave.

He checked his watch. Childers would be taking his siesta now . . . so let him sack out awhile longer and enjoy the sleep of the innocent. Or was it the sleep of the damned? With the spooky Bahamian it was hard to know.

And there was no telling which sleep it was as Cecil Childers dozed in his small stone house a half mile away on the beach—for as he slept, encircled by jungle, limestone cliffs, and the sea, into his afternoon dreams crept the stark, terrible red visions that had been there for as long as he could remember.

In keeping with Post's admonition for thrift, the motel room was budget grade, with sagging bed, bland furnishings, cigarette-burned carpet. A globe of pebbled amber glass slung from the ceiling on a chain was meant to add a decorator touch but only served to collect webs of dust which wavered in the air flow from the air conditioner. Thorne pried off his Hush Puppies, undid his tie, and tugged a can from a six-pack on the bedside table. He rolled the can across his forehead, but the run from the liquor store had leached the coolness from the beer. When the desk clerk who had checked him in learned Thorne was from Martha's Vineyard, she was full of gab about government conspiracies and Chappaquiddick.

Lying on the bed now, inhaling the aromas of fire retardant fabrics and his own stale shirt, he sipped beer. The motel was near a train yard and above the rattle of the air conditioner rose the sounds of locomotives shunting freight cars in the late afternoon heat. He felt a million miles away from solving the case and almost that far from home.

On the Vineyard there was one simple and constant measure of life; something was either on- or off-island. Thorne knew people who had lived there for years, but because they had been born elsewhere, then would forever be off-islanders. Not that it wasn't an amiable, accepting place. It was the only vacation spot he knew firsthand where whites and blacks felt equally comfortable. But as with any small, self-contained place, tedium was a fact of life. Upon turning nineteen he had joined the Navy, and due as much to the whimsical nature of military assignment as to his size, he wound up in shore patrol, rousting drunk sailors out of bar brawls in ports from Villefrance to Gibralta. The summer he mustered out and returned to the Vineyard to take up fishing with his father and Rufus McCoy, he met Lisa.

It was at a lawn party where he'd delivered a hundred lobsters. She was visiting her parents in Chilmark, a "down island" village of whispering willows and vast ocean views. Several years younger than he, she nevertheless had the confident air that comes with money. Like most islanders, Thorne had had his encounters with summer folk, so he regarded her warily, but she'd soon won him over. Twice that summer he drove over to see her.

That fall Lisa started college. Thorne went on fishing and wrote to her diligently (in care of her parents' home, since he didn't know her new address); but after weeks of not hearing back, he stopped. Five days before Christmas he got a terse phone call. It was Lisa. She was in Woods Hole. Could he meet her when the ferry docked?

She labored down the ramp with a dufflebag, a small figure bundled in an oversized peacoat, auburn hair windsnarled. She looked pale and more than a little frantic. Over coffee at the Black Dog Bakery she chain-smoked and told him of dropping out of school just prior to finals. She'd gotten pregnant and had an abortion. He didn't ask any questions. She did volunteer that her parents knew none of this. "I took a train to Boston. I haven't slept in two days. I came straight here."

To see him? Or had it just been the flight of a frightened young woman? Again he didn't ask. He would help her in any case, any way he could.

She stayed for three days, and when Eric rode across on the ferry with her, they had declared love for each other. That June, with her parents' grudging acquiescence (they'd hoped for more than a fisherman), Lisa and Thorne were married.

But that was a long time ago, he thought with a prickle of old despair . . . before he'd let circumstances whip him and send him packing from the city, back to the island, back to safety. He had finally been able to see that in her restless moving Lisa was like a hermit crab for whom he had been a temporary shell, larger than most, perhaps, but in the end outgrown and cast aside. As he opened another beer, the telephone rang. It was Jimmy Dow.

"Sorry I missed you earlier, Ric. How's it going down there?"

"The beer's warm and the trail's cold."

"There's a lot of that going around."

"You?"

"I've been breaking in a couple of summer kids. College types. They may be whizzes at calculus and English Lit. but they've got some cramming to do if they're going to keep traffic moving around here. Anyway, I checked on that

Beechcraft out of D.C. It's listed as owned by a Zeta Company in Ft. Lauderdale. They do import-export trade with the Bahamas. The bad news is that's about all I'll be able to do you for. Post's got me back on doubles as of tomorrow."

Thorne set his beer down. "He told me Saturday."

"Now he's saying 'mañana.' "

"Let me talk to him."

"He's out," Jimmy said disappointedly. "Look, maybe I can help on my own time, if you've got anything specific."

"Yeah . . . well. Thanks anyway. I wish I did."

Bill Rendle, the vice president of the United States and his party's sure candidate in November, had requested the meeting with senior administration advisor John Bricklin and party strategist Ron Zelnick. He had claimed to welcome other perspectives on his campaign, but Zelnick was sure Rendle didn't much like what he was being told.

"Goddamit!" he swore. "I've prided myself on waging a tough, clean war, and you want me to change tactics and start a dirty tricks campaign."

Bricklin was a veteran of four dacades of hard-fought politics who wore his large belly and bulbous red nose proudly, like campaign ribbons. His voice was a cannon rumble as he assured the vice president that he'd already outdistanced any challenge from within the party. "The polls show that if the election were *today*, you'd be president by a five-point margin. But the election *isn't* today, and a lot can happen in a few months."

On the coffee table in Rendle's office were late editions of the *Post* and the Kansas City *Star*, both of which had given a page one ride to the story of Senator Murphy's remarks that morning about legalizing drugs. Subsequent broadcast news reports, however, said that a followup speech in Louisville had defused the earlier statements.

"It's true," Zelnick agreed. "Murphy's campaign has ignited since Shea Stadium."

"But to torpedo him," Rendle said gloomily. "What's that going to cost me?"

'' 'Torpedo' is too strong. 'Deflect the power curve' is better. In fact, sir, I think that could be done without any reference to you at all.''

Rendle's hard Western face masked his interest, but it was there, Zelnick sensed. Peter Hawes's popular presidency had given Rendle and the party elite a sense of security. As a result they hadn't taken the Murphy threat as a real one. Now they had to. Rendle waited. With a look at Bricklin, who was eyeing him guardedly, perhaps even warningly, Zelnick went on. "Sir, does the name Hank Frizzel do anything for you?"

"Makes my skin crawl. His brand of journalism belongs under the urinals in a skid row bar."

"Not exactly Pulitzer material, I admit. But with Joe Sixpack, he's the *vox populi*. When Joe has had it up to here with his boss, city hall, the wife, Frizzel is his champion. They listen."

Bricklin creaked forward in his chair, his large beak as colorful as a puffin's. "What's the point, Ron?"

"The point is, Frizzel has been asking around, trying to get a line on Murphy."

"Who hasn't? The media have been eyeballing the candidates from the minute they announced. It's a given that the ones left are clean."

"Maybe."

Bricklin narrowed his eyes. "Are you saying this drug remark will change things?"

Zelnick gave a dark laugh. "You want to hear something rich? My contact at the *Times* says his paper is about to praise Murphy's willingness to 'broaden the dialogue on the drug problem.' ''

Bricklin glowered. "Why don't they just print that rag on pink newsprint and cut the charade."

"How does Frizzel figure in this?" Rendle asked.

For the past seven years, since his junior year at Vassar, there had been a book on Zelnick's bedstand, as ubiquitous as a hotel bible: Michael Korda's *Power*, so dog-eared and scribbled-in that some passages were difficult to read. But legibility missed the point because Zelnick knew the book by heart. He stood looking down at the seated vice president.

"Sir, Frizzel is an old pool shark. He walks around the table until he finds an angle." He paused. "There just might be an angle."

Despite his curiosity—which was there in his narrowed eyes—Rendle waited for Bricklin to ask the question. Zelnick shrugged. "There was that Murphy worker who was murdered last weekend. Belnap. The word is he was a swordsman."

Rendle cursed. "That's just the kind of thing I'm talking about. So he chased women. What's any of that got to do with *Murphy,* or with the issues of this campaign? *No.* That's mud, and I won't sling it."

Zelnick raised his hands. "I'm not suggesting you ought to. But Washington is a just a big small town. When you're out, you're out—and Frizzel is definitely out. No one's talking to him. But an insider hears stories. Suppose there was a story *I* might hear. Somebody like Frizzel . . . he's got no compunction about slinging *any*thing."

The two other men were silent, waiting. "This is just me speculating," Zelnick went on. "Everything's hypothetical. But suppose I start to check around."

"Snoop, you mean."

"Whoa, you called this meeting yourself, Bill," Bricklin pointed out.

For a long moment the office was hushed; only the faint sounds of construction going on outside penetrated the walnut paneling, like the heartbeat of life in this city, Zelnick thought. Finally, Rendle sighed. "What does the president think about this?"

Zelnick hesitated. Like everyone in public life, he knew that words had a power-to-weight ratio like that of radioactive metals and were to be used advisedly. But he had survived so far partly by being direct when it was useful to be. "We haven't discussed it with the president, sir."

Bricklin stepped in. "Oh, he wants you to kick ass, and

he'll do what he can to help . . . but frankly, Bill, the president has lost the eye of the tiger. He's served with honor for most of two terms, but now he seems just to want to go back to the farm, chop wood, and write his memoirs.''

The muscles in Rendle's jaw bunched. ''A five-point margin,'' he murmured, more to himself than to them. ''Keep me advised.''

At quarter to nine Thorne walked into Houston's on Wisconsin Avenue in Georgetown. There were only a dozen or so patrons in the bar, along with a trio of young musicians setting up shop on a bandstand. It wasn't noisy yet, but judging by the amplifiers the size of burial vaults, it was going to be. Lorraine Patton was sitting amid hanging philodendrons at the far end of the bar, sipping from a silver can of Coors Light.

''You won't kill any werewolves with that,'' he greeted.

She turned and arched her eyebrows. ''Is that the order of business tonight?''

''For me it is.'' He took a stool beside her. ''I'm not a happy camper. I got overcharged for the worst pizza ever built. Then I tried to catch a nap while freight trains went for a new high on the Richter scale. You don't need a Magic Fingers mattress at *that* place. But the rock bottom pits is that the beer was warm. I can remedy that though.''

A few minutes later they were seated in a corner booth, Thorne with a mug of Watney's ale, Rain with her Coors.

''Thanks for getting in touch,'' he said. ''It took me a moment to figure out who'd called the motel.''

''I bet you grilled the clerk who took the message.''

''Bright lights and rubber hose. Rain, huh?''

She shrugged. ''I was a tomboy. Lorraine was too long or something.''

Her garb was no longer T-shirt and jeans, but a less informal white silk blouse and a blue paisley skirt. The blouse didn't hide her athletic shoulders or small, insistent breasts. A blue scarf was knotted loosely at her throat and gold teardrops dangled from where her short hair cut a crisp dark line across her ears. The soft lounge lighting gave her mystery. Her face had a feminine precision, but he had the feeling that she could pluck out the earrings, ruff her hair, and be ready for any sort of adventure.

From her handbag she drew a photograph and put it on the table. It was the photograph he had given her that afternoon. He looked at it, then at her, questioningly.

"The part about the murders is real," she said. "I checked the newspapers."

"You didn't believe me?"

She shrugged. "Respect for the printed word. Two people were murdered last Saturday. Now you show up asking questions, flashing a badge from some quaint little town on Cape Cod."

"Martha's Vineyard."

"Whatever. The point is, how do I know you're what you say you are?"

Thorne frowned. "Why wouldn't I be?"

Her eyes seemed to grow suddenly intent, as though they harbored some secret she hoped he would guess. When she answered, there was an odd, suppressed note in her voice: "Because there's something weird going on."

He felt a small trill of excitement, which prompted him to glance around, making sure no one else was near. Even so, his own voice was low when he prompted her to continue.

"First, I want something," she said.

"Like what?"

"There's a story here. Possibly a big one. I want it."

"That's two of us."

"To report it, I mean. I want to write it."

Thorne controlled himself by taking a long drink of ale. "Look, this is criminal investigation, not a talent search. I can't let—"

"Evidently then we're both wasting time." She took her handbag, slid out of the booth, and started for the door.

What was he doing this for? For thirty grand a year? For

everlasting glory? He was supposed be on vacation now, catching stripers and blues. So let her go. The *hell* with it.

He pounded the table.

"Lorraine . . . Rain."

He motioned her back. "Sit. Okay, I agree something odd is going on. There're lots of questions, but not many answers. I need answers. So . . . I'll make you this deal. You help me, and when the case is solved, you get any story that's in it."

Her eyes held level with his. "All rights."

He was simultaneously awed at his own capacity for stupidity, and hers for toughness, but impressed too. "Sure, whatever that means," he said. "Why not?"

She withdrew a manila envelope from her bag and took out a second photograph. Like a gypsy dealing tarot cards, she laid it beside the one snapped on the Vineyard and turned both to face him.

The new picture was a 5×7 black-and-white of a smiling Senator Murphy in sweatpants and T-shirt and a cap with donkey ears. He stood beside a well-known Southern senator whose cap had elephant ears and a trunk protruding from its peak.

"That was taken last summer, at a benefit softball game. Notice anything?"

"Aside from grown men making fools of themselves?" It took him another moment of studying the photo before he saw it. "This."

Just visible on Timothy Murphy's left forearm was a tattoo of a dragon and, beneath it, some Asian writing.

"He got it when he was a POW," Rain said. "The Vietnamese equivalent of 'Death Before Dishonor' or something."

Thorne didn't need to look at the Vineyard photograph; in it, he knew, the tattoo was gone.

7

The Friday before Memorial Day weekend was beginning brightly, with lifting fog and a mild east wind clanking halyards on the masts of sailboats moored in Vineyard Haven. Alden Post's mood, however, was out of sync with the day. From the window of his office he watched the 8:45 ferry spewing people and cars.

Post often imagined the ferry as a plague ship, bearing to his island a virus, a subtle contagion of prosperity and leisure which infected the natives so that they craved these themselves. The young people of the Vineyard, especially, showed symptoms: swimming bare-assed on beaches, screaming around on mopeds, breaking into places to steal. Or they just moved away, leaving their roots because home wasn't good enough for them anymore. Of course, Post shared his view with no one. They'd call him sour, but that was because they were all infected with the virus themselves. To them the annual invasion of people with green trousers and whale ties, oversize tennis rackets and Swedish cars meant one thing: cash. They didn't see that it also meant bowing and scraping to outsiders; or if they did see, they didn't care. To Post summer only meant more work, toil for which he didn't earn a penny extra. His salary was set by the town council and was barely enough to pay bills and the upkeep on his small house, while summer people had bought up the big old captains' homes that Post's ancestors had built and lived in.

The telephone rang. It was Eric Thorne, still in Washington; now he wanted to go check on the plane that Dow had identified.

"We may be getting somewhere," Thorne explained. "If you call the Ft. Lauderdale police and get a search warrant for the plane, we might be able to tie evidence to the killings."

"What evidence you got in mind?"

"Anything. Fibers, bloodstains, prints. It's possible that—"

The basso profundo warning of the ferry's horn rumbled through the town, drowning out Thorne's words. Post didn't ask him to repeat them. "There isn't enough probable cause," he said flatly. "You know that as well as I do. I'm not going to have us look bad to the cops down there."

"This could be an important line of investigation."

"I said *no!* You listening? *I'm* the one running the show here. You get some solid leads, we'll talk. Anyways, your time's up tomorrow."

"But if I had a chance to—"

Post exploded. *"To what?* Run up more bills against a budget I don't have? I want you back *here*. Period."

When Post returned to the window, a scatter of angry, half-formed thoughts flitted through his head. If he hadn't been overruled four years ago, Thorne never would've been hired. But the town council was being run by an outsider who'd cowed the others with the notion that Thorne was the best-qualified cop the island could ever get—Post included, though none of them had had the gonads to say so. Unanimously they'd offered Thorne a sergeancy. What they didn't understand was that Thorne was a turncoat—and that was another something Post kept to himself. You had to be careful about bad-mouthing people here. Still, the fact was that Thorne was an islander who'd been tainted. He'd gone and married that fancy summer girl and brought her here. Ha. One winter she lasted before running back to Boston, Thorne in hot pursuit. Hell with the island, gonna be a big man in the city now. So he thought. He came back finally, without the wife. But he wasn't ever going to fit in again, and he damn sure wasn't going to run this department, either. Post would see to that.

The ferry's warning horn hooted once more as the boat made ready to cast off and fetch another load of plague.

Pushing a cart down the supermarket aisle, Zelnick saw the little man in the glen-plaid sportcoat approaching. With a nod of his woodpecker nose, the man said, "You Zelnick?"

"Get yourself a basket."

"What?"

"A shopping basket," Zelnick said.

Frowning, Hank Frizzel found a red plastic basket and came back with it swinging awkwardly on his arm. It had been Zelnick's idea to meet in this Safeway in Adams-Morgan in northwest D.C. Most of the other shoppers pushing carts around were black or Hispanic.

Zelnick put a can of clam sauce into his cart. "I'm glad we could meet, Hank." He hoped he didn't sound like a booster club president, but he decided a little flattery couldn't hurt. "I'm a bit of a fan."

"You said on the phone you want to talk about Murphy."

"Actually it seems you're the one who wants to talk about him. You've been leaving messages all over town. Not getting much response?"

"Look, I learned all the hustles and shakedowns by the time I was ten. Let's not diddle each other, okay? You know I've been drawing blanks. I know your camp is nervous about the polls. So we're in the supermarket. Cute. What's on sale?"

Zelnick forced a smile and squatted, pretending to consider jellies and jams. "In 1979 Senator Clarence Winters got caught sacking a quarterback. The penalty was his Senate seat. You know about that?"

"Where do you think I've been the past ten years—Wyoming?"

"Six months ago Murphy's chief competition dropped out of the race."

"Yeah, yeah, he flunked the cola taste test. Is there a point to this? No one's ever tied Murphy to either of those events."

Gripping a jar of Smucker's, Zelnick stood up. The fish was fiddling with the bait but was wary. "No one has because no one's had access."

"Uh huh. So you're telling me—"

"Hold on. There's a biography, and—"

"I read it. I kept waiting for the scene where Murphy walks across the Potomac."

"Okay, it's favorable, but it isn't your typical write-by-number job. The author stayed objective. Now, suppose I told you she was in a Georgetown bar last night, talking hush-hush about a couple of photos she had—one showing Murphy out of uniform, with a blonde woman, and looking angry about something."

Frizzel's eyes widened. "A skin shot?"

"Hardly."

"Then what are you getting hot and bothered for?"

"The writer and her friend seemed to think the picture has importance."

Frizzel looked away, scratched at his eyelid, sighed. "All right, I'll bite."

This was the dicey part, Zelnick knew. His informant hadn't overheard the full conversation at Houston's because the band had chosen that moment to kick in with a million decibels, but the pair in the next booth had been excited about the photo. Frizzel's aggressiveness in riding a story was matched by a reputation for sloppy homework. Zelnick needed a promise from him to check this fully before using it. There had to be evidence, or the thing could blow up in their faces like cheap fireworks, and the thought of facing the vice president if that happened made Zelnick's stomach twist. "The person the writer was with is a cop from Massachusetts. She was dealing with him to get a story she thinks is in the photograph."

"You saying Murphy's porking the blonde?"

"You've got a dirty mind, you know that?"

"I've got a dirty job. Look, I figured the Patton chicky

knows things. I've been trying to open her up, but she's got her legs crossed tight. So if you know anything, *talk* to me. I'm getting depressed watching all the food stamps they use in this joint. You have the photo?''

''No. Lorraine Patton does.''

''So basically you're giving me zilch.''

''Zilch, schmilch! I'm giving you a lead. You've got to do *some*thing on your own.''

Frizzel didn't respond immediately. Finally his mouth twitched downward in a smirk. ''Maybe I'll make this little meeting my story. I can envision tabloid headlines that'd make Rendle squirm in his boxer shorts.''

''I don't think you'd do that,'' Zelnik said quickly.

''No?''

Perspiration was oozing under Zelnick's shirt—he wasn't used to this—but he sensed Frizzel was nearly convinced. The man operated way outside what most journalists would call ethics, but even he had to observe one basic rule: he had to protect his sources.

''Mention this meeting, Hank, and who are you going to get ever to trust you again?''

Acid etched a thin smile on Frizzel's face, and Zelnick knew that the hook was finally set.

''Okay, Okay, give me what you heard. I'll check it out.''

The woman finished her laps and climbed gracefully out of the pool, the Bahamas sun prisming in the water droplets on her sleek, naked body. One question was laid to rest for Hiram Kirk; the yellow hair was natural.

She tugged off her bathing cap, tipped her head back and shook it.

The motion might have been a throwback to films she'd acted in. Kirk stood in the scented shade of tropical bushes, hands in his suitcoat pockets, watching appreciatively. She saw him then and flinched; but she was only startled, not deeply surprised. More than four decades of living had revealed most of the surprises, and apparently a big-eyed male wasn't one of the few that remained. She plucked a beach-robe off a chaise and drew it on. Smiling, Kirk walked over.

"Good workout, huh? You move like a dolphin in that water. Got great form."

"Thank you," the woman said coolly, and turned and headed toward the cabana shower.

She was a tiny thing, but she occupied a lot of emotional space. It was that star quality, Kirk thought. Even though she hadn't been in a picture in fifteen, twenty years, she still shone with a special glamour. He'd love to go to bed with her.

He stood there hearing the splash of the shower, and sounds from a television somewhere inside the villa. He squinted at the place, letting his gaze climb the turret with its draped upper floor windows. Was old Mr. Invisibility up there, watching the tube all day, playing spymaster? Might as well; he damn sure wasn't entertaining his wife, and God knew there was little else to do on this hunk of coral rock. So far, anyway.

Through the bristles of his crewcut, Kirk felt the sun on his scalp like hot oil. It could sizzle a man's brain. Probably *had* fried the old man's. Still, the man had treated him right over the years; Kirk had no beef. But all that woman going to waste . . . now that was a crying shame. He squatted and played his fingers in the pool and put water on the back of his neck.

In a few minutes the blonde was back, settling into a chaise, sleek from her shower, cool, just like in her movies. One of the servants came out of the house carrying a tray with bottled water, ice, and a newspaper, and he set it on a table, casting a sidelong glance of disapproval at Kirk before retiring. Kirk let his hand dangle in the pool and looked at the surrounding jungle. It seemed to watch back. He listened to the sounds of turning pages, the clink of ice in a glass, the muted TV.

"Here's a curious little news item on page six," the woman said, though she could have been talking to herself. " 'Doctor's Death Ruled Suicide.' It says that Martin Ames had been despondent over the recent death of his wife. 'Although foul play is not suspected in the internist's death, a Boston police spokesperson admitted the department has been in touch with police on Martha's Vineyard, where Maura Ames, thirty-nine, was slain last weekend during an apparent burglary. Sgt. Eric Thorne of the Vineyard Haven Police reportedly met with Dr. Ames shortly before he plunged from the top floor of his Back Bay townhouse.' "

Kirk watched the jungle.

"You're not having much luck with your little scavenger hunt, are you," the woman said, addressing him now.

He didn't look over. "My what?"

"How did a Boston newspaper end up here?"

"*I* brought it. Found it on the plane coming down."

He knew her eyes were on him; still, he resisted looking at her. Finally she flopped the paper down. "I know you people are up to something. You think I don't?"

He had to look, just for a second, to assure himself that she didn't. But she was suspicious enough to be fishing. She wasn't the loser she'd played in some of her movies. He turned back to his hand. Oddly angled by the refraction of light in the swimming pool, his fingers looked like broken pencils.

"A man can lose things, sticking them where they don't belong," the woman said, intoning the words as if they'd come back to her from an old film.

Now isn't that the truth, Kirk agreed mentally, thinking about her, about himself, about a cop named Thorne, looking again at the fingers of his left hand, waiting.

Cecil Childers had seen all he could stomach. Easing a concealing leaf of cabbage palm back into place, he turned away from the pool area in disgust and set off toward his house, the tire-tread sandals on his leathery brown feet padding softly on the spongy jungle path. He resented the U.S. government men who came here every few weeks. They had no respect for this place. And he saw the way they looked at Miss Andrea; he knew what was in their hearts.

Everything had changed since the Black Man, Jones, first showed up here a year ago, taking advantage of the old man and using the cay for some scheme. The seaplanes began arriving last month, twice a week, with crates that the men stored in the cave at the south end of the island. Jones had instructed Cecil to oversee the crates, which Cecil did only because the old man had once told him to be ready to do whatever the government men might ask of him. He resented them being here, but he had his instructions. He could only pray things would go back to normal once they left. Which ought to be soon. The cave was starting to fill with their crates. One or two more loads, he'd overheard the Black Man saying, then they would take everything and go. But Cecil was worried about Miss Andrea and even more about the old man.

Having all that stuff in the cave made him think about a night nearly sixty years ago, when he had been a small boy and the cave had been full of another kind of badness.

He twisted free of the memory and emerged on his empty slope of beach. Down past his small stone house at the water's edge, he kicked off his sandals, stripped off his clothes and waded in.

Later, as he took his siesta, his nightmare returned: a hellish red form rushed from the sea cave to gorge on the flesh of his family. Their screams mingled with his own strangled cry as he woke, clammy and cold. Cold, always so cold, he thought as he lay there shivering.

Rain recognized the little man too late. He was leaning against a storefront with a *For Lease* sign in its window, a block from her office, working a strand of green dental floss between his big teeth. Seeing her, he threw the floss down and pushed away from the wall.

"You don't return my calls," he said, grinning.

She decided to play dumb. "I'm sorry, do I know you?"

"Come on, you read the *Insider* like everyone else. Only you do it on line in the supermarket so you can feel superior to the zoids who actually *buy* it, right?"

He looked just like his picture that appeared over his "Crank's Corner" column, even to the sport coat you could play checkers on. "Mr. Frizzel. Well, I would've gotten to you eventually. I've been very busy. I still am." She kept walking, but he fell into step beside her.

"Your *opus* on the man who would be president is coming out in paperback, I hear. You should be unlaxing on a Florida beach." The grin was unrelenting.

"While all my bills resolve themselves into a 'due'? You obviously haven't been calling to tell me you'll do a blurb for the cover."

"My reputation precedes me."

Like stink precedes a garbage truck, Rain thought. Even though his calls had made her curious, she had no desire to deal with him. Frizzel winked at her, a jaunty, gesturing little fellow whose manner suggested he was leading up to the punchline of a dirty joke. "I wonder if any scenes ended up in your wastebasket. Maybe you heard a note that's a little off key. Nothing you can really tune into, of course—but interesting just the same."

Rain quit walking. At five-foot-ten, she stood half a foot taller than he. "Mr. Frizzel—"

"Hank."

"—number one, I don't have any dirt. Two, I won't find any, because that's not my concern. You said it. I'm finished with that project. But most important, number three, even if I had a wheelbarrow full of dirt, I wouldn't let you near it. You're right, I have read your stuff. And I've heard your radio show. What you do isn't journalism, it's character assassination."

"Just tryna do muh job, ma'am." His smile had a blanched, crooked look now, as if his upper lip were too small for the big teeth. The effect on Rain was to stoke her anger.

"You take a few facts and twist and distort them so the only way your victims can try to set the record straight is to bring costly law suits."

"You dumb cooze. Haven't you ever heard of H. L.

Mencken? Izzy Stone? What I do is muckraking! The lampoon is vital in a democracy! Only with Murphy it's fucking gonna be a *harp*-poon! I think the sonuvabitch stinks of virtue!"

"And you don't like the thought that somebody might just *be* virtuous."

"Do I barf now? People *look* clean, but dig through their trash! Poke in their laundry baskets, peek in their nightstands. There's *always* dirt. That's the principle I live by!"

He was hammering the air with such fury, Rain thought he might hit her. "There's dirt on Murphy, and I'll find it! I always do."

Passersby had slowed to watch a fight, but surprisingly Rain found her anger evaporating. The man's attack seemed pathetic, full of a need for self-justification. "Goodbye, Mr. Frizzel," she said, almost pityingly. "This is where I go to work."

He looked at the building, and his anger too seemed to fade. He nodded. "That where you keep the snapshot of Murphy and the blonde?"

Rain's stomach knotted. "What're you talking about?" she managed, but the smile had begun to pull at a corner of Frizzel's mouth again. Had his tirade all been an act? Was the man playing with her head?

He winked. "Told you. I've got sources."

She felt sick. As meticulously as someone assembling a model ship inside a bottle, she realized, she'd been erecting an investigative story in her head. Potentially a *big* story. She would've needed time for research to get the full and fair account before writing it. Frizzel cared nothing for accuracy or fairness or even good writing. He could hack out flimsy allegations in no time, the more outrageous, the more readers would devour them. Her own project would be useless. Worse, word would get out that she had been the leak. She could forget about ever being taken seriously as a journalist again.

With a note of bitter defeat, she said, "It was that Vineyard cop, wasn't it. Thorne."

"Tut, tut. I don't reveal my sources." Grinning, Frizzel took out a money clip, fat with crisp bills. "Now, what do you figure that photo is worth?"

"Go to *hell!*" Rain cried, and she turned and rushed blindly through the doorway of her office building.

Dawn's Early Light

8

Once every ten seconds the oscillating fan swung in Thorne's direction, riffling the limp pages of the *Aviation Week* magazine in his hand but doing little to ease the damp Florida heat. When the proprietor of the small airfield office, a crinkle-faced man with hound-dog eyes, finished barking at someone on the telephone, Thorne peeled himself out of a vinyl chair and went over to make a call. He had the toll put on the Vineyard Haven Police Department account and gave the number for Lorraine Patton's office. Getting no answer after three rings, he hung up before her machine came on. He'd already left several messages since leaving Washington and was low on cute things to say.

"That Beech is comin' in," the proprietor grunted, turning from a window. Thorne thanked him and went outside to wait.

Post used pretzel logic. Without evidence, there was no cause to investigate; no investigation, no evidence. Thorne had decided to drive down here simply to look at the plane, talk to the pilot, try to determine if there might be reason to pull a warrant. If nothing else, perhaps he could rule out the plane and its passengers on the day of the murders altogether. The man in the office had told him Zeta was a courier service running goods between the Bahamas and the mainland—mail and tourist supplies mostly. It didn't sound especially sinister.

Beyond the far end of the tarmac strip, through air made

wrinkly with heat, a metallic glint told him a plane was making its approach. Soon it appeared. She was a pretty craft, trim and white, with a fillagree of sunlight on her wings, and as Thorne watched under the flat of his palm, he found himself wondering if maybe Post was right, if maybe this was a waste of time.

And right then, in a sudden silent billow of fire, the plane exploded.

It had been a month since the rioting in this Cuban barrio in South Miami, but on the sidewalk spills of shattered glass still lay, igniting in the midday sunlight like looters' fires. Oscar Sanchez gazed from the parked Dodge, unsurprised. Over in Key Biscayne or Bal Harbour you could be stopped by police just for being there. Here you might well get away with anything. Sanchez reflected on this for an impassive moment, then turned away. He'd left these streets behind ages ago, with his hardscrabble childhood. But maybe he hadn't left them far enough behind. He was back.

He was hoping to triangulate a source of crack that had been flowing into Little Havana like ice cream. Having linked the drug indirectly to an import/export firm called Zeta, Sanchez had come over from the Bahamas, where he worked undercover. Zeta rented storage space in the Melendez Bros. produce warehouse across the street.

The partner he'd been assigned for the stakeout was a middle-aged black named Wiley, a bodybuilder who sat at the wheel poring over flex mags as though they were Shakespeare. Like Sanchez, he was tough and streetwise and had been with the DEA a long time.

Growing bored with the waiting, Wiley laid his magazine down. From a bag he offered a carrot that he said was organically grown. Sanchez declined. Munching one himself, Wiley said, "You work this area often?"

"No."

"Me neither. Lately they've got me over at the university."

Sanchez didn't pick up the conversation, but Wiley

scarcely seemed to notice. He chewed a moment then gave a soft laugh. "Last week I busted a kid had these little pink tabs, 'bout the size of a toy doll's titties. Lab tested them. Turns out they some kind of maximum strength Lucy. One hit, you're an astronaut. Forty minutes till lift-off, twelve hours till splashdown."

Being polite, Sanchez said, "You don't see acid around much."

"Not like this. Shades of the sixties, man. All that talk about tuning in, dropping out, and turning the world on to everlastin' bliss. You 'member that? What are you, about thirty-five?"

"Just about."

"I'm shaking hands with forty myself. But I tell you what—it was different then, not the shit we lookin' at now. Nobody was killing to get high." He shook his head wonderingly and gnawed the organic carrot.

It *had* changed. More and more Sanchez felt like a man applying a Band-Aid where a tourniquet was called for, offering palliatives for a cancer that was gorging at the country's vitals. He used to think, Give me one year and the power to rescind the civil rights of certain scumbags—just that—and I'll bring the problem to an end. But that wasn't going to happen. Not with the *dinero* that people in high places were making. Though he sure as hell wasn't seeing it.

Wiley came suddenly alert at the steering wheel. "Check it out," he murmured, gesturing with the carrot stub.

Across the street three young males had emerged from the warehouse. One bent to lock the door and they set off, speaking Cuban Spanish.

Moments later Sanchez was studying the lock. He was drawn to locks the way some men were to the engines of cars. He liked the challenge they represented. This one took less than a minute. As Wiley stood watch just inside, Sanchez set off into the warehouse gloom in search of the Zeta company storage area.

He played a flashlight beam over piled crates of produce, mainly to frighten away rats (there was enough light filtering through opaque skylights to be able to see). The air hung with the aromas of onions, and tomatoes, and disinfectant. Wiley had observed the lunchtime habits of the warehouse crew over several days and calculated the place would be quiet for about forty minutes. Sanchez wanted to be out of here well before that.

It took a while, but he located Zeta's space, an area roughly twenty by fifty feet, with heavy wire fenced over two by six studs. The single gate was secured with a sturdy though simple combination lock. Given his leisure, Sanchez could've opened it, but he was conscious of time. The studs went up only ten feet and the enclosure was open at the top, so he walked around to a side no one was likely to inspect, climbed the wire, got over the top, and dropped down inside the enclosure.

Stacked on pallets were ten wooden crates of two sizes, each of which looked like it might hold a table model television set. Stenciled on each crate, along with shipping and packing numbers, was the logo ZETA * SOUVENIRS. There was nothing else in the enclosure.

He inserted a screwdriver blade under the top of one of the bigger crates. The nails gave a screech of protest and came out. Setting the lid aside, he shined the flashlight into the box.

Eyes gazed up at him. About a dozen terra cotta figurines lay in a bed of straw: squat, primitive bodies of dusty orange clay with distended faces and gaping mouths. A chill rippled his spine, like a goose walking on his grave. He flashed the light around quickly.

Reassured that he was still alone, he turned several of the figurines over and peered inside the cavities. No drugs there. He moved some aside and pulled up clumps of straw.

He was startled by the unexpected sheen of metal. A gun barrel.

There were others in the crate too, disassembled parts to as many as half a dozen M-79 grenade launchers. For a moment Oscar Sanchez gazed in bewilderment.

Opening a second, then a third crate—another large and

a smaller one—he discovered belts of ammunition and grenades. He found no drugs.

That's when he knew he'd been wrong. These hadn't
come into Miami; they were headed *out*. But to where? Who
was running them? Had ATF been tipped?

He didn't ponder answers. Time was growing short. He
repacked the weird clay figurines, fitted the lids back on the
crates, and climbed out of the enclosure. As he approached
the warehouse exit, Wiley materialized from the shadows
clutching his .357, and in that instant, Sanchez made the
decision to hold onto his discovery awhile so he could think
about it. Holstering the weapon, Wiley rippled his brow in
question.

"*Nada*, man," Sanchez said. "Souvenirs."

Although Washington could not boast as many secrets
kept as New York, nor as many betrayed as Los Angeles, it
was second in both categories, and therefore first overall.
One of its best guarded secrets was the love affair between
the president of the United States and Prudence Winters.
Not that it wasn't known by others, Peter Hawes realized;
despite the most elaborate precautions, secrets leaked.
Rather, people respected their privacy because both he and
Pru Winters were institutions, and that was both good and
a little sad. Pru often teased that she didn't know which was
worse: venerability or senility. In any event, the two of them
enjoyed the kind of twilight romance that a pair of vital
sexagenarians might. Tonight, though, it was not going well.

"Don't worry about it," Prudence reassured him, "you're
not up for reelection."

"It would appear I'm not up for much of *any*thing," he
said glumly, though he was beginning to see humor in the
situation. "Maybe lame 'duck' is a misspelling."

"Or 'election' is a Chinese pronunciation."

They laughed like two kids secretly awake past bedtime,
and some of the tension melted. They sat against the carved
walnut headboard in the pale light of a single lamp and just
held hands.

After the death of her husband in a car crash six years ago, Pru had gone west. She'd been a longtime friend of Eleanor Hawes, Peter's wife, and when Eleanor died, despite partisan differences, the friendship continued between the survivors. Then, six months ago, here in this third-floor bedroom, where U.S. presidents since Coolidge had slept, the relationship between them had become something more. Nothing steamy—no Jack Kennedy and Marilyn Monroe, Prudence would occasionally sigh. More like Sartre and Simone DeBeauvoir—mind and spirit wedded to flesh. Maybe it would have to be just the first two now, the president thought. He could not keep from taking tonight as one more symptom of what he'd been feeling lately, a sensation he could label only as "off." The maddening thing was that there were no precise symptoms, nothing to convey to anyone. Just a vague . . . unease—lightheadedness at times, nausea in the mornings, some back stiffness. Now this.

Reading his concern, Pru rubbed his hand. But over the soft traces of accent from her Louisiana girlhood, the tough practicality was in her voice. "I want you to go to Bethesda. I know your last physical was fine, but go see Dr. Holsworth again. You've been holding off because you don't want to put anything extra on Bill. Think I don't know that?"

He looked at her, not surprised at her perceptiveness. It was true, he had been giving Rendle time to campaign.

"But if it means you suffering in silence, then I say to hell with it, Peter. Politics will survive till the last of our species goes to her grave—but *you* are not going to be here forever, and I want to enjoy you while you are. I want to enjoy *us.* So if it means taking it slow for a while and letting Rendle pick up the slack, well that's the vice president's job. Call Vern Holsworth."

He promised to call in the morning. Then, although nothing was magically resolved, they held each other tightly.

Later, when Pru had said good-night and retired to the guestroom where she slept when she was in the White House, Hawes turned on another lamp and took a book from his bedside table. It was *The Decline and Fall of the Roman*

Empire, one of the works which, along with *Moby Dick* and the Bible, he had been rereading every few years for much of his life. Tonight, however, Gibbon's prose did not hold him long. His mind was adrift. True, it wasn't a catastrophe when a man couldn't properly satisfy his woman for a night, but maybe it was a sign, an omen of trouble. What Pru did not know was that the party seemed to be in trouble too. John Bricklin, his senior advisor, had been by earlier with poll results that showed the opposing side gaining ground rapidly, and Senator Murphy looking more and more likely to be their standard-bearer. How could you fairly combat a candidate like that? Even when the media attacked him, as they had over that drug decriminalization gaff, he rallied defenders because he tapped into the public's latent antagonism against the press.

Before, it had been a question of how much the incumbent party would beat the opposition by; now it was, would they beat them at all!

The president groaned. Two terms had been barely enough to sow the seeds that he believed would ultimately bloom to make America a great and good nation again. But seeds needed nurturing. A major administrative change would put an end to his hopes for a harvest this century. Worse, change would almost definitely hasten America's decline.

For these reasons, above all matters of mere partisan politics, Hawes's vice president *had* to win five months from now.

Another resolve. See doctor tomorrow; win one for the future in November.

He turned off the lights. For a long time he lay there, his thoughts spiraling with an obscure but growing sense that the unease he was feeling was not just with himself, or with his administration. It was as if some grave trouble were coming to the country.

The orange globe of a Union 76 truck stop beamed from its mast like a hunter's moon in the North Carolina dark, drawing Thorne in. His ears hummed from the miles of highway, and fatigue blurred the edges of his concentration. The sloe-eyed waitress at the counter told him he was forty minutes south of Fayetteville—and a hundred miles east of nowhere, and she got off work at 2 A.M., she said, if he was lonely enough to hang around. Smiling, he stirred his coffee to Ronnie Milsap on the jukebox and took the paper cup and his change back outside to a phone. He fanned away the insects swarming the light, plugged coins in and waited.

"Hey, where've you been?" he asked when Rain said hello. "I've been trying to reach you all day."

"I've been here, listening to you leave messages."

"Really?" Puzzled, he tried to identify her tone, but he couldn't and decided that that could wait. "Well, listen to this. I just came from—"

"No, *you* listen! I've finally cooled off enough to speak to you in person and tell you what I think, you worthless, lying, betraying son of a bitch!"

"Whoa, easy, I'm not good with criticism," he fenced quickly, put off balance by the torrent, which went on unabated. He bumped his coffee and had to shuffle back to keep it from splashing him, but still his shoes got wet. *Damn.* "What did I do?"

"We had an agreement! But still you went and told that slimeball about the photograph."

"What? Who are you talking about?"

"For*get* it!"

"Rain, I don't know what you're . . . Rain? Yeah, right." She had hung up.

As the telephone began to ring again, Rain snapped off her answering machine. Nine, ten, eleven rings, then silence refilled her office. She shut the file cabinet, turned off the lights. Descending the stairs, she discovered her anger was mostly gone, replaced by disappointment. Thorne had seemed straight, and she'd liked that, liked his determination. He'd fooled her.

By the time she reached the street, her mood had shifted.

The book would be out tomorrow, and tonight she was meeting friends to celebrate. She pushed her last worries from her mind and set off with a bounce in her stride.

In an alley, among the night shadows and the scuttling of rats, someone watched her go.

It was here someplace.

Not in the file cabinet. Or the desk drawers. She wasn't carrying anything when she left. So where? Frizzel asked himself.

The wooden floor of the warehouse groaned in the darkness. This place gave him the creeps. He stabbed the flashlight beam around, scanned flyers tacked on a corkboard, shuffled papers on the desk, shook reference books. Nothing.

Outside a sign winked on and off, a web of neon that pulsed like a heartbeat and washed a dim corner of the loft with intermittent red light. If he got caught, he was in trouble. The potential gain, however, justified the risk. The woman's reaction when he'd mentioned the photograph had been the proof he'd needed. Now he had to find it.

Years ago, when he first started doing his *Insider* column, he had been a stickler for legwork and research. Eventually he'd learned they weren't necessary. The average reader wasn't that fussy. Make it sound good, toss in a few facts, close enough. The thing was, people believed what they wanted to. If they figured there were mutant alligators in the sewers, or a race of humanoids roaming the piney woods of Jersey, or that Clint Eastwood was a closet queen for God's sake, then all the proof in the world wasn't going to tell them otherwise.

The photo was tucked in a plastic caddy for floppy disks.

A glance told him it was the one Zelnick had been talking about—someone who looked like Murphy sitting with a good-looking middle-aged blonde. He tilted the print to cut the flashlight glare. Though he couldn't say precisely what, there was something familiar about the woman. He'd seen her before. Where?

With a hissed curse he snapped off the flashlight. Some-one else was in the building.

Earlier he'd cased the outside for an alarm system, but this was just a converted warehouse, office space cheap. Now he could hear footsteps on the stairs. He could wait here, hope it was somebody for one of the other offices. But what if it wasn't? What if someone had seen him and hol-lered cop?

He stuffed the snapshot into his jacket pocket. Not both-ering to try to keep his steps quiet—an impossibility on the creaky old floor—he scurried to the windows. He fought open a heavy sash and leaned out.

Down the side of the building to an alley below zigzagged the fire escape, looking as if it hadn't been used in a dog's age. But the moment wasn't ripe with choice. Lights went on in the hallway outside the office door. He didn't bother to shut the window.

As the fire escape took his weight, anchor bolts grated in the bricks. Panic seized him and he froze. But the contrap-tion didn't collapse. Still holding on tightly, he began to de-scend.

When he reached the first landing, he glanced up and clapped a hand on his thudding chest. For just an instant he thought he'd seen a face peering at him from above, though he wasn't sure. It was gone now.

The final flight of stairs, meant to swing down on a coun-terweight and ease him to the ground, was locked with rust. It halted screechingly six feet above the alley.

With the effort of his descent, his breath was coming in shotgun blasts. Frantically he worked himself onto his belly, clutched the grille with both hands, and flopped backwards.

He hung for a moment, palms blazing as iron scale ripped his skin, then he dropped the few inches to the ground.

Someone grabbed him.

He yelped with terror and tried to look behind him, but he was held fast.

"Whaddya want?" he cried before a hand clamped his nose and mouth.

He lunged, desperately trying to break the grip, but whoever had him was too powerful. His breath began clogging in his lungs. A mist started to settle over his eyes. It was then, at the edge of his blurring vision, that he saw a spike of light reflected off sharp metal. Terror flooded his chest. He bit the hand sealing his mouth, twisted his head free. He managed to shove his own right hand into the side pocket of his jacket, yanked out the snapshot, which tore as it came. Instinctively he knew that this was what his attacker was after. *"Take it!"* he pleaded. *"Don' hurt me! Leemie 'lone—"*

The knife entered, skewering up through his left kidney. Shock took his voice away. His pain-struck eyes swept the photo pinched in his fingers. Unexpectedly, Andrea Wexford was the name that came to him . . . along with another name from long ago, and the thought that, *God in heaven,* this would be the biggest story he ever told. . . .

The blade bit through his heart, and when he hit the packed dirt of the alley, Hank Frizzel was dead.

9

With its white clapboard siding and bell tower, the town hall in Vineyard Haven looked more like the Congregational Church it had been 150 years ago. The tower clock showed 10:40 as Thorne cut out of brisk Saturday morning traffic and squeezed into a doubtful slot behind a Grand Marquis with a neat line of golf caps in its rear window. Thorne's Jeep had 3,000 fresh miles, and the WASH ME someone had scrawled in the body grime seemed desperate. There had been a message in his mail slot to meet Post. He was late.

Warren Stubbs ambled over, bright as a traffic pylon in his orange vest. "Can't leave 'er there," he said. "You're acrost the line."

It was pure Stubbs—no greeting, no questions about the murder investigation, no smile. Strictly business.

"Don't start with me, Warren. I drove all night and I've had three hours' sleep. Ticket that Merc—it's taking enough space for three."

"Already have. You're over the line," Stubbs repeated stolidly. "I'll give you till eleven o'clock, Eric, then I'm gonna have to write you up."

His was a perfect justice-bringer's mind—it allowed no deviation. Thorne had to smile. "Warren, you're one tough cop."

The conference room on the ground floor was like a cavern after the brightness outside. Selectmen Jay Torrey and Bob Sack were seated at the rickety oval table. It took Thorne a few seconds to spy Post perched on a windowsill in a corner. He was twiddling a rubber band with his fingers, clearly agitated. Torrey leaned across the table to shake hands. "Ric, buddy, how's it going?" He was a small, dapper man of fifty with the congenital good humor of a top-forty deejay. He was wearing a red bow tie that looked like it had been rifled from a Christmas wreath. He owned two inns and an insurance agency in town. "Have a sit," he invited.

Bob Sack had summered on the Vineyard for years before suffering a heart attack, ending a professorship at N.Y.U., and moving over permanently five years ago. A lean, bearded man of middle years, he kept fit swimming in the ocean year round. He gripped Thorne's hand firmly. Post wandered over now, without handshake or hello, and sat. Throne gave an account of his investigation.

"Florida, for Godsakes!" Post said when Thorne got to yesterday. "I told you to stay *out* of there."

"You said no warrant. I still had questions to ask. Unfortunately I never got the chance."

He described the explosion of the Beechcraft. The pilot had been killed instantly. Thorne had hung around long enough to make contact with the local police.

"Was it a bomb?" Torrey wanted to know.

"They're trying to determine that now."

The others at the table exchanged a sober glance. Sack spoke first. "Does this tie in with what happened here?"

"My gut feeling? Yeah."

"But the truth is you don't know," said Post summarily.

"No," Thorne admitted, trying to grasp some meaning in what they were not saying. Sack resumed, "We've talked about the deaths in council. A quick arrest would've satisfied everyone, but it's been a week now. Letting things drag on can be . . . well, counterproductive."

"No one's blaming you, Ric," Torrey said quickly, fingering his bow tie. "It's a tough one. We just don't have the manpower. Hell, I'd help you myself if I weren't so damn busy with work."

Thorne's weariness was making him impatient. An image

of Stubbs ticketing his car had risen to mind. "What did you mean, Bob, by 'counterproductive'?"

Sack went to an aerial photograph of the island, which dominated one wall. In his work shirt and Banana Republic shorts, he moved with the cautious zest that an awareness of one's mortality brings. He gazed at the photo. It had been shot on a day of bright sunshine, and the blue-green ocean ringed the coastline with filaments of surf. "While you've been away," he said in his reasonable voice, "the crime has been gradually fading. Oh, it'll come up in conversation, but the story's had its run in the Boston papers, and the TV has moved on to other news, and frankly, no one I talk to is sorry."

"I keep thinking," interjected Torrey, "that what happened at the Captain James could as easily have happened at one of my inns."

"Which would seem a pretty strong argument for vigorously pursuing the case," Thorne said.

"Well, it's pretty darn certain the killer's not still on the island, looking to repeat himself. You'd have got him for sure if he was. No, he's gone, and the quicker we put this whole tragic episode behind us, the better off we're all going to be. People come over here to get *away* from bad news. What's on their minds now is the season."

"Clambakes and lemonade and fun? Two people were murdered here a week ago, Jay. You want to forget that?"

With a glance at Torrey and Post, as if to enlist support, Sack cleared his throat. "A long investigation, especially one that might get into what you've just been telling us . . . that's the kind of attention we need like I need another heart attack. The damage gets done. It's been nearly twenty years, and people still come here every summer and want to go gawk at Chappaquiddick bridge."

"Which isn't even there anymore." Torrey's tone said the perversity of human behavior was beyond fathoming.

"You prefer two unsolved homicides?" Thorne asked.

Torrey glanced away with the rubbery, pitying grin he probably used when he hauled out actuarial charts to show you how grim the odds were. You sold insurance by scaring people, and Thorne had the idea that's what they were trying to do to him.

Bob Sack was still standing, and Thorne had an image of him in front of a freshman class. "Well, there're different schools of thought. In my first year teaching, a group of students took over the dean's office to protest the war. The administration was in a sweat over how to respond. It was obvious that in a few days the students would get hungry and they'd leave. But the president had to save face. He decided on a show of force. Things got hot, heads got busted, and the story wound up on page one. The president learned there are cures worse than the hurt. He got the ax."

Thorne's anger had been rising like a sullen heat; he could feel it burning on his neck. "You want to stop the investigation. Why isn't anyone saying it?"

Post sprang from his seat. "Okay, dammit. I take my lead from the council, and *you're* paid to take it from me! I just pulled the plug. End of discussion." He stalked toward the door.

Thorne managed to keep his voice steady. "I just want to understand why."

Post turned with a look of mock irony that fitted the lines of his face too well. "You want to understand?"

"We're making a big deal about this being a tourist island," Thorne pressed. "What about Vaughan Belnap and Maura Ames? They were guests here too. Or is it just that they were paying off-season rates?"

Sack spread his hands, trying for a reasonable tone. "The crime will get investigated, Eric."

"How? You just told me we're out."

"We are." Spoken from the doorway, Post's words had a harsh finality. "As of now, the case is being handled by the FBI."

Champagne toasts till the wee hours had left cobwebs in Rain's head. Celebrations had gone on until her companions had left, and she'd gone home for a few hours of sleep.

Now, she unlocked the guild and went in, all at once struck with the imbalance in her life. Saturday morning, and instead of waking up with someone who mattered, she was at the office with a paper cup of black coffee. *Heartlander* was coming out in paperback today, and she had a bitch of a hangover.

In spite of herself, she found memory pulling her back to when this place had boomed with Ethan Ross's laughter and with parties and fervid discussions on politics, art, and life. Now silence ruled.

Rain had been the only child of a loving, hardworking woman and a big, rough-sawn miner who'd been a good father in the early years, but whom hard times had changed to where he interspersed long spells of bible-thumping discipline with brief, violent bouts of drunkenness, the latter usually occurring when troubles beset him and the divine delivery system he professed to believe in was too slow for his liking. At such times, Frank Patton might not be seen at home for a week, then he would appear, verbally and physically going at whoever was handy. His family tried to get him help, but the town's services were limited, and Frank's patterns too deeply imbedded to be changed by love alone. Rain's mom eventually found her escape by dying of cancer at fifty-one.

After graduating from high school, where she was valedictorian, Rain lived on her own, supporting herself by waitressing, helping out at home when she could. As an outlet for feelings that seemed too powerful and contradictory to share with anyone, she'd begun keeping a journal and writing poems, some of which she submitted to the local newspaper. Each time one appeared, there would be well-meaning encouragement from townspeople ("That was good, dear, but too deep for me, I guess. Why not write a nice poem about our Lord?"). One afternoon when she was waitressing, there was a disturbance in the adjoining lounge. It was Frank, and he was ranting. The town had been enduring a particularly long miners' strike, and the economy was bleak. Ironically, Frank was in a sober period; but years of binge drinking had altered him. Damning his daughter as a whore for working in a place like that—for working at *all* when honest people were going hungry!—he came at her. His first punch felled her. A huge man, he might have seriously hurt her if he'd continued. Determined not to let that happen, Rain scrambled up. She dumped dishware off a bus tray and brought the tray clanging down on his head. His eyes popped wide with surprise, rolled up like cocktail onions, and he dropped unconscious onto the floor.

For Rain, the incident snapped a final link. Soon thereafter she loaded her car and headed east for Washington, where work proved no harder to find than were men. Unfortunately, most of the former meant waitressing, and the latter were climbing hard on the bureaucratic pyramid (which they made plain), and were married (which they didn't), so what they had in mind for her was sport. She chose not to play; she hadn't left one trap only to fall into another. Aware that drive alone wasn't enough, she tore a card off a poster on a city bus one day and applied to a community college. Thus, waitressing nights, she started school with the intention of taking some basic courses. She wound up in Professor Ross's class, "Intro. to Government."

Medium height, with wire-rimmed glasses and a walrus moustache, Ross sparked with energy, such that around campus he'd acquired the fond nickname of "The Energizer." To Rain, who at twenty-five was older than most of her classmates, he seemed possessed of a valorous honesty she'd never encountered before. He was like one of those Japanese soldiers who crawled out of caves on remote pacific atolls every once in a while years after the war, still brandishing a sword. He'd never surrendered his citizenship in the Woodstock Nation. Addressing everyone as "man," he spoke fervidly of the "heavy numbers" being laid on us all by big business. Get him going on the antics of the sixties, and he was nonstop. By that time, Rain had begun taking courses in journalism and literature, and as a project she wrote a series of articles called *"Profs in Profile"* for the campus paper. The final article featured Ethan Ross. She did her research, unearthing the details behind the legend, and although the hyperbole got stripped away, the person who emerged was every bit as engaging. Ethan had been arrested with Allen Ginsberg, dated Joan Baez, appeared before a senate committee. There had been the comic side too, a cross, as Rain put it, "between Karl and Groucho—ham on wry," as when he'd rented a helicopter and bombed the Pentagon with inflated whoopie cushions.

So amused with the piece had Ross been that he sent a rebuttal, claiming that the author was saying those things only because she was hot for his bod, and bucking for an *A* in his course.

She got the *A*, deserved; as for the first claim, however, although she did find him attractive, it was he who made the overture, which Rain declined on the grounds that going out with a teacher would've posed for her a conflict of interest. Only later, after she'd earned her two-year degree, did she start dating Ethan.

Thirteen years older than she, he was both lover and mentor, a warm friend and enthusiast for her writing, which by then was prolific. She had discovered a vein of material in her West Virginia past as dark and richly shining as a seam of anthracite. For the two years they were together, founding the guild, then the paper, and taking courses, she wrote constantly.

Somewhere in all the busy-ness, a change began to occur in Ethan. Arguments developed over the content and direction of the weekly. What Ethan wanted was a canvas for his increasingly angry vision of Amerika. On some points she agreed with him, the country *had* lost sensitivity and purpose, but although she felt editorial journalism should paint pictures, she was opposed to their having only one single dark hue.

And more and more that's what Ethan saw. Even his humor—that droll side Rain liked so much—began to fail him. He would fret that his students had ceased to care about the world they lived in, intent only on possessions and power. Sex, drugs, music, those avatars of freedom to a former generation, had become destructive, self-indulgent pursuits. He took his fading ability to whip students into scorn for all that as a form of impotence. The world was devolving into an uncaring place, with greedy leaders and numb followers; and fewer and fewer people wanted to hear Ethan Ross tell it.

At last his anger metastasized into full despair.

One night, a week after Ethan turned forty, Rain came home from her restaurant shift and found him overdosed on pills. He never regained consciousness.

Since then she'd had occasional dates, and lots of come-ons from men she knew, but that experience had dislocated some integral emotional part of her that had not been set to right.

Her thoughts might've continued this backward spiral if something else hadn't caught her attention just then.

"That's odd," she murmured. The case where she stored her diskettes had been left open, something she never did.

She felt her heartbeat quicken as she discovered that the picture Eric Thorne had given her was gone. A quick search of the office didn't turn it up, or reveal anything else missing. Had somebody else been here? It was the only possible answer. But who? She pondered a moment, then picked up the phone.

Ray Russo, the Murphy campaign manager, sounded happy to hear from her. "I just saw someone in a donut shop—guess what she was reading?" he said.

"Let's hope she's not the only one. Mr. Russo, the reason I called is, has Senator Murphy . . ." She hesitated.

"Yes?"

"It's rather awkward asking this."

"Please, go on."

"Has he had any threats?"

"Threats. That sounds ominous."

It did, and she realized she'd asked too quickly. "It's just that the senator is public property now. People are watching him closely. The rumor is that Hank Frizzel is one of the watchers."

There was a pause; then: "I heard. Well, he isn't going to

find anything. There's nothing to find. You know that. You wrote the book.''

From all that she knew, Murphy was a man of integrity . . . and yet now she wondered. Had she heard uncertainty in Russo's voice or imagined it? ''Frizzel could invent something,'' she said. ''He's not above it. And even if it's a crock, the damage gets done.''

Russo was silent, and Rain worried that she'd taken the wrong approach. Maybe she ought to have mentioned the photograph outright. Then an idea came to her. ''What if *I* did an interview with the senator.''

''Wouldn't I like that. You'd be a natural. The problem is, he isn't giving any.''

''You couldn't talk to him? Have him do just one more?''

''I wish I could. That's how he insists on playing it until the convention.''

''But people are wondering,'' Rain said tensely. ''This would be a chance to stockpile some good press.'' She hesitated just a second before adding, ''In case anything goes wrong down the line.''

''There's that ominous note again. You sure you don't know something I don't?''

Rain insisted she didn't.

''Well, I'm meeting with the senator later. Let me broach the interview idea with him. No guarantees. I'll get back to you.''

''Gas charges up and down the coast! Motel bills! Probably phone bills coming in too, right?'' Post threw the receipts on his desk. ''I had to pay overtime to cover your shifts while you were out playing Dick Tracy.''

Thorne had too much else on his mind to get sucked into an office war. Reports of the crime so far had called it homicide. There was nothing to red flag the FBI. Why, then, their sudden interest? Violation of civil rights, interstate flight—the customary rationales—might be stretched to apply, but as a policy the Bureau awaited the request of local law enforcement before entering a case. Beyond an initial appeal for fingerprint data, which yielded nothing, there had been no request he was aware of. The Bureau had simply showed up and been given the file. Thorne wanted the details.

Post scowled. "The agent shoved paperwork in my face, and I damn well handed over the file! I was happy to have him take it."

The leash on Thorne's own anger was fraying, but he knew a shouting contest with Post would be futile. Alden would only retrench in his barely concealed hostility. "A lot of what I told you this morning wasn't in that file," Thorne pointed out.

"So there's the phone. Call them with an update."

"The killings happened *here*. It makes sense we should be part of the investigation."

"No. I want you back in uniform."

"I want to find the killer," Thorne said stubbornly.

Post looked at him, an unreadable expression pulling at the edges of his mouth. Just then a young couple wearing fluorescent bicycling clothes entered the outer office and asked directions to South Beach. As Post oriented them on a wall map of the island, Thorne peered out a window and saw a group waiting with bicycles. One woman caught his eye. She was small and pretty, with glossy black hair and umber skin. Native American, he guessed. As the group pedaled off, Post came to the window.

"They'll go back in the dunes to drink and screw. I'll send Dow out there later to roust them."

"They're not hurting anyone," Thorne murmured. Another time he would've pressed the point, but right now his mind would not hold the tack. He was tired. Anyway, Jimmy Dow would handle the situation with tact. Thorne followed Post back to his desk. "What if I cover my own expenses?"

Post shook his head. "A few days ago you didn't want to touch the case, but I assigned you. Okay, now I'm *un*assigning you. You're off it."

Thorne didn't move. For a few breaths he considered simply acquiescing to the demand. The case was hopelessly mired now; and with no backup the difficulty increased.

Why not diffuse the tension between Post and himself and settle into the easy routine of the island? That was what he'd wanted when he left the city, wasn't it? So why was he being perverse?

Yet even as his questions rose, he became dimly but increasingly aware that there was much more at stake than just solving the killings. He sought to identify what it was, but it eluded him, and he cursed his own dullness. Exhaustion was fuzzing his concentration. He tried to think of some further argument, some logic that would sway Post; but there was none.

Taps, played on a bugle, carried in the hot wind blowing off the Potomac, each note etched as sharp as the sun-glint on the intrument's brass bell. Ray Russo knew why they had come to Arlington National Cemetery.

Murphy's habit had developed early in his life, long before his current candidacy—in childhood, in fact. It had been a matter of survival in a sense, a need to go off by himself, away from the turmoil, to gain . . . perspective. Years ago, as a junior legislator from the Midwest, his face had been anonymous. Now escape was complicated. It usually meant getting into a car and driving around Washington with no clear destination. He might stop, unannounced, to tour a museum, a neighborhood, a park, trying to experience the place with the detachment of a visitor, as if to recapture the magnetic charge that had drawn him to this life in the first place.

For Russo, coming today had been an afterthought when the two men met that morning. God knew there was a stack of work to keep him at the office; nevertheless, he'd asked to go along, and Murphy had agreed. Before their morning session ended, Murphy had added one further request to his list of instructions: "Get me a copy of a movie called *Pandora.*" (As in "Box"? Russo wondered. It sounded triple-X.) "Either that or *Mr. Hammond's Secret.* They're old favorites," Murphy said without elaboration. He didn't know if they were available on video cassette. "You might have to hunt around. Okay?"

Why not? If it meant keeping his thoroughbred happy, Russo was game for almost anything, including walking around a cemetery in the midday heat.

As they strolled along a busy path, he spotted a group of reporters, and Murphy touched his arm, shunting him onto a branch path to avoid them. For some reason Russo thought about the day a year ago, in the corn field, when Tim had announced his candidacy. At that moment, Russo realized now with something like nostalgia, everything had felt perfect.

"We needed them then," Murphy said when Russo brought it up.

"We'll never stop needing them."

"I know. I'm not being arrogant. It's just that we have more control now. I've already got visibility, why keep a high profile when the press is only looking for one-breath sound bites? We're not talking about a blackout."

True, there were still the informal conversations with reporters, and the televised debates. Overselling was as much a danger as under, they both knew; Tim didn't want to be one of Andy Warhol's ten-minute wonders. Still, the fuels that ran campaigns were cash and exposure. Tim had already turned down a tempting offer of both by declining an appearance at tomorrow's Indianapolis 500. Russo pushed his point a little harder, but Murphy stood firm.

"I had my say last weekend at Shea. In case you've forgotten, I have a job description that has nothing to do with running for the White House."

"Granted, and that's gotten you good marks for sticking to task, but unless you want to wake up on the first Wednesday in November with that same job, you ought to give the public more."

"More?"

"If only to keep them from saying you're dodging because you've got secrets to hide."

Russo had gotten a rise out of Murphy the way Lorraine

Patton had gotten one out of Russo. Maybe too much rise. Murphy stopped walking and looked at him fixedly. "Is that the buzz, Ray? Why you came today?"

"Oh, hell, I know there's nothing. But, face it—suspicion is in the wind these days. Look at the record. Most of the presidential timber of the past thirty years has been infested with termites."

Murphy smiled, and they resumed walking. Russo brought up the idea of an interview, mentioning Lorraine Patton. "One big free-wheeling conversation." He spanked his palms together. "National pub, then we put the lid on and cruise to the convention."

Tim was noncommittal, but he said he would think about it.

Ahead, on a path which rose along a grassy hill, a sentinel in dress blues, M-14 at shoulder arms, moved to halt them. There was recognition, a greeting; and the candidate, Russo, and the Secret Service man who accompanied them at a discreet remove were permitted to pass. When they reached the crest of the path, they were able to peer down in the distance to where a crowd was gathered in the amphitheater by the Tomb of the Unknowns. The voice issuing from loudspeakers was unmistakable.

As every chief executive before him had done annually since Woodrow Wilson's time, President Hawes had come to lay a wreath at the white marble sacrophagus honoring those soldiers known only to God. Murphy and Russo listened to the words drifting up to them, words about courage and sacrifice and a heritage of freedom. Applause punctuated the sentiments like gun salutes. Russo fidgeted. "Why is it always the ones who never fought that get to say the words? You're an honest-to-God hero. *You* should be telling the country about courage and honor, not that old man."

Murphy turned and started down a diverging path, away from the amphitheater. Startled by the departure, Russo set off after him.

They made their way among oak trees and rows of white stones, each marked with a bright, new flag planted a boot-length from its base. Murphy's stride was long-legged and purposeful, forcing Russo to labor to stay close. The Secret Service man, well trained in his duties, trailed them at a distance which varied according to the surroundings and terrain. Only when they reached a far-off quadrant of the cemetery, where the words of the president no longer penetrated, did Murphy slow. Huffing, Russo caught up.

"If I'd known you were going to put me in cardiac arrest, I'd have stayed in the office." He took out a handkerchief and wiped his face. A few yards farther on, Murphy stopped walking, and for the first time Russo had the perception that this hadn't been an aimless trip, that Tim actually had been checking row markers. But why? Was he seeking a particular stone? He tried to think of whose it might be, but he could come up with no answer.

"Tim?"

"What, Ray? What?" Murphy said irritably.

Russo shook his head. "Nothing."

"You look hot. Why don't you go on back to town. Take the car."

Russo wanted to protest, but something in Tim's manner told him to let it be. "You've got that 4-H group from Indiana at three, don't forget."

Murphy nodded. He gestured toward the Secret Service man. "Take him with you."

"Now, wait—"

"I'll send for another car."

Masking a sullen resentment, Russo did as he was told.

When his campaign manager was gone, Murphy wished he had never consented to let Ray come along. These were his private times to get away. Years ago he'd been able to do it easily, for days at a stretch if he chose. Now a few hours was all he got. And once he reached the White House . . .

He shut off the thought and gazed around.

It was here at Arlington, amid the trees and rows of stone that the Kennedys were buried, and President Taft, along with two hundred thousand other soldiers. He listened to the stitch of crickets, the whistles of birds. The solemnity of the place never failed to move him. However, there was a different, more insistent stirring in him now. He hadn't come today for solemnity.

Satisfied that he was alone, he stepped over a low-slung chain and walked down an aisle between grave stones, his feet falling softly in the thick sun-spangled carpet of grass.

At the eleventh marker he stopped and looked down.

Slowly, as if the slab of white rock were a projection screen and his mind a projector, an image seemed to take form there. Jungle. Sunlight. Birdsong gradually refilling the clearing which had recently rung with the brutal noise of a firefight.

The focus tightened: a hamlet of smouldering bamboo hootches, dead and dying men . . .

His heart, which had slowed after the exertions of the walk only to speed up again with anticipation, now drummed in his chest.

There.

Somebody was moving. Behind one of the burnt hootches. An American, a corporal. Now, a sound which Tim couldn't shut off—an accusatory pain-wracked voice came. *"You were supposed to be there for us. We counted on you."*

Another voice: "You want to kill me, don't you. Don't you!"

"Don't you, Murphy!"

Spoken aloud, these last words pulled him loose.

The images vanished. He squeezed his eyes shut, tipped his head back, drawing breath after noisy breath.

When he looked again at the grave marker, it was only white stone. He was alone.

Then, from deep in his throat, he drew up mucus and saliva, which he spat on the grave.

10

Thorne was being told by an achingly beautiful woman that she loved him. He had not expected it ever to happen again, and yet it didn't surprise him that the woman was his ex-wife and simultaneously someone else too. She touched his cheek. Her lips were about to join his when he opened his eyes. A red slant of sun was in his face. What had wakened him, he realized, was someone at the side door.

Jimmy Dow was on the porch, in his uniform. Thorne pushed open the screen door and stood still for Dow's amused inspection of his rumpled clothes and tousled hair.

"Still decompressing?"

"I was about to find true love," Thorne said.

"I can scram."

"Not unless you bring my dream back first."

Dow followed him in. Thorne turned on the coil under a pot on the stove and offered coffee. Jimmy declined. "I just stopped for a minute to see how you're doing."

"Better. You on till midnight?"

"Yeah, the season is upon us. Rufus McCoy's got a group of bicyclists on the beach for a clambake. There's one I'd like to meet. Talk about cute! She looks like she's one of the tribe, too."

Thorne recalled the small dark woman with long hair whom he had seen outside the police station earlier. "I think I saw her while Post was reading me the Riot Act."

"What happened? Hey, changed my mind—that smells good."

Thorne poured him a cup and told the story.

"I guess I missed something," he finished. "The town council's hot to avoid any bad press, so they give this to the FBI? Does that make sense?"

Dow shrugged. "They're hoping for a fast solve. Post did make the point to them about wanting to keep the news down. The agent was agreeable, said the Bureau likes to work that way too."

Thorne glanced up from his coffee. "You were there?"

"Last night, sure. The agent was a big middle-aged guy with kind of a Southern accent. He seemed to know the score."

"Did he say why they'd gotten involved?"

"Checking the same angle you were, I suppose. The fact that a U.S. senator happened to be here that day."

"He said that?"

"Not in so many words, but that was his drift. He'd come up from Washington."

"Did you catch a name?"

"What was it? Somebody from *Star Trek*. Kirk. Special Agent Hiram Kirk."

They chatted a while longer, then Dow had to get back to his patrol. As he put his cup in the sink, a painting on the wall there caught his eye. He asked the question with his glance.

Thorne nodded. "Lisa's." The painting was one of the oils she had done during the fall they lived here. Chain lightning over a lurching, gray sea. The pigment was crusted on in thick, undisciplined strokes that simultaneously drew the viewer to touch the canvas and had him bracing for the crash of thunder to come.

"She sure caught that storm," Dow said. "She give it to you?"

"I found it in the crawl space when I was getting the screens out last week. I didn't know it was there."

There was a brief silence, occupied with both men staring

at the painting, neither willing to take the conversation further. As Thorne's friend, Dow had been party to the breakup.

"Well, gotta go," Dow declared. At the door he turned. "Oh, Rufus says why don't you drop by later for a beer. If you do, keep an eye on my woman."

Thorne shook off his momentary depression and mustered a grin. "You sound proprietary all of a sudden. Does the lady in question know about this?"

"We haven't been introduced yet, but I asked around and found out she's here for the summer. Hey, you never know."

After Jimmy had gone, Thorne picked up the telephone and called Florida. When he gave his name, the woman on the other end told him that chemical traces among the charred fragments of the Beechcraft suggested the *possibility* that the plane had been destroyed by a bomb.

"That's too vague," Thorne said.

"It's the best we can do right now." The woman hesitated, then added, "There was one other detail though, which is kind of curious."

He waited.

"Well, there wasn't much left of the plane, what with the explosion and fire, but on several components that survived, there weren't any manufacturer's serial numbers."

"Is that unusual?" Thorne asked, knowing as he did that it was.

"Seems like somebody went to some trouble to keep that plane anonymous. The numbers had all been lathed off."

Oscar Sanchez was inspecting Jake Wiley's right arm and listening to the section head of the Miami field office of the DEA deliver a pep talk. Wiley's arm was as big and darkly glossy as the foreleg of a race horse, with veins snaking over the biceps. The section head, who had started with Norman Vincent Peale enthusiasm, had settled into a drone as he opined that even though the agents had got nothing for their effort yesterday at the Melendez Bros. warehouse, it had been worth a try. The drug war could be *won,* he concluded with a weak pop of fist into open palm.

"Better lunch next time, right?" Sanchez stood up and pushed a hand through his collar-length hair.

Wiley shrugged. "Me, when shit happens, I go take it all out on the iron. Turn it into something that's *mine.*"

"Lot of shit must happen to you," Sanchez said.

Wiley grinned and made his muscles leap with a quick flex. They shook hands. "Been a thrill, dude."

When Wiley had gone, the section head smoothed his tie and sucked in his paunch. "You going back over to the island?"

"Soon, but I want to run a few names first. You mind if I hop on your computer for a bit?"

"Another case?"

Sanchez said it was. The section head raised his eyebrows in query but, when nothing was volunteered, said, "Be my guest. Borrow a secretary if you want."

"I can handle it."

It took Sanchez a while to access the file he wanted. When he had it on screen—a lengthy alpha list of companies and banks which had been linked to drug money laundering— he scrolled to the bottom. Nothing. He entered a specific request for information on the Zeta Company. This time he had a response within seconds.

"CLASSIFIED: DATA NOT AVAILABLE"

"As for the stiff back, think of it as giving you something in common with JFK," said Vernon Holsworth.

President Hawes smiled his relief. "Without PT-109?"

Having served as personal physician to three presidents, Holsworth was sometimes said to have cured more of the world's ills than diplomacy could ever hope to. He was a tall, stooped man of sixty-some, with lank hair the color of spoiled cream and a penchant for string ties. His easy Tennessee hill-country voice, in combination with an encyclopedic medical mind, instilled confidence, and Peter Hawes felt that way as he walked out of the examining room at the doctor's Chevy Chase home.

Holsworth, for his part, resisted making a firm diagnosis until he had all the facts. There were symptoms, and he was concerned; still, he had caught a radio broadcast of the president's address earlier that day at Arlington, and Hawes had been in fine fettle. So it could just be the stresses of the job. He intended to find out.

The two men, more than simply doctor and patient, shook hands on the doorstep, screened from the suburban street by magnolias and the warm May dusk. Coach lamps flanking the door threw lattice patterns on the lawn, like a grid the president must get across. He took the first step now. "Vern, I know it goes without saying, but . . . can we keep this quiet?"

Holsworth made a dismissive gesture. "The lab work is all done with numbers, no names. I'll have the results on Monday. I'll phone you at Camp David myself."

"Get y'self a Green Death," Rufus McCoy invited, squatting beside a pit of embers to poke a stick at seaweed-covered lobsters.

Thorne bypassed the *cerveza mas fina*—reserved for paying customers—and drew a bottle of ale from an ice tub. McCoy was nothing if not brand loyal. For most of the thirty-odd years Thorne had known him, Rufus had smoked Chesterfields and drunk Ballantine's ale. A few years back he'd got saved at a tent meeting over in Oak Bluffs, so the cigarettes went, but he still liked an occasional ale. Thorne uncapped a green bottle, hunkered by the pit and took a swig. Laughter drifted from down the beach, where a group of young people sat in merry conversation, their faces aglow in the dance of a crackling fire. Thorne decided he wouldn't tell Jimmy Dow how many of the young men were attentive to his brown-eyed girl.

"When you back on duty?" Rufus asked.

"In the morning."

"You solve those killings yet?"

"No."

"You will."

"No, I guess not."

Rufus looked up.

"Post pulled me off."

Then, with no prodding but his friend's silence, Thorne told the story. Rufus listened, his old face like burled wood in the ember light. When Thorne concluded, Rufus shook his head. "Alden Post always was a narrow-headed fool. For him the world cracks as neat as a Graham cracker. There's them that're on the island, and them that're off. If he had his way, he'd mine the harbor to keep folks out and make us all prisoners in the bargain. So why don't you tell him to take the job and the murder case and stow 'em. You and me could team up and do these clambakes. Why, we could . . ."

Reading Thorne's expression, he trailed off with a laugh. "Naw. Your old man didn't work his tail off all those years so's his only kid had to end up smellin' like fish."

"It's a good occupation, I'm not knocking it." Thorne rose, edgy all of a sudden.

Years ago, in the Navy, it used to puzzle him how some sailors, when their hitches were almost up and they'd soon be free, would get panicky at the last minute and reenlist. But wasn't that how life on the island had become for him? It was as though he still wondered if he could make it outside. God knew his first try had been flop.

He looked up, trying to see the stars, but the fireglow was too bright. When he glanced down Rufus's eyes were on him.

"So what're you gonna do?" Rufus asked.

Thorne drained his bottle and bent to set it on the sand. "Like they say, a bad day fishing is better than a good day doing most anything else. I've got my own fish to catch. I'll convince Post."

"Is that you talking, or that soldier you just killed?"

"I'll investigate on my own if I have to."

For a moment Rufus was silent, solemnly tending his lobsters, as if he had lost interest in the conversation. When he spoke, his mind had angled off.

"You know, growin' up I used to have a young bitch set-
ter. That dog was the chewingest thing y'ever saw. I could
put her out on any king of lead—rope, canvas, didn't matter.
Hated being tied. Wouldn't bark. Nor run round half crazy.
Nossir. She'd settle down and chew. Didn't matter if it was
half an hour or half a day, she'd get through that line and
Billy-be-damned." He jabbed the coals with his stick. "You
remind me of that fool dog."

In another moment he announced that the lobsters were
ready. Thorne helped him serve the feast to his eager customers. When they returned and Rufus settled down with a
fresh bottle, Thorne asked, "What became of your dog?"

Rufus sipped long of his ale before lowering it with a soft
belch. "I finally gave up tyin' her. I let her run."

"And?"

"Don't rightly know. One day she never come back.
Must've got into someplace she shouldn't have and couldn't
get out."

It was after 9 P.M., but Thorne doubted that the hour
would matter. He told the man who answered the phone
who he was and what he wanted, then went through it again
with someone else. He had something they would want. The
third person he spoke with sounded like he had a little authority, and Thorne mentioned the name that Jimmy Dow
had given him.

"Kirk. We've got lots of those. Let's see." Thorne heard
the tweeking of a computer keyboard, then: "Hiram Kirk,
okay. Well, he's not in now, of course."

"Could you tell me when he will be in? This is important."

"Well, I don't imagine it's too often. It says here that
Agent Kirk is on special assignment to the White House."

Russo gazed through the tinted backseat window of the Lincoln Town Car at Holy Trinity Church. It was the church where John Kennedy had attended Mass, and now where Timothy Murphy worshipped on the Sundays he was in Washington. Russo was a lapsed Catholic, had been since the day in 1972 when he sat in a pew while musicians, with electronic feedback skreeling out of their amplifiers, tortured the "Star Spangled Banner" in a requiem for the honored dead of the Vietnam War. He hadn't been back to Mass since.

Bells signaled the end of the service, and the massive doors of the church swung open. As people reached the sidewalk, some turned to gawk at the Lincoln. Even in this city where limos were as common as muggings, Russo thought, people were curious to know who sat behind the dark glass.

He spotted Murphy at the top of the stairs shaking hands with a priest, confiding something that made the cleric's red face glow with mirth. Murphy took his wife's arm, and they descended, a striking pair in the morning sunshine. At the sidewalk there were greetings from well-wishers, then the senator sent Linda and their driver on to the parking lot while he and his Secret Service escort came over to the Lincoln. Russo stepped out. "Good morning, senator. How was the sermon?"

"Did you get what I wanted?" Murphy asked peremptorily.

"Got it all right here." Russo reached into the car and brought out a fat bellows folder. "Rendle's position papers, the week's pending legislation. Oh, and a videotape of one of those flicks you asked about. I couldn't find the other."

Murphy took the folder without comment. He seemed preoccupied again, Russo thought, as he had been yesterday at Arlington. In fact, Tim had not been himself for the last several days, ever since they'd wound up the road trip. The stresses of campaigning were telling on all of them. Only a steady infusion of antacid was keeping Russo's stomach under control. Well, the convention would make everything worthwhile. And then, on a Tuesday in November . . .

As the limousine drew away, Russo found himself thinking that while politics had replaced his religion, nothing had ever restored his faith. What a frail foundation the public trust was, and once the tremors began, how quickly the whole structure of government could be shaken apart. Unexpectedly, he got an image of Tim Murphy sitting alone in a darkened room watching old movies.

He put a Tums in his mouth and chewed it.

The intercom in the Oval Office buzzed. Peter Hawes, dressed in a sport shirt and slacks, listened to his secretary tell him that the Air Force had arrived to take him to Camp David. Through the French doors Hawes had seen the helicopter settling beyond the trellises of the rose garden, where it chomped air now on the rear lawn near an excavation trench for a new water main. "I'm a *lame* duck," he snapped, "not a deaf and blind one!"

"Yes, Mr. President."

A jab of guilt softened him. "I'll be right out, Mary. Thanks."

Across the office his second-in-command, Bill Rendle, was seated on a silk damask-covered loveseat. The irony was not lost on Hawes: love was emphatically not the emotion of the hour. He hadn't intended to let anger beset him this morning, but strange dreams had molested his sleep, and he had awakened feeling out of sorts. He looked forward to getting away from this place for a few days.

"All I'm telling you," he resumed in a calmer tone, "is that for over seven years we've run this official household with an attitude of fair play. You've been a large part of that. So it just makes no sense to go behind my back now to plot dirty tricks. It's not our way. Besides, those plots always backfire."

Rendle, who had sat stoically through the president's reprimand, didn't appear satisfied. He leaned forward, the motion causing his pants cuffs to rise on the western boots he always wore. "Sir, you've seen the polls. The opposition is gaining ground in areas we should own. We ought to be able to steamroller Murphy, yet we're not doing it. He keeps turning up everywhere, like cowshit at a county fair."

Ignoring the crudeness, Hawes took off his glasses and pinched the bridge of his nose. He resisted pointing out that Rendle was the candidate, not he. For his own part, aware perhaps that he'd gone too far, Rendle rose. "You've got the Air Force waiting."

The president exhaled slowly and replaced his glasses. "I'm not saying don't fight hard. Fight *very* hard. And I'll fight with you. Let's just keep it above board, so it doesn't come back to haunt us. I want you to win. We'll talk when I return."

Thorne came out of the terminal at National Airport and bent to the window of the first taxi in the queue. "Is the Senate open today?"

The cabbie squinted at him. "Aside from the fact it's a holiday weekend?"

"What about the Senate Office Building?"

"Give up, pal. Those guys'll be scarcer than tax breaks."

"Make it the White House then."

The driver's shrug said: it's your wallet.

That morning, when Thorne had reported for his early watch, he had asked Post if the FBI agent who'd come for the file had mentioned being assigned to the White House. Post's reaction was annoyance. "He didn't tell me his hat size, either. So what?"

"You don't find it curious? The White House?"

"It doesn't concern us. We went over this yesterday. Let them take it. I want you here. Which reminds me—there's a change on the duty roster. I put one of the summer kids in the car. You're going to handle traffic at Water Street and Union."

Thorne had been thunderstruck. By simple seniority, never mind training, he should be on moving patrol, a beat requiring experience. But Post would hear no appeal, and at last Thorne's exasperation burst forth. "You're being petty, Alden. This has become personal with you."

"What did you say?"

"You're sworn to uphold the law, and that includes investigating those deaths. If anything, you're obstructing the law!"

"And you're out of a job!" Post exploded. "Challenge me on it! Go ahead!"

A kind of electric charge pulsed in Thorne's thighs and down his arms to his fists. But he walked away. He went home and packed a suitcase. He left his Jeep in the public lot and took the ferry to Woods Hole, where he got a bus to the airport in Boston. Now, as the morning's events replayed themselves in his mind, he backed away from probing why he'd left, why he'd come to Washington.

The White House only intensified his sense of purposelessness. He stood among a gathering of tourists and gazed through the tall iron fence as though from behind the bars of a cell. Now what? Take a snapshot? Tell one of the cops on the other side to let him in? Shake a fist? He wheeled away in frustration and hiked ten blocks before he had a notion of what to do.

Infuriated, Ron Zelnick jabbed in the telephone number of radio WENC in New York. He'd been on the tenth green at Burning Tree when word came that he had a phone call from the vice president. He'd returned at once to the clubhouse and clattered across the tile floor to be told by Bill Rendle that all further contact with Hank Frizzel was off. Chop chop. All the planning—gone, canceled at the president's whim.

This whole damn town was one big power ladder, Zelnick reflected bitterly, and he was strictly a low-rung man, with no chance to climb higher. On the fifth tee he and the others in his foursome had been forced aside as a party of Capitol Hill mossbacks played through. According to protocol, their leisure time was more limited—hence, more valuable. Now his own time was taken up, like a divot hacked out of his day.

The producer of *The Crank's Corner* came on the line. No, he hadn't heard from Frizzel in two days. As far as he knew, Hank was still in Washington.

Zelnick frowned. "If you talk to him, ask him to call me. This is important."

"May I ask what it's in reference to?"

"He'll know. Just have him call."

By the time Zelnick piloted a cart out to rejoin his party on the back nine, cool reason had reasserted itself. It was true, there was a ladder, and everyone on it was either too busy clinging or trying to reach the next rung to help anyone below. That didn't mean it was impossible to reach the top; it just meant that you had to do it alone and without remorse. The way to see your ideas work, he determined, was to carry them out yourself.

It was nighttime and snowing. The two people stood in shadows, half lighted by the headlights of a taxi at the curb. The man, who was middle-aged, handsome, was looking down at the woman, who was much younger, lovely, with sprigs of blonde hair sprouting from under a pillbox hat. "Was it worth it?" he asked her in a defeated voice. "To find out all of that?"

She didn't speak right away—couldn't speak—but her answer was stamped on her face. The taxi waited, its windshield wipers slapping at the falling snow. Then the woman said: "I don't know. I guess I wish I hadn't. But . . . I did."

Slowly he bent and kissed her, then turned away and walked to the taxi. He didn't look back. Watching the cab drive off, the woman stepped from the sheltering doorway. Flakes melted on her cheeks, mingling with her tears. The picture faded to black.

Timothy Murphy shut off the TV and the VCR. The film was *Mr. Hammond's Secret,* with third billing going to the young woman in the closing scene.

Andrea Wexford had never got top billing; still, the characters she'd played through a series of films in the mid-1960s evoked sympathy, and in any young actress that was a gift. In the early 1970s, she appeared in a final film, *Pandora;* then, suddenly and without fanfare, she dropped out of film making and left Hollywood.

Pandora, Murphy thought. Ominous title.

In 1969, when *Mr. Hammond's Secret* was made, Murphy wasn't much interested in films. There were too many other things to do—college papers to write, books to absorb, law schools to apply to, women to seduce. And he had accomplished each of those, while all around him the country seethed with protest, flashed with psychedelic energy. A week before graduation he received a letter from his draft board ordering him to report for a physical. Friends offered fervent advice to file for deferment, head for Canada, take the two years—"they're not going to send you to some rice paddy to get your Ivy League ass shot off!". He listened politely. When his parents arrived for commencement, he informed them that he was not going to wait to be drafted. He would enlist and go OCS. He intended to volunteer for combat.

Murphy glanced down and was startled to discover that his arm was bleeding. During the film he had rolled his left shirtsleeve and had been scratching his forearm, so that the flesh over his tattoo was abraded. He hadn't even been aware of doing it.

When he had tended to the injury, he went to one of the

shelves of his library and shuffled among papers until he came up with a photograph. It showed a burning flag and a skinny, bare-chested young man standing before a high bamboo fence. The sight of it now sent a shiver down his spine—as it had that day on Martha's Vineyard when he'd seen it again for the first time in more than a decade.

He thrust the photo into a stack of recent publicity stills and buried the pile on a bottom bookshelf.

Almost at once he felt better.

In 1969, when he had announced that he wanted to go to Vietnam, his father, a businessman-farmer, had harrumphed to neighbors that even though his boy had "gone East to college, he was raised right." In Tim's mind, however, it had nothing to do with patriotism or rearing. It was his own pattern again: in the face of danger, step forward.

He popped the video cassette out of the machine and tossed it on a shelf. It was time to shake off the preoccupation of the last few days.

The abrasion on his arm was dry. He rolled down his shirtsleeve. He reached for a telephone and called his secretary. "Get Ray Russo for me. I'll hold the line."

A man who wasn't resolute didn't deserve to be president.

Seven . . . eight . . . inhale, exhale . . . nine . . .

Rain's home telephone rang.

She shoved the barbell up once more, set it on the rack and peeled herself off the bench.

"I'm glad I got you," Ray Russo said. "I left a message on the tape at your office."

"I've been avoiding the place. There was a break-in at the building two nights ago."

"What?"

"Nothing serious," Rain said, making no mention of the missing photograph. "It gives me an excuse to goof off awhile."

"Well, then, I'm afraid I've got some bad news for you." Russo chuckled. "Guess who's changed his mind?"

"The senator? About giving an interview?"

"No explanation offered, but he'll do it."

"That's wonderful."

"The rest of the news is he wants to do it tonight."

Tonight! There was no time to prepare questions, to prepare herself. She caught a glimpse of her body in the mirror. She was clad in a leotard, and her skin shone with perspiration.

"How does nine o'clock sound?" Russo asked. "At his house."

Rain pulled on a robe, then got a legal pad and pen, and sat in the kitchen with a glass of club soda, letting her excitement settle. For the next half hour she drafted questions to ask Murphy. Before long, however, doubts began to cluster in the corners of her mind, crowding out immediate thoughts of the interview. Why had the senator changed his mind? Was there another, hidden story behind the obvious, or was that just something she'd begun to imagine? For the first time she realized it would've been useful to bounce her questions off Eric Thorne. Except he was gone.

Fortunately, their relationship hadn't proceeded far enough to make its loss painful: merely inconvenient. Practical woman that she was, she wedged him from her mind. If there *were* a bigger story, the hell with him. She'd handle it on her own.

Clouds were massing on the horizon like volcanos, spewing out the sulphurous colors of the Caribbean sunset. In the cockpit of a gently bobbing runabout a half mile southwest of Bootleg Cay in the Exumas chain of the Bahamas, DEA agent Oscar Sanchez stood with one hand on the windshield, balancing himself in the swells. With his other hand he held binoculars to his eyes. Dwarfed by the clouds, a white plane circled and came in low, settling on the sea with a swoosh of pontoons. At the bottom of his field of vision, a rubber launch scurried out from the cay like a waterbug to meet the plane. The only other witnesses to the meeting were a few pelicans that floated near the launch's wake.

In the furnace light of sundown, Sanchez watched two

men transfer a series of canvas bags from the plane into the launch. There were fifteen or twenty bags in all, followed by a heavy wooden crate. Although the distance was too great to make out detail, he would have bet that stenciled on the crate was the name *Zeta*. Soon the launch sped back to Bootleg Cay, and the plane revved to take-off speed and lifted out of the molten sea. In minutes it had faded into the coming night, leaving Sanchez with his questions.

He turned his binoculars to the villa on the cay, where lights had begun to appear in some of its windows. The house stood alone, a Jazz Age extravagance on the otherwise forbidding, jungle-grown islet of limestone and coral. Built in the 1920s, the villa had served as a private paradise for a bootlegger who'd lived in it like a decadent pasha until a rival gang of rum runners beseiged the cay one night, and he had been slain in a hail of gunfire. Now the cay was owned by a reclusive millionaire.

Sanchez studied the villa, noting things like the placement of doors, outside lights, and what security features, if any, existed. He thought about where the crate had gone, and the canvas bags, which interested him even more. At last he put the binoculars away and started the outboard motor. It would be dark by the time he got back to Nassau.

Thorne yawned. He was sitting at twilight on a park bench across the street from the house where Lorraine Patton lived. Earlier he had taken a taxi to the Writers Guild office, but finding it closed, he had called her home telephone number and gotten no answer. On the third try, an hour ago, the line had been busy, but when he located her address, there was no one home. A glance through the first floor windows and at the two mailboxes told him the bottom apartment was vacant, that Rain occupied the upstairs unit. He yawned again. He lingered on the bench in the fading light, suitcase between his feet, and watched her building. Sooner or later she had to return. Lamps in the park and along the street came on. He thought about the Vineyard murders. He wondered what he was doing here. He thought about the past, the present, about the fact that he had lost his job, and sometimes about the woman who lived over there in that apartment.

At Timothy Murphy's home in Spring Valley, a young woman with an Asian cast to her features met Rain at the front door and introduced herself as the senator's press aide. She showed Rain into a library, explained the ground rules for the interview and vanished. Rain set up her tape recorder.

She had put on a long tan skirt with a champagne silk blouse and brown pumps. Although she felt she knew the senator well, she had met him on only one brief occasion, during the writing of her book, and tonight she was nervous. To calm herself she reviewed the questions she had jotted in her notebook.

Murphy appeared on the dot of eight wearing a dark blue suit and a green tie which brought out the sparkle of calm, deepset eyes. He shook her hand and told her how pleased he was with her book. As she started her recorder, Rain knew she would introduce her piece with that overworked but indispensable noun, charisma.

Rehashing some background, she proceeded to probe him on his ideas, especially his controversial stand on decriminalizing drugs. His responses were candid and intelligent, with an occasional jab of wit, and Rain was soon relaxed. When she turned over the cassette, the senator's press aide reappeared and informed him that a courier had arrived with papers for signature. He excused himself.

Alone, Rain wandered over to the bookshelves that lined three walls of the room and examined titles. There was also a collection of phonograph records, which she fingered through. Nearby, stacked loosely on a shelf next to an NBA basketball inscribed with signatures, were some black-and-white photographs. Murphy with a hardhat and ceremonial shovel breaking ground for a fertilizer plant in Indiana, Murphy ringed by Cub Scouts. One shot caught her attention. It showed a skinny young man, shirtless and unshaven, standing before a bamboo fence, the top of which was strung with barb wire. In the foreground an American flag was in flames. On the man's left forearm was a tattoo. Timothy Murphy as a POW, she realized. She took it from the pile.

And what about these others? She stepped over to a portion of wall covered with framed photos: Murphy with a past president, with Jane Fonda, Warren Beatty. Another showed Murphy—as young-looking as in the prison camp photo—standing on a beach with a blonde woman. Rain tipped her head to read the inscription.

"To Timothy, from Andrea."

With sudden certainty Rain knew it was the woman who'd been with him on Martha's Vineyard! And now a name surfaced! Andrea Wexford.

A voice in the hall alerted her. She was still holding the prison camp photo. She hurried back to the bookshelves, but as she reached to return the photograph she bumped the basketball off its display mount.

Grabbing for it, she missed, and the ball bounced on the floor and rolled toward the door which was just swinging open. Impulsively Rain thrust the photo into her notebook.

Murphy stepped in. Seeing the ball, he bent and deftly scooped it up.

"I was . . . trying to read the autographs," Rain said, feeling her cheeks go hot.

Murphy smiled and spun the ball on his hand. "The Indiana Pacers. This is a game ball from the '86 playoffs." He set it back on its perch.

Recovering, Rain said, "I was also looking at your library. I hope you don't mind."

He laughed. "I don't think I'd fully respect someone who *wasn't* curious about what I read."

She smiled too, resettling on the sofa. "I couldn't help noticing some righteous rock 'n' roll over there too."

"The good old days. Please remind your readers that I'm the only boomer in the race."

"Noted," she said.

"It's true, though. That era, the music—it helped politicize me. Dylan, Quicksilver, and Crosby, Stills and Nash. You couldn't listen to it without examining yourself, your values, where you'd been."

He went on about artists and individual songs and how they'd affected him, speaking with fervor about Woodstock and Vietnam. Only later, in a lull, did Rain decide to mention one of the photographs on his wall. "Was that Andrea Wexford, the actress?"

The calmness that characterized Murphy's eyes seemed to dissipate. They darted to the wall, taking on a faraway look, as though he were unraveling a skein of private thought too complex to voice. He said simply, "That was taken many years ago."

The reaction lasted only a moment, and Rain had read nothing clear there, but her heart now quickened. "I used to admire her roles," she said. "Did you know her well?"

"No. I met her only that once."

A lie? Rain was gripped in the talons of some inexplicable excitement, on the verge of asking about Martha's Vineyard. However, something held her back, cautioning her, like a small unseen hand on her shoulder. Just then the tape ran out and the recorder snapped off.

They both looked at it, then laughed with something like relief.

Far out on Vineyard Sound a glimmering mist foretold the moon's imminent rise out of the ocean. Jimmy Dow drove with his windows down, inhaling the cool night. He felt high.

He had just dropped off Maria, she of the long black hair and bronze skin. It had been their first date, dinner at David's restaurant in Oak Bluffs, where, with encouragement from a bottle of chablis and a feast of swordfish and salad, they'd become friends. Maria, like Jimmy, was Native American, from the Penobscot nation. She was a grad student at B.U., active in Indian affairs. And the best part was she was going to be around all summer, staying with a family in East Chop and working as part of a grant to study the Wampanoag culture. They'd talked nonstop for three hours.

One date, one goodnight kiss, and I'm in love. He laughed aloud to the rising moon.

The pair of college boys working the force for the summer would tease him if they discovered he felt like this, but he didn't care. This was the kind of thing he wanted to take slowly: beach walks at sunset, ice cream sodas, even Patti Page singing "Old Cape Cod"—pure capital *C* corn, but he loved it. He beat out a hot little rhythm on the steering wheel.

As he turned onto Sea View Avenue, not far from where Ric Thorne lived, his spirits all at once drooped. That morning Ric had been fired. Jimmy had tried calling, but Thorne wasn't home. He checked the dashboard clock. Just 10:30. Why not? Maybe he could give his friend a contact high.

The house was set off by itself at the end of a short unpaved road across Sea View from Hart's Harbor. There was no traffic. Easing past on Sea View, he leaned close to the windshield to survey the house. He saw no lights nor any sign of Ric's Jeep. Well, he'd have to turn anyway, so he looped and went back and entered the short road.

In that instant, as the beams of his headlights slid across the face of Thorne's house, something pale moved back from one of the windows.

He drew onto the shoulder and shut off the motor. For a full minute he sat hunched over the wheel, staring at the window; but it remained empty. Had it been an illusion he'd seen, caused by his own lights? Ordinarily he might've let it go at that; tonight, though, he wondered. In spite of the island's seeming determination to pretend that the lazy, hazy, crazy days of summer would roll out as usual, last weekend's murders still gripped people's minds. There was an unspoken level of nervousness. He and Maria had discussed it tonight, and although he'd been sorry to see the evening end, he had also felt a sense of relief when she went into the house with other people and locked the door.

In the silence, out on the sound, a fog horn gave hoarse warning.

Each year-round officer had his private vehicle equipped with a radio hooked into the dispatch board in town. He keyed the mike now and got the office. The college kid named Lou was on.

"No, Jimmy," said Lou in response to Dow's question. "Warren Stubbs went off duty a half hour ago. The chief's out in the car someplace. I'm not sure yet how this sucker works, but if you stand by I can try to patch you through."

Dow didn't feel like talking to Alden Post. "Don't bother. Just log my call. I'm out at Ric Thorne's place."

He hung up the mike and reached under the front seat and drew out his holstered off-duty revolver. He slipped the safety strap off the hammer, put the holster and weapon into the pocket of his sportcoat and got out.

As though bloated from having nibbled its way through the bank of mist, the moon hung fat and yellow over the dunes beyond Hart's Harbor. He speculated again on what he'd seen. Could've been a curtain blowing—there was a light wind—though a glance at the windows told him that all of them were closed.

Thorne's front door was locked.

This reassured him some, but he was here; might as well be thorough. There were two other doors.

He walked around to the side of the house and climbed the low porch and opened the screen door. The inside door was secure. Two down. Descending the steps he started for the rear of the house where there was a deck. Drifted sand shushed under his feet. In the cooling night air, he discovered, he had started to sweat.

The sliding door on the deck wasn't locked.

Jimmy's mind snapped into focus. Call it a Yankee sense of stewardship, the lifelong reflex of a careful man—Thorne never left anything unlocked. The door slid open on well lubricated rollers. Dow stepped inside, scanning the dark kitchen.

"Ric, you home?"

He listened. Silence.

His heartbeat quickened.

He edged past a table and chairs, stopped, looked around. On the wall by the sink he made out the shape of the painting Lisa Thorne had done; he envisioned lightning pitchforking downward in darkness, ahead of its thunder.

The refrigerator motor kicked on.

"Ric."

In his years on the force, outside of target practice, Dow had fired a sidearm only once, to frighten off a Doberman that was menacing a child. He eased the .38 from its holster now.

As he went farther into the house, moving toward the front room where he'd first sensed movement, he considered going back outside to radio for backup. But the idea struck him as slightly paranoid. This is a small island, he told himself, not a city.

He had almost reached the entrance to the living room when he was certain that he heard a sound. It was a low, quick shuffling. He froze.

His heart thawed first, beginning to pound. He wanted to put on lights but knew if he had to react quickly his eyes wouldn't adjust fast enough. As it was, his night vision allowed him to make out the shape of a doorway. The living room would be moonlit. He advanced one pace.

"Ric?" he said again; and immediately, because the word sounded hoarse, he added: "*Police!* I'm armed!"

He swung around the edge of the doorway, weapon in both hands. A large shape went past the windows on the far right, swift and dark in a shaft of moonlight. Jimmy ducked back, his heart hammering so hard now that the sound seemed to come from outside him. What if they'd all been wrong? If the person who'd murdered those two guests at the Captain James were still on the island? Had been all along? He was aware of his hand tightening on the weapon, his finger tensing . . .

A lunging movement.

Spurt of orange flame.

Bang!

Thorne jerked awake and sat up. Night mist fell chilly on his face. Whatever had awakened him scurried back down a hole into his subconscious as a more immediate awareness took hold. He was on a park bench in a strange city. He stood up, stiff from the dampness. Across the street there were no lights on in Lorraine's apartment. Was she still out? Asleep? He was startled to see it was about 1 A.M. Over the rooftops a moon sliced thin clouds like a cleaver. He picked up his suitcase and set off to find a taxi.

12

At the presidential retreat at Camp David, it was Peter Hawes's habit to rise early and hike the pine-studded ridges of the Catoctin Mountains. This morning an overnight coolness lingered among the trees, and he had spied a red fox, stopping to observe it before his Secret Service men could catch up and send the animal fleeing as if it represented a danger to the welfare of the nation. Walking easily now, feeling spryer than he had in weeks, he returned to the main lodge in high spirits. His secretary had a message for him that Vern Holsworth had telephoned.

At Bethesda Naval the doctor answered on the first ring. Although Hawes knew that Holsworth was nothing if not efficient, hearing his brisk greeting at eight o'clock on a holiday morning put him on guard. He forced a hale tone into his voice. "Good morning, Vern. I've been up and at 'em for hours, and I feel great. What's doing?"

"Hello, sir. I have the results of your lab tests," said Holsworth without preamble.

"All right. Let's hear it."

Holsworth began with numbers: systolic and diastolic blood pressures, this and that per deciliter, triglycerides, HDL's—all within normal limits, he assured Hawes. He went on with his figures, including what he said was an elevated blood level of the enzyme amylase. Finally the president's patience wore thin. "Words, Doctor, that's the language I understand. What's all this arithmetic mean?"

The doctor paused. "Mr. President—don't misunderstand me—but you are telling me the truth that you haven't been drinking heavily?"

"I've been teetotaling for a month. What's this about, dammit?"

The doctor told him.

Couched though it was in all the empathy and human warmth that doctor and friend could give, the report left Hawes stunned.

Time crept past.

"There's some mistake," he said at last, even managing a flutter of laughter. "The lab mixed up my tests with some other poor soul's. There has to be a . . ."

He stopped, swept with the bleak conviction that Holsworth didn't make diagnostic mistakes like that.

"Sir, in cases like this we always run duplicate samples in separate labs. Plus, I got a confirming opinion, without identifying you. I am truly, truly sorry, Mr. President."

In seven years of being addressed by this title, Peter Hawes had grown used to the sound of it. But it was a meager comfort now. He mustered strength. "I'm returning to Washington at once. I'll want to go over this with you point by point."

"Yes, sir. I've canceled everything else. I'll meet you at the White House."

When Hawes had ordered his helicopter, he summoned one of the Secret Service men and indicated a cabinet near the lodge's fieldstone fireplace. "There's a bottle in there, Ted."

The agent betrayed no surprise that the president was breaking a month-long dry spell, nor that it was barely 8 A.M.; he brought the MacAllan's and left. Hawes poured a large splash into a bone china cup bearing the presidential seal and drank half of it back, aware only of the warmth it brought, like a fleeting sensation of life itself.

★   ★   ★

Rain saw Eric Thorne standing in the hallway outside her door, his brown hair combed back as if he had recently climbed from a shower. She shook off her surprise. "Why are you here?"

He shrugged. "Autograph?" He held up a paperback copy of her book. "There were some in the airport bookstore this morning. I don't know if they were going as fast as Danielle Steel's latest, but I figured . . ."

"What do you really want?" she asked sharply.

"Can we talk?"

"Do we have anything to talk about?"

"Lots. For openers, the worth of contracts made in bar rooms."

"You broke the agreement, not me."

"How do you figure?"

"By talking to Frizzel about the photograph."

His brow furrowed. "Lefty Frizzel? The country western singer?"

"Forget it. He told me. Our deal is void. Bye."

"Wait." He pressed a hand against the door, resisting her. "I've been cut loose once already, Rain. Twice I don't need. I'm serious, who's Frizzel?"

It was her turn for doubt. "What do you mean 'cut loose'?"

"I was fired."

"You're . . . not a cop anymore?"

"As of yesterday. It's a long story with an abrupt ending."

She stared at him, still skeptical, trying to recall her run-in with Hank Frizzel. Had he mentioned a name? No, she remembered now; he'd said he protected his *"sources."* Still, how else would he have known about the photograph except for Thorne's having told him?

She studied the angles of Eric's face, searching for a trace of guile—but it wasn't there. As she had been the day she first met him, she was struck by a congenial intelligence she didn't expect in a man of his rough-cut looks. "Why *did* you come back?" she asked.

"You have reached the dumb answers line," he intoned in a robot voice. "To proceed, please ask a silly question."

She didn't suppress her smile. They sounded like two kids: "did not," "did so." He smiled too and held up his hands. "Truce?"

"Come on in. I'll make some coffee."

"You know, I passed a diner down the road apiece and got my mind set on a stack of pancakes. You interested? My treat."

Rain narrowed an eye. "Can I get that in writing?"

"Andrea Wexford," Thorne said, digging the actress's name from some mental graveyard as they sat in a diner booth waiting for their food to come. Rain had filled him in on her visit last evening to Timothy Murphy's home. "You're certain?"

Her brisk nod left no room for doubt. "She's older now, of course, but it's her. And the only thing missing from my office is that snapshot you gave me. Factor that in."

He stirred his coffee, watching the small vortex the spoon made, his mind aswirl with everything she'd just told him. "And you think this Frizzel must've taken it?"

She shrugged. "No proof, but he saw where my office is. And he sure knew the photo exists, which is why I assumed you'd told him. But if you didn't, who did?"

He could only shake his head, feeling another vortex, this one of questions, pulling him deeper.

"I don't know how it'll affect your investigation," Rain went on, "but if Frizzel did steal it, then I can forget the exclusive I was hoping for. The *Insider* will splash a lot of half-truths all over the newsstands, and no one will ever take the story seriously again. Not to mention my credibility, which'll be zero with Murphy's people."

From his inside jacket pocket he took a photograph and handed it to her. It was a duplicate of the one that had been stolen. "Keep it. I made copies. You can't go public with it anyway because there's nothing else. I'm not even official anymore.''

''But the story—''

''Let the *Insider* risk the lawsuits. If they get some action going, the fallout might tell a lot.'' He hesitated, but he felt he owed her something more. He told what had happened three days ago in Florida. When he got to the FBI's involvement in the murder investigation, Rain was literally on the edge of her seat.

''I'm going to try to contact Hiram Kirk today and see what he can tell me,'' Thorne concluded.

''How? You don't have a badge anymore.''

''I'm hoping Kirk won't know I was fired. The FBI should be interested in what I just told you, regardless. I'll have to improvise my approach. But you're wrong on one point.'' He dug in the pocket of his corduroy jacket and brought out a badge which he laid on the Formica table top with a clack. ''I forgot to turn it in.''

Rain touched the brass and blue enamel shield with a finger. ''Vineyard Haven,'' she murmured. ''That's got a safe sound to it.''

He pocketed the badge as the waitress brought breakfast. After they had eaten quietly for a time, Rain said, ''So why leave?''

He gave her a questioning look.

''The island. I mean, it seems as if you're in the right. Couldn't you appeal the firing? It's not as if they'd banished you from there forever.''

He smiled at the image. ''The selectmen would probably back me. But I don't know. Maybe that's not what I want.''

''I thought you liked being a cop and living there.''

''I do. We're public servants in the best sense of the phrase. The fishing ain't bad either,'' he said lightly.

Rain wasn't to be dismissed. ''The question stands, Eric. Why are you here?''

Silence had become the habit of his years of living alone, a carapace of noninvolvement, and here she was probing for soft spots. What he read in her eyes, though, was interest.

Unexpectedly he found himself telling her about growing up on the Vineyard, taking pleasure in talking in a way he hadn't done for a long time. On the diner's jukebox songs changed, new tempos, different rhythms. He moved the story from the island to the city. He made detective. It was tough work—even tougher on a wife. The marriage went. But when the job brought results, he tried to explain, it was the most satisfying police work there is.

"Once I left it though, I didn't look back. The ones you don't solve always seem to linger too long, like uneasy ghosts." He gave a short laugh, to lighten the sepulchral tone he heard in his voice, then said, "The danger in the job is maybe after a while you'll stop giving a damn."

She shook her head. "I don't see that in you."

"There's no predicting. Anyway, when Post assigned me to the Ames-Belnap killings, I guess I'd grown rusty."

The jukebox stopped. Patrons had come and gone. He paused, trying still to pinpoint some rationale for his recent actions; then he just went on. "It was clear the case was going to be a tough one. The island isn't equipped to deal with that sort of thing. It's quiet there . . . low key."

Rain tipped her head to one side. "Too low sometimes?"

"That's putting it succinctly."

"I was raised in a West Virginia town you never heard of," she said.

"You want to talk about it?"

"Just did. Go on."

Under an odd compulsion to talk, he picked up his coffee cup but set it down again. "What surprised me was, after I got the old habits out of mothballs and dusted off, I didn't feel like putting them away. I'm not going to pretend I was breathing down the killer's shirt collar. The more I pursued this, the more questions I came up with. But I was on some kind of trail. Jimmy Dow, my pal on the force, was getting

into it too. We were building something. Then the chief
knocked it down, whatever it was.''

He had been speaking intently. Now he leaned back in
the booth and drummed his fingers on the green vinyl seat-
cover a moment, discomfited about having said so much;
yet, at the same time, relieved, for he knew that it had
brought him to what he had to say next. It wasn't something
he'd planned, but now it made sense.

"Rain, if I stay with the case, it's all unofficial now. I can't
be responsible for anyone else. I'm afraid our arrangement
is off.''

Her reaction wasn't immediate. She finished her coffee.
Then, without a word, she took her purse and slid out of
the booth. He called to her but she didn't look back. At the
cashier's stand, as he hurriedly paid, he saw her on the street
hailing a taxi.

By the time he got outside, she was gone.

The pair of ground-floor suites that comprised Murphy
campaign headquarters on Delaware Avenue were a frenzy
of activity. A voter poll underwritten by the incumbent party's national committee, and intended for internal use only,
had leaked to the Murphy camp. The results showed that in
some administration strongholds, Murphy held a narrow
lead over Bill Rendle. The staff had given up Memorial Day
to work. A collection had been taken for champagne.

Behind the frosted glass and partition walls of his private office, Ray Russo resisted the activities in the outer
area, but he did kindle a good cigar on the strength of the
news.

Since the rally at Shea Stadium, Russo had narrowed the
possibilities to a pair of scenarios. In people's minds, the
stadium event had thrust Murphy ahead of the pack. They
would act on that perception in one of two ways. Either they
would turn away in pusillanimous fear of the unknown—
thus effectively burying Tim in a reelection landslide—or
they would rally around a man in whom they sensed

strength and courageous leadership. The latter seemed to be happening. It was Russo's job to up the momentum.

There was a knock on his door. He peered over the tops of his reading glasses. An apple-cheeked campaign aide who looked like she should be fox-hunting in Pimmit Hills but instead was working for Tim Murphy, came in. "Sir, here are those phone bills that you asked for."

Russo took the sheaf of printout. "I want someone to get hold of the Park Service about Friday afternoon," he said.

"Taken care of. They'll have the stage and the PA system set up for us."

Russo glanced up, impressed. "Well . . . fine."

"And I had a thought, sir. Uh. Have you got a minute?"

"One minute."

"Well, there's that terrific photo of the senator? Holding the falcon on his hand? We haven't exploited it at all. Blown up, it'd make a wild visual for the back of the stage."

Russo remembered the picture, taken on the farm the day Tim had announced his candidacy. "What's your name again?" he asked the aide.

"Melissa, sir."

"Arrange it, Melissa."

She beamed at him. "We've got champagne out there."

"The night after we take the convention by acclamation, I am personally going to drink a Jeroboam of Dom P. Until then, there's a lot to do. Keep up the good work."

"Yes, sir."

Alone again, Russo felt encouraged. His staff was starting to act like a real team. The campaign was looking more and more like a winner. Why, then, was he also worried?

Murphy had been behaving oddly. One moment he was up, the next testy—or withdrawn, as he'd been at Arlington Cemetery. The change had come on sometime since the California trip. Tim made no mention of anything wrong—possibly it was something he wasn't aware of himself; still, if it was going to slow the momentum, Russo was determined to find out what it was and correct it.

He opened the sheaf of telephone bills. The printout included the monthlies for all headquarters' lines, as well as credit calls made on the road. The FEC was fussy about records. He skimmed the sheets until he came to one particular number sequence: the private line Murphy used while traveling. Listed were just over sixty calls, the majority made to Murphy's residences here and in Indiana. There were a dozen calls to other familiar numbers as well. But there on May twenty-fifth, six days ago, at the Albuquerque area code, was a call listed to a number Russo didn't recognize. It had been placed to Nassau, the Bahamas, and had lasted one minute.

New Mexico. Last Wednesday. The next morning, in St. Louis, Tim had screwed up with that remark about farming marijuana. Curiosity tapped at Russo's mind. He scanned the remaining lists of toll calls and found one other appearance of the Nassau number, on April twenty-ninth. He pushed the printout aside.

The tapping went on annoyingly, like the laggard drip of a faucet, and he knew he had to do something to stop it. He drew over a telephone.

Ten minutes later, after several explanations and a short delay, the Caribbean long distance operator came back with an answer to his request. "I am sorry, sar. We have no record of that number."

"You mean no listing? Like it's unpublished?"

"No, sar," sang the lilting West Indian voice. "There is no such number."

The fact that it was listed twice on the sheets before him did nothing to dissuade the woman: *obviously* it was a computer error, sar; such things happened all the time, she assured him.

Russo leaned back in his chair, letting his gaze slide randomly up ribbons of cigar smoke, as though seeking some wisp of meaning which had escaped him.

Thorne was propped against the headboard of the bed in his motel room, a city map spread across his legs, when the telephone rang. He drew the map aside and swung his feet to the floor. There was only one place where he had left this number. His greeting was met by a brief silence, then a male voice asked, "What is your full name?" He gave it. "This is Special Agent Kirk, Mr. Thorne. Howdy."

So his message had gotten through the bureaucratic net. "Thanks for calling back."

"Thanks a bunch yourself. We're obliged to folks like you for your cooperation. Now, your message implied you may have information on the Belnap-Ames murders."

"There are details," Thorne said, "that aren't in the file."

"Well, I'd surely be grateful if you'd tell them to me." Kirk had that affable, almost lazy, Southwestern voice that airline pilots and military personnel seemed to acquire.

"Actually," Thorne offered, "I was thinking I could come over there so we could discuss the case, maybe pool our knowledge."

"There's nothing I'd like better, honestly. But this here's Washington, land of chapter and verse." Kirk's chuckle made it sound like they were sharing a tired joke. "There are Bureau procedures I've got to abide by which prevent me from commenting on an investigation. You've no doubt got them too, up there on the Cape."

"So when you say cooperation, you don't mean it literally," Thorne said.

"I don't make the regs, sir, just obey them. What I'll do though, I'll send a full report to your office once we've closed the case."

Either Kirk was Uncle Sam's good nephew or he was sandbagging in the most effective way there was: with SOP. Thorne tried to think of a way around it, but he couldn't come up with one.

"What do you say?" the agent prompted. "We in agreement?"

Thorne hesitated. A card perched atop the motel room's TV set—an offer for pay movies—had given him an idea. "Do you follow films at all?" he asked.

There was a pause. "I don't get it."

"Actresses from the 1960s? The woman in the photo that was in the file . . . the one with Senator Murphy on the day of the murders? If you're interested, I know who she is."

In the silence, as he waited with shallow-breathed expectancy, Thorne could hear faint disembodied voices talking somewhere in the circuits, like the overheard confessions of the guilty. After a moment Kirk said, "Where do we meet?"

13

Thorne had not expected to be so moved by the Vietnam Memorial. He had seen it in magazines and on TV, but he was unprepared for the way the reality of it affected him. Like most of the dozens of other visitors spread along the twin lengths of gleaming, black wall, he felt drawn to touch the names etched in the marble. He even had a thought to check one of the locater directories for the names of men he'd known whom the war had claimed; but he was here for a different purpose. Four o'clock, Kirk had said on the phone. By the time Thorne thought to ask how he would recognize the agent, Kirk had hung up.

The afternoon sky was quilted with clouds that threatened rain. He had worn only his corduroy sportcoat. He walked along the wall, scanning fellow visitors, seeking some show of recognition. As it had in the motel room two hours ago, a tentacle of doubt touched his mind. What if the FBI already had spoken with Post and learned what it needed to know? Or discovered he'd been fired? If anyone came to meet him, would it be to arrest him for misrepresentation?

Shaking free of the questions, he turned and began to ascend the cobbled path.

At the far end of the memorial a middle-aged man in an olive-green suit was paging through a directory. Out of respect, or in deference to the Potomac breeze, he gripped his hat behind his back. As Thorne passed, the man looked up.

"America's wailing wall," he said matter of factly. "I'm Kirk."

Startled, Thorne murmured his own name.

"Let's walk," the agent said.

Kirk had a jowly face; a thinning, rusted-steel crewcut; and smoky eyes. His bulk made him appear shorter, but he came near to Thorne's height and looked powerful. His left hand stayed in his pants pocket. As they moved away from the crowd, he pointed with his hat toward a bronze sculpture of three combat soldiers. "That's a bone tossed to the ones who need something concrete. Some folks can't handle abstractions."

Before Thorne could decide if the agent was being metaphorical, Kirk pointed again. "The Lincoln Memorial. You don't know the city, do you?"

"No," Thorne admitted, put off balance by the man's approach.

"Didn't think so."

They walked for several minutes, moving away from the memorials, turning right past lines of idling tour busses. Turning right again, they followed a sidewalk that bordered the park along Constitution Avenue. As they neared the street, Kirk set the hat on his head and belatedly took out an ID folder which he held open for Thorne to see.

"Mr. Thorne, I'm going to be straight with you about the Bureau's interest in those two murders. I could hawk the *official* reason, but obviously you aren't buying or you wouldn't be here." His jowls creased with a tight smile. "In exchange for my telling you, I'd like to learn what you know. Sound fair?"

For the second time today, Thorne was impressed by the agent. Behind the honey-cured ham was a shrewd operator. "You start."

"Well, the way it looks," Kirk began, "there's more to those deaths than anyone knows. So far we're just assembling bitty little pieces, trying to come up with the full picture. But I'm not overstating things by saying that the case involves national security."

In order not to betray his sudden excitement, Thorne glanced away toward the traffic flowing past on Constitution. When he looked back, Kirk was gauging him. "Now, your turn. Tell me what you've uncovered."

Thorne described his trip to Ft. Lauderdale and the mysterious destruction of the plane that had been on the Vineyard the day of the killings. He revealed the identity of the woman in the photograph with Senator Murphy. At no point did he mention Rain's involvement, determined to protect her from problems that were certain to result when his own situation was discovered, as he knew it would be. His best hope was that his cooperation would mitigate for him. At the very least, he hoped the discovery would happen later rather than sooner.

They reached a corner. Kirk stopped walking. The sidewalk continued along the expanse of park toward the pale dagger of the Washington Monument. "Impressive."

For a moment Thorne thought he meant the monument, which Thorne needed no guide to identify, but Kirk was still talking. "Which isn't to say all your suppositions are founded. Still, considering the handicaps you've been working against on that small island, you've shown good instincts. I appreciate your sharing them with us."

Thorne waited.

"Let me offer some perspective," Kirk went on, peering under his hat brim at distant buildings, as if he were talking about architecture. "The Bureau has thousands of employees in over sixty field offices. We've got labs, experts up the yin yang. More computers than IBM." It was an old folks tone—Wilford Brimley selling American ingenuity. "What I'm proposing to you, I'm saying when the case is shut, your department gets a full report. And you personally get a citation for your contribution. How's that sound?"

Gee, thought Thorne, do I get to keep the Ginsu? "Look, I don't mean to sound ungrateful, but what you've told me amounts to nothing. Okay, national security. How about some specifics? What's this about?"

"No can do, I'm sorry. We are grateful to you, really, but

owing to the nature of the case, the Bureau has full jurisdiction now.''

The man's polite affabilty was serving only to fray Thorne's composure. In the heavy air he was perspiring. ''I hear that. But from my standpoint it's a matter of law enforcement. Those killings happened where I live. I'm a duly charged official there.''

''You've got a stake in seeing the killer caught. Understood,'' Kirk said equably. ''You've got to understand *my* position though. This is a federal case. Officially we owe you nothing. Believe me, it's going to get solved. And I'm prepared to update you when that happens. But until then, I'd be obliged if you'd walk away and forget we had this conversation.''

''I can't do that.''

''Can't, or won't?''

Kirk had the cop habit, as he spoke, of moving right into your space, quietly challenging you with proximity. Thorne stood his ground. ''It amounts to the same thing. You said it yourself. I have a stake in this.''

With a gesture that said he was a reasonable man but growing short of patience, Kirk spread his arms. ''So what's the problem?''

For the first time, Thorne noticed that the agent's left hand was encased in a tight, flesh-toned glove of the kind worn over a prosthesis. Kirk slipped the hand back into his pants pocket. ''What you do, you go on home to your regular duties, and I'll be in touch.''

Thorne glanced away in frustration. Holiday crowds drifted past. Afternoon traffic, in smoky profusion, moved along the tree-lined avenues among the massive white edifices of Washington. This was a different world, one where he was an off-islander. His cheeks felt hot. ''I gave you what I had,'' he said, turning back to Kirk. ''Just tell me what's going on.''

Carefully the agent removed his hat. Beneath the bristles of his crewcut, his scalp shone like a ripe honeydew melon. When he spoke, the genial tone was gone and his gray eyes had turned to flint. "Mister, here's some free advice." He poked the hatbrim at Thorne's chest. "Stand back, or you're going to find yourself ass-deep in trouble you definitely don't need. That's a promise. You're out of your depth. I suggest you paddle back to your safe little harbor before you drown."

Kirk looked up then, as the first fat raindrops fell. He put his hat back on. Only after a beige Aries sedan had drawn to the curb and picked him up and Thorne had run for the shelter of a souvenir kiosk to keep from getting soaked— only then did it occur to Thorne that the hat had been a signal to a driver who had been following them the whole time.

Hiram Kirk did not return to the FBI building. At a phone booth he told his driver to wait while he dialed long-distance information. Minutes later, having spoken with the police chief in Vineyard Haven, he had interesting new data. Yesterday morning Eric Thorne had been terminated from his job. Today he was being sought for questioning in the gunshot slaying of a fellow Vineyard cop named Dow.

To Prudence Winters there was no place more romantic than Washington on a rainy night. As she watched from her seventh floor balcony, the light rain softened the city outlines, spun haloes around lamps, and brought a sibilant hush to traffic in the streets below. Such an evening reminded her of her first glimpse of this town nearly sixty years ago, when her father had packed his family into a car and driven for three days to join the faltering law practice of a distant cousin. It was pouring the April evening they had arrived, and cherry blossoms lay pasted to the sidewalks like sodden confetti from a parade. Eight years old at the time, Prudence had been possessed by an excitement at seeing this place she had only heard about. Her mother, on the other hand, exhausted and overwrought from the move and the recent birth of Pru's youngest sister, had wept and pleaded with father to take them all back to Baton Rouge. But Washington became their new home. Over the years there had been increasingly elegant houses as her father had nursed the law firm into one of the city's foremost. There had been private schools, debutante balls, and then Prudence St. Clair's society wedding to Clarence Winters. It was soon after that that Clarence began his long tenure on Capitol Hill.

Over the past half dozen years since her husband's death Pru had become an adopted Californian, favoring the climate and the openness of the people there. Tonight, however, she realized once more how much she loved this city. Especially when she was in love.

She sighed. Unfortunately she was in love with the world's most ineligible man. As a widowered president, whose late wife had been a much-beloved First Lady, Peter Hawes could not consider remarriage while he was in office. It seemed there were some notions of decorum that, right or wrong, were sacrosanct. So Prudence waited, dividing her time between Orange County and here, her regret tempered by the knowledge that once Peter finished this final year in office, then . . .

Ah, her emotion was enough; she didn't bother to try to find words.

The buzz of the building intercom drew her inside, making her curious all at once. Who could that be? She wasn't expecting anyone.

The door captain had an odd excitement in his customarily clipped voice when he announced that she had a guest. "Ma'am . . . it's the *president.*"

A few moments later he appeared, his sandy gray hair windblown, his suitcoat lightly beaded with rain.

"What a surprise!" Pru exclaimed, gripping his hands. "I didn't know you'd returned from Camp David."

"I'm back. No palace guard," he added with a tired smile, seeing her glance past him to the hall. "I came all by myself, like a big boy."

"Well, I was hoping you'd come up and *see* me sometime, Big Boy." She kissed him.

But was he being a little stiff? She would dispel that soon

enough. They moved into the living room, where matching floor and table lamps spilled rich light over the furnishings. Although Peter had been here before, it hadn't been often. Ignoring her invitation to sit, he went to the open balcony door, where a rain-fresh breeze was blowing. She joined him.

"I've just been mooning over the view," she said happily. "I never tire of it."

"It's beautiful," Peter agreed distantly. It was not the tone, she thought, of a man who could justly claim to rule all that he now saw. Her own emotions, though, were full; she would sweep him along with her. "I believe I've caught a belated case of Potomac fever," she declared. "I can feel it coursing in my foolish blood. Peter, I love this city. I love what it stands for. I love what wonderful things can happen to people here." She linked his arms with both of hers and looked up at him.

"You sound so happy," he said.

"I am. I am. I only wish I'd had more hand in the workings of things. Women didn't in my days, and that will be my only regret. Even the great women—the Eleanor Roosevelts and Ladybird Johnsons—had to somehow work their art behind their men." She sighed. "Still, in my life I've loved two men who were giants here. I shall take everlasting pride in that." She quit with an abrupt laugh. "Listen to me. Babble-on revisited. And Peter, poor dear, you haven't said a word."

He turned and gripped her shoulders. There was something in his eyes that she hadn't seen before, an expression that drew out sudden, similar emotion in her: fright.

"Peter—? What is it? What's wrong?"

He took her hand and led her across the room to a sofa, made her sit. "I've been debating with myself all day," he said. "I have decided only in the past fifteen minutes, as I walked several blocks."

"You were walking *alone?* At night? What has—?"

"Prudence, I have something to tell you. It affects you, me, Bill's campaign. I'm very sick, Pru. I'm . . . dying."

★ ★ ★

The taxi's windshield wipers kept cadence for the parade of Ron Zelnick's thoughts. Leading the march, like a determined drum major, was one insistent question: Where in God's name was Frizzel?

That afternoon he had telephoned Frizzel's producer in New York again. No one had heard from the journalist for several days. "Which could mean he's on the track of a good story, couldn't it?" Zelnick had asked, hearing the hopefulness in his own voice.

"That's a nice thought, but don't bank on it. More likely he's holed up with some woman he's met. His girlfriend called earlier looking for him. I think that's what she suspects. I'll check with his editor over at the *Insider*, see what I can learn."

"Please! And get back to me, okay?"

"Hey, you're not the only one who wants him."

That conversation had taken place hours ago, and Zelnick had received no word since. Now the vice president was putting the pressure on him. He couldn't wait for Frizzel to come rolling home in the tomcat dawn; if he didn't make some report soon, telling Bill Rendle that the reporter had been warned off, Rendle was going to land on him with both boots.

When the taxi stopped at the address Zelnick had given, he caught the driver's questioning glance in the mirror. The drab, empty street and dark buildings gave the area the look of a war sector awaiting reparations; surely this was not the sort of place where his well-dressed fare wanted to be. The wink of a sign above a tavern across the way lighted the twenty-dollar bill Zelnick passed through the plexiglass divider. "Keep it."

When the taxi pulled away, swirling the steam drifting from the rims of manhole covers, Zelnick tugged up the collar of his coat.

The front doors of the warehouse building were locked. He stepped back to the curb and squinted against falling rain, trying to see the windows on the upper floors. Except for a weak glow filtering through from the stairwells, the panes were dark; but up there somewhere was the office of the D.C. Writers Guild. And hopefully the secret of Frizzel's whereabouts.

He entered the tavern with a peripheral awareness of the patrons turning to look at him. Mostly they were shabby older men strung along the bar, and a few groups seated at tables. In the smoky heat and under the reddish lights, they could have been sinners occupying small circles in hell. Wordlessly the bartender made change and nodded toward the rear of the dim cavern. The phone's mouthpiece stank of stale smoke. Zelnick fed in a quarter and dialed. Three times the number rang before an answering tape with the woman's voice came on. He hung up.

He chose the alley on the left side of the warehouse, where he could make out a fire escape. Glancing both ways along the empty sidewalk, he entered the alley.

He'd seen the latest poll and the news wasn't good. Rendle was slipping. Or, more accurately, Murphy was surging. Shea Stadium had focused his candidacy. People were starting to say, "Hey, we've heard the rhetoric about a new America—maybe this guy really means it." Editorialists had picked up the theme, offering elaborate analyses of their own. John Bricklin's assessment had been the tersest: "Voters are hot for that Goddamn falcon!"

To Zelnick one thing was clear: something had to be done to hobble Murphy, or Rendle would be out come November. And if Rendle were out . . .

His foot sank in a puddle and he cursed, kicking water off his shoe. Just ahead, rain dripping from the fire-escape railing chattered on a heap of plastic trash bags. The smell of wet garbage fouled the air. Steeling himself, he paused to allow his eyes to adjust to the dark. He grew aware slowly that he was holding one breath clenched in his chest. A rusty sign warned:

NO TRESPASSING POLICE TAKE NOTICE.

But it didn't look as if anyone had taken notice in some time, he saw with a lurch of his heart. Half buried among the sodden rubbish, tended by a furtive scurry of rats, lay a corpse.

"It's Ronald Zelnick," Evy Bricklin whispered to her husband, cupping the phone with a jeweled hand. "Do you want to take it in the den?"

Bricklin took the receiver. "Hey, Ronnie! How was your weekend?" he boomed.

"John, we have to meet right away."

"What? *Tonight?*" Bricklin frowned. It was a holiday evening. He and his wife were entertaining.

"As soon as you can get here."

Zelnick's voice sounded taut. Behind it, Bricklin could hear a buzz of conversation and an intermittent ringing noise that was familiar but not instantly identifiable. "Where are you?" he asked, some of his high spirits fading.

"In a bar."

Pinball—that was the sound he was hearing. "You been drinking?"

"No, listen to me—"

"Well, *I* have! Silver bullets, bone dry, the way God meant them."

"*Listen!*"

Bricklin scrubbed a hand across his face, as if pulling off a mask. "All right," he said tightly.

"I'm sitting on a situation that's got wires and a ticking clock attached to it. You *hear* me, John? If it goes, it's going to blow us right out of the fucking water! Now you quit the martinis. Take down this address. And come *alone!*"

Back at the Capital City Motor Inn, Thorne slotted his rental car between a dumpster and a brown pickup with a white camper-cap decorated with decals of mallard ducks in flight. He climbed the outside stairs to the covered, open walkway which ran along the second floor at the rear of the motel, lit now by the yellow bug lamps outside each door. As he reached the landing, a perception nudged at his mind.

He tried to grasp what it was, but it had fled as quickly as it had come.

Following his meeting with Kirk, he'd gone to a public library branch, where he searched issues of the *Post* covering the past eight days. The paper had carried no report of the murders of Vaughan Belnap and Maura Ames. From a pay phone he called Ft. Lauderdale and learned that laboratory analysis had pushed suspicion a little nearer to certainty that what had destroyed the Beechcraft and killed its pilot was a bomb. The possibility that the plane had been sanitized, all of its identifying marks deliberately removed, had been passed along to the FBI. No one at either agency had any time predictions. Thorne had given the Florida cop his number at the motel. He didn't bother the man with the detail that he was no longer a cop himself.

He was stepping into the darkened motel room when his half-perception of a moment ago was back, and he grasped it.

When he had driven up, the heavy window drapes had been partway open. They were fully drawn now.

That was all the lead time he had as the door crashed shut behind him. Instinctively he ducked, lunging to his left, away, he hoped, from whoever had slammed the door.

The overhead light went on.

He saw a man with red hair and green handyman's coveralls, and hammered a fist at his face. But they were too far apart. The man shook off the blow, then stepped in and threw a punch that sledged off the side of Thorne's skull. Immediately he threw another. The light flickered. Thorne staggered back, just managing to brace himself against the air conditioner. Moth shapes swarmed in his vision.

With no time to get his own fists up, he stumbled inside the arc of Handyman's next swing. The fist went past Thorne's ear, the momentum snaking the arm around his neck, bringing them close. Thorne feinted, as if to move away, then jacked an elbow into the man's ribs.

Handyman woofed and fell backwards, his arms pinwheeling, grabbing hold of the heavy drapes. The drape liner tore off its rod, flapping like a matador's cape as he flung it aside. He seized the lapels of his own coveralls and yanked. Buttons bounced onto the carpet. He shoved a hand inside the open front.

Thorne's head was just clearing. Sizing up the situation, he grabbed the doorknob, got the door open. He plunged out.

As he raced along the walkway toward the stairs, he saw the camper with the duck decals barricading his car. A heavyset man in a black baseball cap was piling out the driver's side, a gun in his hand. Thorne turned and fled back past his room, toward the far end of the walkway, realizing as he ran that there was no second stairway down. The heavyset man was hurrying along below. Handyman came out of the motel room.

For a moment everyone stopped. Three pairs of lungs drew breath noisily. The bug lamps painted the men's faces a jaundice yellow. Two guns to none, Thorne thought. With no means to fight back, he could be dead in an instant.

He bolted.

At the end of the walkway he scrambled over the iron railing. Below sat a dumpster, and beyond it a thicket of bushes. Poised on the outer ledge, he hesitated only a second.

The closed lid of the dumpster boomed with his impact. He buckled his knees to take some of the force, but even so, shock lanced up his legs to his pelvis. He scrabbled to the edge and vaulted into the bushes. From somewhere behind came a gunshot, and a round spanged off steel and whined into the night.

Damp leaves and branches snagged at him. He tore through to where a narrow access road ran back toward a shopping mall, its parking lot deserted at this hour and gleaming wetly. To his right lay a main road. Suppressed but urgent voices rose from somewhere behind the bushes. A motor started and gunned.

Running hard, Thorne reached the main street. Tires yelped as a car swerved to avoid him. A horn blared. His heart was pounding, impelling him on. Sweat stung where branches had lashed his face raw. He ran drunkenly. In the far lane he saw a cab cruising, and he flapped his arms. When it stopped, he got the door open and jumped into the backseat.

The young black man at the wheel eyed him carefully. "I hope you ain't no stewbum gonna get my seat all nasty."

Thorne twisted to look through the rear window. The camper emerged from the motel driveway, hesitated, then turned with a puff of rubber smoke in the opposite direction.

He sank back with a sigh. The cab driver was still eyeing him. "Okay if I ask you where we goin'?"

Thorne laughed. He felt giddy as a kid on the day school let out for summer. "Just drive, my man," he said. "Show me the city lights."

14

The rain had ended and a wind hurried isolated clouds across the clearing night sky. Ron Zelnick stood looking down at them and at the dark buildings of a world tipped upside down in the puddled sidewalk when he heard a car. Bricklin's Audi station wagon approached slowly. Zelnick stepped from the shadows and held up a hand.

Bricklin thrust his head out the open window. "You mind cluing me the hell in?" he demanded.

"Frizzel is in that alley over there." Zelnick pointed.

"Jesus. What are you trying to pull?"

"He's dead."

For a moment, Bricklin sat staring, his face a large, disconcerted moon. Then, shakily, he steered the car to the opposite curb. Zelnick got in the passenger side and cut off the questions with an impatient wave. He started with the call from the vice president earlier that day and told it all. For a long time Bricklin sat gripping the wheel, his face flushed and as soft-looking as his cashmere blazer. At last he said, "We'll go to the police."

"Shit, yes, John. And have them ask what I was doing in an alley with a corpse."

Bricklin frowned. "An anonymous phone call would do it."

"You don't think that occurred to me? I've been running things around in my mind so hard the past half hour my skull hurts. But the police? Figure it out. If anyone starts looking into Frizzel's death they're going to learn he was on an assignment for *us.*"

Bricklin swallowed. "And by extension, for the vice president."

"Even if there were no connection at all, the publicity alone would finish us."

"Wait a—my *God!* Are you saying there *is* a connection?"

"Rendle didn't warn me off till today. Frizzel was already in motion, looking for a lever to use against Murphy. When I met him in the supermarket, I gave it to him. That building is where the writer I told him about has her office."

"Oh, God," Bricklin moaned.

"For all I know, Frizzel took notes on our meeting. At the very least he'd have told his editor, or his girlfriend."

Bricklin cupped a hand over his mouth and blew softly into it. "What can we do? I mean, we can't just leave the poor bastard lying in an alley. We've got to notify—"

"Shut up. Listen!"

The sharpness of the words stung Bricklin into silence, and he sat there, trussed in place by his seatbelt like a fat red-faced baby in its stroller. He was a respected strategist whose ideas on platform and agenda had helped the party hold power for eight years, but in practical ways, Zelnick realized, he was not a smart man. Too many years of the good life had made him complacent. He'd lost his hunger.

In a controlled voice Zelnick said, "If Frizzel doesn't turn up, there'll still be questions, but they can be answered. Maybe he took a trip down to the islands with a woman. His radio producer in New York has it figured that way already. A telegram from Frizzel—'need a break to work on a story, blah, blah'—that would put things on hold long enough for us to decide what to do next."

"But the body . . ."

"Yeah, the body," Zelnick echoed, tipping his head back against the headrest and feeling the first tendrils of hopefulness in many hours. His mind was stoking up to capacity again. "If we get it out of there, John, and put it someplace where it can never be found. . . ." He turned to Bricklin and managed even to smile. "There won't fucking *be* a body."

"Eric."

Even by the weak glow of the hallway bulb outside her apartment, Rain saw the cuts on his face and his disheveled hair.

"Are you all right?" he asked.

"Me?" Of course she was all right. "What's going on?"

"I have to come in. Just for a minute."

Hesitating a few seconds, she belted the white terry cloth robe she was wearing and stepped back to let him enter. Without a word he switched off the lamp in her front room where she'd been reading, went to a window that faced the street and peered cautiously out. She followed, but he waved her back. A moment later, apparently satisfied, he said, "I think you'll be safe."

"From *what?* What's happening?"

"You haven't continued probing that story, have you?"

Her initial puzzlement at his unexpected appearance had begun to shift to irritation. He'd effectively blown her off that morning, so why was he here? "Maybe you'd better tell me what this is about," she said stonily. "Now."

He seemed to debate it for a few seconds, then said, "A little while ago somebody tried to kill me."

Her head whirled with that sensation of standing up too quickly. "Oh, no," she managed. "Sit."

Reluctantly, as though he would have preferred to leave as abruptly as he'd arrived, he took a chair. He told her what had happened, starting with his afternoon meeting with the FBI agent, Kirk, through some library research, to the surprise that had awaited him at his motel room a half hour ago. After riding around Washington in a taxi, checking to be sure he wasn't followed, he'd had the driver let him out across the park, and he had hurried here to assure himself that she was all right. By the time he finished talking, her feeling of safety had grown frail.

"Do you have any idea who they were?" she asked.

He shook his head. "They were lousy communicators."

Thank God lousy aims too, she thought. She realized she was trembling. They both needed something to occupy them.

She led him into the kitchen, turned on an overhead light, and while he sat on a stool at the center island, she washed the cuts on his face and applied antiseptic. When she was done, she went to her bedroom and got the photograph she had taken from Senator Murphy's house last night. Together they looked at the skinny, shirtless young man standing near a high fence of vertical poles of bamboo against a jungle backdrop. In the foreground an American flag burned.

"Murphy with tattoo," Thorne said.

"This has to go back twenty years, to the Vietnamese prison camp. And you know, I have the feeling I've seen it before."

"When you researched your book perhaps?"

She shook her head. "Not then. I'd remember that. No, more recently. Wait." She went into her bedroom and got the print of the Martha's Vineyard photograph Eric had given her. She hunted in a desk drawer until she found a magnifying lens that had belonged to Ethan Ross. As she used it to examine the Martha's Vineyard print, she felt a surge of excitement. "Got it!" she cried.

In the kitchen she placed both photographs on the counter. She pointed at the one Maura Ames had taken on Martha's Vineyard. "Andrea Wexford has something in her hand there. I'd mistakenly assumed it was a postcard." She handed Eric the magnifying glass. "Take a look."

He did. "Well, what do you know," he said. Although the detail was small, what Andrea Wexford held in her hand was clearly the POW photograph. He looked up at her. "As a writer, you make a good cop."

"What does it mean?" she asked excitedly.

"I don't know. Blackmail? Extortion?"

They had no answers. Now he went on gazing at the POW picture, as if something else about it were nagging at him;

but when she asked, he shook his head and put both photographs aside.

"What happens now?" she asked.

"I don't know. Drop back and punt? Got any beer?"

She got two cans from the refrigerator and turned off the main light, leaving on a grow lamp over a cactus garden by the sink that gave the kitchen a lavender cast. Eric took a long swallow of his beer. "Maybe I should call Hiram Kirk," he said.

"Why didn't you immediately? You were almost killed."

"Those people got my name and whereabouts somehow, Rain. They could've gotten yours too. I needed to be sure you were all right."

She gave in to a shudder and hugged herself tighter.

"Now maybe it's time we both got out," he went on. "Tonight has to be connected with the killings on the Vineyard."

"But why? To keep you from going further? Is that why those two people were killed in the first place? To silence them about something?"

And what about Dr. Ames, and the pilot he'd told her about at breakfast this morning in the diner? So many questions, and neither of them had answers. Nor were they likely to get any now. What had begun as fascination for her, the possibility of a gripping story, had turned dangerous. Eric might have been killed tonight. Going to the police made sense. "The phone's over there," she said.

But he didn't move. He was tracing the wet ring his beer can made on the countertop. "Kirk said national security is involved, but he wouldn't say how. If I call the FBI, I'll have to tell them everything—including all the vague links I won't be able to explain."

"That's their job. Let *them* make sense of it." She stopped, struck by a thought. "You'll have to justify carrying on the investigation with no jurisdiction or authority."

He gave a quiet laugh. "The badge won't cut it, huh?"

She ventured a grin too, but both faded quickly. Restless, he stood and walked across the kitchen and leaned on the counter edge. Tonight had made it plain that he was in real danger—perhaps they both were—and this fact filled her with dread; and yet tiredness seemed only to have honed his face to a sharper angle of determination, an intent, self-reliant quality which she found attractive. His presence was reassuring. She was glad he had come back.

She went over and offered him her barely touched beer. "I'll go along with whatever you decide."

For a while he drank in silence, then said, "I guess I'm hesitant because I don't know quite where we are."

"In relation to events?"

"That. And to us."

She blinked, surprised. "Does that really matter?"

"In spite of what I said this morning, Rain, you're part of this too. I can't separate you out. Snatching that photograph took nerve."

"It took a klutz. If I hadn't dropped the basketball . . . well." She shrugged.

"Suppose we waited to call the police? Just overnight, say. To sleep on it."

"Is that what you want?"

He set the beer can in the sink. "Only if it's a mutual decision. I won't endanger you needlessly."

So they were partners after all. She was going to have to trust him, trust the tenacity and the competence he conveyed; and he would have to trust her. "You must be exhausted," she said. "I'll make up the fold-out couch." She took his hand. "Come on."

They stood two feet apart, their eyes intent, her hand on his. This close, he caught her spice, tauntingly subtle, musky, not one of the candy scents that drifted from between the pages of fashion magazines. He reached and took her other hand. Then, slowly, he drew her to him. She may have whispered his name.

Her lips were dry, then softening as they came together with his. The beer on her tongue had the aftertaste of fire.

She tipped her head back and he kissed her throat, working down the column of her neck to the small concavity at the base where her pulse beat with a fragile insistence, like a moth flapping its wings behind a sheer curtain. In his mind were impressions of other throats and pulses that beat there, and some that didn't because they had been stopped, and what a frail thing a life was, his own almost gone tonight, snatched away by men he did not know. . . .

Rain's body was all athletic strength and grace, her arms smooth as banister oak as he ran his hands up them, curving over forearm and triceps to peel back the robe from her shoulders, letting it fall to the floor.

She stood naked.

Blind, her fingers went to work at his shirt buttons, his own fingers joining in a quickening need. Then they were skin to skin, and still their hands went on measuring, reading, charting the unfamiliar and exciting territory of the other's body. He stooped slightly to slide his palms under her thighs, lifting her and entered her standing. She locked her legs around him, keeping them joined; and turning, he set her rump-down on the counter. The small mounds of her breasts were tipped with light and flattened against her chest as she lay back.

They took their time finding a rhythm, but when they had, they moved together in a fevered counterpoint to the world outside this room, this moment.

With his eyes half shut, Thorne was given over to a sensation of them being chased along some unfamiliar strand, their bodies eerily splashed in lavender and leaf-shadow as they strove to escape whatever pursued them. But safety kept eluding them, receding as they rushed toward it, till at last they scaled some immense precipice and paused there, together, breathless. . . .

Then he lost her. She cried his name, and he reached for her, but remained unaware whether he caught her in that instant before he went over the edge in a shuddering drop.

The corpse made Zelnick sick. Blood and water had stained the front of Frizzel's shirt in Rorschach patterns, and there was a bloaty weight to the corpse, surprising given the man's shortness. Rats had found it, but aside from gnawing the fingers, they hadn't gotten far.

The station wagon was backed into the mouth of the alley. As Zelnick and Bricklin struggled to hoist the body over the lowered tailgate, Bricklin lost his grip. The head banged against a tail light, shattering the plastic lens. Bricklin's composure cracked too. "This is crazy!" he cried. "What are we *doing?*"

"Get it in there!" Zelnick barked.

Reluctantly Bricklin resumed work. They covered the body with a plaid wool car blanket whose fringe hung over the top of the scalp like cornrows. Bricklin was shaking badly when they drove away.

On the outskirts of Washington they would buy a shovel. They would go north, head for the Northwest Branch River, drive until they were far out in the country. Before dawn they would carry the body into deep woods and bury it. Zelnick decided these things with a detached mind, some stoic and practical part of him simply taking charge. He had ceased personifying the body with a masculine pronoun; sentiment had no part in this. The presidency was at stake, he told himself soberly. The rest of his own professional life was on the line. The body had to be disposed of as carefully and completely as if they had performed the killing themselves.

As they drove out Route 650, which was flocked with patches of lingering mist after the rain, Bricklin seemed to be balanced on a thin ledge of self-control, his steering erratic. Zelnick resolved that once they got outside the city, he would take the wheel. Right now though he needed to do something he foolishly had overlooked before. He bent over the seatback and slipped his hands under the blanket.

Bricklin sent a glance across his shoulder. "Sweet Mother of God! What are you doing?"

Zelnick could feel a damp dead cold seeping into his fingers, and with it came the stench of corruption which the rain and open air had kept away. He ordered Bricklin to open the windows. After what seemed like hours, though in truth it couldn't have been more than a few seconds, he turned to face forward again. "The wallet's gone."

"Maybe it was taken by whoever killed him. Was it there to begin with?"

"Or did it fall out back there in the alley, when you fumbled the body? Shit. We can't risk going back."

Bricklin moaned. "I knew we never should've gotten involved with Frizzel. He was bad news from the start. In fact, I never would've thought of him in the first place if *you* hadn't."

Their dilemma was swept away by a more immediate concern—a pulse of blue light was splashing the interior of the car. Turning, Zelnick saw a police motorcycle overtaking them. The shaky driving or the broken tail light had drawn attention. Bricklin stomped on the accelerator. The motor whined as if it were hurt, and the Audi jumped ahead.

"You fool! *Stop!*" Zelnick just managed to keep himself from grabbing the wheel.

When they pulled over, droplets of sweat were crawling down his torso like bugs, and his breath came rapidly. Steady, he told himself. Whatever you do, stay in control. Men in jackets and ties, driving expensive cars, have less to fear from the police than other people do.

As the cop dismounted, Zelnick whispered, "How much have you had to drink, John?"

"The hell with *that!* I'm going to tell him. This was *your* idea. We didn't kill Frizzel! We were taking him to the—" He broke off as Zelnick's fingers bit into his arm.

"Now listen to me. Carefully. You can forget about going to work tomorrow—or *ever* if this cop finds what we've got back there. So you scrounge up some balls. You hear me?"

Bricklin's throat clicked audibly as he swallowed.

In the mist, backlit by the headlight of his motorcycle so that he was a large, boot-and-jodhpur-clad silhouette, the policeman could've been a Gestapo trooper. His voice, however, when he spoke was soft, even polite. "Your license and registration please, sir."

"Yes, officer, certainly." Bricklin fumbled with his wallet. "I've got everything right here."

Zelnick had the notion that John might ludicrously haul out family snapshots. As it had moments ago, a hard, practical part of Zelnick took charge. He slipped a laminated card from his own wallet and leaned across and passed it out the window.

"Officer, my name is Ronald Zelnick. This is John Bricklin. We're on a pressing assignment for the president of the United States."

The cop shone his flashlight on Zelnick a moment, then on the White House pass, which was embossed with the seal of the nation and bore a full face shot.

"Mr. Zelnick, perhaps you'd better explain yourself, sir."

"I'll make it brief. If we're not at the White House in ten minutes, we're *all* going to be on the unemployment line."

The cop's decision came quickly. He thrust the pass back into the car. "Gentlemen, I'll escort you."

Bricklin steered through traffic behind the flashing lights. His face gleamed damply and he looked as if he were going to be sick. The fever seemed contagious. Zelnick's stomach was knotting. Nevertheless, he knew that the only thing keeping both of them going was his own appearance of control. "Just follow the cop," he said tightly.

"Then what?"

"Just follow. I'll handle it."

Soon they turned down East Executive Avenue, past the Old Executive Office Building, ghostly now in the mist. To their left, beyond a tall iron fence, was the north lawn of the White House. When they reached the floodlighted rear gate, the motorcycle cop drew ahead to the guardhouse. One of the White House Police officers on duty stepped out, and the two cops conferred. After a moment the White House cop came to the driver's side and put his face close to the open window.

"Good evening, Mr. Bricklin, Mr. Zelnick. I didn't know you were expected tonight."

Bricklin parted dry lips but before he could utter a sound,

Zelnick said quickly, "Neither did we until just a short time ago."

The White House cop took off his cap and scratched his head. "I'm going to have to check this out, sir. The president returned just a short while ago himself. I'll notify the house that you and Mr. Bricklin are here."

"Uh—don't bother anyone, Phil," Zelnick said, pulling the man's name from a place he didn't even know it was stored. "We'll wait in reception. The vice president may join us before we go up."

"Yes, sir."

The cop signaled his partner in the guardhouse to open the gate, then stood aside and waved them ahead. When the gate had swung closed, Bricklin started up the curving asphalt driveway. The Audi's headlights tunneled the steam which rose after the recent rain. Zelnick had the sensation of the night closing in on him at last. Like the adrenalin which had coursed through him before, his bravado had all but burned itself out. If he thought Bricklin could have heard the question without losing all control, Zelnick would've asked his advice. As it was, the older man sat sunken at the wheel like an effigy awaiting flames, so Zelnick asked only himself: What now?

And all at once he knew the answer.

The irony. On Memorial Day. They would do what they had intended all along.

They would bury the dead.

Haven's
End

15

Thorne woke to the clang of iron, and for a moment he was back at the motel by the train yard where he had stayed his first night in Washington. Then he saw he was on a futon, and he identified the sound. Weights. He dressed and went into the next room.

Rain lay supine on her weight bench, pushing a barbell off her chest. She was in a white leotard and black satin shorts, her arms and legs zebra-striped by the morning light streaming into the apartment. He watched from the doorway, admiringly. When she banged the weight into the rack, he said, "Most folks are content sitting in a bathrobe, watching *Good Morning, America*. Now I know why you've got no downstairs neighbors."

Rain sat up. "He wakes, he stirs, and from the dead he rises," she offered between breaths.

"Was I that far gone?"

She toweled her face. "I thought I'd have to vacuum sawdust off the rug in there. How are you feeling?"

"Embarrassed all of a sudden, but otherwise good. You?"

She smiled. "Yeah, me too." Their eyes met for a moment, perhaps in mutual acknowledgement of what had happened last night, then Rain said, "Hungry?"

"I wouldn't say no to some coffee."

"Spot me on this last set, then we'll see about breakfast. My treat this time."

Following her lead, he clapped another plate on one end

of the bar and locked the collar, then she slid under it. Afterwards, when she sat catching her breath he said, "I'm impressed. Have you been doing this long?"

"Most of my life. I grew up in an all-boy neighborhood. It was an Appalachian coal town where being good at sports and drinking beer were prized. Fighting was right up there too. It always seemed such a waste of energy to me. So you break some other guy's face in a tavern brawl—no one ever did much fighting to get *out* of there."

"You seem to have."

She shrugged. "Sometimes I'm not sure. I live here alone, I sneak by. This book has been my biggest break yet, which will put me financially where I'd have been if I'd stayed and kept a waitressing job all these years and married a high school hero."

"Not always a bad deal. Was there a particular hero?"

"I was speaking generically."

"What about love?"

"Back then? That was a word for heavy breathing in someone's pickup and to justify quitting school because you got caught and had to get married. I left town when I knew that was the only thing that might save me."

"Has it?"

She looked at him thoughtfully. "I don't know yet. But I'll take my chances here."

With the sunlight and banter, Rain discovered that the fearful part of last night had been relegated to a dim closet wherein were stored things that held power only in darkness. More interestingly, the intimacy they'd shared felt near, hovering like a spectral presence between them, though for the moment neither of them acknowledged it. As for the issue of contacting the FBI, Eric wanted to speak with a detective named Mike Pulaski in Boston before deciding.

As they sat eating breakfast, it was Eric who returned to the topic of her past. So she told him about her family, and moving here to Washington, meeting Ethan Ross. She went into detail, and Eric proved a good listener. She concluded with a shrug, "Guilt's an insidious affliction."

"Even though you didn't do anything wrong," he said.

"Probably not, but knowing that didn't erase a sense that I'd failed in some way, that it was West Virginia all over again and love hadn't been enough. I debated getting out of the city, going somewhere else. But, in the end, I didn't. I did quit waitressing—except for friends." She winked and got up to pour more orange juice. "I made do typing papers for grad students, and assembling resumés for housewives heading for the work force. I turned the weekly over to others; though I still do a column."

Eric toasted with his juice glass. "And exposés on massive conspiracies."

Their laughter had an empty ring.

After breakfast, as Rain showered, Thorne busied himself washing the dishes. The conversation had stirred memories.

Following their honeymoon, when he had hoped Lisa and he would settle in Boston, she had insisted that they return to the Vineyard. He tried to convince her that year-round life there was very different from the summers she had known; but the notion was fixed in her mind. And so, wanting to please her, he acceded. He fished and she painted, and through summer and fall it seemed a perfect life; but one long winter of isolation laid that idyl to rest for her permanently. Back in Boston, Lisa enrolled in art school. In need of a job, Thorne took an exam and became a policeman: temporarily, he assured himself. The important thing was that they were happy.

And for a year or so they seemed to be. Gradually, however, the common ground of their marriage began to dwindle. Increasingly, Lisa's friends became the avant-garde people on Newbury Street. She was spending little time at her easel. Nights he would come home and she would be out. But he endured the situation, wanting to give her the freedom he figured an artist needed, hoping it would rekindle the spark that made her so happy to be painting, and that her joy would include him.

One evening he came home and found her there with people he didn't know, several of whom were freebasing coke. That her life-style had come to jeopardize her so—actually both of them—was a potent hit of awareness. He had become a better cop than husband—there when you needed him, gone when you didn't. He ordered the people to leave. One of the men came at him in an attack. Thorne handcuffed and arrested him. Later the man, who was a lawyer, sued for assault; he guessed rightly that to protect Lisa, Thorne wouldn't mention the drugs. When Lisa was called to testify, she said that she had not really seen what happened. Soon thereafter Thorne was suspended from the BPD, and Lisa moved out. So he had let circumstances beat him. Rather than stay and try to clear things, he went back to the island.

The telephone rang. Rain answered it in her bedroom. She came back excited.

"That was my agent. I've got to fly to New York and meet her. We're having lunch with an editor at *Rolling Stone*. They want to publish the interview with Murphy!"

Bill Rendle had known the meeting was not going to be an ordinary one as soon as the president had told him to come directly to the White House living quarters.

His partnership with Peter Hawes had begun eight years ago at the national convention, when party officials had given Hawes their recommendations for a running mate. The two men had met just once before then. As a Montanan, Rendle brought a dowery of only twenty assured delegates, but to the people who brokered such things, he was a balancer, representing the West the way Hawes did the East, drawing farmer and sportsman. And even if he and the president sat at opposite ends of a seesaw, with their party as fulcrum, they had nevertheless achieved a good balance. No one who knew either man, however, would call them friends. Despite the fact that Hawes led his campaign, Rendle honestly had no idea whether the president thought he would make a good successor. They had never discussed it.

He was surprised to find Prudence Winters waiting to greet him. Though polite, her smile seemed tense as she invited him in. "Would you like a drink?"

"No, thank you." He was still recovering from his surprise at finding her here not the elegant woman of public occasions. In a simple off-white dress and only a touch of makeup, her hair pulled back, she looked almost plain. He sought a conversational opening, but before he could speak, the president entered from an adjoining room. Rendle felt a cool ripple of uncertainty at the way Peter looked. Informal, yes, in stretch waist slacks and sport shirt—but his face was drawn, his hair wispy. He offered no hand.

"Hello, Bill. How's the weather out on the hustings?"

Rendle didn't misconstrue the question's casualness; in no part of the White House was time a gratuitous commodity. He didn't waste it now by mouthing generalities. "The reporters are being rough. And the voters—who knows? I don't. I can't read them anymore."

Hawes stared, showing no more concern than if he'd just been told that there was crab grass in the Rose Garden. Rendle's uncertainty grew.

"Sit," the president said. "Let's all sit. That's the recommended posture for taking bad news."

The faint grin accompanying the president's words faded at once, and, feeling his chest grow light, Rendle looked from him to Pru Winters for an instant before allowing himself to sink into a chair. Pru sat on the sofa, one cushion's distance from the president, who leaned forward and cleared his throat. "Bill, I've already spoken with Prudence about this. Now it's time I told you. But I want you to understand one thing. I'm doing this for the good of the party, and the country."

The lightness had spread into Rendle's stomach, his knees, and he was glad that he was sitting.

"Bill, what would you say if I asked you to stop your campaign?"

Rendle echoed the words dully in his mind.

He felt as though they, along with everything else in the room—the president and Pru Winters seated there on the sofa—had been carefully orchestrated, and he was powerless to change any of it.

"I'll go into specifics shortly," Peter said. "But first . . . how do you think the country will handle finding out that the president is dying?"

The details followed: a tumor on the head of the pancreas, which had been mostly asymptomatic until it was too metastasized to be operable. Rendle sat stunned, words rising to his mind before falling away dully, totally unequal to the task of conveying the emotions that stirred his heart. Of the people he'd expected to reach old age, Peter Hawes topped the list. The man's unflagging optimism had seemed a guarantee against the wasting of the flesh. Yet now Peter sat with Pru, whose earlier tension had softened and whose love for Hawes shone in her face, and in a weary voice he talked of the hopes he'd had for the country and their administration.

Rendle felt small, diminished by the gulf which existed between them and which they had never bridged with simple friendship. With a crimped heart he listened as Peter revealed that tomorrow he would begin intensive chemotherapy, for which his doctors had given slim odds for success.

"And that," said Hawes at last, "brings me to the point."

Later, when he replayed the conversation in his mind, Rendle would think that if Peter were thirty years younger, he might have asked, "You ready for this?" Instead, he cleared his throat and said, "Bill, depending on what happens in the next few days, I may want you to suspend your campaign and take over my job."

The range officer handed the ID back to Hiram Kirk. "Will you be shooting, sir?"

Kirk said no in a way that discouraged further questions. The officer gave him a pair of ear protectors, then consulted a chart. "Over on the rifle course," he directed. "Second to last lane."

Kirk walked down the fenced-in gravel path at the rear of the pistol range. Only a few of the lanes were in use at midmorning by government people requalifying. He let his gaze roam to the low, wooded Virginia hills, a setting which would've been bucolic if it weren't for the high double fences that stood around the property and the crack of gunfire in the air.

Unexpectedly Kirk felt a twinge in the trigger finger of his left hand. Impossible, of course, because the hand was a rubber prosthetic. Still, at times he felt as if his own flesh were there. His doctor told him it was just a synaptic echo in the brain, a cerebral *déjà vu*—yet it seemed real, the old yearnings to touch and grasp.

He'd been twenty-nine at the time of the incident, a seven-year Bureau veteran with a promising record. In fact, his superiors were so impressed with his performance that they held out the probability of his making supervisor himself before long. But Kirk let neither flattery nor eventualities sway him from his duties, one of which was serving as liaison to a county sheriff's department task force investigating organized crime in Reno, Nevada. One day he and a deputy were searching an old mining camp in the desert where he suspected someone was stashing money skimmed from casinos. Kirk discovered a trap door in the floor. Prying it open, he found several packets of bills, twenties and fifties still in wrappers from the Desert Wind. As the deputy went to his car to radio in the find, Kirk reached between the joists in search of more loot.

That was the last thing he remembered.

When he regained consciousness, he was in a hospital bed, his left arm encased in bandages. The Southwest District AIC came in person and gave him the details. The hiding place had been rigged with a 200-pound ragged-jaw bear trap. Kirk's hand had been gone in an instant.

There were citations, well-wishes, a convalescent leave, but the career that Kirk had planned was over. Unable to fire a weapon effectively, drive an automobile, knot a tie, or cut a steak, he declined a desk job and was pensioned off, doled just enough to pay for the divorce when it came and to keep the bottom-shelf liquor pouring. He learned to use the phony hand (and wear loafers and clip-on ties) though never to like it. When a benefactor heard of his case, there were strings pulled, an offer. He went back to work for the Bureau in D.C., in time got the White House assignment.

The sound of a weapon on full-automatic drew his attention. The rifleman was standing at the head of the next-to-last lane, firing an M-16 at a human-size cutout. Kirk approached from the left and behind, and waited until the clip was exhausted.

"Getting ready for a little action?" he greeted.

The man turned, acknowledging recognition with a curt nod. He set the weapon on a wooden bench and lifted his ear protectors away. "What?"

"Nice day for it," Kirk said.

The man was named Jones. He was muscular; middle-aged; wearing tinted shooting glasses, pale gray pants, a dark blue windbreaker, and just the right shade of cocoa-brown skin, Kirk was convinced, to have levered himself up in government. For that, and because at the moment Kirk was forced to ask a favor, he felt a venomous dislike for Jones.

"I want to update you on that potential problem," he said.

Jones roughed the sides of his head where the earpieces had compressed his short afro. "You mean to give excuses, don't you? For letting that dude make you trip over your dick last night?"

How had he learned about that already? Kirk had just now come from examining the belongings taken from Thorne's room at the Capital City Motor Inn. In an envelope in the suitcase had been copies of the photograph taken on Martha's Vineyard ten days ago. It was incredible how much hassle that one little candid had caused. Well, the hassle would soon be over. One other item found in Thorne's room was a folded publisher's flyer announcing a paperback book on Senator Murphy, across which someone—Thorne, Kirk guessed from the handwriting—had penned two phone numbers. Both, he had learned from the FBI reverse directory, belonged to a Lorraine Patton, the book's author. One number was for an office loft, the other for a residence in southwest Washington.

"Well, J. Edgar?"

Kirk squelched his own bitter retort. "I think I know where he is."

"I'm listening."

Along with who else? Kirk wondered. He wouldn't put it past these people to bug their own nests. Perpetual snoopers, forever looking for toeholds, levers, buttons to push to get people to do exactly what they wanted them to do. That was how Jones had dug Kirk's own name out of the files the old man kept in his villa down in the Bahamas. "I'd like some help."

Jones folded his arms on his chest. For half a minute nothing else about him moved. Bastard. Kirk cleared his throat. "I'd like *your* help," he clarified.

"You mean with a whole federal bureaucracy behind you, you can't *swing* it?"

"You wish. I get to hire incompetents. You're the one with the experts."

"You know the charter."

Kirk had to shake his head. Smug sons of bitches were all alike. They could mount disinformation campaigns that toppled foreign governments and destroyed careers; dose unwitting victims with drugs that sometimes pushed them to suicide; deal weapons to wacko fringe groups. And worse. But when it came to the National Security Act of 1947, with its prohibition against espionage activities on home soil, my God, they were suddenly towers of virtue. Except when they *had* to do something at home. Then they always managed to find a way. Piss on the charter.

"The police are looking to pick up Thorne."

Behind the tinted lenses of the safety glasses, Jones's eyes narrowed.

Gotcha on that one. "He's wanted for questioning in the

death of a Vineyard cop. Another story. The bottom line is, if they get him I believe he'll tell what he knows.''

Jones was motionless for a full minute this time, but Kirk waited him out. Finally the black man turned to the bench and began breaking down the M-16. He could've done it one-handed in the dark. ''Maybe I can arrange that backup. Give me a couple hours, and whatever information you have.''

That was more like it. From his jacket pocket Kirk drew several blowups of pictures taken by his driver yesterday with a long lens at the Vietnam Memorial. He laid them on the bench. ''That's him. I'll tell you where I think he is. The details of stopping him I leave to you experts.''

Lt. Mike Pulaski came on the line, growled a number and a request to give him five minutes, then hung up. Thorne scribbled down the digits. A Boston exchange, but it wasn't the Area C police station. So Pulaski hadn't wanted the call recorded.

Thorne's hope was that Pulaski had learned more details about the case. However, as he waited for time to drag by, he wondered if he had done the right thing in making the call. He laid the POW snapshot on Rain's kitchen counter. As it had last night when she'd first shown it to him, something tickled at the back of his mind, but he still couldn't say what it was. He slipped the picture into his pocket. When Pulaski picked up, he was out of breath and there was a background din of voices.

''Are you at a party?'' Thorne asked.

''The deli around the corner. Where are you?''

''Washington. I need to—''

''Since when, guy?''

''That's two questions in a row. It's *my* turn. Have you got anything more on Dr. Ames's death?''

There was a brief silence. ''You honest to God don't know, do you,'' Pulaski said.

''Know what? What's this about?''

"It's about trouble, for Crissake. A cop was *killed* the night before last. A Vineyard cop. James Dow."

"*What?*" Thorne sat heavily on a stool.

"He was shot in the face in your house. Close range. Your duty piece was the weapon. They pulled it out of a sand dune near the house. Guess whose wheels were in the ferry parking lot?"

Thorne felt a wild, sharp panic filling his chest, and he thought, This must be what a heart attack is like. Dow. He could scarcely accept it.

"Do I need to tell you who your chief is promoting as prime suspect?" Pulaski said.

"Jimmy was a friend. I . . ." Thorne's voice faltered.

"I don't buy it either, if that's any consolation. But I'm here in a pastrami joint saying this, not on the record. I've got to have some proof, guy."

Thorne swallowed. "All right."

"Your friend went down between ten and midnight. You have a story?"

He tried to think. He'd left his car because it was cheaper than parking at Logan airport. "I was here in Washington. I took a morning flight. That's why I left my weapon behind." Even as he spoke, he realized that he could offer no proof that he had not flown back to Boston and returned to the Vineyard.

"Where'd you stay?"

It took a few seconds to remember, and the answer hit him like a falling piano. He'd been dozing on a park bench. He hadn't registered at a motel until long after midnight. "Look . . . all I can tell you is I didn't do it."

"That's not a whole hell of a lot." Pulaski waited as if for more explanation, but when none came, he went on. "Come back here and you'll probably be arrested. That chief of yours is riding hard."

The question came to him: had the men at his motel last night been cops? But if so, why hadn't they identified themselves? He had no answers, but he knew he had to try to find some. If they'd gotten Rain's address from among his belongings at the motel, then they were *both* in danger.

"Check into this for me, Mike, can you? There's a Vineyard officer named Warren Stubbs. He's a Robocop—by the book—but he can be trusted."

"Want me to solve those other killings while I'm at it? Why didn't you just leave this whole thing alone and come back to the city when you had a chance?" Pulaski sighed. "Yeah, yeah. You have a phone?"

Thorne didn't want to give Rain's number; she might not be implicated yet. "I'll reach you," he said. "Soon. I'll give my name as . . ." His gaze flicked around the kitchen before coming to rest on the the refrigerator. "Moore. Ken Moore."

"Sears will love you. Yeah. Watch your butt."

The driver of the pest control van drawn to the curb by the park studied the gray two-floor apartment house across the street. He turned to the man riding shotgun. "What do you think?"

The passenger bent low to peer past the driver. "One way to find out, I guess." He reached over the seatback, hoisted a small cylindrical tank equipped with a carrying strap and a hose and set it on the floor between his feet.

"Careful with that," the driver said.

"Always."

"He's going to be wary on account of those clowns last night. I'll signal you if the woman comes back. Five minutes, right?"

They both looked at their watches. The passenger climbed out, slung the tank on his shoulder like a scuba diver readying for the sea, and walked around the front of the van where he waited for a car to pass. "Watch out for pests," the driver told him. He gave the driver the finger and crossed the street.

Wiping shaving cream off his face, Thorne went quietly into the front room. Someone was on the hallway landing. Whoever it was, was making no effort to be quiet. Thorne could hear low banging and hissing sounds, and somebody whistling. He unhooked the safety chain and opened the door a few inches.

A youngish man with sandy hair spun and clapped a hand on his chest. "Jeez!" he exclaimed. "You startled me. Didn't know anyone's home."

He had on a blue shirt with a company patch sewn above the pocket. *Citywide.* On his back was a metal spray cannister.

"What's up?" Thorne asked him.

The man jerked a thumb over his shoulder. "Landlord wanted the place sprayed for roaches. I did the foundation, so you may be getting some uninvited guests. Seeing as you're home, I might as well do your apartment."

Thorne followed him into the kitchen where the man peered at the baseboards, spritzing occasionally from his tank. Thorne watched for a moment, then went back and finished getting dressed. As he put on his jacket, the exterminator said behind him, "You're all set."

Thorne turned. A mist engulfed his face.

He stumbled backwards, his throat spasming. Through slitted, burning eyes he saw that the exterminator had donned a gas mask. With a thrust of the nozzle in his hand, he released another jet of spray.

Thorne lurched away, doubled over with coughing. Blindly he groped for something, *any*thing with which to defend himself.

He bumped a chair. Seizing it, he whipped it in a sideways arc. The man twisted so that the chair missed him, but it clanged against the tank, knocking it off his shoulder. The cylinder fell and rolled away.

Still blinking furiously to clear his vision, Thorne saw the man pull a large wrench from his pocket and swing it.

The blow cracked down on Thorne's collarbone. The arm on that side went numb. His attacker grabbed the cannister, hefted it, yanked the strap over his shoulder.

If I can get to the door, Thorne thought, get out—

But the man had him cut off and was raising the nozzle again.

With a tingling of hot needles, feeling was seeping back into Thorne's arm. Shuffling sideways, he hit something and saw it was Rain's weight bench. Without thinking, he picked up a barbell plate and, whirling, flung it.

Through the large circular eyepieces of his mask, the exterminator looked almost amused to see the plate wobbling toward him like a five-pound Frisbee. He watched it punch with a puff of plaster dust into the wall and drop to the floor; therefore he didn't see the ten-pounder Thorne threw.

The plate caught him in the temple. His eyes bulged in shock and astonishment. He staggered and collapsed.

Thorne tugged the mask away. The man's eyes were wrung shut, but he seemed to be breathing. Thorne pressed on his chest, feeling for a heartbeat.

That was how he found the shoulder holster and the snub-nosed revolver. A frisk turned up a small walkie-talkie clipped to the man's belt, and a dagger secured by an elastic bandage to his ankle. With an icy sense of mortality Thorne realized the man could've killed him outright with the gun; so why the clumsy attempt with the chemical spray?

He rolled the man over, searching for a wallet, an ID— but there was none, and he eased him down again, thinking. A person's wallet was basic equipment; to deliberately not carry one . . .

The odor came to him then, though probably he'd been smelling it for several minutes. In the kitchen he discovered that the coupling behind the stove had been opened. Gas was flooding the apartment. He flung up a window, then went back to the other room, looking for the wrench. His eyes fell on the walkie-talkie, on the ruby blip winking on top, telling him the unit was on. He slipped to a front window and looked out. It took only a few seconds to spot the van with a magnetic rubber sign on the door. *Citywide Pest Control.* Thorne drew back.

★ ★ ★

The driver kept the binoculars trained on the windows of the apartment, waiting for his partner's signal. Time was up. He checked the van's side mirror. The street was deserted. To his right, across the park, a line of preschoolers and their chaperones moved caterpillarlike toward him on what looked like a day-care outing. He brought the walkie-talkie to his lips. "Fox," he whispered. "Come back."

No response.

"Fox."

When he scoped the windows again, someone appeared in one of them. The guy from the telephoto snaps.

Seven minutes had elapsed. Go with the fallback.

He'd been on missions before. The places and the faces changed, but not the standing orders. Take no prisoners, eat your dead.

From the compartment behind the seats he hauled out a pipe, two-feet long, to which he swiftly affixed a rifle stock and firing mechanism. Onto the muzzle he fitted an incendiary grenade. He butted the stock into his shoulder, cupped his right eye in the rubber flange of an eyepiece. One front window of the second-floor apartment appeared in a circular image quartered with cross hairs. He drew a slow breath and fingered the trigger.

Basic medical sense said you didn't move an unconscious person. Unless you had to. Thorne eased the man onto his back and gripped his jaw.

"Fox," he said, using the name he'd just heard on the walkie-talkie. "Come on."

The man's eyes rolled beneath their lids like those of someone dreaming but remained shut. Thorne lightly slapped his cheek. "Wake up."

It was happening too slowly. It could be many minutes before he recovered. Thorne listened for footsteps, but beyond the low hiss of gas in the kitchen, there was no sound. He slid his hands under the man's armpits and heaved him to a sitting position. Working against dead weight, he hoisted him to an approximation of standing erect, then squatted and hung him over his shoulder. The body shifted slackly, the arms flopping. Thorne felt like he was trying to balance an oversized plastic bag half full of sand.

The inside stairwell was going to be too narrow. The outside stairs wouldn't be much easier, but he'd try them. He felt a prickling, atavistic urge to be gone, away from here. He struggled across the kitchen, where the gas fumes hung poisonously, making his eyes weep. As he kicked open the back door, there was a shattering of glass behind him. The apartment seemed to gasp with a tremendous indrawn breath, then exploded.

Thorne staggered, rammed from behind by a freight-train rush of wind that shoved him onto the porch. Sound burst everywhere.

He fought to hang onto Fox, but his knees buckled, and the man rolled off his shoulder and dropped back into the kitchen.

When Thorne reached for him, a searing heat drove him back.

Rain's apartment had become a cauldron of flames in which everything was being consumed. The walls and furniture blazed. The iron frame of the weight bench loomed skeletally within. He got a hand onto Fox's ankle and started to drag him out, got the limp legs across the threshold.

There was another blast.

Thorne was blown through the porch railing and fell in a clattering of broken pickets the dozen feet to the ground.

With great effort he rolled to one side. For a stunned moment he could do no more. Smoking debris sparked on the backyard grass around him. He was experiencing pain he could not pinpoint. Nor could he identify why he was there.

Slowly, he pushed to his hands and knees. He got up. It came to him then. Fox. Fox was nowhere to be seen.

Still in the apartment, thought Thorne dazedly. If I could reach him, rescue him . . . might still get some answers.

Already the top landing was draped with a bright lace of flame. Shielding his face with one arm, he started to climb. Even before he reached the first landing, his skin felt baked. Acrid smoke scratched at his eyes and throat. He had the thought that his clothes were on the verge of igniting. He climbed higher.

He was finding it impossible to breathe as the inferno gobbled oxygen and spat out carbon dioxide with a roar. The stairs trembled under him, their stringers almost burned through. He clutched the railing and climbed.

At last, through the smoke he could see the lower part of Fox's legs protruding from the doorway. Even as he looked, the man's shoes ignited. There were spasmodic movements, like someone halfheartedly trying to tap dance, then there was another, smaller blast inside—the cylinder exploding?—and the floor upon which Fox lay collapsed.

The legs, with their fiery feet, tipped inside and vanished.

The doorway vomited sparks.

16

Thorne was on the far side of the park across from Rain's apartment, hurrying aimlessly, trying to outrun the pain in his leg, when his head began to spin. His vision paled. He just made it to a bench.

For a long time he sat with his head hanging over his knees, inhaling the stinks of singed hair and smoky clothing, numbly aware of distant sirens and the goosehonk of fire engines. Only gradually did the enormity of what had happened creep over him. Only one thing seemed certain: he had been the target.

The attackers had been professionals of some sort, as the weapons made clear. Incapacitate him; open the gas. Was destroying the house part of it too? Or was that only a fallback when Fox failed with the chemical agent? Who'd sent them? Rain was in New York, oblivious to the fact that her house lay in ruins. Was she all right? Had she been a target too?

He let questions gather in his mind, hoping they might reach a critical mass and begin to provide answers, but what he got for his effort was a throb in his skull. At last he rose, gingerly testing his leg, his shoulder. The knee joint felt locked, but the pain was tolerable. He could manage. But where? Could he reach Rain somehow?

A police car raced past, a blur of lights and sound that drew a serrated edge across his nerves. The car took the corner at speed and gunned out of sight beyond the trees.

On the other side of the park commotion was growing. He could see oily smoke curling into the pale sky.

He considered contacting the police but rejected the idea. They'd be searching for him anyway, and cops looking for a suspected cop killer would be hard people to talk to. In the shape he was in right now, he doubted he could stand up to much. With a wave of desolation, he realized that the notes and data he and Rain had been gathering were gone. He had nothing—no file, little energy, even less fight.

Only this. Remembering it, he took a photograph out of his pocket. It was the picture she'd given him last night of a young Tim Murphy in a POW camp. As he gazed at it, a memory from his childhood came to him of the times he'd gone up to Boston with his father to see the Red Sox play. If the day was overcast, the lights at Fenway would be on, and under them each player became the hub out of which radiated the spokes of many shadows.

What had triggered the memory? Internal injury? Shock?

He gripped the photo tighter.

The effect wasn't so obvious because of the dappled jungle, but it was *there*. They were faint to be sure, but Murphy cast no fewer than five shadows.

"No, ma'am," Cecil Childers said and concentrated on piloting the runabout past the yachts anchored in Nassau Bay. Miss Andrea sat forward as she generally did for the hour-long trip, wind threshing her hair into small curls like licks of yellow flame, not the icy red flames he sometimes had nightmares about! No, these trips were pure pleasure for him. He relished coming into Nassau every few weeks to pick up Miss Andrea to take her back to the cay.

Years ago, before she had left and moved to her small house in town, she used to putter among the gardens and her collections of antiques. Now Cecil settled for having her return to visit. He liked to sit and steer, and watch her, and—although he always felt clumsy in her presence, with his ropy, work-rough muscles and thick native speech—he liked knowing that there was no need to be or say anything more, because she accepted him.

Today though, she wanted to talk, and he was wary because she was asking him about the government men on the cay. He gave only brief responses, but he was sure she knew he was being evasive.

"You honestly haven't heard anything else, Cecil?"

He swallowed. He hated lying to her. "No, ma'am."

"You're sure."

Her look didn't waver. Reluctantly he pulled a piece of folded paper from his shirt pocket. "This came," he mumbled.

She took it and read the brief message it contained. "Do you know what this means?" she asked.

"Not exactly, ma'am. Just that I'll have to work for *them* again." He gave the word a sour emphasis.

"Why do it?"

He didn't answer. There was nothing he could say without it sounding critical of the old man, and Cecil's loyalty was total. She seemed to accept this. She read the note again, then turned and sat staring at the sparkle of afternoon light on the sea and didn't speak until they reached Bootleg Cay. There she thanked him and started up the pier.

He stayed a moment, watching the clench of her calf muscles beneath the hem of her beach robe and the bounce of her golden hair. He was thinking, as he often did, that if she were his woman, she would not go up there alone to the big house with only the old memories and wild flowers to keep her company. No, sir, not if she was Cecil Childers's woman.

But that was not the case, nor would it ever be. Still, he couldn't help thinking it was no way for the old man to treat his wife.

Andrea Wexford opened the note that Cecil had received and spread it on a library table in the villa on Bootleg Cay. It was typewritten on a half-sheet of plain white paper. "Final shipment complete. Squad due Friday 2300 hrs. Be ready."

Friday was two days from now. Then what?

In other circumstances she might've believed the men were just laying their everlasting smoke screens, for no other reason than that was what they did. But she didn't believe it now. To her the note was one more proof that they had to have seen her husband's secret files—which meant they knew about . . . Timothy Murphy.

She thought about her husband, how he'd encouraged men like them, helping them launder money through his island bank connections, letting them use the cay to stage their operations, all because it made him feel like a patriot. The poor deluded old thing. But was he any more so than she?

She picked up a small, framed pencil drawing from the table and looked at the young couple who stood with their backs to the ocean at Malibu. In spite of herself, her eyes filled.

What had happened to those two people?

They'd been young, yes. But what else? They weren't the same people who'd sat recently on Martha's Vineyard. No, that had been another ocean, another lifetime, another *person*. And only now, when it was decades too late ever to go back to that earlier time and place, only now was she beginning to understand what that other person had been running from, and where he had gone when he left her.

"Squad due Friday" . . . at 11 P.M. Would it end after that?

Why did she have the dread conviction that the answer was no?

As if having devoted a fruitless hour to guiding Thorne through the intricacies of the Library of Congress's cataloging system had given her a stake in his search, the library staffer refused to give up. She leaned against the table, her legs crossed at the ankles, pensively nibbling on her necklace of freshwater pearls. Thorne sat behind the stack of fat indexes.

"Tell me again exactly what it is you want," the librarian said.

He had to admit that he didn't really know. Basically he was hoping to get information on an American company.

"Which we got," she said. "Zeta of Ft. Lauderdale goes with Gulf Stream Bank in Nassau. You have the names of the corporate officers, annual earnings, credit ratings."

Which didn't take him anyplace, unfortunately. So settle for having come here because it represented shelter and a place to use the bathroom to wash up, he told himself. He had also tried to telephone Rain at *Rolling Stone* in New York, but they'd told him the editor who'd gone to lunch with her was still away from the office. He didn't have the energy for an intensive research project now. "Look, I'm sorry," he said. "I'm wasting your time."

"This *is* my time. It's my job. Let's try something else. Why are you interested in Zeta in the first place?" She gave a wry lift of her brow. "Planning to buy stock?"

He smiled. "Not if their planes keep crashing."

"Airplanes. You mentioned that. How many does Zeta own?"

He didn't know; he hadn't thought about it. Was it any more relevant than what he'd already learned? "Is that kind of information available?"

"Everything's available if you know where to find it. That's the peg I hang my hat on anyway. Let me just think."

He was willing to give up, but she said, "Wait right there," and walked off on her quiet shoes. When she returned, she was lugging a volume the size of a cinder block, which she set before him with a thud.

"We're building a fort here," he said.

She tapped the pebbled leatherette cover. "This is a leasing index for U.S. companies. It lists data about what equipment they lease, who supplies it, how much, all that good stuff."

"Who on earth needs that information?"

"Leasers, leasees. The IRS." She shrugged. "You, maybe. It's possible this Zeta outfit rents its planes. You can check the table of contents for aircraft-leasing firms and work from there. It's cross-referenced."

"You've been great. How can I thank you?"
She shot him the wry look again. "You pay your taxes?"
"Regular as death."
"You paid me already, then."

Thorne was twenty minutes into his search when the word *Zeta* pricked him from the brambles of microscopic print. He drew the book closer.

Zeta held leases on two aircraft, supplied by a Miami-based firm called IAF—Island Air Freight. IAF was itself a leasee, connected with a parent company called—

He sat back as if he had been shoved.

The parent company didn't need to be cross-referenced. It was no longer a very well kept secret what Air America had been—and by extension, therefore, what IAF and Zeta and the Beechcraft that had flown a killer to Martha's Vineyard that day were. Suddenly it was sinisterly logical that the serial numbers on the scraps of airplane debris had been effaced.

"Damn," he breathed. CIA.

Ray Russo was daubing with a balled napkin at a blotch of thousand island dressing on his tie when he saw the apple-cheeked staffer from the outer office standing in his doorway. She held up a file folder. "Is this a bad time, sir?"

"No, uh, come in." He pushed the remains of a Reuben sandwich into his wastebasket. "Uh . . . Jessica, right?"

"Melissa."

"Sorry. Close the door, Melissa."

Not only had he forgotten her name but also the fact that he'd given her an assignment. Too much paper and not enough time. But she understood that and didn't waste either now. "I contacted the Pentagon information officer and was referred to the Army Adjutant General's casualty office. That question you asked me, sir? There *was* one member of Senator Murphy's infantry company who's buried at Arlington."

Russo felt his heart begin to beat faster.

"A corporal named Charles Evans," the young woman said. "Apparently he was killed in a firefight with the NVA, along with several other members of Lieutenant Murphy's unit."

" 'Apparently?' "

"The Military Assistance Command in Saigon carried him on combat status reports as MIA for a time. There was a mix-up over dog tags and identification of remains, but eventually it got sorted out. That's when it became clear that *Evans* was KIA and Lieutenant Murphy was missing and later reported captured."

She handed him the file folder. "I wrote it all up for you."

"This the only copy?"

"Well, I've got my handwritten notes."

"I'll want those too."

"Yes, sir." She left to get them.

He opened the folder and scanned the top page, which was covered with the acronyms that the military holds near and dear. Stapled to it was a map of Arlington National Cemetery, on which a site was circled in pink highlighter. He was almost certain it was the sector where he had gone with Murphy last weekend. He pressed back in his padded chair. So he had asked for one piece of information and gotten two; but he was as mystified as ever. More worrisome at the moment was the apparent disappearance of Hank Frizzel. That made him nervous. Rumor claimed that Frizzel, perhaps in the employ of the vice president, was looking to find dirt on Tim. Now he was missing. Russo drew no conclusion about these details beyond the fact that others might draw their conclusions.

He found himself thinking back to when he had worked for Clarence Winters and a young FBI agent had come one day to brief the senator. Although it was never mentioned again, that briefing behind closed doors had enabled Winters to save his name by slipping quietly out of politics.

Russo wondered if maybe it was time he himself got out, if perhaps he'd stayed too long. But, no; for better or worse, he was a political animal. The yen for the excitement was in his blood, would be till the day the old pump quit. Still, he half wished someone like that young FBI man were on his own team.

"Sir?"

The aide (damn, he'd forgotten her name again) was holding several yellow sheets of paper and a container of baby powder. "Here are the notes," she said, handing over the sheets. "Also, you don't want to use water on silk. It'll ruin the sizing. Dust a little of this on your tie. It'll lift that stain right off."

He smiled. "Thank you . . . Melissa."

She bobbed her head and went out. His memory wasn't totally shot. He laughed with something like relief—and surprised himself by also recalling the name of the young FBI man who had saved Senator Winters from scandal all those years ago. Special Agent Kirk.

The approaching night didn't dissuade members of the staff of the District of Columbia Fire Marshal's office from continuing to probe the charred shell that had been the house where Rain lived. Rain herself stood motionless under a streetlamp and watched the investigators moving among the remaining walls. The beams of their flashlights, visible in the steam rising from the embers, bobbled and darted, as if kids were playing flashlight tag amid the ruins. Rain held her arms clasped tightly across her chest, warding off the dampness, holding in the flood of her emotions.

She'd arrived from the airport over an hour ago to be met by a crowd of onlookers, and firefighters still pumping water into the blackened remains of the house. The trucks had left a short time ago, and with them, the excitement over, most of the crowd had gone too. The fire marshal's team had been called in because of a reported explosion. Now Rain waited, watching, praying, numb.

Joyce, a neighbor who had given up trying to encourage Rain to go home with her, kept her own vigil a few yards away. They might've been two travelers awaiting a night bus.

The fire marshal approached, and Rain stirred herself. He was a small, round man wearing a waterproof jacket, with kind eyes in a sooty face. "Have you got someplace to go, then?" he asked in a brogue. Rain said she did but that she'd stay awhile.

"You know, miss, if anyone's in there, we'll find them. But a blaze that hot . . . well, it might be easier for you if—"

"I'll wait," she said with quiet insistence.

The marshal nodded. "You have any idea what might've caused it to go up?"

She said she hadn't.

Twenty minutes later the marshal brought her a piece of metal, partly melted by the heat, but otherwise intact. Her chest went hollow. Two days ago in the diner, when she'd fought with Eric, she had fingered the badge. Last night they had laughed about it.

She must have gone pale. The man gripped her arm. "Are you all right, miss?"

Her stomach plunged like a ship in stormy surf. She thought she would be sick, but she held on. "Yes," she murmured.

"What does it mean?" the marshal pressed gently.

"It . . . was my friend's. He carried it on him."

"He was a policeman?"

She nodded. "In Massachusetts."

Just then one of the firemen shouted, bringing the others hurrying to where he stood among the broken walls, pointing down with his flashlight. Rain started forward, but Joyce stopped her, and she didn't struggle. Her eyes filled and she shut them and the tears rolled down her cheeks. Whatever frail hope had kept her here was gone, wisped away like the steam rising from the house. She didn't open her eyes again until the marshal spoke at her side.

"There're medical means of identification," he explained. "Dental records and whatnot. You probably won't have to be any more involved than you want to, but, if you want to be . . ."

"Yes," she heard herself saying. "I do."

He handed her a business card, smudged in one corner with an ashy thumbprint. "Call me." He patted her shoulder and went back to his grim work.

Joyce walked her to a darker section of the street, between streetlamps, where Rain had left her car. "You really should come with me, Lorraine. There's tons of room."

"Later maybe. Thanks. I just want to be alone now."

Joyce was enough of a friend not to push. They hugged and said goodnight. Mechanically Rain opened her car door. *I shouldn't have left today,* she thought. *If I'd stayed . . .*

The *if's*. Were they always there for the ones they took from you? With her mother and with Ethan they'd become part of the cadence of grief. If only I'd said this, done that. . . .

She wiped her eyes, blew her nose, then got in the car. She started the motor.

Someone leaned forward from the backseat and she jumped. *"Eric!"* She flung her arms around him. "Oh, God. I thought . . ."

"It's okay," he whispered, holding her tight. "It's okay."

When they drew apart at last, he said that he would drive. In the few seconds it took for him to get out and climb behind the wheel she noticed he was limping, but a more pressing thought rasped across her mind. "Eric, if it wasn't you in my apartment . . ."

She didn't finish because she saw his face then in the glow from the headlights of passing cars. He looked scared.

Reflexively Thorne poked the door lock down with his elbow. He drove to the first cross street, made a turn, then another, circumnavigating the park. He entered Rain's street from the far end.

The neighborhood was blue-collar residential, quiet now in the aftermath of the fire, tranquility restored. Television sets glowed behind windows in the encroaching dark. He drove slowly past the scene, looking for anything that might

alert them. Nothing did. They proceeded out to a main avenue. Rain told him what she had learned.

"So they think the person who burned up was me," he
said.

"Who else was in the building? Eric, I'm so frightened.
What's going *on?*"

He rubbed his face, trying to erase some of the tension.
The muscles in his arms were knotted, and his knee and
collarbone ached. He started from the beginning.

He told her all that had happened from the time she'd left
for the airport that morning: about the death of Jimmy Dow,
the attack on her apartment, his escape, his discovery in the
library, and his return to find her parked car. When he finished, Rain was silent, and he could imagine her writer's
mind sorting through tangles of data, probing for a central
thesis. At last she asked, "Do you think the men today were
the same as last night?"

He didn't. These had seemed better prepared, more . . .
elusive. It had occurred to him that he hadn't exchanged
fifty words with the exterminator; still, that was usually
enough to get some sense of a personality. With Fox, however, he'd been able to read nothing—if Fox was even his
name; it might well have been a code name, or an abbrevi-
ated version of "foxtrot," the military letter *F.* They were
professionals. No one mounted that sort of attack unless they
were linked to the military, or a terrorist group—either of
which could make sense if you factored in the CIA.

Ah, it was crazy, he thought, brought back by a throb
from his knee. "If only I'd saved that one guy. Maybe . . ."
He clenched the steering wheel.

"What *is* it?" Rain asked.

He shook his head.

The unbidden image of fiery feet doing a spasmodic tap
dance faded. "Nothing."

"You tried your best," Rain said, giving his arm a squeeze.
"I'm sorry about your friend on Martha's Vineyard."

They fell silent. In Thorne's mind one thing was growing
clear: if he was wanted for Jimmy Dow's murder, the report

of his own death in the fire would take the pressure off temporarily. "Where were you headed before?" he asked.

"I don't know. If you want, we could crash at a friend's place."

"Not me. You. You'll be safer without me."

A look of alarm widened her eyes. "Uh uh, no. I want to stay with you. Where are *you* going?"

Unexpectedly he felt buoyed. She'd been through a fire of her own—the scars of a long day were there on her face—and yet she seemed alive with her tension, vital in some way that lifted him. He felt a stir of longing for her. "I'm not sure," he said.

"What about my office?"

He didn't like it. No one had followed him to her apartment last night, yet somebody had known he was there. Those men at his motel room must have found her phone numbers, which he'd written down. If they'd known about her apartment, they would know about the office.

Earlier, as he had lain in the back seat, he had tried to conceive a course of action, but no plan had come to him. Mostly he had wanted simply to see her again, and now perhaps that was enough. The case had grown too dangerous.

"Do you keep backup files in your office?" he asked suddenly.

"Always. Notes and files."

"Let's find a phone booth. I should've done it last night."

As it had in his two previous visits, Thorne thought, the building that housed the D.C. Writers Guild looked forlorn. Except for the tavern across the street, the area of warehouses and commercial lofts held little attraction for people after dark. En route they had stopped at a sub shop, and while Rain got them coffee and sandwiches, Thorne used a pay phone. Hiram Kirk was out for supper, he was told, but was due soon. Eric debated calling back, but he felt vulnerable now, eager to bring in the experts. He left his name and the telephone number of Writers Guild.

They made their way upstairs as quietly as they could. He listened a moment at the door before Rain unlocked it and found the light switch.

She gasped.

Everywhere, as if someone had scattered it to walk on, paper covered the floor. Desk drawers were out, her chair was overturned, office supplies strewn about, mail opened. It reminded Thorne of a vandalized school he had investigated once, except this time the aim had been more than wanton destruction. Someone had been searching for something. Rain stood dumbfounded.

"Don't touch your desk or file drawers," he said. "The FBI must be able to dust for prints."

He checked the door, then went to the windows that faced the street. There was no sign of forced entry, which meant that whoever had been here either had a key or was skilled at breaking in. Outside, other than a few parked cars at the opposite curb, the road was deserted. He saw nothing to put him on guard. "Well, at least we're probably safe here now." He went over to help Rain gather paper off the floor.

When they had picked up most of the mess, he righted her desk chair and gestured for her to sit. "Damage report?" he asked.

"I'm not sure," she said lifelessly. "It appears that my research material on Murphy is gone."

"Big surprise." He picked up the telephone receiver, using only a thumb and forefinger. A second into the dial tone, he heard two soft clicks. When he set the receiver down he realized his hand was shaking. "Is there a public phone in the building?"

Rain frowned. "What's wrong?"

"I think yours is tapped."

"Dear God." She blew her breath out in a fierce sigh. Her listlessness of a moment ago seemed to transform into anger. She pushed out of the chair. "In the bar across the street."

"Come on. I'm going to call my cop friend in Boston."

"No. I have to stay."

"Rain, you can't."

"I want to get on the computer and see if those files have been tampered with. If they have, I'm wiped out."

"It can wait."

She wheeled on him. *"No!* I can't *stand* what's happening!" She flapped her arms, pushing the outburst down. "I can't, Eric."

He went over and put his hands gently on her shoulders and drew her to him. "All right, we'll both stay."

"Please, you go." She pulled away. "I know it's important. Make the call." He hesitated, but she was insistent. "I just need to get organized here, or I'm going to go crazy."

"Okay, don't do that. I'll be right back. Lock the door behind me. There'll be FBI agents here soon. Everything will be fine then."

She nodded and mustered a smile that didn't quite reach her eyes. "I know."

"Post is pushing hard to nail you," Pulaski said. "He's got you on the national wire. They'll be checking airlines, trains, places you're known."

Thorne experienced a sense of being poised on a precipitous cliff with each minute pressing him nearer the brink. He drew a steadying breath. "Did you learn anything?"

"I got hold of your man Stubbs. He's a barrel of laughs. But he talked. Dow was off duty the night he was killed. He'd radioed the dispatch board that he was at your place."

"Why was he there?"

"He never said, but the kid on duty got the feeling Dow thought something was fishy and was going to check it out."

"Something fishy at *my* house?"

Over the long distance line, Thorne heard Pulaski inhale and exhale smoke. "This may mean something, then again it may not. Guy, you got yourself a maid?"

"I don't follow," Thorne answered uncertainly.

"Maid, cleaning lady, whatever. Someone comes in and tidies up after you."

"No. What are you getting at?"

"Nothing. Only, after that doctor what's-his-face, the street diver—"

"Martin Ames."

"Yeah, well, when we checked his place, nothing turned up, the joint was spotless."

Pulaski's obliquity was making Thorne restless, sorry he hadn't let this business wait. He was thinking about Rain up there in her ransacked office. "What're you saying?"

"We found prints at the Ameses' place that belonged to the doc and his wife, and some marks that we figured were from their maid. The state police found similar marks at your place."

"What sort of marks?" Thorne asked, fighting a bad feeling that had begun to creep over him.

"Smudges from a kind of rubber glove with a little grain in it—only not like *ordinary* rubber gloves. Different."

No! Thorne wasn't sure whether or not he hung up the phone upon leaving the booth, but he didn't go back. He shouldered through the line of bar patrons and plunged outside, running as if in a tunnel, at the edges of which pressed a spectral darkness.

He took the warehouse steps in threes, hardly conscious of the struggle for breath or the sear of pain in his damaged knee. If Rain was there it wouldn't matter. If she *weren't* . . .

He flung himself against the door and was startled when it swung in without resistance. The catch was undone.

Rain sat in her chair in an awkward posture, and it took him a few seconds to realize she was tied. A pink necktie had been yanked across her mouth. Behind her, holding a gun, stood Hiram Kirk. "Both of us were hoping you'd return," Kirk said. "Shut the door."

17

"Over here and sit down." Kirk motioned with the .45 automatic. "We've got a few matters to settle, and there isn't much time."

Beneath his cropped brown hair, the FBI man's scalp gleamed with perspiration in the fluorescent light. Catching his breath, Thorne tried to measure the situation. The computer screen was lit and the printer on. On the desk lay a briefcase that hadn't been there before. Rain sat in her chair, skirt drawn up over her knees, watching him. Helplessness, frustration, fear—her look was a complicated mingling of emotions. For his own part, he felt mostly regret.

"Let her go," he said. "This is really between us. She doesn't know."

"Can't do that," said Kirk. "We can dispense with this though." He undid the tie around Rain's face—a clip-on, Thorne saw; a one-handed man's convenience—and stuffed it in his pocket.

"Eric," she blurted, "I'm sorry. He came after you left . . . and I let him in."

Thorne shook his head, almost amused at how it had turned out. "Not your fault. He fooled me too."

"Get over here," Kirk repeated.

Compliantly, Thorne walked across the office. "It was the snapshot, wasn't it," he said when he'd sat down. "The one taken on the Vineyard."

Kirk shrugged. "That was the starter. Somebody saw the

woman take the picture and had to get it. He decided it
made sense to shut her and the lawyer up. That wasn't me,
or my call.''

Thorne tried to identify who he was talking about, but he
couldn't, and he knew Kirk was not going to tell. He decided
to nibble for what he could get. He hadn't fully weighed the
situation they were in; maybe time was their friend; maybe
it just forestalled the inevitable. He said, ''But you made the
call on Dr. Ames.''

''He came in unexpectedly. He was drunk and tried to
play tough guy. Only, he didn't have the snapshot either.
You did. The Boston newspaper said you'd been with him
just before his accident.''

''So you tried my house. *Bastard.* I ought to—''

Kirk leveled the .45. ''Don't make it easy. You're a wanted
man. Maybe armed and dangerous.''

Thorne hesitated, then settled back.

''There was no prejudice involved,'' Kirk went on. ''Dow
was in the wrong place.''

''Screw you!''

''I told you before—this goes beyond you and me.''

''Sure, national security. 'National' seems to be a very
restricted group. Well, you have the photo now. You got it
from my motel room last night. So take it. Whatever the
hell you need, take. Rain, give him what he wants from
your files.''

''She already did,'' said Kirk.

''Then we're clean. You've got everything. Get out.''

''It's not enough anymore. The ante has gone up.''

Thorne saw that Rain's face was gray. Since her apology,
she'd preserved a frozen silence. Her fear was showing now.
She was trembling. He swallowed. He believed Kirk meant
to kill them—he couldn't think otherwise—but not *here.*
Someplace else where they wouldn't be found. Time. He
needed to keep Kirk talking, to delay until he could think
of something. Dammit, *think!*

''What . . . what else do you want?''

Kirk shifted the gun from one hand to the other and

picked a speck off his black trousers. "You're between the dog and the hydrant. You should've visited the tourist sites and gone on home. You've made enemies in high places."

"Who? Murphy? He must be in it somewhere." Thorne hoped his voice held steady. "He didn't want to be seen that day on the Vineyard. He put on sunglasses, hid his tattoo— which is a whole other funny topic. That tattoo and the war."

"See what I mean? You make people nervous." With a glance at his watch, Kirk sprang the hasps of the briefcase and opened it. He laid two pairs of handcuffs on the desk. He set a sheaf of printout into the case and closed the cover. It was as if Thorne's hope was shut up inside too. His heart sank.

Where she sat, Rain was still trembling. Flickeringly, as their eyes met, a perception scraped his mind. Not trembling, *no! She was working to free her hands.* Now she began to move.

He shifted his feet, bringing them under him, simultaneously willing her back, wanting to shout to her. Her move was premature.

In a swift reaction, Kirk swung his hand in a glancing blow against the side of her head and tipped the .45 dead at Thorne.

"Freeze!"

Thorne did. Rain sank back, shaking her head to clear it. Kirk covered them both. "Okay, girl, you've got it loose. Sorry you had to waste the effort. Throw it down. *Now.*"

Rain dropped a loop of wire that had bound her hands. She touched her temple.

"Are you hurt?" Thorne asked.

She shook her head.

"Here." Kirk tossed a pair of handcuffs onto her lap. "Those go on your boyfriend."

Thorne watched her come across the office to where he sat. There were lacerations on her wrists from the wire, but she scarcely seemed aware of them, and he wondered if Kirk's blow had dazed her. "I'm sorry," she whispered strickenly.

He wanted to comfort her, to demand why *she* felt sorry. For getting into this situation because of him? For having had the courage to try to get out? He offered his wrists.

"Don't get cute," Kirk warned.

She locked the cuffs. Kirk called her back over. "Now, put one end of this set on your right wrist. *Right.* That's it."

When Rain had done so, Kirk snapped the open end onto his own left wrist. "I'm going to keep you close so no one tries anything." The .45 touched the side of her head. "Thorne? Understood?"

Eric nodded.

"Okay. We're going outside in a moment. There'll be someone meeting us who's not as nice a guy as I am. So let's just everyone be cool."

He motioned for Thorne to get up.

Inside Thorne's head a machine-like buzzing had started. He began to see the end then. The dark clothing, the good stainless steel handcuffs that a hundred years from now, if someone came upon skeletal remains in a quarry or a sink hole someplace, would still be firmly locked, awaiting the key. Just to alter the pitch of the sound in his head, he spoke: "Whatever happened to that old saw about a G-man being incorruptible?"

Kirk stared at him.

"You're living proof it's a lie."

For an instant there might've been a reaction in Kirk's eyes, a flicker of rage or regret, then it was gone. With it Thorne's momentum seemed to falter too. A faint smile found the agent's lips.

"Admit it, Thorne. You fucked up. But then, when you think about it, you fucked up long ago. I checked on you. A man who had the world by the short and curlies. Big city detective at thirty. A pretty wife. Then you quit and went back to an island that dries up and blows away every year come Labor Day."

"That's not what happened. I made a choice," Thorne said, hearing the defensiveness in his words.

"Bullshit. You cut and ran. You quit. Your chief gave me the story. And now you thought you could take a hack at something big again." He put the gun to Rain's neck. "Maybe get the girl, the glory, the whole schmeer. Well, your judgment sucks. Let's go."

Without a word Thorne obeyed.

Rain stepped onto the sidewalk, shackled to the man who was going to kill them. Eric looked over his shoulder at her, a quick glance, as if trying to tell her something, then at Kirk. "Where?" he asked.

Kirk pointed right, and the three of them started to walk. Rain was only half aware of trash cans at the curb, street-lamps, silent buildings. Her legs seemed to move on their own, numbly, without conscious effort on her part. Every few strides the steel ring on her wrist bit at her flesh, but she scarcely noticed. Soon they passed a final streetlamp and entered a darker block. A scrap of paper blew slowly across their path and she saw the falcon symbol of the Murphy for President campaign. "Almost there," said Kirk.

On the corner at the end of the block Rain noticed a lone automobile. For a moment she assumed it was empty; then the driver's door opened and a tall man got out. He came around to the nearer side of the car and waited. He was black, with hair that flared a little on the sides as if it were thin on top. At their approach he smiled, a chalk stripe in the darkness.

"You did it," he called. "Congratulations."

"No loose ends, Jones," Kirk said, leading them closer. "Now I'm going to get a Bootleg Cay tan and be as dark as you." He gave a bark of laughter.

"Sure," the black man said, and all at once he dipped six

inches on bent knees and brought his hands up and together. "No loose ends."

Rain saw the spurt of flame and simultaneously felt the
impact: a sledgehammer blow that stopped her where she
stood.

The bullet hit Kirk in the middle of his face, whipped his
head back, then forward, throwing the rear dome of his skull
onto the sidewalk. Rain knew he was dead.

In that instant Thorne bulled into Kirk, knocking him so
hard that for an instant the handcuff on Rain's wrist jarred
as if the bones would break—then something came loose.
Eric seized Kirk by his shirtfront and rammed him at the
man with the gun.

"Go!" he shouted at her. "*Go!*"

But she had to look, and like him she saw that Kirk's left
hand had come off! It dangled for an instant in the free-
swinging yoke of the handcuff, then it slipped out and
dropped on the sidewalk, palm up.

Rain was next aware of Eric pushing her ahead of him
across the street toward a dark line of parked cars. They
heard the gun fire again, then again, small inconsequential
noises, nothing compared to the *thunk* of car-door steel and
the gritty crackle of glass in the empty cars between them
and the man shooting. Rain glanced back and saw the killer
stooping over Kirk, lifting him. Then she and Eric were
scrambling, she with one cuff dangling loose, Eric beside
her, his hands chained three inches apart in front of him,
both of them upright now and running hard.

The sound of the hack saw cutting steel set Thorne's teeth
on edge.

"Getting hot?" Rain asked.

"Tolerable."

"Yelp when it starts to burn."

"How's your head?"

"Killing me. My wrist too. How about your knee?"

"Stiffening. I overdid it."

"Dodging bullets will do that."

"Yeh. But overall?"

"I feel like a million bucks. You?"

"Ten million."

Thorne had thought of the tools, and Rain remembered passing this construction site on her way to work. She had been near to hysteria when they got here, and for a time they'd just held each other. The work had settled her down. They were on the unfinished second floor of a building, with the moon shining through the girders above, checkering the concrete where they sat, glinting on the hacksaw frame as Rain worked on the cuff clamped to his right wrist. The steel was of such hardness that each circlet had to be cut twice to be removed. She sawed steadily, her cheeks flushed, her breath coming in small, determined heaves. Etched by the moonlight, her face had the precision and beauty of an Oriental mask, and he watched her, reveling in her intensity, thankful they were both alive.

"There has to be an easier way," she said.

"There's a quicker way. You could cut the arm about here."

Neither of them laughed. He thought of Kirk's hand and knew they'd be dead now if it hadn't been artificial. He quelled a shudder. After a moment Rain stopped to catch her breath and let the steel cool. Some poor worker was going to open his tool box in the morning and find a lot of dull blades.

"Do you think that killer is hunting for us?" she asked.

He said no, sounding more confident than he felt. "You saw how he grabbed Kirk's body and got out of there."

"Maybe he figured we didn't get too good a look at him."

"He's right."

"I'd know him if I saw him again." She shivered. "Not his face maybe, but I'd know him. Kirk called him Jones. Before he pulled the trigger . . . he smiled."

She resumed hacksawing.

Kirk had denied killing Maura Ames and Vaughan Belnap, but he obviously had been involved soon after. Dr.

Ames had died on Tuesday, three days later. What was the connection? Thorne asked himself. Who was Jones? Why had Murphy been on the Vineyard with his tattoo covered up?

At last the circlet of stainless steel on his wrist came apart. Encouraged, they took turns on the remaining cuff and the one on Rain's wrist. When they finally finished, it was nearly midnight. They disposed of the sawed handcuffs in a barrel of construction scraps, then set off to get Rain's car.

Fifteen minutes later they were riding on the broader, better-lit streets of the Capitol area, Thorne at the wheel. They relaxed a little. "I want to take you somewhere safe," he said, "and have you stay there."

He could feel her scrutiny and the questions in it. "Back to where you're from," he insisted.

"Here? West Virginia? There're no such places for me anymore."

He knew she was right. "To the police then. You haven't done anything. We could tell them—" His words trailed off.

"Tell them . . . ?"

True. Were they going to explain how they'd been kidnapped by an FBI agent who later had been shot to death? Where was the body? Would they tell the police why they were even involved? Questions were forcing themselves into his head with frightening speed. What would they say about Rain's apartment, and the man who'd burned to death inside? Where was the proof of any of it?

"What about you?" Rain asked. "You've got to go somewhere, do something."

"We're discussing *you*," he snapped. "You should get out of this while you can. After what's happened—"

"You want to quit then."

He glanced at her. "What?"

But he'd heard her. The word caught him like a small dagger. Quit. Was that what he should've done back when Post had told him to drop the case? Quit. That's what Kirk had called it. Kirk was dead. And they could be dead too. So give up, a firm inner voice said. Go to the cops. They weren't all like Kirk. Keep telling the story, over and over; eventually they'll believe you.

When he spoke, his voice was small, and he had to say the word again to make it heard.

Rain took his hand. "I knew you'd say that. I'm not giving up either."

He drove several blocks in silence. When he looked at her again, her cheeks had wet tracks on them. "You okay?" he asked.

She managed a pale smile. "I'm scared. But we're partners, and partners look out for each other."

He reached and touched her face, and she pressed his hand to her. So the remaining question was, What now?

When he came to an entrance ramp, for lack of a destination he got on the highway. There was little traffic. The fog lamps bathed everything in coppery light, like exaggerated sunshine. After they had traveled for a few minutes, he said, "What's Bootleg K? Kirk said it, remember? Bootleg K tan."

"Skin lotion? A woman? A code word?" Rain shook her head.

"Play with *bootleg.*"

"You mean like free associate?"

"Try it."

"I thought that was a shrink's trick," she said, starting to grin.

"Pretend."

"All right. Liquor. The 1920s, Al Capone," she ventured. "Um, isn't bootleg a play in football? Robert Redford."

"Huh?"

"He played Gatsby. F. Scott Fitzgerald."

"Keep going."

"Booze again. Uh, rum running, rum . . . molasses, West Indies."

He whacked the steering wheel, startling her. "A *destination!*"

"Say that again?"

"Where the Zeta/Air America plane came from, and where Andrea Wexford went after she quit Hollywood. It isn't Bootleg *K*, Rain. I'll bet it's C-a-y—*cay*, or sometimes *key.* A word meaning 'island' in the Bahamas."

18

Miles. Hours.

As Pulaski had said, Thorne was the chief suspect in Jimmy Dow's death. Airports and train stations would be checked. So they drove.

Exit signs on I-95 slipped past. Richmond (3 A.M.). Raleigh (dawn). Columbia (noon). Savannah (4 P.M.). Exhausted, Rain dozed; but Thorne was razor-nerved, beyond fatigue and drawing on the energy of momentum. They kept moving, stopping only when they had to for gas and food.

An hour after dark they pulled into a Rodeway Inn on U.S. Route 1 in Daytona Beach and paid cash for one night. Overtaken at last by exhaustion, Thorne signed the registration card as Mr. and Mrs. Ken Moore from D.C. and fell asleep on one of the double beds without undressing or turning down the spread.

Rain showered and discovered she was hungry. She bought a Washington *Post* out of a coin vendor in the motel lobby and took it with her into the adjoining restaurant. The diners were mostly elderly snowbirds beginning delayed migrations north, and young families with kids in Disney regalia. Looking at them, in their self-contained zones of safety and familiarity, she felt envy.

The newspaper headline hit her with a jolt.

BODY FOUND IN WHITE HOUSE LAWN

Steadying the pages, she raced down through the column of print. A trench for a new water line to the lawn fountains.

A construction worker had spotted a shoe. Police had excavated. The dead man was tabloid and radio journ . . .

She quit reading and looked up, stunned. Hank Frizzel was dead.

Thorne woke from a dream of frightened chase, not altogether sure if he were pursued or pursuer. The bedside lamp was on and Rain was shaking him. He swung his feet onto the floor, scrubbed a hand across his face. "Time is it?"

"Just after eleven. You slept for an hour."

There was a note of urgency in her voice that brought him more fully conscious. He blinked his vision into focus. "What is it?"

She handed him a newspaper. "This."

When he finished reading the account of the discovery of Hank Frizzel's body, Rain said, "The police have no motive or suspect, but I know it's connected to the rest. I can't forget him bothering me the other day about the Martha's Vineyard photograph, and later it was missing, stolen from my office."

"Is there anything in here about Kirk being shot?"

"I didn't get that far."

Thorne shook the newspaper open, restless all over again, with a feeling that their hunters had given him the brief span of sleep; now the pursuit would continue. Together they searched the paper, but there was nothing. What they did find was an account of the fire at Rain's apartment house. Based upon evidence at the scene, the fire marshall speculated that leaking gas somehow had ignited. A body taken from the burnt building had been tentatively identified as Thorne's.

A gas leak . . . an inadvertent flame . . . a victim.

He threw the newspaper aside and got up. So the exterminator had vanished in death as anonymously as he'd lived, and Thorne was presumed dead. Now, except for Pulaski, whom Thorne had telephoned last night, the only people who knew otherwise were the ones who *really* wanted him dead and would kill him, kill Rain too, when they found them.

He went over and chain-locked the motel room door. "I want you to look at something." He got the POW camp photo from his jacket. He pointed out the discovery he'd made.

"What do the extra shadows mean?" Rain asked.

"They could indicate that the photo was staged."

She looked at him skeptically. "Couldn't they just mean search lights at the prison camp?"

"I don't think so. Assuming they even had lights, North Vietnam wasn't wasting money keeping them lit in the daylight. There was a war on."

"Okay, but that still doesn't prove the photo is fake, does it?"

It was a question he couldn't answer. They were trying to form some pattern from what they knew, but he realized it was only late-night maundering, a mosaic of ill-fitting pieces that morning might show formed no pattern at all.

Rain shook her head. "I find it hard to believe. I mean, it's a matter of record that Murphy was a POW. Why falsify the evidence? After all, there's the tattoo he got in—"

"Of *course*," Thorne exclaimed. "That's the answer!"

"Whoa. You've lost me."

"What if," he went on excitedly, "Murphy never got the tattoo in a prison camp at all."

She looked at him in growing puzzlement. "But why would he pretend to have?"

"Because," Thorne said, forcing his voice to stay calm to better convince himself, "he was never *in* a prison camp."

Twilight's Last Gleaming

PART FOUR

19

Nassau's peak season had given way to Goombay summer, and the choice of accommodations was wide. The high-rise hotels along Cable Beach touted special rates, but for privacy's sake Thorne and Rain opted for a cabana in a small resort called the Conch Shell. As protective coloring they presented themselves once again as the Moores, and paid with cash withdrawn from Rain's account in D.C. through an automated teller. That morning, upon leaving Daytona to drive to the airport in Orlando, they'd stopped at a shopping mall, where each bought a carry-on bag and some appropriate clothes.

Rain came in from the bathroom. She was wearing a pastel-green sun dress that tied behind her neck and left her shoulders bare. She had applied makeup, brushed her hair back and put on shell earrings. Thorne paused in knotting his tie. "You look great."

She smiled at him in the mirror. "Not sure I feel it."

He turned and put his hands on her shoulders. "Maybe I'd better go alone and see what happens."

"And leave me sitting here?"

"The beach is fifty feet out the door. Take a swim. Pretend we're on vacation."

"Sure. As if I could relax now anyhow. We made a plan. Let's stick with it."

Earlier they'd decided to split their energies: while Rain attempted to get a lead on Andrea Wexford, he would learn what he could about Bootleg Cay.

"We don't even know if the woman is still in the Bahamas," he pointed out. "That was a long time ago."

"What better way to find out? Journalist looking for mysterious ex-movie star."

He knew she was right. Since the events in Washington, he had to accept that they were being sought. With little idea of who the enemy might be, or who could be trusted, he realized that knowledge might be their only hope for safety. "Okay." He checked his watch. It was just past noon. "I'll meet you back here at five."

"Five o'clock," she said. *"Then* we'll take a swim."

Like a grande dame the Old Executive Office Building was undergoing a facelift in its dotage, but it maintained its public service. As if to snub Washington's favored classical style, the Exec was French Second Empire, sharing with the city's other buildings only a vastness of scale. Here Nixon had taped his secrets and Oliver North shredded his. And here Ron Zelnick and John Bricklin, bearing secrets of their own, hastened along a marble corridor, crossed beneath a stained-glass rotunda dome where work scaffolds had been erected, and entered the office of the vice president.

Rendle stood at a window, gazing at the White House on the far side of East Executive Avenue like a thirsty man eyeing a desert mirage. "Sit," he commanded without turning. "Truth or consequences. I want to know what happened."

Zelnick glanced at Bricklin and saw the older man's face tighten. "Sir," he said preemptively, "we did as you told us. No sneak attack on Murphy, you said, so we waved Frizzel off."

"Waved him off," Rendle repeated, turning now.

"Well, I left word with his radio producer."

The vice president came over to his desk, making a point of not settling into the big chair, and regarded them gravely for a moment. "The chief of White House security phoned me this morning. According to the gatehouse log, two administration aides were on the White House grounds late

Monday night. He called as a courtesy to let me know that those men will probably be contacted by the police investigating Frizzel's death.''

Bricklin opened his mouth to speak but was frozen by Zelnick's look. Since the other night something had shaken loose inside Bricklin and was rattling around. How long, Zelnick worried, before others began to hear it too?

After burying Frizzel, Zelnick had arranged to have a wire sent from St. Croix to Frizzel's producer, claiming to be from the reporter on a getaway vacation. The ruse was futile now, he saw, like all of his efforts. Recently he had watched a woman walking a young, spirited dog in the park. The leash was a retractable affair which paid out line, giving the dog an illusion of freedom—until *wham!* Zelnick saw it as a metaphor for his own situation. He could lie; yes, that was human. Or take cover. But what was the point? Sooner or later Rendle would learn the facts—probably sooner, when Bricklin broke down. By then the damage to all of them would be irreparable. Still, hadn't he acted in the interests of the men he served? Weren't loyalty and drive worth something? Bricklin was a casualty now anyway; a soldier who'd lost his nerve under fire. But Zelnick was younger, stronger, more *ambitious,* dammit! He had a future.

"Sir," he said solemnly, "we buried Frizzel."

The vice president gave both men a slow, measuring look. His voice, when he spoke, was quiet, unprepossessing, but there was no mistaking his tone. "Did you kill him?"

Bricklin cracked then. With a froggy whoop, he pressed his hands to his face and began to sob. Rendle watched for a few seconds in astonishment. Finally, even more embarrassed than surprised, he turned to Zelnick for explanation.

Rain quit walking. Her feet were ablaze with irritation caused by her new sandals. Well, she chastened herself, if she hadn't walked up and down every street in Nassau . . . But her goal was in sight, at last: up there on the top of the hill.

For more than two hours she had tried to get information

about Andrea Wexford. In the few instances she spoke with someone who'd heard of the former actress, she met only with headshakes, stubborn memories, outright *no's*. Gradually she'd begun to sense among the locals a tacit solidarity of protection for the woman, a kind of island *omertà*. Surrendering to the heat at last, and the first warning from her abused feet, she had sought the cool cave of a Bay Street bar. There, over a Planter's Punch, she fell into conversation with some American yachting types. Hauling out the question she'd asked everywhere else, she put it to them. A tipsy, barrel-chested man told a tale of a pass he'd made a few seasons back at a woman who he claimed, "for beauty and wooden aloofness would've made a perfect figurehead on a schooner!" To the scoffing laughter of his companions, he insisted the woman was the ex-film star, Andrea Wexford.

Grimacing with each step, Rain resumed walking. Trees, misshapen by sea winds, clumped thickly on the lower slopes of the hillside but soon gave way to grass and outcroppings of bleached coral. When at last she could see the bungalow, it was as the yachtsman had described it—white stucco with shutters and door painted the aquamarine of the ocean. Bougainvillea, hibiscus and trumpet vines swarmed over trellises, filling the air with heavy perfume. Winded from the steep climb, she approached the doorway and knocked.

After a delay, the door was opened by a small woman in a loose shift of a faded blue that matched inquisitive eyes. Tortoise-shell combs held her hair back in yellow wings.

"Miss Wexford!" Rain said, experiencing the shock of recognition. "I hope I'm not intruding. My name is Lorraine Patton. I write for . . . *Rolling Stone.*"

The woman gave no indication that she knew the magazine, nor, for that matter, that she acknowledged her identity. "I would've telephoned first," Rain went on quickly, "but I understand you don't have a phone. And frankly I was afraid I'd be turned down."

Still the woman said nothing, yet Rain took heart in the

fact that the door had not been slammed in her face. "People haven't forgotten you. Your films play at art houses across America. You've still got fans."

Speaking for the first time, in the unmistakable voice that banished any doubt Rain might have begun to feel, the woman said, "All of that is an image, based on long ago. It has nothing to do with me."

"But what changed?" Rain persisted, expecting any second that the door would swing shut as unceremoniously as it had opened, and Andrea Wexford would retreat into mystery. "Why'd you turn your back on success? Why are you here?"

The questions appeared to have an odd effect, as though they stirred old memories to life. The woman dropped her gaze, blinking slowly. Then, all at once, she cried, *"Goodness!"*

Startled, Rain looked down. The blisters on her feet blazed redly. Taking her arm, Andrea drew her inside. "You've got to get those tended to."

Devoid of windows and clocks, the muted interior of the casino had a disjointed feel, out of phase with the bright tropical world outside. Most of the island's visitors were on the beaches, in pools, or in bed, so afternoon activity at the gaming tables was light. The players appeared mostly to be older women jamming slot machines that formed a glittering gauntlet through which Thorne walked to the bar. He settled onto a stool and was immediately attended to by a large, weathered-faced young man.

"Watney's look good," Thorne told him.

The man laid a napkin in place and set down a foaming pint. With the change out of a twenty, Thorne pushed a ten back into the tip rail. "Are you Dan?"

"Righto, mate." The Australian accent was thick.

"Toby, over at the Conch Shell, said you were the person to see if I wanted some local information."

"Toby's a good man," Dan allowed.

"I'm interested in a place called Bootleg Cay."

Thorne watched for some reaction, but the long, sun-burned face remained stolid. "It's in the Exumas," the bar-man said. "Very small, privately owned."

"Do you know by whom?"

"No, sorry." He drifted off to fill a floor waitress's order. Thorne watched him assemble a pair of pale green drinks with tiny plastic palm trees sprouting from them. When he returned, the ten was still in the tip rail. Thorne said, "I've heard rumors of that cay being a CIA training base."

Dan laughed. "You yanks love a conspiracy. No offense. There's all bloody kinds of rumors around, about all kinds of things. Working in the thrill palace here, I've learned to doubt most of them."

"Have you heard that one before?"

"That one? No."

"Heard anything at all about the cay?"

"Sorry, mate."

Thorne drank some ale. The money hadn't moved. Dan sent a look down the bar where the nearest other patrons were a middle-aged couple in deep conversation. Stepping close, he dropped his voice. "There's a guy who's spent a lot of time among the islands. He might know Bootleg."

"How can I reach him?"

"You can't. He's some kind of undercover copper."

Thorne's curiosity quickened, but he kept silent.

The Aussie rubbed his cheek, as though he might erase some of its premature crow's-feet. "There is a grapevine. Perhaps I could get word out on you."

"I'm interested."

"Nothing's guaranteed. If this fellow's willing to have a go, he'd find you."

Thorne had long-ago learned there are no consumer pro-tection laws for bought information. It was always a gam-ble, and knowing the odds here were stacked in favor of the house, he wasn't overly optimistic, but at the moment this was the best he had.

"He have a name?"

"Sanchez."

Thorne pushed the rest of his change into the rail with the ten. "I'm staying at the Conch Shell, cabana seventeen. Tell him to ask for Mr. Moore."

"I couldn't have got care this good in a hospital," Rain said appreciatively, settling her bandaged feet on a hassock in Andrea Wexford's living room.

The woman had bathed the feet with a boric acid solution before puncturing and draining the blisters, then had applied antiseptic cream and sterile dressings. Rain would have settled for simpler treatment, but she sensed such purpose in the ministrations that to protest would have been to deny Andrea the obvious satisfaction she took in being thorough.

"You don't want to get infected. Tomorrow stay off your feet, and let the blisters air dry."

Rain smiled. "Maybe you should've been a doctor instead of a movie star. Of course," she added quickly, "you were a fine actress."

"Fine? Perhaps. But hardly a Hepburn or a Rita Hayworth."

It was the first direct acknowledgement of her past that Andrea had made, and Rain felt a quick pulse of excitement. "Can you measure success by comparing yourself to others? You certainly had talent. And you were getting good reviews and parts. Why did you give it up?"

Andrea busily gathered scissors, tape, and gauze which she took across the room to a drawer.

"Please, I don't mean to pry," Rain said. "Let's forget the interview idea. You've been kind to me. There's no way I could've walked down that hill to my hotel. I'm just asking questions because . . ."

Because the woman had been on Martha's Vineyard with Senator Murphy, she considered. And because in some way she was linked to events involving deception and murder.

But there was an explanation. *Had* to be. Suddenly, desperately, Rain wanted to find it. "Because I'm interested," she said.

For a long moment, Andrea stood gazing out a window. At last, she turned. "No interview?"

"No."

"Just talk."

"Yes."

Andrea came back and sat down, and although she was facing Rain, her eyes had found focus on some far off point. Her voice also, as she spoke, was distant. "I was nineteen when I got my first film part—just a middle sister in a big family whose father was Pat O'Brien. The next role had a few more lines, and the next more still. I was never offered a lead, but I worked regularly. My life was busy. I had a husband—an alcoholic, womanizing songwriter—a lively circle of friends, parties. Then, something happened to me that I know I didn't really grasp at the time.

"When you're surrounded by people, sought after for what you are, more than who, your perspective gets . . . skewed. Among the admiring throng, you may not have a single real friend.

"In 1970, just after I finished filming *Mr. Hammond's Secret*, I met a young man. We happened to be in an acting class together and sort of fell into chatting one day. He was tremendously perceptive and candid, telling me what he really felt from my performances. He wasn't on the make like so many others. We used to drive up to Malibu in his old car and watch the sun set, and I'd playact all the great roles I was going to perform. He'd playact too, though mostly he was happy to be my audience. For some reason he never got real parts. I don't think he was interested." Andrea hesitated for just a second. "Anyway, my life was busy with roles, and the messy split from that first husband—and then I had my next marriage."

Rain had been a teenager at the time, but she remembered the event—the multimillionaire and the film princess. All the newspapers and movie magazines carried stories.

"But I stayed in contact with my friend," Andrea went on. "He was there for me when I needed to bitch about success, or to lean on and have a cry. But it was all one-sided, I realized too late. I was never there for *him*."

Again the narrative halted for a spell, which Rain made no attempt to interrupt; then Andrea said, "It was when I was doing one of my last films that I heard he'd drowned off Santa Monica. His body was never found, but he'd left a note for me. A suicide note, I suppose. In it he said he had grown tired of his life."

Rain felt pain, as if some link had been forged between the actress and her, connecting them in the tragic consequences of life and love. Her attention latched even more tightly onto what Andrea was saying.

"In the note he thanked me for being his friend. 'Friend.' The word tasted like dust in my mouth. I began to see how desperately unhappy with my life I'd grown, how success had become a trap, and I was the lonely, frightened animal in its jaws. I did the last film, *Pandora,* then I quit. When my husband moved down here to a private island, looking for his own escape from the hard-to-manage world, it suited me too."

Rain said, "That young man—were you in love with him?"

Andrea was slow in answering. "I don't think I was capable of love then. One thing I'm sure of . . . those times on the beach, playing to an audience of one, are the fondest memories I have. But," she added abruptly, looking at Rain with a sad smile, "it's just a past. We all have one. It's now that's important."

Yes, Rain thought. What was going on *now?* Was the woman on the verge of telling her? As she tried to think of a way to ask, there came a tinkle of chimes. Excusing herself, Andrea left the room. Rain heard a door being opened and a man's voice, too low for her to make out words. A minute later Andrea reappeared followed by a brown man in faded chinos and threadbare, striped jersey. He might have been sixty, though his sun-dark skin made it hard to be sure.

"Cecil, this is Miss Patton. She came to interview me for

a magazine. Thankfully I convinced her otherwise. Lorraine, this is Cecil Childers, a very old and dear friend."

He ducked his head in greeting. He had an awkward, shy manner and made little eye contact; but there was no doubt that he basked in Andrea's attention.

"Lorraine, I have to go out," the actress said. "You're in no condition to walk on those feet, so why don't we run you around to your hotel. It's only ten minutes. Cecil, would you carry her down?"

"Oh, no. Not necessary," Rain protested. "I'm much too big to be carried."

"Please, ma'am," said Childers, speaking for the first time. "With bandages on your feet, you never get down the hill."

Before Rain could protest further, he scooped her into his arms. Andrea touched her shoulder reassuringly. "He's carried me more than once when I've drunk too much island rum. You two go ahead. I want to leave a note for the maid. I'll get my things and catch up."

On a back patio overlooking the slope to the bay, Childers said to Rain, "Ma'am, would you ring the wind chimes for me." His voice had the rich Bahamian tones she had already grown to love. "I always do it going in and out," he explained. "Very bad luck not to."

Obliging, Rain touched the dangling shells and bits of coral whose high-pitched music followed them as they descended steps carved in the coral rock of the hill. Rain looked for a car but soon realized there was none; they were going to a secluded cove directly below, where a motorboat was tied at a small pier. When they reached it, Childers set her into the boat.

"Miss Andrea will be right down," he said and busied himself with untying a line.

In the near distance Rain could see Paradise Island drowsing in the afternoon sun. Ten minutes to penetrate Andrea Wexford's shell, she thought—something she had failed so far to do in nearly an hour. And yet she had the feeling the woman wanted to talk, to go beyond details to the meanings they concealed.

Andrea joined them, her hair brushed and shining, sunglasses masking her eyes. She carried a straw tote bag with a big red cloth flower on it. As Childers started the engine, Rain took a chance.

"It's beautiful here. One of the reasons I came down is for a vacation. I need it. Have you followed the campaign at all? I just published a book on Tim Murphy."

For an instant tension passed over Andrea's face as subtly but distinctly as a shadow; then it was gone. Her eyes stayed hidden. "No, I haven't."

"It's getting interesting. He gave that rally at Shea Stadium, and tomorrow he's making some kind of announcement in Washington. I believe he may become president."

Under her tan Andrea seemed to pale, though it might only have been a reflection of light from the sea, which flickered dazzlingly on Rain too as the boat drew away from the pier. She felt a dizzy sense of being on the brink of a discovery which would lay bare the truth of the past two weeks. She started to speak when suddenly a hand clamped over her nose and mouth—a hand holding a cloth.

That smell . . . starting fluid . . . ether.

She struggled, but against Childers's strength she might as well have been a child resisting an adult. The boat gathered speed. The brightness of water and sky intensified, the way a lightbulb will just before it burns out. Rain saw Andrea turn away, like she was waiting miserably for something to end.

Which quickly, woozily, it did.

At 4:45 Thorne put on his new swim trunks and walked the twenty yards to the beach, all but deserted now at cocktail time, and for half an hour he swam. He dried off, then went back to the room to see if Rain had returned.

"Mr. Moore?" someone said as he stepped inside.

Whirling, he saw a dark-haired man standing by the drawn blinds of the window six feet away. Instinctively Thorne crouched, poised to spring, but he made no other move. A snub-nosed .38 was aimed at his chest.

"Be cool," the man said.

"Where's Lorraine?"

"Are you Moore?"

He had to think about it. "Yes."

The man tossed an airline's envelope onto the bed. It was Thorne's return ticket, booked on a credit card in his name. "Not according to that."

Thorne put his towel down. "Who are you? Where's Lorraine?"

Reaching into a pocket of his loose-fitting guayabera shirt the man took out a small ID folder which he flipped open. Thorne made out the U.S. eagle, the words Drug Enforcement Administration, scribbled signatures. "I'm Oscar Sanchez."

The rest of Thorne's tension drained away. The Aussie bartender had earned his money after all.

Sanchez pocketed the ID, slipped his weapon into a belt holster beneath his shirt and came around the bed. With his longish, center-parted hair and hawk face, he was handsome in a hard-bitten way. He moved with an agility that made Thorne think of Jimmy Dow. "Sorry for the scare," he said. "No one was here when I came. The room was unlocked."

Thorne was pretty sure it hadn't been, but he didn't make an issue of it. At the moment he was hopeful Sanchez would help him. He opened the door and peered out, wanting to see Rain returning, but the beach was empty. Leaving the door ajar, he went back in. "I need information. What do you know about a place called Bootleg Cay?"

"Why?"

He made a quick decision. It was time for honesty. He sat on the edge of the bed and gave a brief account of the Vineyard murders, leaving out Washington and the fact of his having been fired. He explained that the phony name was a cover. "I believe the killer could be on Bootleg Cay," he concluded.

Sanchez shook his head. "No chance. Bootleg is rock and

jungle, barely deserves a name. There's no one or nothing on it.''

The words were said too quickly, unequivocally. Thorne didn't believe them. He said so.

Sanchez arched his brows. ''Can't bullshit a cop, huh?''

''My source said you're a hard man to get hold of,'' Thorne countered, ''so why'd you bother to come?''

The agent seemed to decide upon honesty too. ''Because of a bust that's getting ready to happen. Guess where.''

Thorne reacted with surprise. ''Drugs?''

''Pure Peruvian flake. There's a cartel that's been using a cave there to store the stuff. I've had the place under surveillance for months. When I got word someone was asking, I had to check you out.''

''You think *I'm* involved?''

''I don't anymore.''

''When's your action set for?''

'You're not involved; keep it that way.''

Thorne was weighing what he knew, coming to a decision. ''Let me go along,'' he said suddenly.

''No way. I can't allow it.''

''Just as an observer. I'll be under your command. I won't—''

''*Hey,* what is it with you? I could see your ass in jail on suspicion.''

Thorne restrained his own surge of anger. The agent wasn't going to budge. When Sanchez spoke his voice had quieted. ''Ah, there's no need for that. Look, make this your vacation. Swim in the ocean, take your lady gambling. Then go back to where you're from.''

''And the information I gave you? What's that worth?''

The agent's woven leather shoes creaked as he paced a moment. ''Okay, your story's worth checking out. So what I'll do, anyone we bust tonight I'll run them through DEA files and see what comes up. If there's something you can use, I'll get in touch.''

Thorne knew it was the best offer he would get; but there was a time factor. If the killer were on Bootleg Cay, would he be for long? Or would the trail Thorne had been following for two weeks become too labyrinthian, or lost altogether? Perhaps it had already, he considered despairingly. Sanchez's report might take days; meanwhile, someone could be stalking him and Rain, looking to end the search forever.

At a ripple of woman's laughter he glanced expectantly toward the open door. A couple in bathing suits padded by heading for the beach.

Sanchez said, "I've got to go."

"Hold it."

The agent waited.

"Call me tomorrow morning?" Thorne said. "Regardless?"

"Sure. Tomorrow."

20

At 8:30 the casino was busier than it had been that afternoon. Thorne made his way through the throng of players to the bar, where Dan was at his post.

"Hello, mate. A Watney's, wasn't it?"

Ignoring the question, Thorne moved in close. "Do you know who Andrea Wexford is?"

Dan tipped his head speculatively. "The movie actress?"

"She lives here in Nassau, doesn't she?"

"Really? I'd have guessed L.A." The surprise was false.

Rain still hadn't returned from wherever she'd gone. Thorne was in knots of tension from waiting. "Let's drop the silver screen trivia. How much?"

The barman made another faint show of surprise then shrugged. "A tenner would do nicely."

Under a glassy skin the sea lay undulant and green, like some leviathan stirring itself awake after the torpid afternoon, thought Andrea Wexford. Daylight too was fading as Cecil slowed the outboard and steered toward the island. Andrea sat forward beside him, her attention now on Bootleg Cay.

Lorraine had recovered quickly once they'd gotten out on the water, by which time Cecil had tied her hands and feet. For a while she'd seemed groggy but full of questions. Only gradually, having gotten few answers, had she settled into silence. The experience had been hard on Andrea. She hated

to see anyone suffer; but Lorraine's prying had left them no
choice but to take her with them. Most likely they'd hold
her only overnight, then take her back to Nassau tomorrow.
If the message that that government man, Jones, had sent
to Cecil was true, this was the night when he would take
his damned cargo away and be gone from their lives for
good.

She hoped. She also knew that there was the potential for
danger tonight.

Although she hadn't seen or spoken directly to her husband in years—at his wish—Andrea nevertheless felt a sense
of responsibility for him. If by being here tonight she could
somehow protect him, she would.

"Where are you taking me?" Lorraine demanded from
the stern seat. "Bootleg Cay?"

Cecil glanced nervously at Andrea. "Will you steer the
boat for a moment, miss?"

"What are you going to do?"

"I won't hurt her, miss. I promise."

Reluctantly, Andrea took the wheel. When Cecil had rendered Lorraine unconscious again with the starting ether,
he set her gently on seat pads in the bottom of the boat and
returned to the controls. Soon he cut the motor. In the dwindling light they drifted quietly toward a small private dock.

"Well now, Childers."

Cecil's stomach tightened. Standing on the rocky beach,
some twenty yards away, was the man who had spoken.
Jones was his name, but Cecil thought of him as the Black
Man, which had nothing to do with the color of his skin,
which was lighter than Childers's own. No, the blackness,
Cecil imagined, lay beneath the skin.

"I thought you'd skipped out on the job I've got for you.
Evening, ma'am," Jones greeted Andrea. "Nice to see you
again."

Childers felt loathing coil in his belly—and alarm, as Jones
started down the beach toward them. Had he seen the girl?
No, they'd been out too far for that. But he would now.

As Cecil reached to help Miss Andrea onto the dock, she whispered, "I'll keep him occupied. Can you get her to your house?"

"Yes, miss, but—maybe you should come too. You'd be safer."

"I think I should be at the main house. If it seems okay later, I'll get word to you. Make sure Lorraine's comfortable." She sent a quick glance along the dock as Jones stepped onto it. "My tote, Cecil," she said in a louder voice.

Shouldering the bag, Miss Andrea strode directly toward the man. "Would you walk me up please."

"My pleasure. Childers, you know what needs to be done."

Cecil muttered acknowledgement. On his own he'd never do anything for these people, but the old man had agreed to it. Why, Cecil didn't know; though he didn't question it either. In fact, for this once he was glad to help. The task Jones had for him was to ready the crates in the cave for removal. So the time was near. Jones's men would arrive soon and, please God, be gone soon too. He could guess the type of people they'd be: riffraff desperate or bloodthirsty enough to take on Jones's kind of job. He felt a coldness settle over him, the way he always did when night fell, even in this tropical place.

"God bless you, miss," he breathed, turning to look at Andrea, but she was already gone into the dark rim of jungle at the top of the beach. He wondered if she had touched the wind chimes for luck.

"Going to be a beautiful evening," Clement Jones said.

The woman's grip on his arm was as stiff as if he'd offered her a snake, but he didn't care. His mind was elsewhere, stirred by the excitement he'd always felt before an operation, going all the way back to his days running spec ops into Laos. He'd stayed in the Corps for three tours as one of those few good men they were always looking for, and afterwards others had wanted him. All that was history. He was twenty pounds heavier now, and he needed glasses when he peered through a gunsight—but tonight he felt higher than he ever had. Jesus, if this worked . . .

From day one it had been tricky. Over the years the U.S. had grown shaky about covert activities, hobbling the intelligence community, sicking legislative watchdogs on the people who planned operations, even when such plans were in the country's best interest. Fortunately there were still people in the Company who believed in the old values. They'd given him an okay, though with the standard disclaimer: get caught, and it's *your* ass in the wind.

The key had been enlisting the old man. With his mania for keeping secrets, he hadn't been hard to persuade. The old man had scrubbed the cash through Bahamian accounts and let Jones use Bootleg Cay as base. Jones handled the details personally: buying the hardware, having it flown in in small consignments over a period of months and stored in the cave, assembling the team that would get the weapons into the hands of the people who'd use them—everything squeaky clean, no tracks back to anywhere. Then he had gotten his true inspiration, for which the arms plan was just a fuse. In a matter of eight or ten months, Christ, he could name his wish, and the new president of the United States would jump to grant it.

The villa loomed ahead as he and the woman stepped from the jungle path. She drew her hand away as if she were snatching it from a fire and after a brisk thank you went on alone.

You, too, lady, Jones thought, though he really did have Andrea Wexford to thank. It had been her unthinking little bolt up to Martha's Vineyard that had finally clued him about Senator Murphy.

He pried his attention loose from her swaying hips and surveyed the villa in the waning light. Like the woman, it belonged on the Riviera somewhere, not rotting away on this hunk of rock, vulnerable and unprotected. Sprouting from the roof was a satellite dish, and in a turret on one corner, through the shutters on its top floor window, he could see the nervous flicker of a TV set. Was the old dude up there? Funny, in the year Jones had spent developing the operation, he'd never once laid eyes on or even talked to the man. All contact had been through notes delivered by Childers, couched in indirect language because the old man enjoyed playing spy. Jones never liked that part—anything on paper was a potential trail—but now it didn't matter. After tonight no files or witnesses were going to exist.

He whacked a mosquito and picked his way back through the jungle.

Twilight was tingeing the sea like a spill of lavender oil as he emerged on the beach. Although the plane was still an hour away, he felt eager. At the periphery of his vision he saw movement and noticed a person scuttling along the beach toward the far end where the stone shack and the cave were. Childers . . . and he was carrying someone in his arms. By the dress, Jones realized the someone was female. Well, what do you know. The sly devil was taking a lady down to his crib for his own private stash.

Thorne was breathing deeply as he climbed the steps etched into the rocky hillside outside of Nassau where the Aussie had directed him. He felt as if he were swimming in the heavy air. The city lights had faded behind him like dying stars, and the spreading dark enclosed him. Somewhere down there, waiting, was the taxi.

It was a tired Chevy wagon driven by a cocoa-brown man with a personality as bright as his island shirt and the unsettling habit of peering long over his shoulder to give a tour commentary, never mind the mad Nassau traffic. Riding here, with his emotions wound tight as fencewire, Thorne was bothered that so many contradictory thoughts could exist simultaneously. Now they sought to cancel each other out, to paralyze action. Was it still possible to get out of this? To find Rain and go back to the Vineyard?

He pushed upward, one thought urging him on: Rain was four and a half hours late.

The bungalow sat on the hill crest, dark except for lamps flanking the raised entry. At this elevation a sea breeze prowled through the high grass and bushes like an unseen animal. Shivering as it cooled his perspiration, Thorne stepped to the door and knocked. Briefly, over the rustle of palm fronds and flowering vines, a faint tinkling sound reached him.

A remote house on an island, by the ocean. . . . The perfect sanctuary for someone in retreat. . . .

Cut the self-analysis, he told himself. He knocked again.

Trying to ignore his growing disquiet, he followed a garden path to the back of the house. The tinkling sound was louder now, and he saw the source: wind chimes dangling by a rear door. He rapped on one of the jalousie panes.

He had to believe Rain would've come here. She was resourceful and determined enough to have found out where Andrea Wexford lived. But why hadn't she returned or at least called? Impatiently he put his hands against a pane and peered in. By the filtered glow of lamp light from the front of the house, he surveyed the room. Chairs, a table, a sofa.

All at once, an object on the floor beside the sofa grabbed his eye. A sandal.

He drummed the door with his fist but got no response. Gripping one of the louvered panes by its bottom edge, he pried up against the pressure of its crank until he could snake a hand inside and unlock the door.

He moved across rattan mats and bent and picked up the sandal. Yes! It was one of the pair Rain had bought that morning in Orlando. The mate was under the front edge of the sofa.

"Hello?" he called, his voice sounding forced with the accelerating pound of his heart.

He began to search, checking other rooms, fighting a sense that he was moving too fast, missing some vital detail. But he didn't slow down. He opened doors, switched on lights.

But Rain wasn't here. No one was.

Outside, the wind plucked eerie music from the chimes.

The taxi driver, straw hat tipped over his eyes, sat up as Thorne came.

"Where can I get a boat?" Thorne demanded.

In the island mode that knows little haste, the driver reset his hat, scratched his chin. "You want a sailboat ride?"

"A motorboat. Tonight."

The driver wagged his head. "Very difficult, sir. Tomorrow, maybe we—"

Thorne took two five-dollar bills from his wallet. "I need one with a large gas tank. And navigation charts for the Exumas."

The money vanished into the driver's shirt pocket.

The derelict oil dock was as the driver described it, a mass of ragged palm trees, mechanical equipment, metal-roof sheds corroding in the salt air on the coast road. The planks of the wharf groaned beneath Thorne's steps. The driver had telephoned his brother-in-law and made the arrangements, negotiating a price which included a cut for himself. That had been forty minutes ago. The brother-in-law would be waiting.

As Thorne passed the conglomeration of machinery, which loomed like an abandoned amusement park, he wondered if he was doing the right thing. Besides the sandals, there had been one other clue in Andrea Wexford's bungalow that might indicate Rain's whereabouts—a note left on a hallway table. "Lucretia, laundry in the basket. I've had to leave unexpectedly." Assuming Andrea had written it, was the destination Bootleg Cay? He knew he was taking a chance by going there; and yet not to go might cost Rain her life.

Hastening his steps, he soon made out the pale shape of a runabout tethered alongside the end of the dock. It was an old craft, he saw doubtfully as he neared, a sixteen-footer with a Mercruiser outboard, likewise old. Water lapped the stained fiberglass hull. A man in the cockpit quit picking his teeth with the corner of a matchbook and stood up. Thorne introduced himself and jumped in beside him and began checking the boat.

He wasn't encouraged by his inspection. The motor housing was rusty, the deck scabby, hardware neglected. In the U.S. the craft would have failed even the most general safety inspection. A question rose in his mind as to whether the boat could make the sea journey he intended for it; but it was already ten o'clock; the likelihood of securing another boat now was almost nonexistent. On the plus side there were two full ten-gallon fuel tanks. And the Merc started right up.

The brother-in-law got a chart from a drawer in the dash panel, along with a flashlight. Unfolding the chart on the front seat, he pointed out where they were. Thorne followed the marked channel down the western flank of Great Exuma to the chain of little islands. He didn't see names.

"Which one is Bootleg Cay?"

"Here."

The island the man pointed to was small, with the general shape of a painter's palette, an area of cleared land as its thumbhole. Thorne judged it to be eighteen to twenty nautical miles away. He refolded the chart in such a way as to display the channel routes.

"Do we go there, boss?" the man asked.

"*I* go. I'm a fisherman. I've been around boats all my life. I'll have yours back by morning." He took out the agreed upon one hundred dollars American—three twenties and four tens—and handed it over. "Your brother-in-law's waiting for you on the road."

If the owner felt uncertain, he didn't show it. He put the money carefully in his pants pocket, then climbed onto the dock and began to loosen lines. Thorne got his notebook out. He wrote quickly, "Rain, if I missed you, I'm sorry. I'll be back later and will fill you in. *Please* be all right.— Thorne."

He hesitated, then wrote "Love" before his name and folded the note. He instructed the boat-owner to bring it to the Conch Shell and leave it at the front desk with Toby. For an instant, as he settled at the wheel, he had the impulse to take the note back and scratch out the added word, but he let it stay, like an echo from long ago, or a growing hope.

With the lines cast off, he switched on the running lights. He could see by the wharf pilings that the tide was rising. The newspaper had listed a midnight high. His hunch was that Sanchez and his people would time their raid accordingly to make the landing easier. Shifting into forward, he aimed the boat at a channel signal that glowed green in the darkness. When he remembered to, he glanced over his shoulder and saw the taxi groping back toward town.

21

The beach house was rustic stone and timber, with slits for windows, through which a rising moon spun lemony webs of light. Rain had awakened on a scratchy, straw-filled mattress. The door was locked from the outside. There was no electricity, but she located an oil lamp and got it lighted. On a table next to the bed was a note, penned in an uncertain hand. "Dont wory. You are saff."

"Saff" from what? she asked herself now. From whom?

Answers were few. The big dim room she was in made up most of the interior. Tools, a rusty trident, fishing tackle, and clothes hanging on pegs by the door appeared to belong to a man. The room's only decoration was a faded sacred-heart portrait of Christ. In the adjoining corner was a soapstone sink with a hand pump. The ether had made her mouth dry, so she worked the pump until water splashed cold on the soapstone, and she cupped her hands and drank.

Refreshed, she continued to explore. At one end of the room was a propane stove and some cupboards with food in bags and cans. Adjacent to the kitchen, behind a curtain, was a toilet. Her explorations done, she considered again the problem of getting out. The windows were glassless but constructed like the slots in a medieval fortress, too narrow to get through.

You are saff.

And imprisoned. Battling frustration, she sat on the bed.

Where was Eric now? Surely he'd have been alerted by

her absence, but where would he begin to look for her? Even assuming he located Andrea's house—a reasonable assumption given his skills of detection—what would he find there? Andrea was gone.

As she sat, raising questions without answers, Rain found herself thinking about dolphins and their special ability known as echolocation, by which they were able to find things through the use of sound waves, including members of their own pods. She longed for such a talent now, some way to reach Thorne and bring him to her.

Dont wory. You are saff.

But she was worried. And afraid.

"We're out of here at dawn, takeoff at oh-six-hundred."

Clement Jones crouched inside the anchored seaplane, balancing against the bobbing motion caused by the small waves lapping at its pontoons. In the weak battery light he surveyed faces, like a battlefield commander inspecting troops. The seven men who sat before him had been picked from personal ads placed in *Soldier of Fortune* magazine. All had been warriors in the service of their country once; had sampled the flavors of danger, fear, and blood; and had liked them. Doubtless some had been trigger-happy misfits long before they'd ever donned their first uniform. A few, perhaps, were seeking to live out childhood dreams of comic-book heroes. Most probably had tried to readjust to civilian life but hadn't made it. So they were here, his. They weren't the strackest squad ever assembled; in fact, they were pretty woeful soldiers, he judged. But that didn't matter, because what he had in mind for them didn't require Green Berets.

"Takeoff at oh-six-hundred," he repeated. "Meanwhile, the hardware gets loaded, then I want you armed and on the beach in forty-five minutes. I've got one extra little assignment for you tonight."

"Yo, chief," said a rangy, muscular man with a Zapata moustache. "Didn't see nothing about extra assignments in my contract."

The protester was clad in fatigue pants and an OD T-shirt

with the sleeves cut off. Jones nodded. There was always one; somebody who, no matter how many armies he'd served in, could never quite take discipline.

Jones said, "What's your name, troop?"

The man smoothed his moustache. "Neeley."

"You have any complaints about the pay, Mr. Neeley?"

"The pay? No, uh uh, but—"

"Any of you?" Jones walked his gaze slowly across the other faces before, finally, bringing it back to Neeley, who had fallen as silent as the rest. "Outstanding, gentlemen. Tonight'll be easy, just a little game. And Neeley, you get to be squad leader. Pick one man to pull guard duty here. I'll see the rest of you on the beach in forty-five minutes, locked and loaded. Then I'll tell you how it's played."

On a sheet of stationery embossed with the vice presidential seal, Bill Rendle typed: "Dear Mr. President. . . ."

An hour ago he had deplaned from Air Force Two at Dulles and followed his Secret Service detail through a gauntlet of reporters. The questions had been the same he'd been hearing all day at stops in New York and New Jersey. "Who killed Frizzel?" "When did you first learn about the body in the White House lawn?" "Any comment on Senator Murphy's lead in the polls?" Doggedly he had tried to turn attention back to the issues, but no one was listening. However, real despair hadn't hit until a short while ago when, having arrived home to the empty house (his wife was at a League of Women Voters forum in Chicago), he got a phone call from the White House.

The conversation had been brief. "Bill," the president said, "I'd like you here at eight A.M. I'll make the formal announcement at nine. I want a minimum of fanfare. You understand."

Underlying the thickness in the president's voice, brought on, no doubt, by the cancer treatments, had been an edge of the considerable pain he must be feeling. Yet, in spite of that, Peter's optimism came through, like bubbles welling to the surface of dark water. He knew the baton was being safely passed, etc., etc. The president's final words, before he'd hung up, had been: "I've got full confidence in you. You're the one for the job."

Now the man who tomorrow would take charge sat alone in his empty house and felt afraid.

All the years in politics, he reflected, and it wasn't enough. Because what he wanted was not a job, power, glory. It was purpose; as simple—or as complicated—as that. And all at once he felt his muddle had become too great. Those reporters' questions tonight had no easy answers. Not any more than the big questions about foreign policy, national defense, the economy, or a thousand others did. Yet, people would look to him to supply answers.

The only honest thing to do was resign. He typed:

"Dear Mr. President, It is with great personal regret that I. . . ."

He did not know how long he sat, nor why he found himself remembering a camping trip he had taken many years ago with his two young sons. They'd hiked into the Bitterroot Mountains in western Montana where, although it was September, a snow squall blew up their second day out. When it was over, the terrain had altered. They discovered they were lost. The Bitterroot range is jagged, unforgiving country where human error is often punished with swift indifference. Justly so, he had been frightened, though not as much as his sons. The younger one, Ned, had started to cry, prompting his older brother finally to say, "Quiet. We're with dad. He knows where he's going." In truth, Rendle *hadn't* known. But, at that moment they needed to believe he knew exactly what he was doing. By keeping his wits, relying on experience, and praying, he led them all to safety.

Unexpectedly now he discovered tears in his eyes.

For the first time in his memory, his ambitions seemed to dissolve. He had no time to concern himself with whatever the future might be. In a practical sense, he was president. Conceivably the term would last only a few weeks. If the Frizzel squall became a storm, it could be far shorter. But it might be very long too.

He blinked away his tears. Eight A.M. the president had said. He needed to sleep. He yanked the sheet of stationery from the typewriter and climbed the stairs to the accompaniment of his resignation letter being ripped into halves, quarters, eighths. . . .

Rain could not have said just when her eyes had come to rest on a box in a corner, but she'd been staring at it for some time. It was wooden, charred on one side, and bore the faded label *Rum XXX*. Curious, she stirred herself and carried over the oil lamp.

The box evidently was used for storage now, the top secured with a simple hasp, no lock. Inside, under some folded clothes and a carved wooden crucifix, she found a scrapbook, its pasteboard covers frosted with mildew. She lifted it out carefully. Opening it, she stared at a sepia-toned snapshot. It showed a villa, in front of which posed what looked like an island family—man, woman and three children. Behind them stood a middle-aged white man in a white tuxedo jacket. Judging by his hair style, the scene dated from the 1920s.

On following pages of the scrapbook were articles clipped from movie-fan magazines. With surprise Rain saw that they featured Andrea Wexford; speculations about a possible return to the screen, accounts of her private wedding to the much older man she'd married. More recent still were snapshots of Andrea sitting by a swimming pool, and then in a boat that might've been the one they'd been in today. With dawning awareness she realized that the scrapbook—and this stone house—belonged to Cecil Childers. But why was she here?

She sat bolt upright, startled by a crunching sound from outside. She replaced the scrapbook in the box, blew out the lamp, and felt her way to the nearest window slot. Only a slice of beach was visible, but she saw a man picking his way across the stones toward the house. He was large and carrying what appeared to be a stick.

Reflexively she shrank away from the window, but not

before she realized that what he held was in fact a rifle—and that she recognized him. She'd seen him in Washington two nights ago—when he'd executed Hiram Kirk.

Stars shone in the sky like brass buttons. During most of the run from Nassau, Thorne kept the outboard wide open. In the distance, to port, lay the low, dark mass of Great Exuma. Otherwise, except for the occasional faint light of yachts, like fireflies in the June night, the sea was empty. At last, spotting his destination, he eased the throttle back. When he made out the headland at the southern tip of Bootleg Cay, which would be the logical place for the cave Sanchez had mentioned, he switched off the lights. He knew where he would start looking for Rain.

Ashore he tipped the motor, drew the boat above where the tide was likely to reach, and secured it. Over the sea a waxy yellow moon had begun to rise. In the moon's glow, a craft perched several hundred yards offshore caught his attention. It was a deep-hulled seaplane, and in a curved oblong of light from a hatch in its fuselage he could discern a rubber boat tied alongside. There were several figures in the boat, and they looked as if they were carrying rifles. DEA people getting ready for their raid. If Rain was somewhere on the cay, he needed to find her quickly. It was 11:15.

Hollowed by the sea over ages, the cave had enough clearance so that a boat could enter directly or a person could climb in on a tilting walkway, which Thorne did now. Thirty feet inside, the cave angled so that the large natural room at its center was invisible from the ocean. It was lit by torches set atop tripods on the walkway. He crouched behind an outcropping of stone and scanned the flickering interior for people, but there were none. He moved forward.

On a ledge a foot above tide level stood a number of various-sized wooden crates. Each was stenciled with the words: ZETA * SOUVENIRS.

Zeta. Gulf Stream Bank. Island Airways. Air America. CIA.

The tempo of Thorne's heartbeat kicked up. He looked around for a tool of some kind and found a boat hook. He pried up a corner of one of the boxes, doing it carefully; even so, the hoarse, seal-barking sounds of nails drawing free echoed in the cave. He pulled the lid off.

Torchlight shone on oiled brass. He lifted out a canvas strap of large-caliber ammunition.

"And Sanchez said it was drugs," someone said.

Thorne dropped the ammo belt and spun to see a figure emerge from the shadows and step into the torch light cradling an M-16. Oscar Sanchez. He was dressed in camo fatigues and jungle boots, wearing a black nylon backpack. Holstered at his waist was a big handgun.

"Couldn't stay away, huh? In spite of my warning. I wondered who belonged to the runabout."

Sanchez's gaze went to the open crate. "Machine gun ammo," he said, nodding as if this explained something. He kicked lightly at several other boxes, then looked at Thorne. "What's your story?"

Thorne decided to be direct. "Lorraine is on the cay. I'm almost certain of it."

Quickly, he recounted his trip to Andrea Wexford's house and the discovery of the sandal and the note he believed had been left for a maid. When he finished, the drug agent said, "Flimsy. But, if she is here, it'll be in the villa on the other end."

"You told me the cay is deserted."

"I lied. The villa's owned by a flaky *viejo* who lives here with his wife and a few servants."

"They're the ones you're after?"

Sanchez hadn't lowered the M-16. "I'm not after anyone."

"You brought a planeload of men for nobody?"

"I came alone." Sanchez dug a roll of tape from one of his fatigue shirt pockets and bit off a long strap.

For a moment, Thorne thought the man was putting him

on; then, with frightening speed, parts began to stack up. The structure was still rickety though. "Those people in the plane then . . . they've come for what's in here," he said, trying it out.

"Mercenaries, if I had to guess." Sanchez stuck the strip of tape lightly on a crate and bit off another. "I've been working the islands undercover for two years," he went on, talking between bites. "I stumbled on this place in March. The seaplane activity got me curious, so I staked it out. I discovered just recently it isn't drugs they've been bringing in. We're only eight hundred air miles from Central America. A few hours."

He shrugged off his backpack and dug out several extra ammo clips, which he taped to the stock of the M-16. Pieces of an explanation were coming together in Thorne's mind— the CIA, guns—not enough yet; but far more pressing was his feeling of time slipping away, turning like the tide. "If Rain's here, I've got to find her."

With a quick movement Sanchez tipped the muzzle of the rifle up at his belly. "Hold it. You crazy? There's a squad of them, with weapons that make this look like it came off the back of a comic book." He paused, peered around quickly, brought his eyes back. "There's also money. A *lot* of money. I saw the bank bags."

So that was it. This wasn't a heroic, single-handed bust at all. Thorne stared past the flash suppressor, then slowly nodded his understanding and his disappointment.

Sanchez read both. "Man, for years I've been chasing scum. For an honest paycheck I see slimeballs raking in more in one score than my pension's going to pay me till I'm dead. The hell with that. I grew up hard too, but I *worked* all my life for what I got. I'm sick of it."

"If you can't beat 'em . . .'"

"One time, man. Once. Put the money in a Nassau account."

"And then go back to being straight? What's a little tarnish on a badge," Thorne said sardonically.

"Screw that, man." Sanchez kept the rifle aimed. "Everybody expecting you to put your ass on the line, while they sit back and bitch about how we're losing the war, things falling apart. But the politicians keep getting fat, and the bad guys keep walking."

The rationalizations didn't surprise Thorne—every cop thought them—but the pain underneath did. Unexpectedly, it drew him to the man. There was truth to what he was saying. Society did have a lot of priorities wrong. It was sorrowing to see the world growing colder year by year, being taken over by people who were greedy or just didn't care. But the flaw in the cop's thinking was the notion that you could swerve across the center line just once, then go safely back and never be tempted again.

"So why toss it away?" he asked. "They don't issue a claim check for you to get it back."

Sanchez seemed not to be listening. He was squinting into the greasy torchlight of the cave. "The money will be here," he said in a hushed tone. "Help me, then I'll help you."

There was no time. Thorne started to move.

"Stop."

"I have to know if she's here."

"I'll cut you a slice."

"I'm leaving."

This time Sanchez raised the rifle to his shoulder and sighted.

"Hey," Thorne said nervously. "I'm not going to interfere with you."

"I've got the gun and *you're* not going to interfere with *me?* I call that cojones, man."

Thorne wanted to wipe his face, which was streaming with sweat, but he didn't move. "I have to find her."

Sanchez frowned. "You're in it just for that? For her?"

"I thought there was more, but I was wrong. Right now she's all that matters to me."

Sanchez threshed a hand through his dark hair, and once more Thorne was reminded of Jimmy Dow. Again, in spite of the gun, he felt drawn to the man. With a sigh Sanchez lowered the rifle. "If she is here, the villa is the likely place. You could make it up there."

"And the mercenaries?"

"Their business is in here. I think they plan to move the guns tonight. If they head ashore . . . I'll come get you."

Thorne considered, and though he didn't like any of it, he was out of options. Armed soldiers aside, once the tide turned they'd have to fight the offshore currents to get free of the cay. He took a few steps then stopped. "How about a weapon?"

"What's my guarantee you won't point it the wrong way?"

Thorne shrugged. "There is none. But each of us is the only family the other one's got right now."

Sanchez hesitated a moment then unbuckled his gun belt and handed it over. Thorne drew the revolver: a blue steel Colt Python, .357 Magnum with a 4-inch barrel, a round in each chamber. He strapped it on. From his pack Sanchez replaced it with the snub-nosed .38 he'd had at the cabana earlier.

"Use this too," he said. "There's a moon."

It was a tin of greasepaint. Thorne smeared some on his face and the backs of his hands. Sanchez did likewise. When they finished, Sanchez consulted his watch. "It's eleven-thirty. We better be at the boats by midnight."

The witching hour. With a cold tightening in his belly, Thorne started over the rocks for the mouth of the cave.

Like something out of a calypso version of *Gone With the Wind,* the house sat dramatically in the clearing, ringed by jungle, three stories of whitewashed stucco with a tile roof and a turret at one corner. The ground floor lights were on, and Thorne squatted in a thicket of bushes, watching. When he was reasonably sure no guards were patrolling the grounds, he hurried across the yard to an overgrown clump of hedge and melted into shadows.

Evidently the cay had no roads, even if there were vehicles; but apparently that hadn't mattered to the villa's original owner. The facade featured a porte cochère over a curving shell driveway, which was puddled now with light that spilled through the panes flanking the front door. Although he saw no movement inside, he decided against approaching so directly. Instead he skirted left, moving toward the rear, slipping past a terrace with a swimming pool and cabana before making his way to within a dozen yards of the house.

As he paused, he had a feeling that things were happening too easily. There should be watchmen, a dog, *something*. But there wasn't. Except for the soughing motion of palm trees and the faint noise of a TV, which seemed to be coming from the shuttered upper room of the turret, no other movement or sound disturbed the night.

Under different circumstances he would have waited and watched, but the thought that Rain might be inside urged him on. He crossed the terrace to a double door and gripped the handle. It was unlocked.

Again he had his sense that this was easier than it should be. Where was everyone?

He opened the door and stepped in.

He was in a kitchen, though it appeared as if little cooking had taken place there in a long time. Cobwebbed pots hung on hooks over a dusty wooden counter. He hesitated, listening, then made his way along a hallway toward the front of the house. He soon reached a broad foyer aglitter with light from crystal chandeliers. A veined marble staircase swept to the upper floors. To either side, arched doorways opened to other rooms. There was a decadent richness to the house—silk damask, dark furniture, Renaissance paintings—but the enthusiasm for decor had stagnated. In this climate, surfaces were deteriorating. Wall coverings had started to peel, and the ornate ceiling bore stains. The fustiness of dry rot prickled his nostrils.

He moved to the first archway and peered into a ballroom. Vast, vacant. He came successively to a drawing room, a billiard room, a library. What was this place? Where were the people? *Where was Rain?*

Farther along the hallway he came to a closed door. Easing it open, he discovered a small office. The walls were lined with empty bookshelves. There was a desk whose surface was bare except for a small gilt-frame drawing. Perhaps because there were people in the drawing, like a token of life in this palace of decay, he went over and picked it up.

It was done in pencil, a detailed rendering of a young couple standing on a beach. In the blink of time it took him to see the faces, he grasped who the people were.

It was the only thought he had time for.

At a sound, he whirled, drawing the Colt.

A small woman had entered the room, and they saw each other simultaneously. She gaped in surprise that was the mirror of his own.

He had the advantage, however. He knew her.

22

Thorne realized all at once how he must look, face smeared with greasepaint, gun in his hand. The woman had not moved.

"Miss Wexford," he said quickly and gave his name. "I'm trying to find a friend of mine. Lorraine Patton."

"How do you know me?" the woman asked.

"There isn't time for that. She visited your house in Nassau tonight, didn't she?"

"I don't know who you're talking about."

But she did know; he was pretty sure she'd brought Rain here. He hadn't lowered the gun. "I don't want to hurt you, but I have to know where she is."

Half a minute dragged by. Finally, the woman closed the door and leaned against it. She shut her eyes and blew her breath out in a prolonged sigh, as if release had come at last. "You don't have to worry," she said. "Lorraine is safe."

Exhaling with relief of his own, Thorne holstered the revolver. Andrea nodded at the drawing he still held. "Do you know, then?"

"You and Timothy Murphy?"

She searched his face a moment then came forward slowly, reaching to take the portrait. In a soft voice she said, "I knew and loved him as Charles Evans."

Thorne didn't understand.

When Andrea set the drawing back on the desk she said,

"I told Lorraine tonight about a young man I knew long ago, who I thought took his own life. All this time, I privately mourned him . . . loved him. Yes, loved. I didn't tell Lorraine that because I didn't know it. But I do now. It's true."

"Please," Thorne said, "where is she?"

But the woman was not to be hurried. She leaned against the antique desk. "About six months ago I saw Senator Murphy's picture in a magazine. I spoke with my husband's servant and asked for some files. My husband has a trunk of notes and memos upstairs somewhere. Cecil, the servant, was reluctant—he's very protective of me, believes there are things I shouldn't trouble myself with. But I insisted. Among the files I found a Los Angeles private investigator's report written many years ago, with an update made later. Evidently my husband was suspicious of the time I spent with Charles Evans, so he'd had him checked. The past that Charles claimed hadn't borne out. I began to understand. In the files I also came across a prison camp photo."

Thorne felt drawn in, despite his sense of time passing. Rain was safe; that much he knew. This information was the point in their being here. "The one with the burning flag?"

"Yes. Charles had faked suicide, I believe, because he had to go back to being who he'd been *before* he became Charles Evans. Gradually I began to think: if *I* knew this, who else might?

"My husband must, of course, but he's no threat. But there have been two men here at various times this past year—government men—involved in some plot. If they knew, I had no doubt they'd use the knowledge to destroy Timothy Murphy."

"So you went to Martha's Vineyard to confront Murphy?"

She seemed to debate whether to say more than she already had. "Not right away. First I decided to make indirect contact, give him time to react. Remember, it had been a long time since we'd seen each other, and he'd led me to believe he had drowned. I needed some message that would get past his protective ring of aides and staff, a token that would immediately persuade him I was for real." She paused. "I chose this." She had picked up the pencil drawing again. "I sent the photograph this was made from actually. I inscribed it from me to Timothy Murphy, to show him I knew.

"It worked," she went on. "He wrote back to a postal box in Nassau and suggested we meet. Martha's Vineyard was his idea, a quick stop before he headed west. So I went. To warn him. And because I wanted to see him again. That part was a mistake. He isn't Charles Evans. Oh, it's the same man, but the personality . . . Charles was gentle, nurturing. Senator Murphy's reaction when I confronted him was resistance, like I'd made up everything as a plot against him. Then, when I finally felt he believed me, he got angry. I left with a sense that he wasn't going to do a thing about any of it."

"When you met him—you didn't notice a tattoo on his arm? Here." Thorne touched the inside of his left forearm.

She shook her head. "He had rubbed calamine there, said he'd caught poison ivy."

"Miss Wexford, would he have had somebody killed to cover up your meeting?"

Her eyes widened. "Those killings *were* linked then. Oh, God. Awful. But, no. I'd never suspect him of that."

"Do you suspect anyone?"

She shook her head—a question mark, not a denial.

"Have you had any contact with him since?"

"Once. After I'd read of those two people being stabbed. I didn't think he saw the real danger of his situation. I secretly used a secure telephone line the government men set up here. I left a message for him to call back. When he did, we spoke for less than a minute. He totally denied the killings were connected in any way. And I guess I believed him, because I wanted to. But he also sounded . . . very strange."

"What do you mean?"

"It was like our meeting hadn't really happened for him. That . . . none of the past between us had happened."

Her eyes filled, and she choked off a sob. Thorne was conscious of time slipping past. Sanchez had said midnight— it was already quarter of. Just another few minutes would tell him what he needed to know.

"Andrea," he said gently, "you got the prison camp photograph in your husband's files, you said. Had it been there long?"

She blew her nose on a silk handkerchief, cleared her throat. "I think so. I think it must've been what started my husband doing certain . . . things behind the scenes. To boost Murphy's career. One of the government men I told you about, he's someone my husband once helped get a job. I'm convinced he collected information to use against people who stood in Murphy's way politically. He'd have access."

"Hiram Kirk?"

Andrea's surprise was as great as his own. "You know him?"

"Please. Go on."

"Well, my husband has always occupied himself with what he considered patriotic duties—doing favors, arranging money mostly."

"For running illegal arms?"

"I honestly don't know. In fact, I doubt even he knew what's involved. He's very old and . . . removed. Our marriage hasn't been very conventional. The truth is, I haven't actually seen or spoken with my husband in five years."

Thorne was confused. "I thought he lived here."

"As a recluse. He communicates only by notes through the one servant. I've lived my own life for a long time. I suppose memories of past glory—and having known Charles—sustained me. Until I found out the truth." She used her silk hanky again. "You know, I once portrayed a woman who discovers the truth about the man she's loved. *Mr. Hammond's Secret.* In a strange way, I've been living a version of that these past few months. I thought maybe I could save Timothy. But now . . .'' She shook her head. "I guess what I've tried to do has been too little, too late. I should've acted. I suspect the others have won after all.''

"You mentioned two government people," Thorne said. "Who else beside Kirk?''

"The one in charge. His name is Clement Jones.''

The CIA man. Links were snapping into place for him. More than ever, though, he was aware of time racing past, and now there was none to waste. "Where's Lorraine?''

Andrea was clutching her arms across her chest, as if warding off a chill, but it couldn't be cold she was experiencing; the room was warm. "I have . . . a bad feeling. You should get her now, both of you should get away from here.'' She looked toward the door, wanting perhaps to get out of there, get to safety herself. Her revelations had made her vulnerable. Or maybe she felt she'd been safe long enough . . . hiding, waiting, keeping herself. For what? Thorne wondered. Her husband? Charles Evans?

"Where is she?'' he asked again.

Andrea squared her shoulders, and when she spoke her voice was steady. "Lorraine's questions today stirred up ghosts I thought I'd put to rest long ago. Now they seem to flit around this old place.'' She gazed at the portrait as if drawn by one final tug of longing, then said, "Maybe it *isn't* too late. I'll take you myself.''

Sanchez pried open the last crate.

With a gasp he stepped backwards, dropping the lid. An array of the weird terra cotta figurines he'd first seen in Miami gaped at him. As he had that other time, he shuddered with the sensation that a goose had walked on his grave. Peasant superstition, he chided himself, but quite unconsciously he made the sign of the cross.

He dug past the figurines and clumps of straw, though he already knew what he would find. More weapons. With a sigh of frustration, he replaced the lid and gazed around the cave.

Rockets, assault rifles, ammo . . . and a lot of coke. That was the puzzler. Why would anyone conspire to smuggle drugs *into* Central America? It was like taking cigars to Cuba. It made no sense. But he didn't belabor the question. What he was really after was not here. The cash was gone.

With a gnaw of anger, he kicked at an outcropping of wall and was startled when his boot met with little resistance. In fact, what he had taken for rock was actually a tarpaulin which had been flung over something. He pulled it back.

There they were.

There had to be thirty or more heavy canvas sacks, each the size of a throw pillow and sealed with a padlocked metal clamp, each printed with the words GULF STREAM BANK NASSAU.

Slinging the M-16, he hefted one of the bags. It must've weighed ten pounds. He drew a pocket knife and made an incision in the canvas wide enough to slip several fingers through. The feel of money brought an almost electrical surge of excitement.

There was no way he could score it all in a single trip. Fully loaded, his pack would hold maybe sixty pounds' worth. He calculated two trips, possibly three, 180 pounds of paper. Depending upon the denominations, it could be a huge take. He started to grin. He pinched one packet of bills and tweezed it out through the incision.

His grin faded. He held the money up to the torches' light. Instead of green twenties, fifties, or hundreds, as he had hoped and expected, the notes were a muddy brown. Inspecting them, he saw each bill was inscribed with the seal of the *Banco de Nicaragua.*

He tugged more packets out of the bag and saw the same thing. He sliced open four other bags. Nicaraguan cordobas.

And all at once he thought of himself as the butt of a joke, the funny one about the cash going with the guns for buying munitions, bribing officials, paying informants, whatever was needed to fund a secret little *yanqui* war. To him, the money was utterly worthless. Even if it were not marked— which the CIA or whoever was supporting this thing might have managed—at an exchange rate of five or six hundred cordobas to the dollar, he couldn't carry enough to bankroll a night at the slot machines in Freeport.

Laughter began welling up inside him, brackish and bitter, searing away his disappointment, mocking his lapse into greed, dissolving the tarnish, as Thorne had put it; cleaning off his whole damned soul. Laughter rang off the cave walls. He flung a packet of bills into the air, where it sprang apart, filling the air with flapping brown notes as if he'd spooked a flock of bats off the ceiling. Cordobas fluttered to the water to float on the turning tide. Still laughing, he grabbed his pack.

As he reached the mouth of the cave, he heard something which choked off his humor and brought a quick dazzle of alarm. Far out on the water, by the moored seaplane, an outboard motor had started up.

In her pale dress Andrea Wexford appeared to float like a wood sprite through the thickets of jungle. Thorne still had questions for her, but now he was thinking only about Rain. They hurried, not speaking, their attention on the trail and the swarms of mosquitoes that had found them. After a few minutes Andrea turned to him and put a finger to her lips. He followed her several more yards, then they emerged from the trees onto a sloping, rocky beach. Farther down, near the ocean, a glow visible through its narrow windows, was a stone house.

"She's there," Andrea whispered. "The house belongs to Cecil Childers, the servant I told you about. He's a good man."

As they started down the beach, the mosquitos' whine faded from Thorne's ears. That's when he heard a sound that turned his blood cold. A shriek had risen inside the house, clawing raw from a woman's throat. Rain!

The rocks made treacherous footing, and he ran stumblingly, barely avoiding falling several times. Even though the house wasn't far, he was panting when he reached it. The door hung open. He listened for sounds from within, but there was only the crunch of Andrea's steps hurrying over the stones behind him. He waved her back. Then, pulling the Colt, gripping it in both hands, he went through the doorway.

The interior was low-ceilinged, dim with smoky light. He moved in in a crouch. To his right was a kitchen area, empty. He swung left. In a corner, kneeling on a low bed, was a man whom he recognized instantly as the one who'd killed Kirk. He was struggling to hold Rain down.

In the slice of time it took Thorne to register this, Jones swung a pistol up from the mattress, jammed it to Rain's ear.

"Don't!" Thorne shouted.

"Give it up!" cried Jones. "Now!"

Rain fought, but Jones kept a hand clamped on her throat, the pistol to her head.

"Your *weapon!*" he said. "Down, or she's dead!" He grabbed Rain's hair and began getting to his feet, pulling her with him. Through shifting shadows, Thorne saw that her cheek was discolored, one eye swollen nearly shut.

He felt the moment hanging by a thread. He could not forget how, two nights ago on a Washington street, this man had shot Hiram Kirk dead.

Thorne's grip on the Colt was loosening—like his grip on the situation—yet he couldn't let go. If he lost control of his mind and his weapon, he lost his only chance to keep the thread whole. Lose them and it would snap.

Jones slung a heavy rifle over his shoulder by its strap and crooked an arm around Rain's neck. Keeping her between himself and Thorne, the muzzle of his pistol pressed into the hinge of her jaw, he began dragging her toward the door. Thorne backed off. His heart was pounding wildly.

Jones reached the doorway and backed out, pulling her along.

Before Thorne could react, there was a thud, then two explosions shattered the night. Rain flew back through the doorway.

He got to her in three strides and threw himself over her. Wheeling the Colt up to cover the door, he cried out her name, the word implying a dozen questions.

Andrea Wexford lay on the rocks, her arms spread as if she had flung them in welcome. Her face was tipped away from Thorne and Rain, her hair tossed in a soft golden fan, as graceful and perfect as a palm frond.

Thorne tore his attention away to look for her killer, who was scrambling up the beach. *"Jones!"*

The man turned and fired a wild round which whined off the stone house. Thorne fired two of his own before Jones flung himself over the ridge into the refuge of the jungle. Stillness poured back in.

Rain was kneeling at Andrea's side. The woman's face appeared relaxed, untroubled, as if she were only acting a part and in a moment she would stand among them. The vacancy of her eyes, however, belied this. After a moment Rain looked up at him and shook her head. "She was right here. She smashed him with a rock. She saved me."

The pointlessness of the death grieved Thorne. He was stricken with a sense that he'd contributed to it by having pushed the case too long, too far. "Better get inside," he murmured.

When he'd assured himself that Jones was gone for now, he carried Andrea's body into the house. He set her on the pallet bed and covered her with a blanket.

Rain had washed her face, which looked better but was still swollen. She was starting to shiver with the aftershock and the cooling night. He put his arms around her. "You okay?"

She nodded. Then, as if some frozen core of her had thawed, her words began to pour out in a tearful rush. She described what had happened since she'd left their cabana that afternoon, coming at last to how Jones had arrived, thinking at first that she was a girlfriend of Childers's, but then recognizing her.

"He was trying to find out how much we know and to

make me tell him where you were. He would've killed me after.''

"It'll be okay very soon," he said, hearing the dull timbre of exhaustion in his voice. He told her about Sanchez and the waiting boat. "Let's get you there, then I'll come back for Andrea.''

"Cecil Childers should be told. I found a scrapbook. I think he was secretly devoted to her.''

"I loved her.''

Startled, they drew apart. The man had come up quietly and was standing in the door.

"Cecil,'' Rain said.

He winced at seeing her bruised face. "Miss . . . you're all right?''

"I am, yes. But Andrea . . .''

Childers took the oil lamp, went to the bed and drew back the blanket. Squatting, he brushed a strand of hair away from the face, which was as dully gray and still as the stones on the beach outside. For a long moment he only looked, then he said, "You both should go, get off the cay. Dangerous here now.''

"What about you?'' Thorne asked. "And the others in the main house?''

"I will attend to things. The staff's already left. Best go quickly.''

They hesitated several seconds, then started for the door.

"Miss,'' Childers said, "you can't walk without shoes. I've got some old sandals. They're big, but you'll want them for the rocks.''

Thorne found the sandals, fashioned from tire-treads, and Rain strapped them on. Childers did not look up as they set off.

There had been two gunshots; then, a minute or so later, three more; five shots in all, the sounds carrying ominously across the calm night. Crouched behind an outcropping of rock, binoculars pressed to his face, Sanchez saw just how far.

The Zodiac zoomed out of the cave. He counted seven men aboard, heavily armed by the looks of them. The boat cut a tight arc which would shortly take it past the cove where his own boat and Thorne's were tied. If by a remote chance the men hadn't discovered someone else had already been here, they would in a matter of minutes. They would either post a guard or seize the boats and simply sink them, then sweep up the headland on foot and along the length of the cay until they found the invaders. Whatever they were up to here, he knew, was illegal, so they wouldn't look kindly on any witnesses.

He did a quick calculation. It was almost midnight. No Thorne. The percentages lay in reaching his own boat pronto, ahead of the mercenaries, and just getting out.

The idea tickled his brain. Since those five shots there had been no others. Maybe Thorne had gotten careless. Maybe the poor bastard was already dead. If not, he was almost definitely going to be. A revolver against what they were packing? No way.

For the moment the moon was tucked under a cottony blanket of clouds and darkness obscured the landscape, but he could still hear the buzz of the Zodiac as it headed for the beach below. And he thought: if you're going, amigo, *el tiempo es ahora.* Just haul. Who'll ever know?

He didn't move.

One person would know. An idealistic young cop would know. A cop who'd grown up in Little Havana—who'd seen the drugs take over, seen his friends become junk, a lot of them in jail now, or in hell—*he'd* know. A cop with brave, simple parents who had put him through schools with hard-ass nuns and later two years of college, after which he'd shocked everyone by going back to that world he'd escaped from; only this time he wore a badge. A cop who'd survived a dozen years of street work undercover, a loner, parents dead, without close friends—he was the only person who'd ever know, and the one who would never forget.

With a curse Sanchez shoved the binoculars into his backpack and yanked the pack on. Carrying the M-16, he moved inland at a jog.

"Not much farther," Thorne urged.

Rain's ordeal had taken its toll. Her hand gripping his was like a claw, her steps tentative, as though the ground were threatening to open beneath their feet. He was drawing her along faster than she wanted to go but not half as fast as he knew they should be moving. During the past half hour something had come to near certainty in his mind. On the day Maura Ames and Vaughan Belnap were killed, someone had flown to Martha's Vineyard on a plane owned by the CIA. He thought he knew who.

Overhead the moon sliced out of a net of clouds. As much as possible, Thorne had been trying to keep hidden, but the jungle lay at the other end of the cay; here, on the windward coral spine, trees were few. Now they might as well have stood on a spotlighted stage. He had just turned to help Rain across a crevice when he saw her eyes go wide. He spun. Running at a crouch across the open, moonlit ground in their direction was a man with a rifle.

Thorne motioned Rain down, then scrabbled forward on elbows and knees. As the runner neared, he sprang up with the Colt. *"Stop!"*

"Whoa! For God's sake," the man cried, stumbling to a halt.

They gaped at each other. Then Oscar Sanchez said, "Am I glad to see you. I heard gunfire. I thought—"

Thorne was still aiming the gun. "Where's your money?"

Sanchez wiped a forearm across his streaming brow. "Yeah, well, that's a story in itself. I'd have to go south to spend it. *Far* south. *Comprendes, amigo?"*

Growing aware that he'd been holding a breath clenched in his chest, Thorne let it out and lowered the Colt. Sanchez exhaled too. Thorne called Rain out of hiding and made the introductions. From a pouch in his backpack Sanchez took an oblong plastic packet which he kneaded with his hands a moment and then handed to Rain. "Chemical ice. It'll take some of the sting out of your face."

As Rain applied the cold pack, Thorne said, "We'd better get to the boats."

Sanchez shook his head. "I'm not the only one who heard the gunshots. The mercenaries will have found the boats by now."

Rain looked from one to the other of them with growing recognition. "We're trapped?"

"It seems that way," Sanchez agreed.

"Couldn't we just *talk* to these people?" Her voice was muffled by the cold pack, but the note of alarm in it was obvious.

"Could you have talked to Jones?" Thorne asked, taking her hand. "Just our being here threatens them. They mean to fly the guns out tonight. We're an unwanted complication."

Sanchez said, "There's a piece that I can't figure. I found cocaine with the guns."

"That's your job," Thorne said.

"But running it *into* Central America? Makes no sense."

It didn't, and all at once Thorne found himself thinking of something Andrea Wexford had said, about not knowing what might be in her husband's files. If Jones got his hands on them, what kind of leverage could they buy him? What hold might he already have on Timothy Murphy? And if Murphy got elected . . .

All at once he felt as if something were spinning a web of ice around his heart.

"The coke is meant to stay," he said suddenly. "The guy running this arms operation, Jones, is CIA—or at least was. He wants some files that'll be at the villa, but he won't want witnesses. The coke is a screen. To make what's supposed to happen here tonight look like it's part of a drug war."

"You lost me, Eric."

"Yeah, man, explain."

"Before Jones's soldiers leave," Thorne said impatiently,

"I think they mean to attack the house and kill everyone they find."

"No—" Rain whispered.

The sound Thorne's whiskers made as he dragged a hand over his cheek might have been the feeble rasp of an idea. He gripped Rain and Sanchez by their upper arms. "We've got to reach the villa before they do. It might be the only chance we and whoever's still there will get. We have to find the old man."

23

The anchored plane rode deep on its pontoons, its belly full of the weapons that had been in the cave. Childers circled it once before twisting the outboard's throttle shut and allowing his boat to slip under a wing and bumble against the fuselage. As he reached for a handhold, a cargo door flush-mounted in the aircraft's side curled open with a hydraulic sigh.

A muscular man with a shaved head appeared in the hatchway, back-lit by light from inside the plane. He wore ammo belts crisscrossed over his shirt guerrilla-style and pointed an automatic pistol. "What do *you* want?"

"I've . . . got a message for you," Cecil said.

He'd been hoping everyone had gone ashore, but obviously they had left a guard, which was going to complicate things. He would have to improvise.

"Well?"

"Mr. Jones . . . wants you to come ashore."

"And leave the plane, right?"

"That's what he told me. You can radio him and confirm it."

The solder spat into the black water. "Naw, Jones wants radio silence; fuck it. Wait one." The man disappeared into the plane a moment and reappeared carrying a machine gun. "Slide over, pop."

As the man lowered himself, he spotted the tarpaulin draped over the cargo on the floor of the boat. He'd seen too many such cargoes in his time to mistake its shape. He looked up sharply, spooked and off balance. That's when Cecil picked up the rusty trident he had brought along. As the soldier levered his machine gun up, Cecil thrust forward with the spear.

The three prongs hit the man's chest where the ammo straps crossed. The heavy webbing and brass casings took the force, preventing the barbs from penetrating very deeply. With a gasp and a look of stupid surprise, the man was jolted back against the fuselage of the plane. As Cecil tried to recover his spear, the man grabbed the crude weapon by its shaft, yanked it free, and flung it into the water. Defenseless, Cecil knew he had failed, had let down Miss Andrea and the old man. The soldier would kill him.

The man got his rifle up, trying to aim. But with his feet in the boat and his back against the plane, he found the boat suddenly sliding out from under him. He shoved away from the plane in a desperate lunge, trying to get fully into the boat. He missed and toppled backwards into the water.

Instinctively Cecil reached for him, but the weight of the weapons was too much. The shaved crown of his head gleamed underwater briefly like the descending moon of a jellyfish, before fading into the depths.

Shaken, Cecil drew the boat back to the plane. He had much to do and not much time to do it in. He reached for the hatch.

A red tongue licked out of a black mouth. . . .

He grabbed the hatch frame, hanging on, certain that he would follow the mercenary to the sea floor.

The terrifying image receded, but not the icy sensation of dread that had accompanied it. Such images had disturbed him since childhood; but before now they'd always been confined to his dreams. Were they seeping into his waking life at last? He shivered.

Willing himself not to think about any of that, to ignore the coldness settling into his bones, he drew the tarp away from the floor of the boat.

Miss Andrea looked at him. She was still lovely, and his

mind filled with tender memories of the years he had served her. Gently, as if she were sleeping and any sudden movement might waken her prematurely, he lifted her through the hatch. He climbed in, picked her up again and carried her forward past crates of weapons and ammunition, into the crew quarters. Tents, duffle bags, cookstoves and lanterns were stacked against the bulkheads. He set her down on a pile of sleeping bags. Stooped there, with moonlight falling through a tiny window and igniting Miss Andrea's hair in a silken fire, he felt a throb of desolation. While she had lived, he'd known love in his life. Now only duty remained. He bent and kissed her brow. It was cold to his lips.

Unscrewing the caps of several lanterns, he sloshed fuel around the cabin, dousing tents and duffle bags until the tanks were nearly empty and fumes hung poisonously in the air. He drizzled the last of the fuel over Andrea's body, like a blessing.

Outside he started the outboard, letting it idle in neutral while he used a match to light a strip of blanket which he'd dangled out of the hatch. Flames scurried up the cloth into the tomb.

Thorne, Rain, and Sanchez swung their heads at the sound of the explosion. Out on the water a fireball broiled up into the sky, white at its core, going to crimson. Thorne realized at once what it was. The glow was like an arc light turned upon them as they crouched among trees a hundred yards from the villa. A series of secondary explosions popped sparks into the air, but soon the intensity of the blaze began to dim. Behind them, the presence of the villa seemed to reassert itself, and the three of them turned toward it.

Moonlight lacquered the facade. Lamps still glowed in the lower windows and threw spidery lines of shadows among the trees. Thorne searched for signs to indicate that the mercenaries had arrived, but, as earlier, everything was still.

"Maybe they cut their losses and left," Rain whispered.

"They'll be coming," Sanchez said. "They won't take

prisoners.'' He thumbed the M-16's selector switch to automatic.

''What's the plan?''

Thorne decided quickly. ''I go first. I'll signal you if it's safe.''

Before they could argue, he jogged across the yard, past clumps of overgrown shrubs, slowing one last time to survey the house, then dashed across the curved driveway, his feet making a quick clatter on the broken sea shells. From beneath the porte cochère he waved to the others. In a few moments they stood beside him, catching their breath. The door was locked. Had Andrea Wexford locked it? He couldn't remember.

Sanchez knelt to examine the lock. With his back to them, they couldn't see what he did, but when he stood up he swung the door open.

After the dank enclosure of the stone house on the beach, the villa seemed totally out of place here, Rain thought—out of time. It was as if they had dreamed themselves into a gilded past. She half expected a slightly disheveled butler to come down the marble staircase to greet them. The door's closing behind her drew her back to now.

''I don't know about this,'' Sanchez said skeptically. ''If the mercs surround it, they've got us.''

Eric's face was shiny with perspiration and the remaining smudges of greasepaint. ''We'll have to hurry. It'll be best if just one of us went up. There's a billiard room through there. Why don't you both rest for a few minutes. I'll be back as fast as I can.''

Rain squeezed his hand for luck then watched him climb the stairs to the first sweeping curve where he slowed to glance back. She waved, but he was already out of view. She followed Sanchez through an archway into a side room.

There was a billiard table all right, its baize faded to a mossy green, the balls, which were the color of old teeth, cued up in the center. She tried to imagine men in baccarat shirts and cummerbunds, with cigars and brandy, but she couldn't expunge the image of Jones bending over her, or of Andrea lying dead.

Sanchez said something and she turned abruptly. "What?"

"You mind if I douse the lights? I don't want us to be any more of a target than we have to be."

"No, it's okay."

When the room was dark, he went to one of the big windows that faced front and swung open the hinged outer shutters. Air smelling of jungle and sea and decay drifted in. He drew over a chair for her, then went to extinguish the hall lights.

She sat and looked out. The throbbing in her swollen cheek had eased, and she set the cold pack aside. For the moment, with the moonlight dappling the jungle with mosaic designs, the night seemed almost peaceful.

The second floor was not as bright as the one below. Electric sconces burned with faint amber light, throwing crab-patterns on brocade-covered walls as Thorne moved along the hallway. Doorways opened into large rooms full of elaborate old furnishings. But there were no signs of life.

A thread of misgiving had begun to unspool slowly in his mind. Being here might serve no purpose. What if Andrea's widower were too old or too sick to help them? Did he even exist?

From somewhere outside came faraway shouts. Thorne heard Sanchez call his name, and he backtracked hurriedly to the stairwell. "What is it?"

"Find anything?" Sanchez hollered up.

"Not yet."

"The mercs seem to be moving this way. I'm going to kill the lights down here, okay?"

Thorne waited until he saw the foyer go dark, then resumed his search. He was moving more quickly now.

The last room off the hallway looked lived-in, and he guessed from the items on a dressing table and bed that it had been Andrea's. He tried to picture her in it—primping before the mirror, sleeping in the satin sheets—but all he got was a feeling of loneliness.

He'd reached the end of the second floor hallway. With growing doubt he began to climb the final flight of stairs.

The only light on the shadowy top floor was reflected from the sconces below, revealing walls that were an abstract of old water stains, a ceiling liver-spotted with mold. The oriental runner in the hallway was threadbare. Dust prickled in his throat. He could not imagine a wealthy man living in the house. For the first time, his misgiving turned to near certainty that he was here for nothing, that the villa was a white elephant, empty, that he'd wasted precious minutes.

That's when he heard the voices.

A muted conversation was being carried on beyond a door at the dark end of the hall. He swallowed. He tried to make out words but was too far away. With a sense of inevitability, he moved toward the door.

Hardwood, with a lidded slot halfway down and below that a shelf, the door baffled him for the moment it took him to realize it was like something formerly found in an asylum or a prison for passing through meals and notes. Pausing only a second to let this sink in, he knocked.

The door had neither knob nor keyplate, so he laid a palm on the wood and pushed. The door didn't budge. He put his ear to the panel.

He was startled by the voice of Jay Leno.

"Guy walks into a bar on Sunset," Leno said. "He's wearing this T-shirt that on the front says . . ."

The *Tonight* show. Thorne stepped back, then lunged.

He drove his shoulder against the point where the lock edge met the frame. The door shuddered but held. Leno's punchline drew laughs. With the third blow a sabre of wood ripped from the frame and the resistance was gone. Thorne opened the door.

The air that hit his nostrils had the odorous warmth of an animal's den, and yet there was more to it, which he couldn't identify. The darkness whirled with the kaleidoscoping images of a TV screen and the slices of moonlight through the slats of barred blinds—just enough light to throw grotesque shapes onto the room's curved walls and crowd shadows into corners. In contrast with the scale of the rest of the villa, the size of the room amazed him. It was scarcely more than a closet rounded in the shape of the turret it was part of. Most of the floorspace was taken up by a steamer trunk, and a bed pushed catty-corner against the innermost curve of wall.

In the deepest shadows, something with a faint, scaly shine was moving on the bed, and he had an impression of two snakes sliding away through dead leaves. A rash of gooseflesh had spread across his shoulders and down his arms.

With apprehension he realized they were legs—skin on bones—which had drawn up. Now feet patted dryly on the floor. Instinctively he took a step backward. At the wide-eyed limit of his vision he saw a low silhouette rear up against a shuttered window.

His heart was banging. He was straining to make out human features in the TV light, but they wouldn't coalesce into a face. Torn between stepping forward and fleeing, he stood rooted in the threshold when a hand fell on his shoulder.

He whirled with a gasp.

Childers. A reek of kerosene was coming off him. His hair and clothes were singed, but his face was the same impassive mask as before.

"What did you want, sir?" the servant asked.

Like the hand on Thorne's shoulder, the voice was quiet yet insistent, just audible over Ed McMahon's guffaws. Thorne gestured toward the indistinct form crouching on the bed. "Is that—? Can he *help* us?"

Childers shook his head. "He's beyond helping."

"Andrea said there were documents . . . ," Thorne began.

The hand and eyes held him a moment more, then Childers nodded at the steamer trunk inside the room. Glancing once more toward the bed, Thorne stepped to the trunk and lifted the top.

The trunk was stuffed with paper—handwritten notes, clippings from newspapers, yellowed file folders. Suddenly, being here seemed utterly pointless. It would take weeks or longer, to go through the haphazard collection to find whatever secrets, if any, the recluse had squirreled away. Thorne turned to Childers. "We were hoping . . ."

He let the words die. Hoping for what? Help? Shelter?

All at once, over even the woozy stench of kerosene, he identified the smell in the turret room: The mingled odors of medicine, unwashed bedclothes and sickness. The old man was in the process of dying. He was certain of it. Childers and Andrea probably had been keeping him alive in hopes of holding Jones at bay.

Outside there were gunshots quite close by, followed by muted shouts. Abruptly Childers said, "Use my boat. Miss Lorraine will remember where it is. You'd best get away from here now."

Thorne stared into the turret room, making a futile last attempt to see the man. He turned back. "Come with us. Bring him."

"He'd never survive leaving here, sir. This is his refuge. We'll be all right. Go now, while you can. Already it may be too late."

Childers's voice was sepulchral, and Thorne had the impression that the Bahamian was barely seeing him, involved instead in some potent, inevitable drama of his own.

Gunfire from downstairs broke the spell.

Rain looked up as Thorne rushed into the darkened billiard room. The half of her face that he saw was moonlit, expectant. Sanchez was crouched at an open window, cradling the M-16. "The mercs are arriving," he said. "I've spotted several."

Thorne knelt beside Rain's chair. "There's a boat. Do you remember where you landed?"

Her expression clouded.

"When you arrived with Andrea," he pressed. "Childers said you'd know where he left a boat."

"Before we landed . . . I remember seeing a pier. That would've been . . ." She frowned in concentration but finally shook her head. "I'm disoriented."

The *ether,* he thought. She'd been blacked out. "Was it on the high end or the low end of the island?" he coaxed patiently. "Can you remember that?"

She thought hard about it for a moment before shaking her head in frustration. "I'm sorry."

"There's no pier on the other end that I know of," Sanchez said. "Must be near here."

Suddenly the outer wall of the room shuddered under a barrage of weapons fire. A window next to the one where Sanchez crouched dissolved in a hail of glass and shattered wood that clattered across the parquet floor. Thorne quickly got Rain behind the billiard table, then drew the Colt. Ice-skating on broken glass, he moved to the big windows. Sanchez poked the M-16 through an empty sash and fired a burst. Thorne squeezed off a couple of rounds at shadowy figures flitting in the jungle beyond the cleared land. He didn't think he hit anyone. "Have they surrounded the house?"

"Don't think so, not yet. But they will." Sanchez glanced over. "What's the plan?"

Fueled with adrenaline, his mind was regrouping. "Can you nail them down for a while?"

"Got the hammer right here." Sanchez fired another burst.

"There's a back entry. Give us a couple minutes. Hit them *uno mas* and then *vamanos.* All right?"

This time Sanchez didn't turn from the window. "You planning to stand there all night speaking lousy Spanish?"

24

Moonlight brushed the rear grounds of the villa with interlacing shadows, giving the night a deceptive tranquility, Thorne thought. No sooner had he done so, however, than there was gunfire and more glass exploded in the house. As Sanchez answered with gunfire of his own, Eric took Rain's hand and they ran across a terrace to a cabana, where they pressed into darkness against its stuccoed wall. Ten feet away lay the swimming pool. As if attuned to some vibration in the coral foundation of the cay itself tonight, the smooth surface of water rocked gently, fractionating the moonlight.

All of the lights were out in the house, and for a moment Thorne wondered if the power had been cut. Then he heard the television still playing in the high, turret room and made out the furtive glow. It would almost certainly draw fire if it weren't shut off. But that was no longer his concern. He held the Colt ready to cover Sanchez.

Childers set the old man up in bed. The skin on the frail body was papery and damp, the muscles underneath it flaccid from years of self-imposed inaction. Leaving the TV picture on, Cecil turned the volume down. He spoke soft words to reassure the old man, though whether they were understood he had no idea.

His plan was to get him down into the cellar, where there was a hidden tunnel to the cave. There the Zodiac and enough food and water for two waited. First he needed to find some clothing and a blanket to protect the old man from the elements as they made their way to another cay that Cecil knew. He peered around.

This had once been Cecil's room, ages ago when he was a child and his family lived in quarters up here and served the villa's original owner. Then had come the night when a rival gang of rum runners invaded the cay. Cecil's father, convinced that security would be with the currency these men traded in—the liquor itself—had ordered his wife and children into the cave. But his father had been wrong. He and the owner were murdered on the beach. Cecil had just gone out to them when fire erupted in the cave. The alcohol burned wildly. As the boy struggled back toward the screams of his mother and sisters, there was a thunderous explosion, and he was hurled into the sea.

He alone survived. Raised as an orphan in a Freeport slum, haunted by dreams of that fiery night, he eventually returned. But as if the cold sea had gotten into his bones that long-ago night, he had never felt truly safe or warm again. He built the stone house on the beach and lived there, fishing, eating jungle fruits. Twenty years ago, when the old man bought the cay and the villa, Cecil had offered his services. It was not long thereafter that Miss Andrea came.

Like a man gentling a spirited horse into a stall, Cecil eased thoughts of her back into his memory. He opened the wooden blinds on one of the turret room's windows. In the flood of moonlight he found a blanket, which he swaddled around the old man, then stooped to pick him up. All that money, and the man was as light as a basket of bamboo sticks. As Cecil turned, the window blew apart.

He was flung back across the bed. He lay dazed for an indeterminate time. Seconds? Minutes? Over a ringing in his ears, sounds of distant gunfire and shouts wove in and out of his consciousness, like jumbled segments of a dream. Then he grew aware of another sensation, that of something wet spreading across his chest. Forcing himself to a sitting position, he saw a jagged glint of moonlight on the shard of glass lodged deep in the old man's throat.

Thorne felt Rain's hand tighten on his. Turning, he saw a man with a Zapata moustache step out from the opposite end of the cabana. He carried an assault rifle in one hand, a walkie-talkie in the other. Apparently he hadn't seen them yet, but he'd have to pass them to reach the villa.

". . . still taking fire from the front," came a voice over the walkie-talkie. "I can't reach Jones."

The mercenary put his unit to his mouth. "Forget Jones. Let's move on the house *now*. No prisoners. That's an order."

To Thorne's right, Rain began edging noiselessly away along the wall. She reached the corner and disappeared. Thorne had just started to follow when the mercenary turned. The rifle whipped up fast.

"Hold it!"

Thorne froze. Standing in moonlight, the man squinted into the shadows, his eyes alight with a cold savagery. "Out here where I can *see* you!" he growled.

Thorne gripped the Colt alongside his thigh. He had no idea whether the man knew he had it. Carefully edging away from the wall, he brought his free hand up into the light to show it was empty.

"Got me one," the man mouthed into the walkie-talkie.

There was no way Thorne would be able to conceal the Colt. He should surrender, give Rain a chance to get to Sanchez—

"Turd brain," the mercenary said brutally, stepping nearer. "You screwed up my war. You're *dead!*"

In that instant Rain lunged from the other corner, crashing against the man's shoulder. Upended, the rifle spat a useless burst. The radio unit flung loose and skidded across the tiles. Thorne took a short run and swung a foot into his crotch. The man yelped. The impact of the kick spun him backwards into the pool.

He resurfaced immediately, bellowing, still gripping the

rifle. In that instant, Thorne had the impression of silver rain lashing across the surface of the pool. The man's voice died in a gurgle of bubbles as he slid back under the darkening water.

Sanchez. Thorne covered him as he ran to join them. Sanchez yanked an empty clip out of his M-16 and flung it aside, ripped loose the last spare taped to the stock and locked it home with a gritty snap.

"Neeley," spoke an incorporeal voice from the walkie-talkie. "What's your location? Come back."

Thorne kicked the unit into the pool.

In death the old man was cold, scarcely heavier than a bag of palm husks, thought Childers as he laid the body on the bed. Solemnly he crossed the stick-like hands on the chest and said a brief prayer. He pulled off his own blood-speckled shirt, tore it into strips, several of which he brought into other rooms on the upper floors and set afire. He waited just long enough to be sure the flames took. Almost done.

Carrying one more strip of cloth, he descended to the ballroom on the ground floor. He lighted the strip. Still pungent with kerosene, it took flame quickly and he held it up, peering into the surrounding darkness where he could make out the glint of crystal and antique brass, the mouldering shapes of furniture. He had a flickering memory from his boyhood of watching through a window one night as gloriously-dressed people danced in here. He chose a slender wooden chair and sat down. As the flames nipped his fingers, he dropped the cloth.

The house shuddered with a blast of gunfire, making the crystal pendants of the chandeliers tinkle. Cecil thought of wind chimes. He shut his eyes. No lurid red visions stole forth to trouble him. Instead he was aware only of the dance of light through his closed eyelids, like a soft violet, mist. And then warmth.

They had reached the encircling jungle when the villa began to burn. Fire seemed to break out in many places at once, sprouting brightly from the house like the crests of rain forest birds.

"Those idiots torched it," Sanchez said. But Thorne was pretty sure that wasn't what had happened.

They resumed their march, moving through the jungle toward the beach. Sanchez set the pace, wielding the butt of the M-16 like a machete to clear the trail. No one needed to tell them to hurry.

Soon the foliage thinned and they found themselves on a low ridge where they could look back to see the villa burning. Ahead the trail dipped into a final shadowy thicket between them, the beach, and, Thorne hoped, the boat.

"Let me just check it out," Sanchez said. He loped forward alone.

Rain looked up at Thorne, her face lit and shadowed by the wildly mounting flames far behind them. "Thank you for coming to get me."

He smiled tiredly. "Thank you for saving my neck back there. And for being here." He put his arms around her and kissed her forehead.

"Save it for later, you two," Sanchez called. "We're home free! I can see the end of the pier."

On the moonlit ridge, some thirty yards ahead of them, Sanchez pumped a celebratory fist. As he did so, Thorne had the impression that invisible hands seized Sanchez and gave him a rough shake. He gazed back at them, his face full of surprise.

Thorne turned now too drawn perhaps by a peripheral muzzle-flash, though it could have been a spark from the burning house. Was that a man-shape in that tree, backlit by a curtain of orange smoke? Sniper? He squeezed the Colt's trigger.

It was hard to know if he hit anything. The shape in the tree remained, though smoke was rolling thickly through the foliage. He tugged Rain down the slope into dense shadows. The shape, obscurer now, didn't move, making him wonder if it were a person at all. "Stay," he ordered Rain and scurried forward.

Sanchez lay curled on his side, a spreading star adding a dark new pattern to the jigsaw of his camouflage shirt.

Thorne pushed down a rush of panic. His hands were damp and his chest felt light, but mostly he was conscious of the painful throb in his lower back, in the adrenals, where the core of the fear response lay. "Oscar," he said, aware that it was the first time he had used the name, "I've got you."

Sanchez groaned.

Thorne pried his knees away from his chest, trying to be gentle, but even so, Sanchez's face clenched in pain. Two holes below the collarbone, to the left of the throat, made a soft slurping sound, like the last water down a drain. Around the holes bubbled a bright froth of arterial blood. Thorne swallowed. "Chest wounds. Have to get pressure on, get the bleeding stopped," he said in a rapid voice, as much to himself as to Sanchez. He dried his palm, pressed it flat on the holes and felt their kiss, sucking at life.

Rain came alongside. He wanted to scream at her for leaving cover.

"How bad?" she whispered. She put a hand on Sanchez's forehead. Below it, his eyes were preternaturally bright.

"We must be close to the boat," Thorne said. "Maybe there's a first aid kit."

"I'll go."

"We've got to move fast. Can you start an outboard motor?"

"I never have."

"I'll do that. Just get the lines untied. Find a first aid kit. If there are any cushions or life vests, lay them in the bottom. Wait for us. I'm going to tie something over the wounds before I bring him down."

"I'm on my way."

Thorne caught her arm with his free hand. "Take that."

She looked at the revolver holstered on Sanchez's belt, but she shook her head. She was trembling, he saw. For a moment the three of them formed a small tableau, their faces—his and Sanchez's mottled with greasepaint and sweat,

Rain's bruised—like tragic theatrical masks. Then she was gone, darting down the shadowed slope of jungle.

A hand gripped Thorne's wrist. "Go with her, man."

Sanchez's eyes were on him, and Thorne fought off the idea that they weren't as bright as before. "Did you hear the plan?" he asked quickly.

"Scrap it. Go."

"Like you did when you had the chance?"

"*Voy a morir*," Sanchez breathed.

"Shut up and rest a minute."

The suction from the wounds was weakening. The fingers on Thorne's wrist felt cooler. Repositioning his hand, trying for a tighter seal, he saw a foam of new blood at the heel of his palm. He pressed harder. But all at once he realized that not his hand, not their combined strength, nor hope nor good deeds was going to be enough to keep the life from seeping out. The light was fading from Sanchez's eyes.

No! The word beat in Thorne's brain like an auxiliary pulse: twice, three times, then it too began to die. From the direction of the villa there was a muted burst, like a TV tube imploding, and reflexively he looked to see a wraith of sparks swirl up over the jungle into the night where they faded like stars before the coming of day.

The hand on his wrist let go.

The boat. Down a slope of beach Rain saw it tied at the end of a narrow pier. The same boat she had come in. Only had to get to it, find a first aid kit, undo the ropes . . .

The sandal on her right foot caught, and a stone went ticking down the slope. From nearby, something that did not belong in the woods barked fearsomely. A blinding pain hit her, and she pitched sideways into black.

". . . place is an inferno! I think they've escaped. Where the hell's Neeley? *Where's Jones?*"

The mode switch on the walkie-talkie had snapped off in the "standby" mode. Jones could only monitor; he couldn't send. He flung the useless damn thing aside and nearly screamed with the motion.

The clouds of mosquitoes chewing his face were nothing compared to the agony gnawing the bottom half of his body with a mouth full of razor-sharp teeth. He lay sprawled on the upper slope of beach, a hundred feet from the ocean and the boat. A hundred feet, but it might as well have been miles.

He lowered his head between his spread arms, breathed through clenched teeth. Seemed like days ago he'd been hit, after killing the movie star. Thorne had put a round into his hip. That's when he'd dropped the radio. He was making it, though. Humped all this way. Just a little farther. First though, rest. . . .

He jerked his head up. Had to pay attention, or he wasn't going to get out of this.

He could just make out the form of the woman lying face-down off the trail fifty feet away. He watched her, hoping she didn't get up, praying he wouldn't have to hoist the ten thousand pounds of rifle to shoot again.

Bitch had spooked him, appearing like that. Somehow she'd escaped his men. She'd been going for the boat. He watched another minute. She didn't move. Good. She was dead.

Bracing for the torment of motion, he looked toward the sea. Moonlight sparkled on its surface, and he tried to draw calm into his mind. It didn't help. His eyes, swollen from insect bites, burned with sweat. Not much farther, he told himself.

The op was blown all to hell, weapons gone, his worthless fucking troops scattered. He scarcely cared. Still had the leash on Murphy. That was what mattered.

Right now though, there was this agony like tracer fire shooting up his legs.

He touched the rifle, slid his hand onto the grip, finger into the guard. At the back of his throat, bile rose in a brackish churn, and he tipped his head aside to retch. The effort made him whimper. Bracing himself, he heaved his weapon ahead a few feet. He crawled after it.

★   ★   ★

Thorne stepped from the undergrowth and saw the boat. It rode on moonbeams, still tethered at the end of the pier. But Rain was nowhere to be seen. Instantly wary, he started down the slope clutching Sanchez's M-16. A voice howled at him to stop.

It took a moment to make out the partial figure of someone leaning on a boulder near the water's edge. Moonlight glinted dully on the barrel of a big rifle. One of the mercs.

"Where is she?" cried Thorne.

The man levered himself into a straighter position, adjusting the aim of his rifle. With a jolt, Thorne recognized Jones.

"Rid of the gun," Jones said.

Thorne realized he was using the rock to prop himself up. He looked in bad shape, his face slick with sweat, shirt in tatters. "Where *is* she, Jones?"

"You want to see her again, do what I *say.*"

Rain was alive!

"Drop it," the man commanded.

Thorne flipped the M-16's selector switch to safety, gripped the weapon muzzle and butt for Jones to see, and threw it. The rifle clattered on the rocks, losing half its plastic stock before coming to rest.

"Step nearer."

Thorne obeyed. Jones's face and neck were knotted like mangrove roots as he fought off pain. "Now . . . bring the boat."

"Where is she?" Thorne asked again, battling an undertow of dread that wanted to sweep him away.

"Do it!"

He moved down to the pier and stepped onto it, tracked by the rifle in Jones's hands. The craft was wooden hulled, old but well kept. In the moonlight the varnished brightwork gleamed. The motor was tipped up out of the water. Thorne bent and freed the stern line first and looped it into the boat. He did the same with the bow line, holding the gunwale steady with his foot.

"Bring it here."

From where he stood, Thorne could see partly behind the

boulder where Jones was propped but not completely. Was Rain there?

"Let me see her," he said.

"The boat," Jones croaked.

"Just answer that one thing."

"I have her."

Fear had rekindled Thorne's sense of time running away, like breath, the tide. . . . He needed to seize a little of it. Could Jones get to the boat without him? Thorne had no idea. "Why'd you kill those two people on the Vineyard?"

Jones exhaled noisily. "Shut up."

"What's Murphy's connection to arms dealing?"

"Nothing. Shut up."

Thorne waited.

"He was the old man's private project. Till I found out too. Murphy's screwy . . . double personality. The old man figured it out years ago. He'd hired a dick to shadow the guy. Wexford must've finally put it together and gone to warn him. I trailed her and watched them meet. Now, come on!"

"The Ames woman spotted Murphy just by chance and took a photo, so you had to get it back or risk losing everything. You blew up your other plane too, because I got nosey, right?"

"No proof of any of that."

"Like a partial fingerprint left at the Captain James Inn? I couldn't figure why that never got a match, but Kirk could've wiped you out of the Bureau files. Could've even shelved the Florida police request for analysis on bomb fragments. Kirk was a handy ally. But expendable."

Jones's breath dragged in and out with a sound like heavy paper being crumpled. "The boat."

Sweat was stinging Thorne's eyes. He had the answer he'd originally set out to find. He had located the killer. And all at once he was struck by what a precarious and meager triumph the moment afforded him. There was only one thing he wanted, needed so desperately that even his fear had shriveled to a tight and stoney focus. "Where's Lorraine?"

"Now, by Christ! Or you're gonna be as dead as *she* is!"

Until that instant Thorne realized he had been delaying so as to cling to a thread of hope; now it snapped. His heart convulsed in rage. He lunged, dropping into the boat hard on his right shoulder. A deafening blast of gunfire punched through the hull, splintering wood, paralyzing him.

"I *wasted* her," Jones yelled. "She's lying off the trail."

The gun roared again, and a geyser of seawater splashed over Thorne's back. The paralysis was terror; and now it left him. He felt void of any human motivation except survival. He began to inch toward the small deck at the bow, his shoulder numb with a gritty sensation inside it, like Velcro fasteners being ripped apart.

There was another blast, and the runabout's windshield was torn away.

Going by touch, keeping his head down, Thorne located a drawer in the dash panel. He clawed at it and it fell, spilling fishhooks, sinkers, maps. His hand closed on a short steel cylinder. A flare pistol. Useless. Even if he could've stood up to fire it, it would do nothing at this range.

"That's your *coffin,* Thorne!"

Maybe it was the ultimate ring of that phrase—or that he no longer could hope Rain still lived; in despair he pushed up against the broken-glass sensation in his shoulder, the stone in his heart, and plunged over the side of the boat.

The Caribbean closed black and blood-warm over him. With no plan in mind beyond escape, he kicked and stroked down with his good arm, under the boat, beneath the pier. He groped until he felt a piling, prickly with marine life, and drew himself shoreward to the next. He did this twice more, but the water didn't grow any shallower. His eyes had begun to adjust to the pale light filtering down, and he could see that the coast here was ledge. The water was too deep for him to stand and try to run up the beach. If he swam to shore and pulled himself onto the ledge, Jones would shoot him. Too late he realized he should have swum in the other direction. Way too late.

Even as he rebelled at the idea, already the dance of moonlight on the stones far below was becoming a flickering in his brain as oxygen dwindled, and he knew he had staked everything on a last chance and lost. Jones would be waiting to kill him and that would be what all this had come to—crabs picking his bones clean. Thoughts of Rain ticked through his mind, and of Dow and Sanchez and Andrea Wexford, all the dead, and there was a kind of freedom in knowing there was no longer any hope of winning, so that even losing ceased to matter, and thus from the depth of exhaustion he kicked once more, fighting back under the pier to the last piling, lungs burning, mind almost all gray now as he reached the ledge and broke surface.

Both had guessed wrong. Thorne came up gasping, only feet from where his enemy was bracing on his rock, facing too far to his left. Startled, Jones began to swing the heavy rifle around. It was then, with his shoulder out of the water, that Thorne grew aware of the weight at the end of his dead arm. The flare pistol.

He tried to lift it, but his body balked at the sear of pain, nearly making him pass out.

"*Your* turn!" Jones cried and steadied his rifle.

Thorne seized his own forearm with his good hand—damn the agony!—and hoisted it and the pistol, its muzzle as big as the sudden gape of Jones's mouth . . . and squeezed the trigger.

Nothing happened.

With a shriek of victory, Jones fired.

Thorne was lunging sideways away from the muzzle-flash and roar of the rifle when the magnesium cap burned. The flare exploded from the gun in his hand.

Jones's face burst into flames.

Thorne dragged himself out of the water. He started to stumble up the rock-strewn beach. The only thought in his mind was Rain. He had to know.

25

The homely, noble face of the nation's sixteenth president appeared tired, although it could have been projection, Thorne considered. He certainly felt that way himself. What Lincoln clearly did not have was the shakes. He sat in marble effigy inside the massive memorial where an afternoon group of Asian visitors gazed up to read snatches of the Gettysburg Address and the Second Inaugural, trigger their cameras, and shuffle off. The attraction today was Senator Murphy's speech, scheduled to begin in half an hour at the far end of the reflecting pool, near the Washington Monument. From a stage that had been erected there, a public address system sent inspirational strains of music across the intervening sunlit distance.

Thorne turned his attention to a pair of dark-suited men climbing the monument steps, the one in front young, large, with red hair and sunglasses; the other middle-aged, wire-haired, short, clearly the one with authority.

"Mr. Thorne?" Like his footfalls, the short man's words had a flat echo in the stone portico.

Thorne nodded.

Russo had the twitchy watchfulness of a plump squirrel on open ground, but there was nothing timid about the man. In his crisply tailored suit and red tie, he conveyed tough assurance. His glance took in Thorne's rumpled chinos and sport coat, the sling on his arm. For a moment Thorne sensed that he was found wanting, that Russo would change his mind. But the man's presence belied that.

"I mentioned on the telephone there'd have to be a security check," Russo said matter-of-factly.

Thorne submitted to a deft frisk by the red-haired escort. When the man nodded his satisfaction and had backed off a discreet distance, Russo said, "I did call Lorraine at the Nassau hospital number you gave me. The doctor permitted me all of thirty seconds. She okay?" The concern was brisk but genuine.

"They'll hold her another few days. She's groggy but she's mending."

"Those damn mopeds ought to be outlawed." The story Thorne and Rain had agreed upon was a vacation mishap. In truth, a round from Jones's rifle had grazed her scalp, resulting in a fall and a concussion. He had gotten her back to Nassau in the badly damaged boat and had stayed with her until he was sure she was out of danger, then he had flown to Washington.

"Anyway, here we are," Russo said. "You get the nickel tour—five minutes. After that your best bet will be in writing, care of sixteen hundred Pennsylvania Avenue."

"You're confident."

"Why shouldn't I be? Hell, we even made *Rolling Stone*."

Doubtless Murphy's appearance on the cover, along with Rain's interview inside, had contributed to Russo's magnanimity in consenting to meet with him. Thorne had known time would be limited, so he'd planned his approach carefully. In spite of that, as he cleared his throat now to speak, he found that the words had fled. The skein of recent events was coiled so complicatedly in his mind that he could find no string with which to start unravelling it. Growing impatient, Russo glanced sidelong toward the red-haired guard, then back. "Well?"

Thorne swallowed. "Murphy is a fraud."

For a few seconds Russo regarded him with an opaque stare. "You better explain that, mister, and explain it well."

"I'm convinced the photographs claiming to show Murphy in a POW camp are fake, staged much later."

"*What?*"

"To cover the fact that he was a deserter in Vietnam."

"That's crazy. Who are you working for?"

"Murphy was in California two years before he claims to have escaped. He lived there under the name Charles Evans."

Was the name familiar? Russo's brow lowered, deepening the seams of his face. For a breath his gaze appeared to turn inward. "That's crazy," he said again, though with diminished force.

Thorne took him from the killings on the Vineyard to the plot by the CIA man, Clement Jones. When he finished, he had far exceeded five minutes, but Russo didn't seem to notice or care.

"You asked me before if I was working for anyone." Thorne shook his head. "I'm not."

Russo remained silent for a half-minute more, then said, "What you've told me is regrettable, tragic. I'm sorry people have been hurt. But look at the situation . . . pragmatically. I mean, what's any of that got to do with the senator? Is there anything saying he knew about the killings or the gun-running?"

"I think that was strictly Jones," Thorne admitted. "My guess is he'd uncovered Murphy's past. It would have been worth his while to keep that quiet too, for obvious reasons if the senator reached the White House. Through Hiram Kirk, it's likely someone engineered at least part of Murphy's rise. That could've been Andrea Wexford's husband."

"Why? I mean . . . *why?* You haven't offered a single reason for Tim to have been party to any of this."

"Maybe it just . . . happened."

"Shit. The big bang theory."

The man was right; where was the hard evidence? Still, Thorne had to try to convince him. "Desertion from an infantry unit that's seen almost continuous combat isn't far-fetched. It would've been possible to build a whole new identity, backfilling as needed." He considered something Jones had said too. "It could also be that Murphy had, *has,* a serious personality disorder. What do you know about his early childhood, for instance? Lorraine told me he resisted talking about it."

"Is that your diagnosis, doctor?" Russo said sardonically, but he no longer appeared to be invested in his counterattack. His energy had sagged. He looked like a man whose last illusions had finally foresaken him. "This is all your story, and a lot of wild-ass suppositions," he pointed out listlessly. "You have the photos?"

Thorne didn't. He had nothing. All graphic proof had been destroyed. Andrea Wexford was dead. Kirk, Jones. Murphy could walk free and rally his supporters. "No," he said.

Russo studied him a moment. "You're a dumb son of a bitch, you know that? I could have you arrested as a crank, a potential menace to the senator."

It was true. Furthermore, when it was revealed that Thorne was being sought for Jimmy Dow's death, had been present at the killing of Kirk but hadn't reported it, there would be trouble that could take months to sort out, by which time Murphy might already be nominated.

Russo fingered his lips and chin, as if stroking an invisible beard. When they came, his words had a faraway sound. "Do you know where the campaign logo came from? I selected it myself. When Tim was a teenager, he kept a falcon *and* doves. I've always loved that. Seventeen years ago, after he came home a hero, he worked hard, went to law school and has served the public unselfishly ever since. That damn fool gunrunning plot doesn't affect us. Hell, if that got out, it could well sink the Hawes administration. But that's not what this campaign is about. We want what's best for America."

Thorne said nothing.

"This could just . . ." Russo made a gesture like he was releasing a bird, "go away."

Far down the park, the band music had ceased. The crowd by the speaking platform had swelled. Russo began to rock from his heels to the balls of his feet, as if new energy were fueling him. "Does any of it amount to much? I mean, isn't what matters the good the man has done? Can *do?*"

Still Thorne did not speak.

Russo glanced at the huge seated figure to his right. "Do people remember that Lincoln was a waffler on emancipation? That JFK played dicksie with movie stars? Or that the Reagan administration had the moral leadership of a street gang?"

The questions were rhetorical; he kept talking. "There's a point when myths become more vital than reality. They give people the power to dream. Good God, that's what America needs right now. We've run out of dreams."

Thorne sought words to counter with, but the campaign manager was looking at a watch as slim as a nickel. "He's about to go on. Come on. We'll have to hurry."

Russo was late and had to sit two rows back from his accustomed spot on the platform. He patted his pockets for a roll of Tums. He felt like hell. There was a real possibility that Thorne was a crank—or worse. What the guy had been saying sounded just plain nuts. Nor could one discount the possibility of dirty tricks. After the revelations of those Rendle aides, with their scheme to use Hank Frizzel, anything was possible. And yet, there had been a Corporal Charles Evans in Murphy's infantry company who hadn't immediately been identified as killed. And what about Tim's sudden interest in Andrea Wexford's movies? And that unexplained phone listing for Nassau?

No. He shut off the pernicious spin of doubts.

Tim was at the podium, beginning his remarks. Willingly, Russo let his attention be drawn there.

Today's event promised to be as shrewd a tactical strike as Shea Stadium had been. With enough delegates already committed to assure a first-ballot nomination at the convention in a few weeks, Murphy was going to call for a cease-fire on in-party fighting and urge a unified offensive against the opposition. The war chest was brimming again, and yesterday morning's surprise announcement from the White House had effectively rendered Vice President Rendle *hors de combat* by putting him temporarily in the Oval Office, out of active campaigning. Even so, Russo intended to see that the press didn't let up on the Frizzel affair.

To assure that Thorne didn't interfere right now, Russo had ordered an aide to keep tabs on him at the back of the stage. If Thorne were part of a plot to derail the campaign—even if only one of his allegations were true—it could shatter Tim's composure. Russo had seen how overtaxed he was lately. One good crack . . .

He squirmed in his chair. People seated around him on the platform were engrossed in the speech, he saw, their faces rapt. He tried to concentrate on Tim's words. But other words kept invading.

Thorne had sounded convincing. And Lorraine Patton had vouched for him. Could she be part of a plot too? It didn't make sense. Her book had played such an important role in spreading Tim's name.

He found himself thinking about an incident that had occurred a year ago, at the farm in Indiana. On the evening before Tim would officially launch his candidacy, Ray and he had taken time to stroll around the property. Russo had asked to see the small family graveyard where Tim's parents and forebears were buried. Murphy had snapped: "Let them lie! This is *my* time." Neither of them had said another word about it, and Russo hadn't remembered the incident until today. Now he wondered. Were there things in Tim's past that he didn't want to explore?

He felt perverse, like an old man harboring dirty thoughts. Sweat oozed from his brow in the afternoon heat. His stomach burned. What should he do?

He listened to the candidate's words, trying to focus his mind on November, when Tim would be elected President.

After a minute, he uncapped his fountain pen. Controlling his hand, which wanted to shake, he wrote on a notecard and folded it. With a gesture he summoned the red-haired

Secret Service man. "Get this to the Senator," he whispered.

"Are you sure you want to watch this?" Pru Winters asked.

Peter Hawes sat in pajamas and bathrobe in front of the TV set in her living room. Spindly and exhausted, he had been given a few days' reprieve from the chemotherapy and radiation treatments. "I'm sure," he said.

On screen Tim Murphy was speaking to a crowd gathered by the Washington Monument. Behind him hung a gigantic black and white blow-up of himself holding his arm aloft with a falcon perched on his wrist. Beyond that the flags ringing the monument flapped in a breeze. What theater, Hawes thought.

"Peter, I'm sorry about our fight this morning."

He looked at Prudence and smiled weakly. He had asked her to marry him, and she had argued that it made no sense, that it would only further complicate his party's fortunes. "I'm sorry too," he said.

"I know you will do what you believe you must. And I hope you know that I'm with you, regardless of what happens. I love you."

He touched her hand. "I do know. That means everything to me."

Together they watched Murphy talking about the future. In the forty years of his own public career, Hawes had said and heard all the words. America, family, work, sacrifice, peace. Most of the time they were as empty as prayers to extinct gods. The cold truth was that politicians no longer used words because they believed in them; they chose them because consultants who earned more than they did advised them that that was what an audience wanted to hear. Thus, politicians had lost any hope of leading the people; they could only follow. They picked their spot on the wave of public opinion and rode for dear life. Murphy was using the words now.

So why were the ideas so gripping today? Hawes wondered. Oddly disturbed for reasons he could not name, he held Prudence's hand more tightly and listened.

Timothy Murphy had never imagined it would be this easy. The audience was his. He felt the power.

Like a falcon circling in, he sensed that the moment to strike had come. The nomination, the presidency . . . , the whole country was his for the taking. He was the man America needed.

At the corner of his eye he noticed a member of the protection detail holding a folded notecard. It would be from Ray; that was how they worked it. Something to add or to watch out for, or a change of emphasis. He took the card, still speaking as his fingers plucked it open on the podium. When he reached a natural pause between breaths, he dropped his gaze.

He blinked. What was this?

Obviously there was an error. This wasn't for him. He craned a glance over his left shoulder, looking for his campaign manager, but Ray wasn't where he usually sat.

He looked at the notecard again. Something fluttered in his mind. Ray had written a single sentence:

"Charles, Andrea is Dead."

Thorne felt a leaden despair. Two much effort with too little sleep had depleted him. His body clocks were out of synch. Worse though, he had failed. Russo hadn't believed him and, in fact, had brought him here as a cruel taunt. From where he stood at the back of the stage, Thorne could see the campaign manager sitting up there in his chair, listening to Murphy. The bastard wasn't going to do a thing.

Affixed to the upper rear stanchions of the platform superstructure, flanking a huge portrait of the candidate, was a row of speaker horns, out of which Murphy's words were issuing crisply. In his torpor, Thorne gazed up at the portrait . . . and began to listen.

This close, the portrait could be seen to be composed of seemingly random black pixels and white space. From even a short distance, however, the abstract patches recomposed themselves into recognizable form. He was taken back to the day—it seemed so long ago—when he'd watched the event in Shea Stadium on his little TV. He remembered the cards held by that crowd, each holder blind to, yet essential to, the whole. Murphy's words had that power as they flooded out of the speakers in individual wavelets of sound, recombining when they rolled across the sea of listeners, sweeping doubt and confusion before them, leaving calm, so that Thorne found himself wondering if he'd been wrong, if his riprap of suspicions was so flimsy that it must certainly be dismantled by the currents of Murphy's power. Maybe Timothy Murphy was the best man for America after all.

The candidate paused. As the hush stretched on, Thorne broke free of his musings and glanced toward the podium. Murphy seemed to be looking down at something in his hands.

Elsewhere on the stage people began to stir, puzzled by the delay.

"Dead?" Murphy said all at once, the word crackling through the PA system.

"Dead?" came the echo.

Thorne tried to edge past some of the people near him in hopes of getting a better view, but the backstage area was too crowded.

Then "No, no, no" rang across the mall in a strangled voice that wasn't Murphy's own.

With rapid swings of his head, Murphy looked left then right several times. "I *know* you. You wanted me dead, so I wouldn't bother you. *You* did it!" he cried, words overlapping echoes. "Just like you killed me, Murphy."

What was going on? Thorne wondered. All around, people were moving, shifting position to try to get clearer lines of vision. Thorne spotted Russo, who was sidestepping toward an aisle, frantically sawing a hand across his throat as he attempted to get someone to turn off the microphones. The red-haired security man was wedging through knots of people toward the podium.

"You left me to die there in that reeking jungle!" Murphy shouted. "Then when you saw your destiny, you killed me again. Now you want to bury me for good!"

"*—for good!*" came the echo.

The red-haired agent reached for the microphone. Startled to discover him there, Murphy cried out and grabbed him.

Thorne was able to see little else of what was happening, until the gun went off.

At the sound, people began dropping, chairs collapsing. At last, over the tumult, Thorne had an unobstructed view.

The bullet's impact knocked the agent into the laps of spectators in the front row. Screams erupted, amplified so that the entire area reverberated with alarm.

From everywhere on stage, it seemed, weapons materialized as government agents and plainclothes policemen reacted. Murphy spun, holding the fallen agent's automatic, and for a weird instant Thorne had the idea that the candidate had identified *him* as the cause of what was occurring, singled *him* out for execution. But there was no recognition in Murphy's face, only wild-eyed terror. With people diving for cover, he emptied the weapon into the huge portrait at the back of the platform.

Agents were on him quickly, without themselves firing a shot. Murphy was wrestled to the platform and held there shrieking.

At last, mercifully, somebody shut off the microphones.

26

In the meadow where Queen Anne's Lace, goldenrod, and thistle bloomed wild, flowers were a redundancy, but Thorne bent and placed a bunch of roses beside the headstone. It was nothing more than a boulder actually, with orange lichen flecking it, and yet here amidst the dust of his ancestors Jimmy Dow lay at rest.

A lot had occurred. Murphy's breakdown had been followed soon after by his withdrawal from the presidential race, his manager citing total exhaustion. Thorne had returned to Nassau to await Rain's recovery. In late June, back in Washington, he gave closed testimony to various agencies, including the FBI, by whom it was confirmed that a body pulled from the Anacostia River was that of Hiram Kirk. The left hand had been missing, but tests showed that a prosthesis of the type Kirk had worn would have caused the smudged prints discovered at Dr. Martin Ames's house in Boston and on the revolver which killed Dow. Other evidence bore out the claim of two former administration aides that Hank Frizzel was already dead when they found him. One theory was that Frizzel's killer had been hired by Kirk, though it probably would never be proven.

The Vineyard killings had been laid to Clement Jones. A check of military files had produced a match for the partial fingerprint lifted from room twenty-three of the Captain James Inn. And that's where the matter lay. By having closed ranks and dismissed Jones as a renegade "former in-

telligence officer," the CIA had remained untouched; and
Vice President Rendle was too busy trying to run the country in Peter Hawes's absence to pursue the matter further.

The details that Thorne found most disquieting, however,
were those included in a psychiatric evaluation of Timothy
Murphy made after his nervous collapse. Rain had gotten
access to portions of the report through Ray Russo.

The profile revealed a deep personality split which probably had originated early, when Murphy took on an imagi-
nary persona to mitigate the stresses of childhood trauma.
It was likely, the examining doctors wrote, that later, under
the strains of military combat, Murphy had reacted with a
psychogenic fugue episode. Deserting from Vietnam by way
of the Philippines, he eventually reached California, probably still in a state of confusion. There, the doctors reasoned,
as an unconscious defense response designed to relieve his
anxiety, Murphy had taken on another identity, that of
Charles Evans, whom Army records depicted as a withdrawn young soldier, the ideal foil to the hard-driving Lieutenant Murphy.

Only later, as more and more recall of his "erased" past
began to occur, did Murphy return to the Philippines, where
he got tattooed and staged photographs to support his fab-
ricated story of escape from a POW camp. Thus, having
reintegrated his original personality, for the next decade and
a half Murphy had been the hard-driving achiever once
more.

It was the opinion of the doctors that the unexpected return of Andrea Wexford to his life, on top of the escalating
pressures of high public office, had begun to erode Murphy's ego structure once more, driving him to escape to his
alter ego. Incidents of odd behavior reported by close aides
and Murphy's wife tended to corroborate some of the psychiatric findings. It was noted that Ray Russo did not testify.
Perhaps, the profile concluded, the subject had sought to
protect himself by symbolically killing the Murphy persona.

It was intriguing speculation, and Thorne had little doubt
Murphy was disturbed in some way; unfortunately, the

analysis skirted details which he had put together in his own version. For one thing, he suspected that Murphy's desertion was more willful, that following a Viet Cong ambush, which left Corporal Evans and other members of Murphy's platoon killed or dying, he had fled in hopes that he would be believed dead. In this version, when the mix-up was revealed, Murphy thought of a way to return to civilian life by inventing the POW story.

There was some evidence for Thorne's case—chiefly in Murphy's having left his own dogtags behind, and Evans's tags never having been found—but it was skimpy, so Thorne left it as speculation. Murphy had been hospitalized for observation and since released. There was no talk of charges being brought, nor of a return to public life. The red-haired Secret Service man had healed quickly from a superficial gunshot wound.

Rain recovered from her injuries and spent the summer in Washington undergoing physical therapy and writing. Thorne returned to the Vineyard.

Now, with Labor Day come and gone, the island was finding its slower rhythms. Sadly, Jimmy Dow wasn't there to enjoy them. Saying goodbye to his friend, Thorne walked to his car and drove to Vineyard Haven.

The *Nantucket* was wedging into her berth. Warren Stubbs stood unobtrusively in the canopied waiting area, a spot he occupied lately for most arrivals. "Eric," he greeted in his laconic way.

Thorne nodded. "Hello, Warren. Nice day."

"It is." Stubbs had his arms crossed, his eyes taking in nothing in particular, everything in general. "Meetin' someone?"

The question was amiable. Stubbs had none of Alden Post's xenophobia; he just believed it helped him do his job if he knew who was on the island. Since Post's dismissal for what the selectmen termed "irregularities," Stubbs had held the job of acting chief. Thorne had been reinstated with back pay and granted a leave of absence.

Rufus McCoy clattered up in his truck and switched off the motor. He fitted a cardboard sunshield in the form of an enormous pair of sunglasses across the dashboard and climbed out.

"Life's a beach," Thorne greeted him.

"Amazin' what summer folks'll throw away," Rufus said.

His bib overalls were sequined with fish scales, and it didn't take two cops to guess where he was coming from. "Today the day, Eric?" he asked, though he knew it was; he wouldn't have turned up otherwise.

Thorne was noncommittal. Eager to change the subject, he said, "Warren, I almost forgot. I ran into Bob Sack last night. He asked how things were getting on. It seems the selectmen want to fill the chief's job permanently."

Stubbs looked at him questioningly a moment, and Thorne grinned. "Congratulations." Stubbs took his offered hand and pumped it. He shook Rufus's hand too.

"You had me worried, Warren," Rufus said. "For a second there, I thought you were going to smile."

And for a second Stubbs did. Then, catching himself, he scrubbed the smile away, but every few seconds little brushfire grins kept flaring at the corners of his mouth.

Thorne's attention returned to the ferry, where the deck crew bulldogged a gangway into place and tied it off. The boat schedule had dropped back to fewer runs now that the summer mobs had thinned, and Thorne watched passengers beginning to disembark. He could feel Rufus's sidelong glance, and he was aware of his own slow, expectant breathing.

After Rain left the hospital in Nassau, they had been together briefly, but there'd been much to do, so many things pulling them separate ways. He had been occupied with filing reports, clearing his name, presenting testimony to the DEA that Oscar Sanchez had died in the line of duty. The cocaine found in the cave on Bootleg Cay convinced them. Finally, what Thorne had needed was rest.

Rain had been busy too. *Heartlander,* having suddenly become obsolete, dropped off sales lists like a stone. Nevertheless, there were contract offers to write a book about what had happened. She resisted most of the hoopla, and she and Thorne had kept in touch by telephone. Somehow, though, the intensity of what they had been through had eroded the common ground they'd established, as if it had been built on shifting sand. Although neither would admit it, it was apparent to both that someone you had brushed death with could only remind you of the encounter. In the end, each had sought easier circumstances closer to home, without the reminders.

Six days ago, on September tenth, she had called. She wanted to come see him. His week had been haunted by the memory of how his former wife had fared here, and his worry that Rain would change her mind.

A final trickle of passengers was coming down the ramp. She was not among them. His chest went tight. "Come on, Rufus," he said with false heartiness. "I'll buy you an ale."

As he started away, Rufus caught his arm. He turned. And there she was. She came out of the cabin, and he realized she'd waited till last because of the enormous suitcase she was lugging two-handedly. A young deckhand with a bandana tied pirate-wise around his head hustled forward and took it. Spotting Thorne, Rain waved.

"Wow," Rufus murmured. Stubbs, as if having had a mystery solved, murmured agreement. When Rain stood at the top of the gangway, Thorne went forward.

She was browned, and her dark hair, which had been shorn because of her head wound, was almost fully grown back. She wore a blue and white flower-print dress which the salt breeze pasted crisply to her hips and long legs. As she got to where Thorne stood, he experienced a stiff little moment of inaction, then he reached for her and the awkwardness dissolved. Following introductions, Rufus and Stubbs fought each other over the suitcase until both ended up carrying it to the Jeep.

"It looks heavy," Thorne said. "Bring your barbells?"

"Books, clothes. I wasn't sure of the official uniform here, so I brought a lot. No coveralls though."

"We'll get you outfitted. You look great."

She shook her head as though in wonder. "God, I've missed you, mister."

When the suitcase was loaded, Stubbs shook hands, wished Rain a good visit and sidled off toward the police station. Rufus said, "You've just seen history made, young lady. Warren smiled *twice* today and said more than he normally does in a year."

Rain was grinning warily, as if suspecting a put-on, but Thorne assured her it was true.

"Course, getting that chief's badge permanently was something," Rufus pointed out. "Funny you being the one to hear the news first."

Thorne didn't take the bait. In truth, *he* had been the selectmen's choice for the job, but he'd thanked them and declined, saying that as soon as they could get a replacement he'd be leaving the force. A few weeks ago, Mike Pulaski had let him know there was a gold shield for him in Boston if he wanted it. Thorne was in no hurry to make decisions. Maybe he would stay on the Vineyard. He understood now that it wasn't as if you had to leave, but that you could.

"You can always come into business with me," offered Rufus. "Can turn you into some kind of local attraction. You could write up his story, couldn't you, ma'am?"

Rain shot Thorne a sly look. "Oh, there's a story to tell all right."

"Y'see?"

"Stow it, Rufus."

"Just funnin'. Anyways, I'll let you two be for a while. You'll want to catch up. I don't know about down there in Washington, Rain—always seems to be the same bad news to me—but a whole lot's been happening here. A new wing's goin' on the post office, and my neighbor's dog is about to whelp, and just the other day—"

"Bye, Rufus," Thorne said.

"Glad to meet you, Rain. See you again if he doesn't hoard you."

"He's nice," she said when Rufus had gotten into his Studebaker, folded the sunshield and puttered off.

"Don't encourage him."

Thorne put his hands on her shoulders and held her at arms' length, finally free to really look. The post-hospital pallor she'd had when he saw her last was gone. She was tanned, her eyes were clear and her smile shone. Radiant was the word that came to his mind. She sat two feet from him as they rode out of town, and that reality brought back the awkwardness he had felt on the pier. He was aware that she experienced it too. They were going to have to become reacquainted.

They drove across the lagoon, where a clamdigger was bent over the twisting furrow of his labor, sharing the tidal flats with seagulls.

"This would be a peaceful place to write a book," Rain said.

"You didn't tell me you'd decided not to write yours."

She looked at him, surprised.

"You brought a lot of clothes," he said, "and no typewriter."

"Anyone ever tell you you'd make a fair detective? I was going to discuss the decision with you. Somehow that particular ambition burns a little less hotly. Maybe writing was something I needed to bring me fully away from my past, into who I am now. Who I want to become." She laughed. "That sounds like marshmallow psychology."

"I think you're a writer. I read the retrospective you did on Andrea Wexford's films."

She was watching him, gauging his response.

"I liked it very much," he said. "I think she would've too. You kept her confidences."

"Not easy," Rain confessed. *"Vanity Fair* wanted the whole juicy tale."

"You'll write other things."

"Maybe. It could be I just want to take a break. Am I crazy?"

He glanced over at her. The wind through the open window riffled her hair, and her eyes shone brighter than he had ever seen them. In fact, everything about her seemed to crackle with health. He took her hand. "I'm hoping."

The September afternoon was mellow, somnolent with the languid drowse of insects and songbirds from the salt marshes. After a silence Rain said, "Ray Russo called the other day to say hello."

"Has he gotten another racehorse yet?"

"No. But he claims that his faith is back. Now that the president's cancer is in remission, the new First Lady is putting energy into some projects of her own. Prudence Hawes has talked Ray into joining her and some others in a nonpartisan group to promote leadership. I was thinking maybe there's an article in it somewhere."

"Something to prime the pump?"

"Or whatever."

"Sounds promising."

"There wouldn't be the fat advance."

"Uh huh."

"And you won't get to be the hero of the story."

"Hmm. Would I still get the girl at the end?"

"Maybe."

"Is that a definite maybe?"

"It might be."

"We'd have to negotiate it, huh?"

"Probably draw up a contract."

"Your agent and my attorney?"

"I've got a better idea," she said.

When he had brought her suitcase into the little house and showed her around, he popped a bottle of Korbel, bought that morning for the occasion. He set it in a bait pail full of ice, and they drank a toast: to her, to him, to them. Afterwards he shucked her out of her dress, and together they slid her panties down over long legs, so smooth and brown they looked polished, and without the fear and rush of the first time, they made love, slowly, tenderly, nursing old hurts as they nurtured new hopes. At sunset they climbed over the dunes to the beach.

The sand was empty, still printed above the high-water mark from the feet of summer bathers but otherwise as bare as the moon. They took off their shoes and strolled along the margin where the ocean held the Gulf Stream's warmth. The light began to fade. A distant bank of fog swirled like a magician's cape, transforming the sea to a pearly iridescence. A few yards from shore Thorne saw a sudden broil of baitfish. He pointed. Something was feeding—probably mackerel. He had an urge to run and get his spinning rod. But the temptation passed without regret, and they stood there for a long time as the colors dwindled, an arm around each other's waist, not bothering to speak, just looking.

By twilight's last gleaming they made their way up the beach to home.